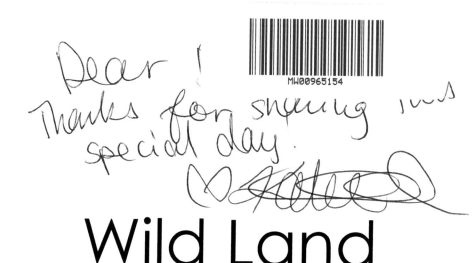

Wild Land

Kathryn Hogan

A Limber Pine Press Book

A note from the Author:

You are holding the first edition of my first novel. I really hope that you really enjoy it, a lot.

For more about me and my books, check out: www.kathrynhogan.ca

LIMBER PINE
PRESS

Published by Limber Pine Press
P O Box 1466
Cochrane, Alberta
T4C 1B4
limberpinepress@gmail.com

Printed in the United Stateas.
ISBN: 978-0-9877883-0-6

I dedicate this book to Will Dinghum, who proves that nice guys don't always finish last.

Acknowledgements:

The production of this book resembled a barn raising in several ways, primarily:

1. Neighbors and friends all helped
2. It took way longer than expected
3. Now that it's done, it's party time
4. God willing, it will put a roof over my head.

To those friends and neighbors in point 1, thank you so much. Especially thank you to my Beta Reading Attack Force, who made me think this book was actually pretty good. The feedback from these good looking people was indespensible.

Thank you to Cammy Nice Guy, Jodie and Ian, Norja, Toby, Vikki, Basia, Julia, my parents, Sharon and Mike, Dave and Kara, most of the people I'm related to, and so many others for all of the help and support you have provided.

Without you, it is entirely conceivable that I would be a raving-mad, half-naked lunatic trying to join a wolf pack out in the woods somewhere.

And now, thanks to you, book purchaser! You're making my dreams come true.

Thanks, guys!

Chapter One

Everything about her bag was meant to remind the others that she was just like them. It was light enough that she could outstrip the toughest of them at a run and empty enough that they wouldn't tease her about bringing all of her girly belongings, the kitchen sink or whatever else the morons could think of.

Hopefully.

"Need a hand there, my dear Miss Dizzy?"

Elizabeth almost snarled at Mark. *Moron*, she thought. He certainly sounded like a moron, talking like a hillbilly all the time. Especially now that they were finally *here*.

A few of the other boys laughed. Elizabeth managed a lighthearted smile, and rolled up her sleeve to reveal the bicep underneath.

She winked at her cousin as she kissed it, then heaved the next bag at him so hard it almost knocked him over.

"Ok, Dizzy. No need to put on a show," Mark chuckled, tossing the bag on down the line. Stupid Mark, goofy Mark, always taking everything so easy. He had a permanent farmer's tan, always-tousled hair, dirt always under his fingernails; and none of it bothered him at all.

On her other side, unloading onto the dock next to her, Dinky shook his head in quiet disapproval. While the others liked to take their shots at the only girl on the squad - *or almost any squad, for that matter, thank you very much,* she thought - Dinky was too grateful for her company to care about her gender either way.

"You wait till you see 'em, Dizzy," he said, his sporty spectacles gleaming. "One of the greatest mysteries we know of. Can't believe you never saw a picture in school or anything; they're so beautiful and spooky. I can't wait."

Elizabeth smiled, grunting just loud enough to save her the effort of a response. Dinky hadn't stopped talking about the statues since they left home three days ago and had spoken of little else for the weeks leading up to the groups deployment. The damn statues had better be amazing after he hyped them up so much.

The next bag was so light that she nearly fell over backwards when she heaved it up off of the deck. In the moment it took her to regain balance, she saw that someone had painted crude, hairy lady-parts in childish red strokes onto her brand new duffel bag, purchased just for this mission.

She shook her head to clear the colour she knew would be rising in her cheeks and passed the bag on silently. Beyond Mark, Ray started to laugh wildly and tossed it hand to hand like a hot potato, his dark red hair glinting as it was tossed back and forth.

"Look out!" he shouted, "Here comes the pussy bag!"

"Say it again, Ray," Elizabeth said with a smile, trying to sound as relaxed as he did while shouting just as loudly, "and I'll kick your sorry balls so far up your ass that you'll have a nice little pussy, too."

There were sniggers at this, and a cat call from down the carry-line.

"Oooh," Ray cooed, tucking his elbows to his ribs and letting his wrists flop in front of him, "would you let me bowow one of the pwetty dwesses that you keep in your pussy bag?" Despite with his wide, well-muscled good looks, Ray's antics rarely qualified as attractive. But his attempt at humour, however heavy-handed, was desperately needed by the group – they were arriving in the infamous wild land, after all. They all laughed, and none realized that it was at Elizabeth's expense.

Elizabeth's eyes flared. She was about to scream that she hadn't brought any goddamn dresses when Dinky put a warning hand on her shoulder. She whipped around and froze. Standing among the duffel bags and crates of supplies, the group's Captain was glaring down at Ray.

There was a moment of silence as his features shifted from a patronizing sneer to an expression of true contempt.

"Didn't your mother teach you a goddamn thing!"

Ray swallowed audibly. Another silence passed.

"Dinghum."

The Captain turned to Dinky, who shot Elizabeth a concerned look. "Yes, sir?"

"Tell this worthless country bonehead why spiteful talk is not permitted on this ground."

"This ground is holy," Dinky muttered, to no one in particular.

"Why is that, Dinghum?"

"The Ethos chose this place to make their stand."

Now the Captain swept his eyes over the line of boys. Very few of them over twenty. His lip twitched as his gaze passed Elizabeth.

"And why," he whispered, turning towards the water with the sand flats beyond, "why is it that saying anything..." he turned back to Ray, who flinched, "*ungentlemanly*, is likely to lead to expulsion from this mission and the Peacekeeping Core altogehter!"

"Because of the Mother, sir." Dinky blinked.

As the Captain was still watching expectantly, Dinky went on, "The one at the front. If we disrespect the Mother, then motherhood will abandon us. We'll be childless, probably wifeless."

"Do you want to go home, son?" The Captain asked Ray.

"No, sir," Ray said.

"What was that?"

"Sir, no sir!"

"Then apologize to the lady and get back to work. It's bad luck for all of us."

The Captain trotted away before Ray could protest.

"Sorry, Dizzy," he mumbled, tossing her bag on down the line.

"Whatever," she said, "how do you know all that stuff, Dinky?"

"My mom taught me," he answered, as if it were obvious.

"Mine, too," Eddie called. He was six spots down the line and the only city boy on their squad, besides Dinky. "she told me about the ethos when I was little."

"I know about the fucking ethos," Ray mumbled, "Ok? Who doesn't. I just didn't think it was a big deal to do a little horsing around."

"Probably isn't," Dinky said, wiping sweat off his forehead, "The statues *stand* for the ethos, but they aren't actually the ethos. It's a metaphor."

"Don't know why the ethos had to pick the frickin' wild land to set up camp, that's for damn sure," Ray muttered. "Spooks me out here already."

"Well," Dinky went on, and Elizabeth saw that he was about to broach a topic of interest to him, which likely meant it was going to be boring. "don't worry to much, Ray, it just seems spooky because we've heard so many stories, but those stories are likely metaphorical as well, not real, objective records of history."

"Nerd," Mark said, loudly enough that even the boys at the other end of the line started to laugh. None of them had wanted to admit that this place already seemed spooky, and they especially didn't want to be reminded of the stories that made it seem that way.

Elizabeth laughed too and adjusted Dinky's glasses for him before tossing the next bag to her cousin down the line.

By the time the supplies were loaded on top of their personal belongings, the sun had gone from mid afternoon hot to early evening warm and cozy, the kind that usually meant a nice hammock nap back on the farm. Elizabeth was so tired that she didn't know if she would be able to lift her duffel bag, light as it was.

"This is the last one, Lizzy," Dinky said, struggling under the weight of yet another tent kit.

"Whatever," she grunted.

She heaved the plastic pack off to her cousin and almost gagged. She could smell his sweaty feet despite the meter between them; she was covered in sweat herself, hungry as hell and bug bitten from the river delta's many insect inhabitants.

"Ugh," she said. She collapsed against the dock's railing behind her. Dinky grunted, supporting her sentiment. Once the last tent pack passed out of his hands down the line even Ray was too exhausted to mock anyone.

The Captain appeared on deck of their barge, laughing.

"You poor kids look like you're ready for bed!"

There were murmurs of agreement and a handful of chuckles. It seemed like when he wasn't being a jerk, the Captain wasn't such a bad guy after all.

"Well then," he jumped down to the loading dock with a robust, explosive bang and strutted past them to the waiting carrier ship, "let's go."

Elizabeth found herself smiling with the others. A hard day of work had a way of making evenings seem sweet, especially this one. Finally. She was finally here, in the Wild Land, finally in this new and utterly foreign place, one of the first from her country to settle there, finally going to see the new colony, finally, finally, finally. Mark clapped her on a work-sore shoulder and she even felt like she might be sort-of part of the gang. Mark clapped her sore shoulders and she even felt like she might fit in with the gang, eventually.

"Not so fast, boys," Captain said, holding a hand up as he walked. He reached the end of the dock and clasped his hands behind his back, "ladies first."

Elizabeth's heart sank. Was this a joke?

"Please sit at the front, Miss Walker, in the place of respect."

The Captain and a few of the more religiously inclined boys bowed their heads and stepped out of the way. Elizabeth looked to Dinky for support, and gaped at seeing his head bowed, too. The others quickly followed suit, leaving a more or less empty path between her and the ship. Mark gave her a mystified look, the best reassurance he could have offered her, though he may not have known it. She shook her head at him, equally confused. She and Mark were supposed to be the hillbillies, the uneducated, the backwater kids. But the worldly Captain was the one following superstitious nonsense about the Mother statue!

Elizabeth gulped and started to walk down the makeshift aisle to the ship. That the Captain believed in the old myths was acceptable, sure. To be so afraid that he would follow protocols so old that they were barely mentioned, even on Sundays? That was enough to make her forgo her exhaustion and excitement in favour of embarrassment.

She forced herself to walk slowly, in imitation of the regality this protocol required of her. Dinky was first, he touched his stomach as she walked past him and she looked him in the eye, trying to convey her confusion and apprehension without letting the others see. He didn't look up.

Fine, she thought, *but you'll get it later, Dinky.*

Even Ray gave her the ancient salute, albeit perfunctorily.

Elizabeth hurried to her seat at the front of the ship once she had jumped onboard. She stared ahead at the water and waited for things to go back to normal. It wasn't enough that she was *the only girl* on the team, oh no. Maybe the Captain was a jerk after all.

Dinky sat next to her without a word. She shot him an angry glance and went back to staring.

"Anchor away!" Captain yelled, and a few of the boys cheered. Once the engines were loud enough that she could talk to Dinky without the others hearing, she leaned towards him.

"What the hell was that?"

"It was the fertility –"

"I know that," she whispered, "but why? Are we going to sacrifice a goat, too?"

Dinky rolled his eyes and looked at her. She forced herself to look back without blinking. For some reason, doing so made her mouth feel extremely dry.

"You think that it's just superstition."

"Yeah. Or... I don't know. I just don't know why it has to be such a big deal."

"It *is* a big deal, Liz."

"It was embarrassing."

"Really?" he smiled at her. "I thought you looked pretty... womanly. Beautiful, actually."

Elizabeth blinked. Was Dinky flirting with her?

"Yes, really. I hate being singled out."

"You're the woman, you know that. It's an honour. Just like bearing children. That's why the Mother is at the front of the Statues of the Ethos, after all."

They both looked out at the gentle hills that led down to the sand flats. The ship would go up the river's deepest arms, slow and lazy against the current.

"We'll be able to see them, soon. I'm pretty sure that they're just around those hills."

"Mm-hmm."

They sat in silence for another moment, the sun turning the air around them a soft gold, unlike anything she had seen before. In spite of the strange incident she felt herself relaxing, felt the expectation and excitement return. She was really *here*, on her first mission. Really a peacekeeper, really living her dream. The one that almost everyone had told her was *just* a dream, something unrealistic bordering on impossible, that would never happen. She had shown them, and wasn't done yet. She'd be the best damn peacekeeper in the corps, climb the ranks, do important things and be someone important...

The wind picked up and her eyes slipped shut. For the first time in three days, she could smell something other than sea water; damp smells, earthy, like an ancient evergreen forest in a cool place. Her heart skipped into higher tempo. She couldn't wait to see it! The forests, the new colony... even the statues.

Elizabeth inhaled deeply and opened her eyes.

But instead of breathing out, she felt her throat close. Instead of sweet anticipation, she filled with dread and her heart continued to skip ever faster, tripping over itself and pushing up with each beat.

Instead of a brand new place, she saw a familiar one.

I'm running down the beach, she thought, *trying to reach Cameron before it's too late, before the bomb hits. The sky is purple, like a bruise, like scraped knees. He's running to me, too, Dana's with me, holding my hand hard and whimpering. She's too young for this, I think, and I'm surprised at how calm the thought is. Is that how I'll die? Calm and cold?*

The feeling of betrayal is so strong I can taste it, can't get it out of my mouth. The beeping, so loud and getting louder, everyone's running; it's chaos. I yell, Cameron! I love you! We reach each other just in time, just in time for the untura. I squeeze his hand, and Dana's. She's almost screaming with fear now.

Then everything goes white.

Elizabeth's mouth hung open, staring at the statues, just down the beach. There they were: Cameron, her parents holding each other not far behind. And Dana, olne hand covering her eyes, while the other hand...

The other hand was holding the hand of the lead figure.

This is impossible, she thought, *I'm one of the statues.*

I'm the Mother.

Chapter Two

The memory had only been a flash, only a handful of seconds, but it had been so real and vital that Elizabeth could not find a way to convince herself that it was untrue.

I'm exhausted and I've been overthinking. It's just because of Dinky and his obsession with the statues, she thought. She was beginning to panic. *Am I going crazy?*

The statues grew closer and closer as ship travelled lazily upstream. Every moment revealed more details - most of them so achingly familiar that Elizabeth slapped her hands over her eyes in fear. But the memory was there: waiting, replaying itself over the backs of her eyelids. *The arm-bands that are beeping, they're a warning of some kind but...*

No. Elizabeth forced her eyes open and her hands to her sides. It was foolish to indulge in silly fantasies like this one. It was impossible. *The statues aren't of people: they're a metaphor, like Dinky said. They're certainly not of real people. And even if there were a possibility that these millennia old statues had been based on real people, those people would have had to pose to create them.*

Right?

Besides, Elizabeth knew who she was, had her own set of memories binding her to this life and to her far away home, not to age-old phantoms from this strange and foreign place.

Just my imagination, she thought stubbornly.

Except Elizabeth had never been known for her imagination. She was literal, realistic, pragmatic. That's what had gotten her into the corps and onto this mission, she felt sure of it.

Still, no surprise that I have a weird imagination attack now. This is an emotional moment, she retorted to herself, heart still pounding and a cold sweat popping up on her forehead, *I probably fell asleep and just had a weirdly vivid dream. That's all. And I'll prove it.*

She closed her eyes again, letting the dream play itself out. This time, she paid attention to the details of the sand flats and the gentle, grassy hills behind. She wasn't sure exactly what she was looking for, only that she would know when she saw it. Sure enough, there was a very noticeable stream feeding into the many arms of the river from the hills behind the statues – or rather, the people that were about to become statues. It seemed to be the only tributary into the delta, the only one that she could see in her mind's eye.

"Ha!"

Her heart sank immediately. There was no stream. In its place, the hill had been worn down to a shallow gully. Almost as if there had been a stream there for hundreds of years, one that slowly dried up. Given the age of the statues, it made sense that what was a stream then would be gone now...

"Oh no..." Elizabeth whimpered.

"What's up?" Dinky looked her over, eyebrows drawn together behind his glasses.

For a moment, Elizabeth couldn't answer.

"Nothing. I'm just really tired, I think."

"You sure?"

"Yes. Definitely. I just... fell asleep, I think. I had a weird dream."

"You fell asleep?!" Dinky nearly jumped up, "Haven't you been listening? That's them, Liz! Those are the statues! The oldest things anyone has ever... I mean... Man!"

Elizabeth tried to laugh. Dinky's consternation was so characteristic and so loveable. She managed a smile.

"Don't worry, Dinky, I hang on your every word."

Dinky blushed.

Chapter Three

The loosely braided river wrapped around itself tighter and tighter until it was a unified thread that led their ship into the hills. They reached the end of the delta just as the sun disappeared over the horizon and into the sea. It wouldn't be long before they reached the dock, the colony and everything else.

Everything.

Elizabeth couldn't wait to get to bed. The sooner her head hit the pillow, the sooner she could forget the strange dream, and move on with this new life. She would wake up in the morning before she knew it, see the new colony, and get to work building and keeping the peace. It would be glorious, just like she had imagined.

"Alright, kids," Captain called, as the ship busied itself with the delicate work of approaching the dock slowly and sideways, "what goes on the ship must come off the ship."

They moaned. Elizabeth wondered if she would collapse during the manual labor that was to come, but knew better. Even if her body gave up, her pride certainly wouldn't.

"The faster you get done, the faster you get to set up your tents and make yourselves dinner!"

The boys closest to the Captain jumped up and led the others onto the dock.

"We still have to *make* our dinners?" Dinky whispered, exasperated. He was clearly as hungry as she was.

"We have to unload all those supplies, carry a hundred pounds each and you're worried about *cooking!?*" she whispered back, "Bet you can't blame me for having a nap now."

They unloaded in silence, barring the occasional grunt of effort under the cumbersome loads. Soon there was rhythm to their work. Elizabeth let it dictate her movements, her breathing.

Just a dream, she thought, over and over. It soothed her.

When they finally breasted the hill leading up to new colony, she kept her promise to herself and led the group, relishing the pain in almost every muscle of her body. She was disappointed it was too dark to see this place that would become her new home. One more thing that would have to wait until morning. It felt like the eve of her birthday, just waiting to wake up and be showered with gifts. Only this time, this time...

It was just a dream.

Alphabetical order dictated that she share a tent with Mark, as they bore the same last name.

"Just my luck," he muttered, as they set up the tent.

"Just like old times? Is that what you said?" Elizabeth said, somehow finding the energy to tease him, "You mean, just like the first time we went camping and you peed in the tent?"

"Ah, shove it," Mark said, but he smiled.

Country boys though many of them were, most of the group had to read the instructions in order to set their tents, checking and rechecking the pegs and poles with each other. The cousins had no such problem. They had camped together on so many occasions that they set their tent the same way they might have set the table. With barely a dozen words of coordination between them, their tent was raised and ready.

When they finished, Elizabeth looked up to see Dinky struggling with the instruction manual while his bunk mate, Tom, read the labels on each of the pieces out loud for him. At each one, Dinky scanned each page and nodded his approval. At one point, he turned the booklet upside down while scratching his chin.

"Need a hand?" Elizabeth said, walking over to them.

"Don't tell me your girlfriend is gonna come for sleepovers, city boy," Tom moaned.

"Very funny," she said.

"We do need help, yes," Dinky surrendered the paper to her, "we shamelessly beg for your assistance."

By the time Elizabeth completed Dinky's tent Mark had finished making their dinner.

"Can of beans, my favorite!"

"Maybe you should be grateful I didn't leave you to make your own."

She rolled her eyes and took a fork from her gunny sack.

"I'm too tired to taste it anyways."

Mark grunted in agreement.

Elizabeth expected that they would both pass out as soon as they were in their sleeping bags. Instead, she found herself afraid to fall asleep. Thoughts of the strange dream lingered. She argued with herself, *I'll feel better in the morning once I've had some rest.* It didn't help.

"Lizzy, you still awake?" Mark whispered. She had thought he was asleep, lying in his bag beside her.

"Yeah."

"Do you... miss your mom?"

"Why, do you miss Aunt Linda?"

"Yeah."

She considered for a moment. It was their first night away from home for good, so it was no wonder that he missed his mother. Elizabeth had barely thought of her own since the first night away, when she had cried quietly in her bunk while thinking that her mother would never come to tuck her in before bed, ever again.

"I guess so," she finally answered.

"Sorry about today."

Elizabeth yawned, her exhaustion finally overtaking her. "What about today?"

"You know; Ray, and the paint on your bag. I swear I don't know who did that."

"Yeah well ... " she considered saying that he was just as bad as whoever it was for making fun of her, or pointing out that Ray seemed to get away with just about anything, because everyone else found him inexplicably charming, but thought better of it,"...whatever."

"Okay," he whispered.

There was a long moment of silence. Not exactly silence, she corrected herself: she could hear soft voices as the other boys got into bed. Some of them she had known her whole life - many of the boys she grew up with had enlisted and were assigned to the same unit. The soft orange of firelight dappled the tent skin above her. There was a clang as someone dropped a frying pan or a plate, and hushed giggles

Like a little village, she thought. Elizabeth felt her eyes closing.

"Lizzy?"

"What."

"It was weird, the fertility rite today, wasn't it?"

"Yes, it was definitely weird."

"I thought that was just something you see in plays and stuff. Not something people actually *do*."

"Maybe Captain's from the city."

"Why do city folks care about fertility? Don't have no crops."

"I thought it was weird, too."

"Lizzy, do you think... that it's safe, just in tents like this?"

Elizabeth rolled her eyes in the darkness. "Yes, I do. They wouldn't have us in tents if it were dangerous. All of the noise will keep the wildlife away."

"Even the... bears?"

" Even the bears."

Mark grunted. Elizabeth knew that he was afraid of the many strange, giant, beasts native to the Wild Land.

"What about... witches?"

Elizabeth had to chuckle, throwing an arm over her eyes as she settled into a comfortable position. "There aren't any witches, Mark. Those are just stories."

"It's still the Wild Land."

"I know. How about this, Mark: I'll protect you. Alright?"

Mark grumbled inaudibly.

"Goodnight, Mark."

Chapter Four

"Goodnight, Cam," I say, sighing.

He murmurs, perhaps trying to say something. I know exactly what he means, either way.

"I hope it worked this time, too," I whisper and sigh again. No amount of sighs can capture how utterly wonderful I feel. It has to have worked - how can two people feel so close to each other, to God and to creation without conceiving?

He rolls onto his side and pulls me towards him, kissing my neck with a gentleness that tells me he is falling asleep. I can feel my muscles releasing, the sweat on my skin drying. My eyes are starting to close, as his breathing evens and slows. I let my eyes rest on the wall, logs roughly cut and painted with a clear lacquer to help them keep. Sparsely decorated for now, but soon I'll make curtains and quilts, and Cameron will build us better furniture. It will be the perfect little home.

I pull the blanket closer around our shoulders. It's the thin one. It's warm outside now, the leaves tinkle gently in the late evening wind in the garden, just outside our window. We are far in the North, and late evening lasts almost all the way to early morning during the summer. I think of the garden we planted, the shoots taking shape in patches among the skinny poplars. The white poplars, with their tiny leaves always tinkling.

I sigh again, my last thought before falling asleep is -

"Our food grows to the sound of chimes..."

"What did you say?"

Elizabeth sat bolt upright, hitting her head on the diagonal support beam of the tent.

It was Mark, she thought, Mark asked me what I said. There's no one else here.

"Nothing, Mark," she said, lowering herself carefully back into her sleeping bag, "It was just a dream."

Elizabeth pulled the sleeping bag up and under her nose, staring at the fabric of the tent. Outside, the only sound was river roaring faintly in the distance. Not even the birds were awake yet, despite the muted greys illuminating the tent exterior.

Not another dream.

Fear and despair worked her into wakefulness. Two didn't mean a pattern, but this dream had felt the same as the other one: as if it weren't a dream at all. A memory. And such a *clear* one. She couldn't remember what had come before it but she could certainly extrapolate that it had been sex. Something that Elizabeth had little knowledge of; her experiences limited to what she could do under her blankets once her younger sister Mira, (with whom she shared a room) had fallen asleep. Her lack of real life experience with sex only made this dream more unsettling. She felt sensations that she had never experienced before and certainly hadn't imagined as linked to the act of love.

That's because it was just my imagination, she thought.

Elizabeth sniffed, then forced her eyes closed. But as soon as she did, she again saw what she had in the dream: the knitted blanket that had seemed so comforting and familiar; the log walls of the tight space, bathed in a glow that could only be dusk filtering through forest and window-shades; and most of all, the side of the man's face, just a profile in the warm glow. *It's the same man as from the other dream,* she thought, *Cameron. His name is Cameron. But I call him Cam, or Cammy.*

Her eyes flew open with surprise. She was shocked with a flood of intense longing, a sense of profound loss. *I miss him,* she thought. *I miss him so much…*

She had to blink quickly to force the tears back. *Dreams can be powerful, dreams can seem real, dreams can make you cry.* Elizabeth knew that. She remembered dreaming that her mother had been killed, when she was a child. She had woken up wailing with fear and grief, inconsolable. This felt the same. The realization was a relief - of course it was just a dream. And the more she thought about it, the more it made sense that she would have these dreams *now*. The man in the dreams, Cameron, was the Father. The statue bound forever with the Mother, holding her hand with one arm and comforting her young child with the other. The *Ethos of Fatherhood* had appeared to her in two dreams. It must simply mean that she was reaching the stage of her life in which there was a place for a father and a husband. Becoming a woman. Especially after Captain's fertility ritual, it made sense that she would start to see the two Ethos of parenthood in her dreams. What had her mother said? Something about "becoming a woman once your womanhood is acknowledged". Elizabeth's womanhood had certainly been acknowledged by the fertility ritual. But there was something else. Some familiarity to the romantic feelings in the dream, a sense of magnetism or internal animation.

Dinky, she thought and blushed soundlessly. *Dinky acknowledged my womanhood.* As corny as it sounded, Elizabeth knew it was true. The way he looked at her sometimes, the way that he, among all others was aware of how she felt. She wondered if he had had any dreams about the Mother.

She wondered if Dinky had any dreams about *her*.

In spite of the intense fear she had upon waking, Elizabeth found herself smiling and biting her lip, contemplating this new, strange development. She giggled quietly, pulling the blanket up and over her head to hide in her own little world, wondering if her best friend did feel something for her.

Chapter Five

"How could you be more excited about the market than you were about about the *Statues of the Ethos*?" Dinky was past the point of feeling incredulous, he was looking at Elizabeth as though she were truly absurd. "Sometimes you are like a different *species*!"

Elizabeth smiled and shook her head.

"I'm not *more* excited, just excited. Unlike some pretty city boys, I never got to go to market whenever I wanted, and if I went I had to go with Mark to sell crops, and he would always try and flirt with ladies, which is really hard to watch, believe me."

"I heard that," Mark hollered from a few feet behind them. As always, Elizabeth was at the front of the group with Dinky marching faithfully beside her. This was to be their morning route to the colony and so far Elizabeth was enchanted by it. In spite of the early start to the dawn the sky was still soft and glowing as they packed their lunches, strapped their peacekeeper belts on and set out for the day. The hills sweeping up from the river valley to the west and the delta to the east undulated around them. Long, graceful grasses of a light yellow green played lazily in the light wind. There was sand in the soil but up ahead it transformed into a lush hummus that supported a plethora of evergreens and -

White poplars with their tiny leaves always tinkling

Elizabeth shook her head and shot a look back over her shoulder at her cousin. A smile played at the corners of her lips as she called, "Yeah, and Mark is pretty bad at selling tomatoes, as you can imagine. His smell always scared the customers off."

Dinky laughed and replaced his spectacles.

"Sure is pretty here, eh Dinky?" Elizabeth said quietly, as she breathed deeply of the sweet air. Everything looked pink, thanks to the sun's slow ascent, and there was a dewy smell that reminded her of spring time. Dinky nodded at her, making brief eye contact. In spite of herself, she felt a little quiver snake down her belly.

The quiver was a good thing. So was having Dinky and the beautiful landscape to consider. Those things prevented Elizabeth from admitting to herself that she knew what the leaves of the poplars looked like before she ever saw them, knew the species' without ever having learned it, knew that even the slightest wind would cause the tiny leaves to slap against each other, producing a sound not unlike a fountain or wind chimes. For some reason it seemed natural that she should know these things, so much so that it didn't even occur to her. If she had thought about it at all, she would have simply thought, *Well, of course I know. They grow right outside our window, all throughout the garden.* Had she thought that, she may have realized much sooner what was happening, what was at stake. This wasn't her garden, this wasn't her land.

Once the barely-there trail brought them into the forest, Elizabeth's sense of familiarity and welcome grew. She mistook it for simple excitement, the fulfillment of a wish. *To be somewhere else, to make something of myself, to see this sacred place with my own eyes...*

"Honeyberry!" Elizabeth cried. She sprang off the trail like a doe towards a wildly scrubby bush with lopsided blue berries dangling merrily from it. She tore one off and popped it in her mouth, savouring the bitter, nutritious treat. "Mmm, I love honeyberry!" she mumbled, shoving a handful of them into her mouth.

"What are you doing?" Dinky appeared at her shoulder, examining the bush while the others continued down the path, forgotten, "you're going to get us in trouble."

Elizabeth smiled playfully at her friend. She touched his chin with the tip of her finger before she realized what she was doing. Her hand withdrew, but she had liked the way it felt, to touch him that way. She carefully picked another of the plump berries and pressed it through his lips, deliberatly allowing her fingers to linger there for just a moment.

Dinky was so surprised by this tender action that he simply knelt there staring at her. Then he spit the berry into his hand to examine it.

"It's ok, they're edible, and rich in vitamins. I've eaten them my whole life!" She laughed at his incredulity. It was such a common emotion for him. "You city boys are so funny."

Dinky grunted to indicate his dislike of the term and popped the berry back into his mouth as he stood up.

"Come on, Liz, let's go. Maybe they'll have some of these berries in the market. Maybe they'll even be washed," he added, pointedly, giving her a look of confused exasperation. What was she thinking, eating wild things, dirty things, and here of all places?

Elizabeth nodded and followed him back to the path, oblivious of his concerns. They walked in companionable silence for a few more moments. When she wasn't looking, he touched his lips briefly, then his chin.

The forest opened ahead of them and the boys at the front of the line began cheering. Elizabeth felt her heart pounding as she walked the final distance to the edge of the colony. Then she was out of the trees and evering was in front of her - the path widened to a packed-down road with small tent-houses on either side. There were skinny little spruce trees lined up in front of some of them which gave the impression of a standing sentry lined up along the path to a great castle. But instead of a castle there was a giant white hall, lit by the morning sun with banners of white raised into the sky. It was one of the biggest buildings that Elizabeth had ever seen and certainly more clean and modern than anything she was used to.

"Hot damn, Dizzy," Mark grunted from just beside her, "that dog'll hunt."

"Once backwoods, always backwoods, eh Mark?" she whispered, elbowing him in the ribs.

"Sure don't feel like it here, though," he said seriously. "Nope. Here, feels like I could be part of somethin' new, and special.

"I know what you mean," Dinky said. There was awe in his voice.

"Come on," Elizabeth said.

She took a deep breath and led them all forward without looking back.

Chapter Six

"Welcome to the Wild Land."

The peacekeepers had been chatting excitedly, waiting for their briefing to begin. When it finally did, they all hushed immediately. They waited.

"You are the hope of the next generation." The voice echoed in the large hall, filled less than half to capacity between the two peacekeeping crews. Elizabeth was pleased to see a young woman in the other crew – she wasn't the only female peacekeeper in the Wild Land.

Dinky sat to Elizabeth's right, and Mark to her left, with Ray right beside him. Elizabeth glanced past her cousin at Ray and was surprised to find him totally enraptured by the Chief's speech. She realized that she hadn't been paying attention for a minute at least and turned her attention back to the speaker.

"...may be myth, or legend. But we are real. The ethos are inside of us, in each of our lives, in our history. We are the perfect form of the ethos of humanity - incarnate in our physical bodies, in our choices. Our people are resilient, capable and you are testament to that! Each of you has been given a holy mission - to help this settlement grow, to foster everything that we are and everything we will become! Here, we fortify humanity's stand against eternity!"

Elizabeth blinked, bewildered by the sudden applause that broke out all around her. Her surprise lasted only a moment and then she was on her feet with the rest of them, cheering, clapping and nodding at what he said. A holy mission – sounded alright. Just not exactly what she had expected.

Although each crew had their own Captain, it was the Chief who was really in charge. He was a big man with an impossibly large, round moustache that climbed his cheeks in twisted knots at each side, reaching towards bushy eyebrows. He was otherwise bald, and the contrast between his bald head and hairy face was impressive.

"Thank you! Welcome to you all! It's wonderful to have such distinguished young men and women among us! Are you excited to be here?"

Tumultuous cheers and applause. Elizabeth clapped politely, never one to let excitement overcome her while Mark and Ray barked like coyotes beside her. On her other side, Dinky unsettled his spectacles, fidgeting with them on the bridge of his nose. When he saw Elizabeth looking at him, he leaned in and spoke so quietly that it was barely a whisper,

"Why does this feel like a pep-rally instead of a briefing?"

Elizabeth gulped. She didn't have any idea. Their mission was simple enough: armed with polished-every-night leather boots, black baton and taser they were to be a combination of low-level police officer and tour guide for the settlers and visitors that would eventually arrive. In the meantime, they would be responsible heavy lifting involved in turning a colony into a settlement, to get everything set up for civilians from their homeland, patrol streets and provide a sense of security. Elizabeth didn't bother to ask herself for whom that sense of security was being created.

Instead, she wondered about the Chief's dramatic speech. If this colony was really so important, why was it's peace being entrusted to a crew of untested rookies?

"Thank you, that's enough," Chief held his hands up until the crowd had settled down. "You're all going to be getting your first duty assignments today. You'll be in rotation, performing all duties for at least one week. As time goes on, your propensities will determine your permanent positions."

"What's a propensity?" Mark whispered to his cousin.

"Like a talent," she whispered back, "or a natural ability."

"Oh," he said, but he looked confused. His brow furrowed and his lips pursed together for a long moment. Then he opened his mouth, but all he managed to say was, "Oh."

Elizabeth realized that there was silence in the hall. The Chief was waiting expectantly.

"What did he say?" she asked Dinky.

"He said 'what I'm about to tell you is the greatest secret our people have ever uncovered'. I think he's pausing for effect."

The Chief's eyes flashed at his young audience.

"As you know, there have been scientists studying the Statues of the Ethos for decades here, with little success and few important discoveries." He said it flippantly. Dinky snorted, indignant. "Until this year. An extremely rich field of ore has been uncovered. It has the same mineral composition as the statues themselves: impervious to environmental decay and unbreakable with conventional tools."

Low gasps from the crowd. Dinky shot Elizabeth another look. She nodded, just a quick movement of her head to confirm what she knew he was thinking: that this still didn't feel right. Felt more like a preacher trying for a conversion than a civil employee briefing important information.

"Not only will further expansion and mining operations help us to finally uncover the mystery behind the Statues, but access to this mineral will improve the lives of all of our families, our neighbours, our whole civilization!"

Mark hollered his support. Elizabeth figured he was thinking of the barn that he and his brothers had to rebuild just that year after a particularly fierce windstorm destroyed it. Were it constructed with this wonder mineral, it would have lasted for generations.

"Now you can see that your recruitment officers were not exaggerating when they said that this was a special mission. Now, our people will be able to build monuments to their lives that last forever! Now, everything we build will mirror the glory of the Statues of the Ethos: a testament to humanity and it's future!"

More cheering.

"The local indigenous population have been given homes here and will work in the mine. They will be our only civilian population until the settlers arrive, and have already been put to work constructing suitable homes for our permanent residents."

As the Chief turned his speech to the specific duties on roster, expectations, free time, meals and all the rest, Elizabeth realized that most of the boys in the crowd had been entirely won over by the display of the morning's speech. They would be loyal, hard working and most of all, unquestioning for the duration of their time in the colony. Mark included. He sat beside her with his mouth hanging open, slouched forward as if trying to physically swallow the man's presentation, the images of their glorious future, the idea of being something great. She remembered what he had said when they first saw the majestic Central Building - that he didn't feel backwoods anymore, not here.

"And finally," the Chief said, "each of you will need to undergo a full medical exam including a special body scan that can detect pathogens specific to the Wild Land. I know it sounds intimidating, but it is perfectly safe. We will visit you at your work stations throughout the week to administer the scan."

The Chief went on at length about the scan and some new medical procedures that Elizabeth thought would do little more than inconvenience her.

"Dinky?"

He raised his eyebrows at her in response.

"I'm really glad you're here with me."

Dinky turned a deep red but held her gaze. She wondered if he felt the same kind of pandemonium in his diaphragm that she did.

Chapter Seven

To her immense excitement, Elizabeth's first assignment was to monitor the market. To her immense relief, Dinky had the same assignment, which meant a whole day to be spent together. They hurried through the complex's massive central courtyard to the half-indoor, half-outdoor market, directly across from the auditorium. There were ponderosa pines that were small enough to have been planted just that spring. The plants, native to Elizabeth and Dinky's homeland, didn't seem to be taking to this northerly climate. They were a faded yellow colour and spindly. As obviously new to the courtyard as the trees were the river-stone walkways, droopy flowers, berry bushes and the massive stone fountain. Just beyond was a low stone wall that acted as a partition into the market. A faint, rusty yellow had been painted on the stones to imitate age and wear. There was a mass of ivy reaching it's way up and across this wall. From a distance, much of the courtyard looked ancient, established and dependable. But each element was revealed as new and curiously fraudulent as they approached. The ivy had been tacked in place, transplanted from another wall, stolen from some distant place.

"My mom would say that this is charming and she would mean tacky," Dinky said as they rounded the fountain\.

"My mom would say it's charming and mean it," Elizabeth replied.

They cleared the low wall into the market, the conversation consumed by giggles. But the market wasn't as friendly and bustling as Elizabeth had been hoping it would be. Only about two thirds of the stalls were occupied. The others were swathed in dirty, white canvas that looked like old sails, giving the area an unused, seedy feel. The sellers there stared baldly at the newcomers, as did the few patrons. Elizabeth tried to turn her giggles into a cough and ended up swallowing them painfully. Dinky cleared his throat and managed a polite smile. They shared a nervous look and imitated the military posture that their Captain so often bore.

The outdoor portion of the market was lit naturally by the sunlight of the courtyard, the indoor by squat lamp-posts. The two peacekeepers found those lights to be dim and tarnished compared to the light outside as they made their first, slow rounds of the markets indoor interior.

"Oh, look at this," Elizabeth cooed. They were passing the stall of a mountainous, dark man who stood smoking an intricately carved pipe. His stall stood between two of the lamps and what little light it received from them was shrouded in sweet smoke. Instead of acknowledging his potential clients with a smile, he focused his eyes deliberately on their peacekeeper belts, and gathered his chest and shoulders up until he stood towering above them at his full height. The effort forced his thick neck taut and his head back. He observed them down a nose that had been broken often and never well set in the weak light.

Elizabeth fingered a richly ornamented wool dress and sighed. "I think this is charming and I mean that. You see? This is why I was so excited about the market. I've never seen anything even remotely *like* this before in my whole life!"

"I guess I didn't really appreciate this sort of thing until now," Dinky said. The corners of his mouth fluttered and his eyes softened, seeing something faraway as he looked at his friend. Tentatively, he placed his hand on the small of her back to lead her to the rest of their rounds. Elizabeth managed to make her surprise at his gentle touch look like adoration of the brightly colored scarves and dresses. She fell into step beside him.

After walking past the remaining stalls of the ground level in silence, Elizabeth regained enough control over herself to speak again. Plus, she couldn't stand walking in silence anymore - it felt so strange to be with Dinky and have nothing to say. Even worse, most of the market goers and stall attendants – the local indigenous population that the

Chief had mentioned in his speech, went silent as they approached and only began to speak again in whispers once they had passed. The whispers were harried and agitated. It made Elizabeth uncomfortable.

"What's with these people?" she whispered.

Dinky raised his eyebrows at her, in a helpless gesture. "We should probably talk about it somewhere else."

"Right." Elizabeth cleared her throat awkwardly. "I guess that you got to go to market all the time, eh?"

Dinky chuckled. "You said 'eh'. If my dad heard me say something like that instead of using a proper sentence, he'd probably wash my mouth with soap. Not that I mind your hillbilly sensibilities or anything."

Elizabeth wrinkled her nose at him, marching up the spiral stairs to the second level of the market where the foodstuff stalls were located.

"I went pretty frequently," he said, "my mom took me a lot when I was a kid, she was always looking for new things for the house and her wardrobe. It usually felt like a chore."

They passed a woman with heavily charcoaled eyelids and an impossibly gold afghan matched to the ring in her nose. She watched them silently, then turned to her neighbour and said something neither of them could understand.

"This is starting to feel like a chore, too," Elizabeth whispered, trying not to turn around and look at the woman. "What is going on here?"

"They don't seem particularly happy to see us, do they?"

"Don't see why they wouldn't be. Chief said they got nice homes and now they've got jobs, too. What more do they want?"

The second floor was small, the stalls loosely packed with many empty slots. The savoury smells of roasting meet and exotic spices were diluted by the dusty scent of as-yet-unused construction. It all had a makeshift feel. They followed the outer wall slowly until they were standing at the balcony that looked down into the courtyard, some distance from the nearest marketeers. Dinky said, "It reminds me of the police downtown, in Lila. Some people would look at them suspiciously, as if they were afraid that the police would just turn on them."

Elizabeth nodded. "I seen the same thing in town once, when Mark and I were loading up his dad's stall for Sunday market. Two policemen came in and just stood there watching us. Everyone felt like maybe they were doing something wrong, and everyone acted real careful, not talking much, not touching anything they weren't going to buy in case it looked like they were trying to steal it."

"We're not the police," Dinky said.

"We're the closest thing there is here."

They were standing at the end of their route through the market, less than an hour after arriving for their shift. They stood silently for a moment, then Elizabeth tapped her foot and let out a long sigh.

"What are we supposed to do now?" she asked.

"Do the round again, I guess. Or just... stand here and watch them."

"No. That won't do. Let's talk to them, be nice, ask about their day, show them that we're not to be scared of."

Dinky tried to object, but Elizabeth had already set off resolutely towards the woman with the gold scarf. Elizabeth smiled and nodded in greeting. She gestured to the woman's wares: an assortment of dried herbs, wound in colourful twine, berries wrapped in cheesecloth, and dried meats.

I'm walking through the grasses over the hill from home. It's the time of year when there are tiny blue butterflies, and a hundred floral colours dotting the grasses all around me. I'm holding the sage grass loosely in my hand, walking slowly to feel the warmth of the sun on my bare shoulders and the wind stirring the grass around my legs. I almost have enough to braid for the cleansing of our new home. Once that's done we'll be able to...

Elizabeth smiled again, this time to herself. She remembered walking through a field, collecting sage grass.

"This all looks delicious," Elizabeth said slowly, "you must be a very successful saleswoman here."

The woman blinked. She was surprised by this young woman's pertness.

"How long have you been in the colony?" Elizabeth continued.

Now the woman tilted her head to the side and narrowed her eyes.

"I'm Elizabeth, by the way. And this is Dink- Dingham. Will Dingham. We just arrived last night. We're both really excited to be here."

"Pleased to meet you," Dinky put in nervously.

The woman licked her lips. "You want to buy?" She had a thick accent unlike anything Elizabeth had heard. She looked to Dinky for reassurance, assuming he would have been exposed to people of all kinds thanks to his inner city upbringing.

Dinky held up his palms, to indicate "no" but Elizabeth pulled them back down. "Yes," she said, "I'd like some of the sage grass. I'm in a new place after all. A new home."

There was a silence so deafening in response that Elizabeth had to glance between the woman and Dinky, hoping to understand what she had said wrong. "What?"

The woman shook her head as if to clear it and handed one of the braided herbs wound in blue twine to her. As she did so, she made a spirla gesture with her left hand. Elizabeth smiled and returned the gesture. She held out her payment, but at the sight of Elizabeth returning the blessing of the sage, the woman blanched. She extended a shaking hand to take the money from Elizabeth.

"What was that?" Dinky asked, as they walked away.

"I have no idea! What was wrong with that lady?"

"No, Elizabeth," He turned to face her and stopped walking, "You. What was that weird thing you did with your hand? And what is that stuff you bought? You freaked that lady out. And you sort of freaked me out, too."

Elizabeth turned red as if she had been slapped. "It's sage grass! Maybe you don't know about it because you didn't grow up near any wild fields. You pick it in late summer, braid it and then burn it in your new home. It clears bad spirits."

"Bad spirits? What are you talking about! What is a 'bad spirit'?"

Elizabeth opened her mouth and closed it. She honestly didn't know.

How *could* there be a 'bad spirit'? Spirit was a word for someone once they had died and left their body behind. They couldn't be bad, once that happened, because then they were freed of all the modes of humanity, all of the different roles that they may have had to play, all Human Ethos. A spirit was naturally good, untarnished and immaterial. Even if bad spirits were possible, they wouldn't be able to do harm. They wouldn't be animated by Ethos of any kind - good or bad.

"It's... it's got something to do with plants and animals, and..." Elizabeth scrunched her face together in concentration, "Look, I don't know. I must have heard it when I was a kid. From an aunt or an old lady in our village. Must just be an old wives tale. Anyways, there's no harm - sage smells real nice when it's burned, so our tent will be nice and aromatic."

Her last sentence was meant to be a joke, but Dinky barely smiled. Could there really be such differences in culture, belief and knowledge between city and village, apartment and farm? She supposed that must be it.

"You're a funny girl, miss Lizzy," he said.

"Hilarious." She turned and began to walk again, this time back towards the spiral staircase that led to the ground floor. "I think that went well, anyways. Let's try it again, only this time you do the talking. I don't want to be broke after my first day."

Chapter Eight

Elizabeth and Dinky passed the day attempting conversation with the market goers. Most were antagonistic, many didn't seem to understand a word that they said. Dinky was mesmerized by Elizabeth's sustained politeness and spirit. Even though he knew her energy had faltered, she managed to introduce the two of them to nearly all of the stall attendants. They didn't learn much, few responded to their questions and those who did mostly answered yes or no. Still, at the end of their shift, when the market had emptied and they walked slowly back to their camp, they agreed that it had been a successful first day.

There was an unspoken tension between them, a curiosity and a nervous energy. Neither had mentioned it, and after that first touch on her lower back, both strove to maintain a professional physical distance. Elizabeth wondered if that was as hard for Dinky as it was for her. She wasn't yet willing to risk complicating her only friendship in this progressively stranger place, nor her position as a peacekeeper. She could have a career here. There were actually no rules against romance between peacekeepers, but she posited that was because up until six months prior no women had been allowed in the program.

By the time Mark returned to the camp, Elizabeth had already burned the small braid of sage grass in the tent and around it's perimeter.

"What's that smell?" he asked, immediately.

"Something from the market," she replied. She didn't want to go through the same awkward conversation with Mark that she had with Dinky.

"Huh," he grunted, and collapsed onto the foldable chair that Elizabeth had set out beside the fire pit for him.

"You look bushed, baye," she teased, falling into her natural accent to make him feel more comfortable, "Whatcha seen? Tough day?"

"You dunno the half of it, dear. Been a tough one alright. Big fight with one of the boys from the other crew."

"What happened?"

"Well, they been here a few days already, right? And I'm teamed up with one, name's Bill. He comes from across the lake from us, actually. Quite a ways away, but somewhere we know, by Big Rock, south of Lila. Anyways, those fucking coal-eyes been causing trouble the whole time the other crew's been here so far, that's what Bill said. Been *soliciting*." Mark said the final word with great emphasis and palpable embarrassment.

"What's soliciting?"

"You know!" Mark threw his hands up, exasperated.

"I don't."

"God, you're such a baby. You know, when a lady tries to sell... herself. Tries to get with guys for money."

Elizabeth blushed. "Oh."

"Yeah, exactly. *Oh*. Well, some of the guys from the other crew, they're tougher'en us I guess. Rougher. Come from cattle country, way down to the south from us and our farms. Bill says they got a funny way about em, real... personal. Anyways one of them cattle-boys took up a coal-eye's offer, no joking! Right on shift, too, when he was supposed to be patrolling with us. Me an Bill, we were chatting and joking and then we realized he was missing. So we started walking around and looking for him, not real busy like, but just looking."

Mark took his shoes off and started burying his toes in the sandy earth. Elizabeth's eyebrows drew together. He was upset.

"What happened then?"

"Well, we heard a commotion. Lots of fucking coal eyes yelling and things getting thrown. We run over right, through the neighbourhood we were patrolling, to this little hut. Rusty, this cattle-boy, he's getting thrown from the hut all naked, holding his clothes and his peacekeeper belt in his hands and yelling all sorts of swears. There's this giant coal eye fella following him out of the hut, yelling at him about something, we don't know what. The coal eye is pushing him, spitting on him! There's some other coal eyes around, they're yelling too, and they start spitting and throwing little rocks at Rusty. Little at first. Well, Rusty didn't waste any time. Dropped everything but his baton and his taser and zapped the big guy, naked as the day he was born. The guy dropped as soon as he was tasered, started shaking on the ground. Don't know why, but Rusty hit him with his baton, hard as he could. Right in the head, too. Look, Lizzy I don't know if I should tell you the rest." Mark didn't have to say the rest – he was her only male relative here, and that meant he was supposed to protect her.

"Just tell me, you moron," she said, with just enough acrimony to remind him that she was as tough as he was even if she didn't know what soliciting meant.

"Yeah, right," he mumbled. "The other coal eyes went right at Rusty. Some throwing rocks, some hitting. I couldn't believe it. The woman, she come out of the hut by then, tits all hanging out. She just watched, quiet as a mouse. Bill and me, we ran in and tried to push them away from Rusty. Bill got hit in the head with a rock, but he's fine. Just three stitches. Me, I just got a couple bruises. But Rusty, he's still in the infirmary, in the town centre building. Hadn't woken up yet when we left. All the guys there that beat up on him got put in jail, don't know how long they'll be there. Didn't even know we had a jail, don't even know where it is. And the one guy... the one coal eye guy, well the woman saw him, right as soon as we got everyone quieted down a bit. She started screaming, shaking him. He was still twitching a little, in his fingers. Doctor said that in rare cases, the tazers stop the heart. The guy died, Dizzy. Rusty killed him."

Elizabeth sat beside her cousin silently. A peacekeeper, one of the supposed 'good guys', had purchased sex illegally and then killed the man that tried to stop him. Had nearly caused a riot by doing so.

Looking back over her own day, she was suddenly convinced of how well she and Dinky had done by comparison.

"I'm sorry, Mark," she whispered.

"Yeah, me too."

"It'll go better tomorrow, don't worry."

"Easy for you to say. I'm gonna have to see that lady every day for the next week, until my next assignment comes in. Bill said that we couldn't tell anyone about the... soliciting, because then Rusty'd get put in jail too. Maybe worse, even. I bet that she'd a got put in jail if we did tell, but we didn't. Then once we were all taken care of at the infirmary, another of them cattle boys said that the lady got what she deserved, because..." Mark's face went dark, "only sluts would do that anyways. I thought that was real rough."

Elizabeth swallowed. She wished there was something she could say to make her cousin feel better. Even though he was a few months older and much wiser when it came to things like soliciting, it often felt like she was the one that took care of him. She wished there was something she could do. Even more, she wished that dinner would go by quickly so that she wouldn't have to wait to tell Dinky everything that Mark had just told her.

Chapter Nine

"...This Rusty guy is still in the infirmary, and when Mark and Bill left this afternoon he still hadn't woken up. The guy he tazered is *dead*. His heart stopped, when the taser hit him. And the rest of the – the coal eyes, I guess that's what everyone is calling them, they were all put in jail."

Dinky let out a whistle, long and low. They were sitting on the ground, at the very outer edge of light cast by Elizabeth's dying fire. Mark had gone to bed early and she couldn't blame him after the day he had. The two of them sat with their heads close together, whispering at each other.

"This is *not* how it was supposed to be," Dinky said.

"I know. That's what I thought, too. It's just like in the market today. Remember the brochure they gave us, back at the start of training? About how we were gonna be part of the colonial community."

"There are lots of colonies. This one is just new, that's all. There's bound to be some bumps along the way."

"This was a *big* bump," Elizabeth said.

Dinky sat silently for a moment. "At least you and I did well today."

"That might all change tomorrow. What if the rest of them, the coal eyes, find out what happened? What if they blame *all* of us?"

"Don't worry too much, Lizzy. There's nothing we can do about it anyways. Besides," Dinky looked at her full in the face, his eyes soft and dark in the firelight, "if you're as friendly and charming tomorrow as you were today, we won't have a problem."

Elizabeth's worries evaporated instantly. *Charming.* He thought she had been *charming*.

"Thanks, Dinky. That's sweet of you." She pulled her knees up to her chest and rested her chin on them, looking at the fire.

"Well, I mean it." Elizabeth watched quietly as he reached his long, slender fingers slowly towards her and touched her knee with his fingertips. Then he swallowed audibly and retracted them. "Goodnight, Lizzy. I should get to bed." He stood and walked away.

Elizabeth sighed and let her head rest on her folded knees. She could hear the tinkle of the white poplars just over the hill and let the sound wash over her. In spite of everything, she couldn't help but feel this was a good place, a special place. Almost like she belonged here. As she lay on her little mattress that night, falling asleep, she remembered Dinky's hand stretching out to touch her. Such a simple thing and so clear in her mind's eye: his fingers looking waterstone smooth in the low, orange light. They move slowly and cautiously. She fell asleep.

There's chirping. It's evening and we're sitting on a fallen log. The sky is fading from brilliant blue to a smokey dusk and the air is warm and golden. The river runs nearby, I can hear it and it makes me smile. Cameron smiles back. I look away, at the broken horizon of mountains and forest. I listen to the birds and the busy tree rodents singing happily as they finish another summer day's work. I look down. Cameron's hand, large and rough is moving towards mine, resting on the log beside me. He takes my hand, gently, and runs his fingers over my knuckles. His skin is like sandpaper but it's warm.

It's winter now and I'm sitting on the floor, on a thick rug beside our old stove. It's fire crackles inside and I work quietly by the light it casts, sewing up the hole in his sock. He kneels beside me and takes my hand in his. The cold weather has coarsened it.

Then I'm running down the beach of the river delta. We've been betrayed and I am desperate. It's too late, there's nowhere to go and it's my fault. Everyone is wailing and screaming. The beeping of the radiological detectors on our armbands is incessant. I see him and he sprints towards me, beloved, rough hand outstretched. I know that I'm screaming, too, but can barely hear what I'm saying. That I love him. We must reach each other before the weapon destroys us, for the Untura. Dina is ahead, alone, wringing her hands and sobbing. She's so young. How could I have done this? How could I have trusted them? Just in time I see his hand lace tightly around mine, connecting us in our moment of death. I grab Dina with my free hand: she will not die alone. I will create Untura with both of them, if my will is strong enough. I step forward, and everything goes white.

Chapter Ten

"Lizzy come on, what's wrong with you?"

Elizabeth saw a shape that must be Mark. He was blurred and moving back and forth. Vertigo corrected her - she was the one moving back and forth. She tried to push him away and hide under her blanket but her arms were weak and unresponsive.

"Fine! Miss breakfast. Be late. Whatever." Mark's angry voice again. He stopped shaking her and disappeared from her line of sight. She tried to push her eyes open but they were sticky, resistant and closed as soon as there was any small break in her will.

Elizabeth was still lost in the memories. She had expected to wake up under the thin quilt, in the log cabin, with the garden outside. With Cameron. At the same time, she was not surprised by Mark being there. Of course Mark would be there - he had been there most of her life, hadn't he? But something was wrong. There had been a tragedy. Something terrible had happened...

everything goes white

Elizabeth's eyes flew open, the dew and dust finally clearing from them. She sat upright, disoriented. *It's alright,* she thought, *I'm in the tent. Because I'm on a peacekeeping mission. My first. I'm in the camp outside the colony. Dinky and I are going to the market again today to patrol. Everything is alright.*

But it wasn't. Because there was something else. There was another place and another time. She could remember them; at least, she was starting to.

This doesn't make sense, she thought, pressing her hands against her eyes. *This isn't happening.*

"This is your last chance, Dizzy, you've got ten seconds before I eat your breakfast."

She jumped off her mattress and unzipped the tent. The bright morning sun made her blink and she had to shield her eyes with the back of her hand before she was able to see. Mark pursed his lips at her and handed her a plate of eggs that had been sitting on his lap.

"What is with you this morning, Liz?" he asked, tying his boots.

She shook her head without answering. Growing up, Elizabeth had been the one to wake Mark up. Time to play, time for chores, time for market - whatever the morning's activities, Elizabeth would be ready and Mark would take his time. Remembering their childhood lives left her with an overwhelming sense of doubt. The memories in her dreams, they weren't real. They couldn't be.

"I had some really weird dreams last night," she finally answered.

Mark nodded.

"I know. You kept waking me up because you were talking."

Elizabeth's stomach dropped. It was bad enough that she might be going crazy. She didn't need her cousin to find out.

"You kept saying 'I'll see you again, we're connected, I'll see you again'. You seemed upset over it. Must have been some mighty nightmare."

Elizabeth let out a long sigh. "You don't know the half of it."

"Well, you're out of it now," Mark said. Then he thought better and punched her in the shoulder. "Try not to be such a girl all the time," he chuckled and ducked back into the tent to get dressed.

Chapter Eleven

They are just dreams. Elizabeth was still trying to convince but in her heart she knew better. They were not dreams, or at least, not just dreams. They were true events. As real to her as her recollection of that morning's breakfast. Strange as it was, seeing as she had only started to remember these things in the last three days, she felt that they were a part of her identity.

In other words, real. Real things that had really happened to her.

She grumbled quietly, unsure if her reasoning was sound. Even if it was, she was very concerned about where this conclusion would leave her.

"What's wrong?" It was a statement, not a question.

"I told you, bad dreams."

They had walked back to the colony in general silence. The excitement of the day before had been replaced by somber vigilance as the news of yesterday's death spread through the group. Some were worried, others seemed curious or confused. The chatter of the first day's march from camp was replaced by conspiratorial whispering.

Now, she and Dinky were making their way through the courtyard towards the market, and Elizabeth was just as subdued, even though they were alone.

"You're angry at me, aren't you. Is it because of... last night?"

Elizabeth blinked at Dinky, surprised.

"No, it's not that," she said, remembering his slender fingers and the slight pressure of them on her knee. As soon as she did, her mind flooded with the other images; the bigger, stronger and rougher hands of a man that she could remember, but that she had never met.

Elizabeth shook her head, trying to clear it. She forced herself to focus on the one memory - the one that made some semblance of sense - of Dinky reaching out to touch her. It brought a faint smile to her face.

"Dinky, that was *nice*," she looked at him in the eyes and her smile grew. "Really nice." She blushed and looked away. They had stopped walking, standing just outside of the market. Just as tentatively as he had the night before, she reached her hand out to his where it hung at his side and squeezed two of his fingers firmly before letting go. It *did* feel nice. But that other man's hands, Cameron's hands... Elizabeth felt tears welling up in her eyes at the thought of Cameron and turned from Dinky abruptly.

"Come on," she said over her shoulder, trying to keep any indicator of inner turmoil out of her voice.

I've never met him, but I know him. I remember him. I remember touching him, being with him, believing that I had a future with him... She couldn't think straight. None of it made any sense. *But something went wrong. Something terrible happened. I've never met him, and now I'll never know him, because of... whatever it was.*

Elizabeth tried to remember his face or any other details about him. She went over her sparse memories of him again, frustrated by their limitations. His face was always in shadow, or just out of her sight. Even at the end, when she had been running, his features were blurred by movement.

At the end, she thought. *then everything went white. That... terrible thing that happened. It killed us. It killed all of us.*

And somehow, it was my fault.

Chapter Twelve

Any progress that Elizabeth and Dinky made their first day in the market had evaporated overnight. The narrow paths between the stalls grew oppressively quiet wherever they went, but exploded into angry whispers once they had passed by.

"My question is why they're here in the first place."

"What do you mean?" Elizabeth asked. They were walking slowly, almost strolling and speaking in whispers.

"I mean, if they came here for work opportunities, then you'd think they would be more upbeat."

"That's true."

"Another question: *where* are they coming from?"

"You've never seen people like this before?"

"Like what – with coal on their eyes, this kind of dress, the sort of dark skin and all that? No. I've seen lots of different kinds of people. My dad's a diplomat, and we've had people over for dinner from all sorts of places. I've had to play with their kids and act polite and charming my whole life. And I've never seen... coal eyes before. By the way, I don't like that name. It's condescending. And it's going to encourage the wrong attitude in the others."

"Maybe."

Elizabeth listened as Dinky postulated about the origins and circumstances surrounding the colony's only colonists. She tried to focus on what he was saying but found herself revisiting the shadowy dreams again.

Even if things happened and not just my imagination getting the better of me, they aren't mine. They don't fit with my life. And if those events are real, somehow, they all happened a long, long time ago. So even if this Cameron guy is somehow a real person instead of a figment of my imagination, he's dead. Long dead.

But that doesn't make sense, either... because if he's dead, then I ought to be, too. And if you're dead, you can't remember things. I'm alive, and so are the memories. If they're real, that is. But they have to be! I've seen those things, felt them, smelled them!

"Are you even listening to me?"

Elizabeth stared at Dinky, open mouthed.

"Sorry, Dinky. I just got distracted. What were you saying?"

"I was wondering why we aren't building more permanent settlements for ourselves here."

"Good question."

"I mean, both crews are full of people at the start of their careers, besides the Captains. Doesn't that seem strange to you? Especially after what the Chief said about how important all of this is? The whole thing just doesn't make sense."

"No."

Dinky examined his friend out of the corner of his eye. Distracted again, it seemed. She was shuffling along beside him, barely paying attention to anything, with a faraway look in her eyes and a small frown knit into her forehead.

"What's wrong with you?"

She blinked. "Nothing."

"Come on, Dizzy."

"I'm fine. I mean it." She glared at him, eyes as wide as they would go and eyebrows lifted. Hopefully he would understand not to push the issue any further.

"Right." Dinky sighed. They continued along the narrow corridors between stalls, examining the wares silently. Elizabeth tried to snap back into her immediate surroundings. She didn't want to push her only friend away, not now. Besides that, she had never been one to let herself be overrun by any situation, especially one as bizarre as a psychological invasion by ancestral visions. She immediately noticed many coal rimmed eyes watching them as they passed.

"I feel like a celebrity," Elizabeth whispered, "and not the good kind."

Dinky raised his eyebrows in agreement. "Do you remember, a few years ago, the riot in Mount Ganai?"

"I think so. I heard about it from a girl who lived down the road from me."

"I live just north of there, in Lila, the main city. There's a pretty popular entertainment district in Ganai that my dad always really liked."

"Right, I've heard of it."

"Even when things were getting worse and worse in Ganai, my dad took the whole family for a night at the theater. Said he had better things to do than be bothered with people who wouldn't be happy anywhere. Walking into the theater back then felt sort of like this does now."

"Why were the people in Ganai upset?"

"It wasn't all of them. Thing is, there were a lot of people there from... somewhere way far south. Can't remember the name of the country, but it was some colonial holding or other. Kids at school called them Azies. Some of them had been living in the city for their whole lives. But their religion warned against animated technology, and they had this superstition that we were part robot, or something like that and so they were terrified of us. They only socialized with each other so that even Azies who were born in the city never really learned our language. Most of them ended up working pretty menial jobs because of that – cashier clerks at the theaters, holding up signs or handing out flyers, stuff like that. They weren't happy and they wanted to go back home, but they didn't have enough money. They didn't have enough money for a lot of things. I remember someone saying that the Azies thought we had a plot to keep them poor and use them like slaves."

"Hold on. You're telling me they thought we were robots?"

"Something like that. I can't remember exactly. It had something to do with our technology. They were almost totally agrarian in their home country and thought that most technology was evil."

"Huh."

Dinky smiled at his friend. Her brow was scrunched tightly together, one eyebrow raised slightly.

"Anyways, almost all of the theater district employees were Azies. They looked at us like we were a different species or something. Like we had personally done something terrible to them, something that we could never, ever take back."

"I see the similarity," Elizabeth replied. They were walking the darker, stuffier lane of the market now, the indoor section of the first floor. There were fewer occupied stalls here but there were still more than enough people for her to feel their antagonism. She could see something akin to hatred in their eyes. But it was not pure. It was mixed with a harried fear, the kind that one feels if the object of their anxiety is incomprehensibly, entirely evil.

"A few days later, the whole of Mount Ganai was shut down. The Azies trashed everything they could get their hands on. It took almost a week before it was open to the public again. Another two years of constant peacekeeper supervision before it was deemed to be a safe area."

"Are you saying that you think there's going to be a riot here?"

Dinky thought about it. "Not necessarily. I'm just saying that I wouldn't be surprised. It's like I was saying before. Why send in new recruits, why not build permanent houses for the peacekeepers, why aren't there any settlers here from other places if this is such an important colony? Something isn't right here."

Elizabeth nodded. The question she couldn't shake: what would happen next?

"What do we do about it?" she asked.

Dinky blinked in surprise. "I have no idea," he said with a sad chuckle.

Elizabeth laughed too, giving him a lopsided smile.

"We *are* peacekeepers, Dinky. If something isn't right, it's our job to fix it."

He nodded, unconvinced.

"Why did you enlist, anyways?" Elizabeth asked. They had reached the stairs to the second level and stopped there, facing each other. Their slow, measured rounds suddenly seemed sort of useless. If these people wanted to riot, it wouldn't matter if these two young adults with tasers and clubs strapped to their belts were shuffling down the corridor or standing still.

"You first," he said, narrowing his eyes at her playfully.

"To show Mark up, obviously," she said. "Seriously, I did because I could. I was always faster, smarter, worked harder and I was tired of being told that was strange. I wanted to get away from farmland but obviously couldn't just up and move to the city all by myself. I saw a poster at market one day, when I was twelve or so, for the corps. My cousins laughed at me when I said I wanted to do it. But I trained for it every day and two months before my seventeenth birthday they passed the law saying girls could enlist for this mission. I enlisted on my birthday, as soon as I could. My mom cried, but she didn't understand. Wait until I'm Captain, or even a Chief. I guess I was never one to just... do what everyone else expected."

Dinky smiled at her, holding her gaze.

"You're amazing, Elizabeth."

She tried to swallow and sort of choked instead. Then she cleared her throat. "Your turn. Why'd you join?"

Well it's sort of a funny story..."

"I'm prepared to laugh. Give me a signal if you say something you think is supposed to be funny and I don't."

"Shut up. I went to grammar school. You know, supposed to be for smart kids, actually for rich kids. Did you know I can speak four languages?"

"Ha... ha," Elizabeth said flatly, then smiled, "sorry, I'll stop. Go on."

"Everyone in grammar school was going to the north to study. Everyone including me. The thing is, I started thinking about life in a monastery, even if it was just for a couple of years and I realized that I didn't *want* to go. It seemed like I didn't have an option. Everyone expected me to become a doctor. It felt like I had no say, no influence, and the next thing I knew, I was already enrolled for a residency at Sensacordica, this sanitarium monastery two hours north of Lila. I had some sort of scholarship where I would live in a little cabin on site and I they even gave me a schedule of everything I would be doing, every day, for the next two years."

"Woah."

"Yeah. Exactly. I got that schedule and I spent a few hours sitting in my room just staring at it. Then I spent the night writing down things that I liked, or didn't; things I wanted, things I didn't. I woke up the next morning and went to the enlisting centre instead of to school. Training started the day after I graduated. I figured I could do this until I figure out what else there is."

"What else there is to do?"

"No, what else there is. In general."

Elizabeth smiled. *"You're amazing, Dinky."*

He blushed furiously and led the way up the spiral staircase to the second floor of the market.

Chapter Thirteen

Elizabeth and Dinky spent the rest of the day in close conversation about what more there could be for two young and adventurous people to discover. They made a total of fifteen slow laps around the stalls of the market. Neither of them kept track. It was only by the bright liveliness of the conversation that the pervasive sense of discord surrounding them began to fade. They barely noticed the grim silences and the evil looks aimed at them. Nor did they attempt to philosophize further on a solution for the surrounding hostility. Everything seemed momentarily lost, pushed away by the connection that had sprung up between them. Elizabeth even forgot about the strange memories.

When they arrived back at camp that evening, the Captain was waiting on the path with a clipboard and a frown.

"Dinghum, Walker," he said, nodding pertly, "There will be a mandatory meeting tonight back at the Centre to address the unrest that we experienced yesterday. Are there any issues that you would like addressed?"

Dinky blinked, looking to Elizabeth for guidance. She shushed him with her eyes.

"No, sir." She said. "The market's been real quiet."

"Hmph," Captain made two checks on the paper in front of him, already turning to the next peacekeepers down the path returning to camp. "Six sharp. See you there."

They set out to Elizabeth's campsite for dinner, and Mark emerged from the tent as they approached.

"Hey Dizzy, Dinky. You hear about the meeting?"

Elizabeth and Dinky nodded, settling into folding chairs side by side.

"I'm glad about it, actually. I just wonder what they're gonna say." Mark said, sitting down in another of the folding chairs in front of the tent.

"Procedures," Elizabeth said, and stood back up. She stretched, then opened their food locker and handed each of the boys a dehydrated meal ration.

"Maybe they'll finally tell us what the hell is going on around here," Dinky said. He was going to say more, but Elizabeth elbowed him in the ribs as she handed him his meal.

"I just hope that I'm not in trouble," Mark said, the corners of his mouth edging downwards, "I mean, about yesterday. I did my best, ya know?"

Chapter Fourteen

The three of them sat near the back of the room. It seemed they had taken longer with their dinner than most of their camp mates and had to rush to the open seats before the Chief started speaking. Electricity was palpable in the air as Chief made his way across the stage to the podium in long, confident strides.

"I wonder where he lives," Dinky whispered to Elizabeth. "Probably not in a tent."

"Shh." She turned her attention to the Chief.

"Welcome back, everyone!" Chief boomed. "How are we enjoying our first assignments?"

There was a low, ambiguous murmur.

"I said, how are we enjoying our first assignment?!"

The peacekeepers applauded generously. There were a few whistles and Dinky cheered, winking at Elizabeth as he did so. Elizabeth bit her lip. A sudden flash of heat kissed up her inner thighs.

Dinky winked at me, she thought. *Hot.*

"Good. I know what it's like, being dropped in a new country and told to call it home. I was once a recruit myself after all, though I've stopped counting the decades since," the Chief added. A few of the boys laughed uncomfortably.

"I know that you have already heard about what happened yesterday." The Chief paused, scanning the faces in his audience. His own visage was supremely, regally cold. "There is always a first incident and it is always upsetting. Disturbing. It is difficult to understand why people choose to spit on the offer of order and safety we have made them. Remember the statues on the beach and you will begin to understand. The Ethos operate within every one of us. And while the people that we protect may choose to act on the madness inside, we must never waver in our resolve to keep the peace. Yesterday a drunken boor tried to beat his wife in public, thinking us impotent and incompetent to stop him. Several brave young recruits proved him wrong. I congratulate all of you that were involved in yesterday's unfortunate event for your level-headedness and bravery. You kept our mission alive and that makes you our first heroes but certainly not our last. There will be more tribulations in the weeks to come and I can only hope others will follow your example."

Mark's mouth fell open. A few seats ahead of him Bill was wearing an identical expression of disbelief. They both were inundated with pats on the back and handshakes from those nearby, while those further away applauded heartily.

"Weird," Elizabeth whispered to Dinky.

"Yeah," he replied, "looks like you were right not to say anything to the Captain."

"I had a feeling."

Elizabeth sighed, and to her surprise, Dinky responded by laying his hand over hers and squeezing gently.

So hot. She smiled, suddenly breathless, and squeezed his hand back. As the applause blew over, the Chief's stance relaxed and a playful smile flitted across his face.

"Alright, alright, quiet down." He raised his hands congenially. "Now. To help get everyone settled in, your Captains and I have planned activities every night for the rest of this week. They aren't mandatory, but we do encourage you to come out, meet your fellow peacekeepers and enjoy yourselves. For the next hour, we're going to do a tour of the whole colony. Anyone who wishes to join us is more than welcome."

The Chief stepped down from the podium. , the crowd realized that the presentation was finished and tentative conversation resumed.

For a moment, Mark continued to look as surprised and worried as he had when the Chief lied so blatantly about what had happened the day before. Then he shrugged, and his face lifted.

"For sure, eh?" Mark said to the others, frowning appreciatively. "Definitely want to go. Nothin' better to do and besides, there's a lady in the other crew and I'd sure like to meet her!"

"Sure you do." Elizabeth said. "But does *she* want to meet *you*?"

Dinky snorted. "Why not, I guess. This could be fun," he said. They followed the crowd towards the grand doors leading past the stage and out to the main hall of the town building. Dinky leaned his head in to Elizabeth and whispered, "I've already met a girl." She looked at him, confused and he pointed to her with a playful, unsure smile.

"Oh," she said. Then she punched him in the shoulder and they both burst out laughing.

Elizabeth's cheeks were cherry red, her eyes shining. Her skin felt warm. The energy of anticipation and curiosity between her and Dinky was intoxicating and she laughed and giggled and carried on like a drunk. The best part was that he looked and acted the same way, so that it felt they were in a little world all their own. To the men around them he betrayed no sign of the bubbling chemistry between them, something for which she was grateful. He joked, traded jibes and treated Elizabeth with the same quiet courtesy that she had come to depend on since they had met. What had happened between them and what might still happen was in a little world all their own. He did this with such gravity that Mark too became caught up in their lightheartedness, making jokes and teasing his friends as the casual tour plodded on. Soon Ray, Bill, several of his rancher friends and a few others were grouped together at the back of the crowd, laughing and talking, paying no attention at all to the Chief's presentation, or to the courtyard, infirmary, market, or squat little neighbourhoods with nauseatingly cute names like Babble Brook Corner and East Birch Meadow Road.

When the tour was over, the group of about a dozen sat on the steps of the grand town building, joking and swapping stories, until well after dark. They told a few dirty jokes and a boy named Nate from the south called Elizabeth a gash, which Mark had to explain referred to her girl parts, but she took it in stride.

"I don't know about you guys, but us rancher folk need our beauty sleep," Bill said, once there was a lull in the conversation.

"True enough," Nate put in, his voice low and gruff. "Nice talkin' to y'all, even you, bearded clam. Not as bad as I 'spected." The other ranchers bawled with laughter at this, but Elizabeth gave him the finger and pretended that it didn't bother her at all.

"We might as well turn in, too," Dinky said, taking his glasses off with one hand in order to rub his eyes with the other, "I don't know about you country people, but in the city, they say the early bird catches the worm."

"Didn't know you had birds in the city," Mark said. "Or worms."

They said their goodnights amicably and soon it was just Mark, Elizabeth and Dinky again, heading back to their camp.

The tipsy, spirited state of the evening began to fade from Elizabeth as they walked through the little pocket of trembling, white trees in the moonlight. She found herself becoming acutely aware that she would soon be going back to sleep and that more disturbing dreams likely awaited her. Her nervousness and confusion about the identity Cameron, her own identity, the doubts about her sanity all returned at once, flooding her gut with tight, heavy, cold fear.

It was fear. Now, in the moonlight, as she came crashing down from the high of too much laughter and too little food, it was blinding and deafening. What was she going to do? She didn't want to go back to sleep, didn't want to be alone. Alone with more memories. And when she woke up the next morning, she would have to mind the mounting evidence that Rivertown was itself some sort of conspiracy. As she had told Dinky, if they didn't, no one would. Besides, if they didn't do something, they would likely end up entangled in whatever the conspiracy was.

I can't deal with this, Elizabeth thought morosely.

Mark yawned, scratching his belly. It was an early childhood mannerism that he still clung to, one that Elizabeth had once found annoying. It was comforting now. She knew that he would head straight for bed and would not interfere if she claimed she wanted to wash up first. Dinky would stay up with her. Elizabeth felt a quick flutter climb through her chest at the thought of being utterly alone with Dinky in the dead of night. He had done well distracting her from her worries through the day, maybe he could continue to be a distraction into the night...

Elizabeth exhaled forcefully, the heat between her legs pulsing, intensifying. Dinky was a distraction alright. She hoped he would stay up with her. Wondered if he was thinking about it, too; if he would want to touch her, if he knew much about sex. She suspected she had the mechanics down pretty well thanks to her aunt's gruesomely informative dinner table tales and the compulsive remarks of her male cousins. All that remained was putting the knowledge into action. Again she felt a flutter of clandestine excitement and moaned quietly to herself. She glanced at Dinky and a jolt went through her when she saw he was watching her, a painfully serious expression on his face.

Just as she had predicted, Mark mumbled goodnight and crawled immediately into the tent when they reached their campsite.

"I'll be a little while, Mark," she said. He mumbled some form of agreement and his breathing evened out almost immediately.

Elizabeth gulped, then turned to Dinky. He was still watching her, still earnest and unsmiling. She cleared her throat. "He's fast asleep."

Dinky nodded and pursed his lips.

"Will you stay up with me for a while?" she asked, heart pounding in her throat, heat and tension spreading through her groin.

Dinky nodded again. Neither moved for a moment. Then Elizabeth walked to a fallen log nearby and sat on the ground with her back against it. Dinky crossed the space between them quickly, eagerly and sat next to her. They looked at each other for a long, silent moment. The only sound was the distant rustle of the birch leaves and the rush of the river.

"I'm scared that I'll have more dreams," she said, finally.

"Elizabeth," he whispered. It seemed he had more to say, but he didn't finish.

Elizabeth turned her shoulders and inched towards him, closing the distance. He was breathing hard, watching her slow movements. He reached tentatively to her, tracing her cheek with three trembling fingers of one hand, cupping her head with the other. She closed her eyes and pressed her lips against his, painfully aware of her heart pounding. Then she pressed her body against him so that she could feel his heart beat, wrapped her fingers through his hair and around his shoulders, pulling him into her. He moaned quietly as she did and his hands lost all of their hesitation. He pulled at her shoulders, her waist, her hips and wrapped one arm around her to hold her more tightly to his body.

They lost track of time in their embrace. Finally Dinky pulled away. He sighed heavily, a small smile pulling at his lips. To Elizabeth, he looked almost relieved.

He thinks we're just going to kiss, she thought. She considered it for a moment. It would be easy to just say goodnight and go to bed. Continue on tomorrow, maybe, and prolong the anticipation for a few more days. But the thought of trying to sleep in her overstimulated state was a treacherous one. She would surely have more dreams, or memories, whatever they were. Elizabeth set her jaw and stood up to her knees. She reached first to Dinky's face, taking no time to caress him before taking his glasses off of his nose and placing them on the log beside her. Then she untucked the hem of her shirt and pulled it over her head.

The shock on Dinky's face was almost comical, but then he grew deadly serious and together they learned the serious business of love.

Chapter Fifteen

They lay silent except for their heartbeats. Elizabeth could feel the cascade of Dinky's pulse slow to a trickle. His breath became even.

She sat up, and Dinky sat up beside her, clearly unsure about whether he should cover himself or simply be naked. He watched her breath rise and fall, and the faint tremor of her breast in time with her heart.

"Wow."

She smiled at him. "Yeah."

"Are you leaving already?"

"It's late." she said.

"Yeah, it is." He sat up and watched her collect her clothes.

She smiled again, barely more than tightening her lips. "Thanks."

He pushed his hand through her loose hair, touched her cheek and pulled her into a gentle kiss. "This was ok, right? You're not leaving because you're upset?"

"I'm fine," she pulled her shirt on and fumbled with her belt, "and it was definitely ok. Better than ok. Ok?"

Dinky laughed quietly. "Ok."

She brushed her lips against his and left him sitting naked on the cool earth. As she ducked into her tent, she heard him whisper goodnight. It made her stop and truly smile to herself. She poked her head back out of the tent-flap and gave him a small wave before closing the zipper. Then she climbed into her sleeping bag, amazed at how utterly exhausted she was. It was a relief: she never remembered dreams after being this tired. As she fell asleep, she thought about Dinky and sex. About what it had felt like, looked like, smelled like...

Honeyberry. It smells like honeyberry, spruce and tamarack; like softwoods burning and cold wind. I'm lying on the bed and he's sitting on the edge of it, watching me. His face is clear in the soft evening light. It is our first night together and our wedding was just hours ago. He climbs forward carefully, covering my body with his, covering my face with light kisses, murmuring all the while that he loves me, loves me, loves me...

Suddenly, we're both laughing and crying all at once. Then he's jumping on the bed, triumpant, laughing. We're always laughing.

We undress each other slowly. Scared, apprehensive, electrified. I put my hand on his chest. His heartbeat is thunderous. I giggle and then we're serious. Naked. Afraid and exhilarated. We kiss, then kiss a dozen times, then three times more. He runs his hands over my body and I run mine over his. I'm surprised by how desperately I want... these unknown sensations. For now it's a nameless need, pulling into me, heating me up. Yes, this is serious, very serious. I love you, Maria, he says.

Come on, I say, no one will see us! I'm laughing, not just at the prospect of sex right here in the woods where anyone could happen by and see us but at how aghast Cameron is at the idea. He shakes his head silently, eyes wide. I laugh again and dart into the trees, towards a bed of moss hidden from the path by low brush. I look over my shoulders at him and bat my eyelashes, unbuttoning the simple wool dress clinging to my damp skin. I drop it on the ground next to me and let the sight take effect. Not always serious.

There is a tinkle of leaves in the warm wind outside our home. I hold his hand over my heart, he holds my hand over his. This is more than sex. This is the greatest act of humanity achievable by two people - the act of creation. We will create a child tonight. Our first. Ours. Blessed with a love as perfect and genuine as ours, this act is the fulfillment of our destiny. When we're finished, he begins to fall asleep almost immediately.

"Goodnight, Cam," I say.

He murmurs, maybe trying to say something. I know exactly what he means, either way.

"I hope it worked this time, too," I whisper and sigh again.

Chapter Sixteen

Elizabeth woke to the sound of frying grease. She kept her eyes closed, savouring the recollection of love making from the night before.

He's already making breakfast, she thought, *probably eggs. Butter eggs, just like he knows I like. Like my mom used to make.*

After a long moment, she opened her eyes. She was instantly overcome by panic.

Where am I?

Elizabeth shot out of bed, bumping her head again on the low ceiling of the tent.She tugged at her hair. It was shorter than she remembered.

The tent. I'm at Rivertown.

She started to get dressed and caught a glimpse of herself in the mirror.

I'm at Rivertown...that means I'm Elizabeth, not Maria.

If I'm at Rivertown, she thought, biting back a swelling panic, *then it's not Cameron making the eggs at all. It's Mark. Cameron's dead - worse, I've never met him. We weren't together last night! I was here, in this tent. And Cameron was dead. Long dead. Maybe he never existed at all.*

Grief hit her like a wave. She was overcome and collapsed back onto her bunk, sobbing. It was the first time in her memory - in either memory - that she had sobbed so abundantly and inexhaustibly. How could it be? How could he be dead? She loved him so much, everything about him, every little thing... and he was gone. More than gone.

It was worse than just that. She knew that these two people in her mind, Maria and Cameron had planned a destiny together, as domesticated and cheesy as that sounded to Elizabeth. They had something they were supposed to do, not just for themselves, but for all of creation. They were meant to have a family. To raise souls out of purgatory and breathe life, form and future into fleshly shell. To love each other. To be human. In a way that Elizabeth could not begin to fathom.

The sobs subsided. Elizabeth rubbed her nose back and forth, trying to regain a semblance of control over herself. In spite of everything, the tomboy inside still balked at the prospect of Mark, Dinky and the other boys seeing her this way.

She emerged from the tent with dry eyes and a smile, her hair tucked back and dressed for the day.

"Mornin' sunshine!" Mark exclaimed, "Got eggs for ya', just the kind you like."

She ambled to the small fire he had constructed for the task and examined the eggs with a frown. There was red spice covering them and no smell of butter at all.

"What *is* that stuff?"

"I know you're surprised," Mark said proudly, "but I snuck us some from home. Figured it wouldn't do to go without it!"

Elizabeth stared at her cousin blankly.

"Paprika, stupid!" he exclaimed, pretending to box her on the side of the head.

"Paprika?" She looked confusedly between him and the eggs. "I like butter eggs."

"Butter? With eggs? Ahh, I see. You're jokin. Well laugh all you want, just eat your damn breakfast, alright?"

He served her a plate of the strange, red specked eggs and raised his eyebrows at her expectantly. She realized, with sinking heart, that he thought this was a game. He really didn't know anything about butter eggs.

She lifted a fork of the new concoction to her mouth and gave a grunt of surprise when she tasted it.

"These are alright!" She said.

Mark chuckled, his brow drawing together. "Well, yeah. Geez, what's wrong with you, Dizzy? Course they're alright. They're only what you've had for breakie every morning since you were born."

"Yeah," hiding her mounting fear, "right." *I know that. Of course I know that.*

They ate the rest of their breakfast in silence. Elizabeth was almost too preoccupied to notice, let alone to realize that it was strange for Mark not to be yammering his head off. After she had gobbled down the simple meal, she looked up at Mark and realized that she ought to try and say something.

"Are you... still assigned to that neighbourhood for today?"

"Yeah, tomorrow's my first day off."

"That's good, you can get good and ripped tonight."

"Yeah, with them boys from last night prolly. I like them, eh."

She had no idea what he was talking about. Elizabeth was saved from having to make more conversation by the timely arrival of Dinky. He had run water and a comb through his hair and even parted it cleanly to one side.

"Morning guys," he said, sitting in the open chair.

"Mornin Dink," Mark mumbled.

Elizabeth smiled at her friend. He smiled back, then blushed furiously. She frowned.

What the hell? she thought.

"Are you ready, Liz? I thought we might go a bit early and see if we can learn about market set up and all that."

"Sure, sounds great. See ya, Mark."

Mark tipped an invisible hat to his cousin in a mock cowboy salute.

When they had passed around a stand of spruce trees and out of Mark's sight, Dinky stopped and grabbed hold of Elizabeth's hand. She stopped too, looking at him questioningly. He dipped his face down to hers and kissed her, right on the lips.

"Dinky!" she pulled back, surprised. "Wow, I didn't... expect that."

"Is it ok?"

"Yeah, it's fine." Elizabeth smiled at him, but pulled her hand free and started walking again. It should have been fine but it wasn't at all. She had started the day grieving for one man, she couldn't very well be kissing another right after breakfast.

Dinky jogged two steps to catch up to her. "No I mean, ok, like last night. I was trying to make you laugh."

"Oh," she said, "I didn't get it. Sorry."

"It's ok." He smiled at her broadly. She stared at her feet unresponsively.

Once they were out of the camp and walking towards Rivertown, Dinky made another attempt at conversation: "I barely slept. I just... couldn't stop thinking about it. Felt like I'd been hit by a train. You really caught me off guard. I really liked it. Not just the... but being with you. You know."

I don't know.

Elizabeth racked her brain, trying to remember the night before. Upon waking, the sensation that she had fallen asleep in Cameron's arms was so strong as to be beyond question. Now, she knew that hadn't been the case. It was a false memory - had happened either thousands of years before to some woman named Maria, or had never happened at all.

What *had* she done the night before? Something with Dinky, obviously. She remembered being with him, Mark and the rancher boys, sitting on the steps of Rivertowns central building, chewing the fat. Laughing. She remembered that it was late when they finally went to bed. One of the rancher boys - Tim? Ned? - had made a joke about beauty rest. That much was clear. She remembered walking back to camp, too. Then it was a jumble - Maria or Elizabeth? - and she was waking up expecting to be one woman, only to discover that she was another.

I'm missing something, she thought. *Something very important that I should have remembered by now.*

"Elizabeth?"

"Yeah, I know," she said, forcing a smile.

You know what you're missing? Your mind. she thought. *What is wrong with me? I'm Elizabeth. I'm a country girl who has finally got the job of my dreams.*

"I just had... those bad dreams again. I'm feeling really screwed up now. That's all."

Dinky nodded and walked silently beside her. He seemed hurt.

How can I go from spending the night with him, to waking up and discovering that he was never there at all?

"Elizabeth?" Dinky's worried tone woke her from her thoughts.

"What?"

"You're crying! Are you alright?"

"I don't know," she answered, her voice breaking. She cleared her throat. "Yes, I'm fine. Just... bad nightmares."

"Why don't you tell me about them?"

"It's hard to explain... I guess I died in the dream and I was sad because I wasn't ever going to get to see anyone I cared about again."

That's not right, though! There's something else, something that I only half remembered...

"That does sound scary. Don't worry, Lizzy. I'm right here."

Dinky took her hand again and squeezed it gently.

Oh shit...did I sleep with him?

"There was something else," she said. She hoped that talking about it with someone would help her remember, even if she had to leave out most of the specifics. "The... *untura.*"

"Untura?"

"You know, when you forge a connection at death. It can only be done with someone of the same mind, when the death comes before its time and... oh. Oh..."

"What? Elizabeth, what is it? What are you talking about?" Dinky looked worried, had stopped and was staring at her. She realized that she had stopped breathing steadily. That she had probably gone white. That her mouth was hanging open.

You form untura in order to complete a destiny that the untimely death has robbed you of. That's what it is. Untura means you get a second chance. Elizabeth couldn't believe that she hadn't remembered this part before. And she knew that it wasn't something that Dinky would know... because Elizabeth hadn't known it.

Dinky's gaze pierced Elizabeth's. He looked between her two eyes, searching. Finally, he let out a sigh, scrunched his forehead together and turned back towards Rivertown.

"Sounds like you had some very intense dreams last night, Liz."

"I guess so. Sorry," she almost yelled it, as an afterthought, realizing how crazy she must look, "I didn't mean to scare you. I guess I just hadn't fully woken up yet. You know, when you're still sort of in the dream that scared you so much."

Chapter Seventeen

Fooling Dinky was hard. More than hard. It felt like he could see right through her. He seemed more and more worried throughout the morning, watching her when he thought she might not be looking. The attention and care that he devoted to her as the hours trickled by showed Elizabeth very clearly what she couldn't remember from the night before.

Dinky loved her.

It broke her heart to realize that only half of her loved him back.

The other half loved Cameron. They had a destiny to fulfill. They had to complete something they had started together a long time ago. She couldn't stop thinking about him, even with Dinky right beside her, obviously worried, obviously willing to help in any way he could. He couldn't help though, Elizabeth was sure of that. How could she even begin to tell him what was happening? Despite his concern, despite his feelings for her, he was sure to think she was crazy.

Maybe I am crazy. Dinky's a great guy. Cameron doesn't exist.

Elizabeth scratched her throat tiredly. They had done their rounds already, of course and were not surprised to find nothing to report outside the tangible antagonism. It was becoming clear to her that These were just people going about their business; not criminals who needed to be watched. It had been quiet between them as well. Dinky tried to make conversation a few times and Elizabeth could only mumble a reply. She was thinking about Cameron. Trying to reason a way that he might be alive, or that she might reach him. The thought of going her whole life without him was becoming unimaginable, at least it felt that way when she allowed herself to remember her time with him in the cabin, making a home for their future family.

But it was true that Dinky was a great guy. Better than great, if she was honest with herself. And it was also true that Cameron might not exist at all.

She looked at her friend, remembering the evening before when he had said that he already met a girl and pointed at her. It made her smile, a real smile.

"Oh, thank you Ethos!" He said, breaking into a broad smile himself, "I'd been making all my best jokes all morning. I thought maybe I had lost my touch."

Elizabeth reached out and touched the tip of his nose. "Nope. You've still got it."

They walked into the courtyard to have their lunch and sat at the fountain. A few of the other peacekeepers were there already and more trickled in as noon hour wore on.

"I guess the market isn't the only place with nothing to report," Elizabeth said.

"It's better than the alternative. Still, we both know it's not right. There's something very strange going on. This whole thing is…"

"Yeah. I know. They tell us to watch, to keep the peace. But it's have only been necessary once, on one shift, in one neighbourhood and because a peacekeeper made a bad call. It makes me wonder what we're *really* here for. What we're *really* supposed to be doing."

"Maybe they expect us to make bad calls. To cause trouble and then blame the coal eyes. Did you notice that the Chief never talks about permanent homes for the coal eyes, just for the settlers from home?

Elizabeth nodded. "You may be right."

Mark and Bill came into the courtyard under an arch that led down a windy, cobbled avenue to one of the neighbourhoods of Rivertown. Like most of the surface décor the arch appeared ancient, with an intricate, seemingly weather-worn design etched on. Closer inspection revealed the pattern and its wind-scarred motif were painted on. The rock was new.

"Howdy," Bill grunted, as he sat next to Dinky. He hooked one thumb into his belt while the other held a sandwich. Mark sat on his other side, and greeted his cousin and her friend wordlessly.

"Busy day?" Dinky asked.

Bill responded with another grunt, this one clearly meant to indicate that their day was anything but busy.

"Yeah, us too" Dinky said.

"This is boring as heck," Mark exclaimed, throwing his own lunch down beside him, and looked at his cousin imploringly. "Dizzy, would you do one o' your crazy stunts or something?"

"Crazy stunts?" Dinky asked, raising one eyebrow.

"Hell yes!" Mark responded, slapping his thigh. Dinky nearly jumped. "This girl's like a tornado. Nothin ever stopped her. One time she locked herself up in a little room of the barn most of the winter. When she came out, she had a new addition for the tractor. She wanted to upgrade the old one's it would be a self-run, you know. This thing was so ancient, they prolly never even heard a self-run or smart machines back then. Well, instead a tellin us about it and lettin our dads do the work, she up and rode it out a the barn, just like that, if you can imagine, so's to show it off. Sure enough, she ain't done the work quite right and that old tractor started spinning, instead of sayin' good morning or howdie do. But our Dizzy, she's too tough to let a little spinning bother her. So she held on for dear life and it just kept goin faster and faster. Finally some wire crossed and the whole thing stopped. Poor Dizzy tried to stand and couldn't. Course, that wouldn't stop her, either! She just kept on trying to stand and then fallen down again and throwin' up cause she was so dizzy. By the time we got her inside, she was covered in puke and bruises from all the things she landed on when she fell down."

"Is this true?" Dinky gasped between laughing.

"Unfortunately, it is. That's where the nickname *Dizzy* came from."

They all burst out laughing again.

"How are the heroes of Rivertown faring today?" Dinky asked, once the laughter had died down.

"We're alright," Bill answered in his slow drawl, chewing his sandwich thoughtfully.

There was a long moment of silence in which the others expected Bill to go on. Instead, he looked up, confused and they all burst out laughing again.

Chapter Eighteen

Mark leaned in to his cousin once his lunch was gone. "You alright, Dizzy?"

"I'm fine."

"I just wanted to make sure, no need to getcher panties in a knot. Just, after this morning you seemed a bit upset or somethin."

"Just bad dreams again, that's all."

"I heard you talking in your sleep again, so that's what I figured."

"Do you remember what I said?"

"Well, it wasn't quite words..." Mark took on a thoughtful look and blushed.

"What was it then?"

"You were makin... *noises*. All sexy like."

Remembering the vivid things she had seen in her sleep, she was not surprised. "Sorry, Mark."

"Ah, hell. At least one of us is gettin' some." Mark yelped. He said it loud enough that Dinky heard. Dinky gulped audibly, and tried to smile at Mark in a 'please don't kill me for sleeping with your cousin' type of way.

Bill looked cautiously between them and chuckled under his breath.

I think I know what Dinky and I did last night. She pressed her eyes closed. *But why can't I remember something so important? Why can't I remember something that happened just last night?*

"Elizabeth?"

She didn't open her eyes to see who was speaking. She couldn't. Her voice caught in her throat and she had to fight against tears. Great - just great. How could she succumb to such a characteristically girly thing; crying? There was no way she would be able to restore her reputation if she burst into tears, here, in front of all of these boys. Why did this all have to happen now, when she was finally starting her life, finally doing something important?

No. She wouldn't cry here. Instead, she stood up, mumbled that she had to go to the bathroom and raced away, towards the main hall of the building. There was a large bathroom there where she could hide until she had regained control of herself.

"What's with her?" Bill asked.

"Don't ask me," Mark replied, "she's been real strange almost since we got here. Talkin' in her sleep, actin' all weepy like in the morning and... sayin things... *wrong*"

Dinky perked up and said, "What do you mean, wrong?"

"Well, like this morning. I made her favorite, just like her mom made it every day and my mom too and their moms before: eggs with paprika on top. Only it was like she... didn't know what it was. She said somethin' about *butter* eggs. Never heard a such a thing, myself."

"I knew something was wrong. Things she's been saying just don't seem to fit. She keeps telling me that it's just the difference between city people and country people, but..."

"Well I'm a country people, so's Bill here."

"Sure am," Bill put in.

"So ask us. If somethin's wrong with our Dizzy, we oughtta be the ones to know so as we can help her. That's our duty and I'm not shamed to say it's a duty I'd gladly do for such a wildflower," Mark said and nodded solemnly.

"Do you know what honeyberry is?"

"Don't think so," Mark answered. Bill shook his head no.

"It's a low bush with dark green, oval leaves and weird, misshapen berries that taste sort of bittersweet. A little bit of a mix between blueberries and crabapples. I'd never seen it or heard of it until we got here, not even in biology lessons. Elizabeth saw it on the first day and said that she had been eating it her whole life. She said it's full of vitamins and naturally good for you. I was in pre-med. I did a course about primitive, natural medicinals and didn't learn about it."

"I've never seen it at home either."

"You sayin' she made it up?" Bill asked.

"That's the weirdest part: I don't think she *could* have made it up. She recognized it. Maybe she just read about it before we arrived and wanted to pull my leg, but she seemed serious. She seemed genuinely excited to see this berry bush. She said it was delicious."

"Delicious?" Mark asked.

"Alright, *that's* the weirdest part. She actually ate half a basket's worth without even washing it first."

"Is that it?" Bill said. He waited a moment, then added, "Because if that's it, then it just sounds to me like she's a bit out of sorts, being in a new place and all. 'Sides. She's a woman, ain't she? Maybe she's just got her monthly."

"No, she doesn't." Dinky said. The other two men looked at him. He realized what he had said and clamped his jaw shut, turning a deep red.

"Excuse me?" Mark said, puffing his chest up.

"No, I, uh, we just, it wasn't..."

"Is there something I ought to know, Dink?"

"No."

"Even more reason not to worry," Bill interjected, "My dad says women always get crazy when they're twitterpated." Bill nodded matter-of-factly. "Now you both're worried and gettin' at each other's throats. No wonder they don't usually let ladies into the corps. That's what I say."

Bill nodded again to himself, made a deep snorting sound and spit in the dirt. Then he stood, hitched his pants up with one hand and tipped his head to Dinky.

"See ya." He hooked his thumbs in his jeans and sauntered away.

There was a long moment of silence as Dinky and Mark sat next to each other.

"Was she cryin' cause of you?" Mark asked, finally.

"I don't think so. I'm not the sort of guy who hurts girls and lets them walk away without saying sorry."

"Hope not." Mark said to the ground. Then he looked Dinky straight in the eye. "And you better hope you're not, because if that girl gets hurt, it's me who'll be makin' you pay. I take it seriously."

"Don't worry, Mark." Dinky adjusted his glasses, frowning. "I take it seriously too."

Chapter Nineteen

Dinky sat on the edge of the fountain as the other peacekeepers finished lunch and slowly returned to their posts for the afternoon. They spoke of their anticipation for the evening's activities and there had been a few snide references to the corps' women. Dinky was beginning to realize how lucky he was to have a relationship with Elizabeth, as confusing and messy as it had become lately. Of course he was lucky. The woman he cared about seemed to sort of care about him, too, or at least be interested in... sex.

Dinky sighed deeply and looked around. Nearly everyone had gone back to their stations for a long afternoon of fruitless watching. Elizabeth had been gone for well over a half an hour already and Dinky was unsure about mounting a pursuit. He flexed his hand open and closed, watching the shadows appear and disappear, tracking the path of veins along his slender fingers. Was she crying because of him? His experience was limited: as a boy girls had never looked at him twice. His father would laugh gruffly whenever the subject was breached. *You just wait until your a doctor,* he would say. *Same girls that turned you down will see things differently.*

There was the implication that once he was a doctor Dinky would cease to be. He would be William Dingham, so he had been named at birth, so his destiny had been decided. The glasses, love of books, fear of heights and genuine, aching desire to help other human beings would cessate.

But I'm not a doctor and Elizabeth might be crying about me. Dinky thought. *What a mess.*

Dinky's father had provided only a few nuggets of wisdom about women and he had been Dinky's only quasi-reliable source. It had been wisdom for a distant future in which Dinky was successful and established. The reminder that he was neither left him even more unsure of himself.

Well then, I guess I'll have to do what I think I should. Thanks for nothing, Dad.

He followed last of the peacekeepers into the main hall of the building, hoping he would find Elizabeth without having to invade the ladies room.

At least she'll be the only girl in there, he thought.

Chapter Twenty

Elizabeth had also considered the limited number of peacekeeper women and also came to the conclusion that she was lucky. Lucky, because she had the whole women's bathroom to herself. It was a spacious room carved out of imitation marble with stalls that were more like personal powder rooms than the utilitarian public rest stops back home. Each other these stall was furnished with plush, purple armchairs. She wondered why Rivertown was able to afford this opulence and to what purpose. Then she splashed cold water onto her face and locked herself in one of the little rooms.

She collapsed into the chair, letting the cold water drip off of her face and onto her shirt. She hugged her knees to her chest and closed her eyes, sobbing freely.

This isn't me. I don't cry like this. I'm tough and brave. I don't cry.

But then she thought about Cameron, whom she loved despite the mists through which she remembered him. Their time together was blurry but consuming, like the smell of spring on a winter morning or a recurring childhood dream. The loss was fresh, the grief insurmountable and she burst into tears again.

Control yourself.

She tried to divert her attention and immediately thought of Dinky. It only brought more fear and confusion.

Why can't I remember what happened?

She slipped her hand down her pants and touched herself, checking for any signs of intercourse. She didn't find much but of course she didn't really know what she was looking for.

Maybe I'm going crazy. Maybe I'm just... sick. They have medicines for that. I could go to the infirmary and tell them everything.

At the thought Elizabeth felt deep revulsion.

I can't. They know. They know the truth, even if they don't realize it.

Elizabeth stopped. That wasn't her voice, those weren't her thoughts - not exactly.

Hello, Maria.

That woman and her memories again. But Maria was more than a stranger, more than just some woman who lived - and died - so long ago.

You are Maria. You are the same. We're the same.

It seemed impossible, but felt too true to ignore. She knew it had to do with the Untura, somehow. If only she could remember more...

There is not enough room in my brain for both lives. Every time I remember Maria, I forget Elizabeth. The overlap isn't possible. Which means that I don't know who me is.

At this, the tears stopped.Her shoulders and knees stopped shaking and her lip stopped quivering. If it was true, Elizabeth would be lost. She would be Maria.

Someone knocked on the door of the palatial bathroom.

"Elizabeth?" Dinky called.

She let her eyes drift shut. Dinky. What about Dinky? Maria was devoted to Cameron. The more Elizabeth remembered of their life together, the more she felt the same way. But now... she cared about Dinky, too.

My head is going to explode.

"Can I come in?"

Elizabeth wiped at her eyes and nose with the back of one hand, using the other to unlatch the door to her parlor-sized stall. What could she tell him? She didn't want to lie. But he would never understand the truth.

Whatever happens, they cannot find out who I am. All will be lost.

She sighed. Unfortunately, she had no idea who 'they' were and even less idea how to hide herself from them. In the meantime, Dinky was waiting. There was nothing for it - she couldn't very well hide her tears. Could she trust Dinky? Her one true friend, the only living man she cared about? She wanted to, desperately.

"Come in."

She heard a gentle swish as he pushed the door open and let it fall back closed, then the tap of footsteps across the grey and white faux-marble floor. Finally he appeared in the doorway to her little sanctuary. He wanted to move forward, to comfort her. But then he stopped, unsure.

"Are you ok?" he asked.

"I don't know."

"What is it? What's going on with you? Ever since we got here, it's like... something is wrong."

She clamped her jaw shut, fighting back tears. Of course he had noticed, she shouldn't be surprised. And was it really a bad thing? Did she really have to hide this... whatever it was from him? He cared about her, after all.

"Tell me. I want to help."

Elizabeth looked to the ceiling. Tears pooled in her eyes, blurring the bottom half of her vision.

"I don't know how to tell anyone. And if I tell you, you can't speak of it."

"I promise."

Elizabeth felt a deep fear and foreboding. A warning, telling her to shut her mouth and be done with this. Play the game, pretend and wait until she remembered enough to... do whatever it was that Maria had been given a second chance to do. But she was still Elizabeth and Elizabeth was head-strong. Elizabeth didn't let fear stop her.

"I trust you," she said. "I keep remembering these strange events, from another... world, or life. I thought they were just dreams, but they're too real. I thought I might be going crazy. But I do not feel crazy. It just can't be that. I know it can't."

Dinky blinked, colour rising in his cheeks. Immediately, she knew it had been a mistake. She shouldn't have told him, shouldn't have told anyone. She shook her head, galvanizing herself to think quickly – to cover up what had just been said.

Just lie.

"I know it sounds crazy,"

"No, it's alright," Dinky tried to sound reassuring, but Elizabeth interrupted him.

"In the dreams, I died and I'm crying because of my brother. Cameron. He died, too. Only, he's not my brother in real life. That's what I meant when I said it was another life. I don't know why I'm letting it affect me so much, it's just... it really shook me up. Losing a brother and having it seem so real. You know."

Now, Dinky smiled gently. It seemed he was relieved. She was, too.

"Sounds awful."

"It was," she said, "but I feel better now. Now that I've told someone. Thanks for listening."

Dinky glowed.

Chapter Twenty One

It took another half hour for Elizabeth to get herself sufficiently cleaned up and calmed down to return to their post. She splashed cold water on her face and patted her eyes dry with the fluffy towels in little baskets beside each silver-painted sink. Dinky watched her silently and rubbed her shoulders. It was nice to have him there and she was glad for it. As she washed her face again and again, she went over their conversation repeatedly. She knew that she had started to tell him the truth. But he did not need to know everything.

Finally, Elizabeth examined herself in the mirror and nodded.

"Ok, let's go."

They walked through the echoing main hall and into the courtyard, just in time to see several of the stall keepers leaving the same way that Mark and Bill had.

"Hey! Where are you going?" Dinky called, "It's only afternoon! You're supposed to stay here until dinner."

They ignored him and continued on their way, chatting with each other.

Dinky and Elizabeth hurried into the market and found it already mostly deserted. There were few stall attendants left and they were all busy wrapping their wares in rough linens, pulling curtains down in front of their stalls and scurrying home. Dinky called after several of them as they walked passed him but none answered. Finally, Elizabeth approached one of the men she had spoken with the afternoon of her first shift. She watched him for a moment, then said "Excuse me, sir."

He looked up at her, surprised. Clearly, sir was not something he was often called.

"Where are you going? Why is everyone leaving early?"

He shook his head and resumed his work of packing. "You not understand this."

"Try me. Please, sir."

The *sir* got him again. He sighed as he finished packing his wares and circled the counter of his stall to close the curtains on its front. When he was standing next to her, he said, "We want to work, we will do good. They say we work, they talk about mine and city. We don't see mine. We don't see city. We come back in morning and leave when we are finished, like today, we think is good enough. Will you kill us?"

Elizabeth balked. The man spoke with no fear, only a mild expression of distaste. She looked at Dinky, whose mouth hung open with disbelief.

"Of course we won't kill you!" Dinky exclaimed.

"Yes, that's right," Elizabeth added, "we would never hurt you."

He leveled his gaze at her, a profound frown on his mouth, then thought better of speaking and lowered his eyes slightly before walking away after the others. Dinky and Elizabeth were left alone, a faint breeze stirring the dull coloured canvas and linens.

"Are we going to be in trouble?" Dinky asked. "I mean, we weren't at our post. We left. If we had been here, we could have kept the peace, kept everyone at their stations."

"We won't be in trouble, because no one will know." Elizabeth said and started back in the direction of the main hall.

"How will no one know?"

Elizabeth ignored Dinky's question. She was thinking about a group of people Maria had met, other refugees. There were striing similarities between them and the coal eyes, in dress, culture, and looks. It was possible that the people Maria knew had been their ancestors. They said that the enemy held some of them as slaves, holding them to very strict rules. The punishments for breaking any of the rules was death.

It could be a coincidence, Elizabeth thought. But after her experience buying sage grass, she wasn't sure. What if Maria had truly known the coal-eyes' ancestors?

*If that's the case, then the enemy is still here, still holding the coal
eyes as slaves, and still killing them if they break the rules, just as that
man thought would happen.*

They're still here.

"Elizabeth?"

"Do you still want to go to that group activity tonight?"

"Yeah, I guess so..."

"Good. Me too. But I'm exhausted after all that crying. I'm not used
to doing that. I'm going to go back to camp and have a nap. Make
sure you wake me up before Mark finds me."

"What?"

Dinky ran after Elizabeth, who had already crossed half of the
courtyard.

"But, what about the market?" he asked.

"If anyone asks, we'll say we let them go home early, because there
were no buyers and it was a waste of everyone's time. That is if anyone
asks. And they won't. I don't think they expect anything to get in the
way of Rivertown. If something strange happened, they would start
watching everything closely." Elizabeth listened to the words as they
came, effortlessly, from the dark, growing place inside her that was
Maria's home.

"But not yet."

Chapter Twenty Two

"They're watching us. They have been for weeks."

There are cries of shock and fear. The whole village is gathered. I'm in the middle, my arms crossed in front of me, Cameron's hand on the small of my back.

"We don't know what they want, or why. We don't know how they have been able to keep us under surveillance for so long without our knowledge. We only know that it is their nature to destroy. The village will burn. We must leave. All of us. Take what you can carry and nothing more. If the creator wills it, we will return. If that is not possible, do not fear. We will be granted a new home. A place to create in. We have beautified the Earth. We have planted gardens. Perhaps this is our chance to do more. We must have faith..."

Elder Jared goes on. He explains we have little time, we have but an evening to pack up our lives and leave. That our neighbouring village was burned in the night and everyone there, cut to pieces and left to roast. Some begin to cry. Others are resolute. I look to Cameron for reassurance, or maybe just to see his face. To know that he's still right behind me, that he will be no matter what happens. He is already looking at me. We lock eyes and I kiss him gently.

"We'll be fine," he whispers, "we'll build a cabin that puts this one to shame, you just wait."

I smile in spite of myself.

"I still don't understand," I say, "what are they?"

Elizabeth woke up.

She blinked, looking around at the tent, focusing on her surroundings, her identity. It was becoming more difficult to do with every memory she recovered... with every recollection of Marie's she regained, she lost one of Elizabeth's. Truly, she didn't know how much longer she could pretend, or how much longer she would even remember what she was supposed to be pretending. In the meantime, she had found another piece of the puzzle, but not, it seemed, the key piece.

Now that she was beginning to remember the war - had it been a war? Cameron, their people and herself had been refugees. She had the distinct suspicion that Maria's destiny had a lot more to it than raising a family. A sinister force had destroyed her people with a terrible weapon, butchering every human settlement they came across.

Something destructive, technologically advanced and very inhuman.

If only Cameron was here, she thought. Immediately she regretted it. Hot tears sprung up and she pushed her eyelids closed, trying to fight them. She couldn't have imagined, in her life as Elizabeth, ever feeling such grief and loss and heartache. Even in her life as Marie, she had scarce imagined that such darkness could fill her spirit. How could he be gone? Of course, the question ought to be wrong. 'How could he be *not* be gone' made a lot more sense. At least it should have. But she felt certain that they were supposed to be together.

Either way, she couldn't succeed alone.

Chapter Twenty Three

"You didn't wake me up," Elizabeth said. She was standing with her arms crossed, watching Dinky from the bushes that lay between their two campsites. The bushes were low, but he sat with his back to her and hadn't seen her. He whipped around at the sound of her voice and chuckled nervously, adjusting his glasses

"You scared me," he said and chuckled again to himself, "I thought I should let you sleep. You looked peaceful. Besides, Mark isn't back yet."

"Yeah, alright." She stood with her arms crossed a moment longer. It was how she had been standing what felt like only moments ago... in reality, it had been millennia. Still, if she closed her eyes, it almost felt as if Cameron was right behind her.

I can almost feel his breath on my neck, his hand on my back...

"Dizzy?"

"Oh, sorry," she said, quickly uncrossing her arms, "I'm still half asleep. I don't nap much."

Dinky laughed. He had a book on his thigh, which he set on the ground beside him. Then he held out his hand to her silently. A little smile tickled the side of his mouth and his eyes lit up.

She smiled back, crossed the distance between them and sat beside him.

"You don't cry much," he murmured, brushing his lips against her eyelids, "you don't nap much... you sure are tough, Miss Dizzy."

"You have no idea."

Elizabeth was tough, no doubt about it. Maria was still a mystery. She didn't know enough about Marie to know whether she had been brave. Elizabeth was a soldier in a time of peace, but Marie had lived during a war. A terrible one that stole her home, her family, and her life.

Dinky touched Elizabeth's cheek with two fingers and kissed her.

"That's nice," she cooed. Maria was in love with a dead man. But Elizabeth - what was left of Elizabeth - felt very pleasant things about Dinky.

"What are you thinking, Liz?"

"Nice things... like that you're cute." she smiled at the happiness that radiated from him in response. "And sweet." he smiled broadly and she giggled. She bit her lip to look provocative, "And sexy. And... I don't actually know very much about you. I mean, we've been friends, but there's still a lot to learn."

Dinky's eyebrows shot up and he started to blush.

"Well," he stammered, "if you want, we could find a quiet place and... learn more about each other."

His hand had found its way from her face down her throat. He traced slowly down the line of buttons on her shirt. Elizabeth moaned, suddenly overwhelmed by the heat between her legs.

1 hour

What about Cameron? she thought.

What about Cameron, indeed. *He's dead. But I remember him and it's driving me crazy. What about Cameron is, that I'm never going to see him again. I've never actually seen him, except in my head. What about Cameron is, that Dinky is a good person, a good friend... and...*

Dinky moved towards her, tentatively. Elizabeth's eyes slid shut as he nibbled her throat, his hand now boldly caressing her breasts through the fabric of her clothes.

What about me?

"Let's do that." Elizabeth smiled and nodded enthusiastically.

They jumped up and scurried away like excited children. Elizabeth ran ahead, through the camp and into the vast, rolling land between camp and river. She sprinted flat out, her heart thundering in her throat and chest and arms, the expansiveness of the land filling her. Finally she slowed, opening her arms to the sky and the sun, still warm in the late afternoon. She remembered this place, remembered loving it, feeling safe here.

At one time, she had thought herself to be a part of this land and it a part of her. She breathed in deeply, the scent of the river in the distance and the grasses, low shrubs and stands of trees between filling her. She listened to the sound of birdsong, smiling lazily as she identified some of the creatures that were singing. Some she didn't know and wasn't sure if that was because she hadn't known them back on the farm where Elizabeth grew up, or because she hadn't known them back in the forest, where Marie had.

Dinky's footsteps sounded behind her on the hard, grassy ground. She turned to face him, smiling hugely. Maybe it wouldn't last, but for a moment, she felt like everything made sense.

He smiled in return, finally catching up to her. The sudden assertiveness in his manner as he took her in his arms and kissed her and ran his hands up and down her body betrayed his feverish desire; the clumsy way that only a young man can, groping, pushing, with mouth hanging open. But Elizabeth was herself quite a young woman, despite memories that were centuries old and her own body responded the same way.

"Listen, Lizzy," Dinky panted, "I just... wanted to say that..."

"Fine, whatever," Elizabeth didn't seem to have room in her brain to consider whatever it was that Dinky was trying to say, "just take your pants off."

They both laughed and then Dinky undressed and stood naked in front of her. Elizabeth stopped laughing and quickly undressed, too. They stood for a moment, looking at each other silently. Then they lunged at each other, desperate, pushing their mouths together.

They fell to their knees clumsily, trying to stay entwined in each others' arms.

"Your lip is shaking," she said and giggled.

He grunted in response, his eyes so bulged out she wondered if he was more scared or aroused.

She quickly found out that it was the latter. So much so that he accidentally threw her off of him and onto the ground, when the moment came too suddenly for him.

Elizabeth lay beside him on the warm earth, panting. He was panting, too, his thighs covered in semen. She opened one eye and squinted up at him. The sight made her laugh. He looked like he had seen a ghost. A sexy, sticky kind of a ghost, apparently.

He looked down at her, her knee scraped from the suddenness with which he had thrown her to the ground and laughed too. Then he fell onto his side and nuzzled up to her.

They lay naked in the sun for a few moments.

"I love you, Elizabeth."

Elizabeth closed her eyes, torn between enjoying the tender moment and fighting against it. Dinky was far too intellectual, had an embarrassing sense of humour and the thought of telling him the truth of what was happening to her filled her with real fear. At the same time, he was gentle, smart, adventurous… and right here. Right now.

"Ah, Dinky, I'm glad you're here in Rivertown so that I'm not the only girl."

He pushed her hair back from her face.

"Very funny. But I do mean it. Even your confusing, tough parts."

Elizabeth didn't know what to say, so she didn't say anything.

After a long, lazy snuggle in the sun, the young lovers dressed and returned to camp in search of food. Mark rose immediately as they approached his and Elizabeth's tent site. He crossed his big arms in front of his chest and raised an eyebrow significantly at Dinky.

"Dingham."

Dinky blinked. "Mark?"

"Elizabeth."

Elizabeth cocked an eyebrow. "Mark."

"Where have you two been?"

"Walking. I think you're taking this peacekeeper thing a bit serious, huh? Walking isn't a crime." She punched him in the shoulder as she passed him, on her way to the gunny containing more dehydrated meals.

Mark hmmphed.

"You coming with us to the activity tonight?" Elizabeth asked.

"Yeah. Bill's comin' too.

"Bill?" Elizabeth feigned consternation, "you two seem to be spending a lot of time together. Should I be worried?"

"Very funny Dizzy, but *Bill* can't get pregnant."

In the silence that followed, Dinky could be heard gulping.

"Go wash up, Dink. You smell like dink. And... lady flower."

Dinky blushed bright red, stammered something about dinner and scampered away.

"If you think you're going to give me a talking to, Mark, you're dead wrong."

"I dunno about no talking to, but I do know my place and that's as your cousin. Your brothers ain't here, but I am. So I'm gonna do my part to keep you safe. Dinky's alright, that's true. But any girl worth her salt has a brother or a cousin around to scare other guys off. That's the way the world works. Then if the guy keeps comin' back anyways, well. There you go. See?"

"You're sweet, Mark. Misguided, confused and drunk on your own power. But sweet."

"Mm hmm."

"Don't worry, Mark. I think Dinky's more than alright."

"Mm hmm."

Chapter Twenty Four

"You know Mark wouldn't actually *do* anything to you, not unless you did something stupid like cheat on me, which I might point out would be virtually impossible." They were walking the now-familiar path to Rivertown, Mark and Dinky's tent-mate Tom walking close behind them. They were in the middle of a long, lazy procession of off-duty peacekeepers to the evening's promised activity. As they crested the hill leading down to the settlement, they saw another snake-like line coming to meet them from the other camp.

"Either way, I thought it was respectful to leave. He clearly didn't want me there at the time." Dinky whispered back.

"Whatever. We're ok, though?"

Dinky beamed at Elizabeth. "Oh yeah. We're more than ok."

Elizabeth kissed Dinky on the cheek. Sounds of retching came from behind them.

"Almost two hundred strapping young men in Rivertown and sexy miss Dizzy chooses the only nerd. Do you get it, Mark?"

"Sure don't, Tom. If I were Lizzy, I would go for a strong, red-necked, tough and rough kinda fella, one who's sure to treat her right."

"Like me!" Tom exclaimed.

"Hell no. Like me," Mark retorted, then looked puzzled. "Only, not me, cause I'm her cousin."

"What you guys are forgetting is that Lizzy is already as tough as the two of you put together. She's rough and tough enough for the both of us, aren't you Liz?"

"And then some, Dinky. You can be as nerdy as you want."

They all laughed. Elizabeth was amazed at how distant the worries and concerns of Maria seemed. For the moment, she felt like Elizabeth - nothing more. Maybe it was like her grandmother had always said; that there's more to the earth than we can imagine, more than we can understand and sometimes we get caught in seasons that we can't see. Maybe she had experienced something like that and maybe it would stop before taking over her life entirely. Elizabeth had never been one to let the past stand in her way. She didn't need precedent and didn't let it stop her, if it conflicted with her ideas and goals.

"What do you think the activity is going to be?" Dinky asked.

"Prolly pushups. Too bad for you." Mark said.

Elizabeth whispered something romantic into Dinky's ear and the two other boys made retching sounds again.

Chapter Twenty Five

The Chief stood waiting at the top of the short flight of stairs leading into Rivertown's main building. He watched, silent and smiling, as the two groups poured down the wide main street and milled about on the packed earth before him. New friends from different camps greeted each other, albeit less raucously than they would have done if not under the vigilant gaze of their Chief.

Elizabeth was relieved when the young woman from the other camp arrived. She felt she had been ogled enough, in the time since they arrived at the square, to last her for the rest of the month. She was just about to make a saucy comment on the topic when the Chief, ever so quietly, cleared his throat.

Immediately, the peacekeepers gathered below him went silent and looked up at him expectantly. It was attention he seemed to bask in, he didn't move or make a sound for almost a full minute, instead just looked down at them with a look so benevolent and wise it bordered on a sneer. Finally, he cleared his throat again.

"In the interest of building team spirit, our two camps are going to compete in a friendly game of disks in the field behind town."

The roar and cheer that followed was deafening. The Chief certainly understood his young audience.

Chief made to try and speak over the sound, but instead, made a gesture over his shoulder meaning 'follow me' and set off down the stairs and around the group. The excited gaggle bounced along behind him.

"Didn't know you boys even knew what a disk was out there with them goats or whatever it is you sleep with at night!" Mark called at Bill, who he had spotted up ahead, over the excited crowd.

"Ah, hell, Mark. Least we don't got no city boys on *our* team."

"Actually, I'm pretty good at disks. I was on the school team one year." Dinky adjusted his spectacles unconsciously as he spoke.

There were whoops at this and a couple of yee-haws from Bill's tent mate.

"Man, I love disks!" Tom beamed, "You know, I was feelin' a bit down about Rivertown but if we get to play disks, well, I think these ranch boys are alright and I think Rivertown's alright, too."

Elizabeth shot Dinky a concerned look. The Chief knew his audience well, indeed.

"Why is it that we only keep the peace during the day?" she whispered.

Dinky raised an eyebrow at her in response.

"Disks is fun, Dizzy. Let's just enjoy it, huh?"

Elizabeth scoffed. She started to walk faster than Dinky, trying to push her way into the crowd and away from him.

From the other side, she saw the other girl approaching.

Great, Elizabeth though, *I'm no good with girls*.

She considered for a moment. If the memories she had recovered were part of her identity because they were part of what she remembered of her life, then she could use them, even if they were so old that they were practically from a different world. Maria was great with other women. Had lots of close women friends, if Elizabeth remembered correctly. Taking a steadying breath, she threw her shoulders back and made straight for the other girl. The girl smiled as they approached each other through the moving crowd of boys, most of whom were already sweating in the early evening sun and with the excitement of play. It was a big, warm, friendly smile and entirely genuine. Elizabeth was so taken aback that she didn't know what to say when they finally reached each other.

"Nice to see another human being, 'stead of these nan-der-thals," the girl drawled, in almost the same way that Bill would have.

"Tell me about it," Elizabeth fell into step beside the girl. It was easier than she had believed it would be.

"I'm Stephanie, by the way."

Stephanie burst into a playful smile, her eyes sparkling.

"I'm Elizabeth. The other girl in my unit's my friend Dinky, but uh... well he *is* one of the boys, if you know what I mean."

"I think I seen him with ya before, back in the atrium. The one with glasses, right?"

"Yup. That's my Dinky."

"He seems nice," Stephanie bit her lip, mischievously, "and he's cute, too."

Elizabeth blushed. "Yup. That's my Dinky."

They burst into giggles, more girlish than either would have expected.

"How about you?" Elizabeth asked. "Any of the boys here to your liking?"

"Not entirely. Sure, there's lots of cute ones, 'specially in your unit. And I made a friend, with my tent-mate. Name's Will. But he's not feeling too good so he's stayin' back fer now. So I'm sure glad I found you!"

Elizabeth beamed. She felt quite glad, herself.

"Tell me which ones you like. I'll tell you if they're worth your time."

"Well," Stephanie leaned in to her new friend, "that one fella, Ray. I think he's mighty fine."

"Ray? No. Just no. Sorry, girl. He's uh, a moron. Also rude about women, if you know what I mean."

"Hum. Too bad. Nice, big shoulders. How about... that Mark fella? You're friends with him, aren't ya?"

"Mark? Really?"

"Oh, yeah. He's a real looker. Also seems to have nice, kind eyes. Or maybe I'm just gettin' ahead a myself."

"Mark is... definitely kind. Yup, a girl could do much worse than Mark. He's real... chivalrous. Actually, he threatened to beat Dinky up if he ever got me pregnant." Seeing the confused look on Stephanie's face, Elizabeth laughed and added, "He's my cousin. Like an older brother, really."

"Oh, heavens! Hush my mouth, I'm sorry Elizabeth. I didn't mean for you to feel uncomfortable."

"Don't worry about it. As long as you don't go for Ray, I'll be happy."

"Alright. And I promise, if things do get interesting, I won't tell you the dirty details." Another impish smile. She was used to teasing.

"Sounds good to me."

"Do I get to hear your dirty details?"

"Stephanie!"

"Just wond'rin! No need to get all fussed. Tell me if you want to. Besides, I'm mighty curious. Only been with a couple boys, myself."

"A couple? Already? Dinky's... sort of my first."

Sort of because I remember sleeping with a man named Cameron several thousand years ago, but that probably doesn't count, right? Elizabeth thought.

"My, my. They say you farm girls know how to keep your legs closed. I guess they're right." Stephanie giggled, shoulders raised and hand over her mouth.

"You know, Stephanie, I've never told anyone this, but you are actually adorable."

"Shucks. Thanks, Elizabeth. You can call me Steph, if you want."

Elizabeth called her Steph from then on, very gladly at first, until the day they both died.

Chapter Twenty Six

The game of disks, under the still-warm evening sun and on grasslands of a home half remembered made Elizabeth feel like a child again. She had a friend, a female friend, a Steph friend... and it felt like she was with her sisters again. It was something she hadn't realized she missed.

Stephanie and Elizabeth managed to switch so that they were on the same team. They had to trade players, which required convincing and Elizabeth found herself uncharacteristically feminine in handling the task. Somehow, that made her uncharacteristically convincing as well.

In place of a gymnasium wall, the Chief and his unknown helpers had set string along the length of the cleared, level field. Many of the boys tried to show off, performing gravity-defying stunts as they ran from the line of string into the playing field for their shot with the disk, dodging opponents' balls and sprinting back. The girls realized their intentions when each looked glanced expectantly in their direction after their turn was over. Subtlety wasn't yet a strength in the young peacekeepers. One boy even did a back flip, then blew a kiss in the direction of the two girls.

Despite the requirements of the game, the girls were inseparable for the whole evening. Dinky looked on longingly and Stephanie shrewdly commented that he might be getting jealous, as he was used to being Elizabeth's only girl friend. For her part, Elizabeth couldn't have been happier. It was more than the affinity with her new accomplice -- it was a sense of finally being able to tap into something inside that she hadn't known existed. Why had it been so difficult before for her to be herself? To be friends with other girls? To enjoy the moment.

She realized the reason half way into the game. She had the chance to run into the field and throw her ball, as the other team had run out of their own for the round. It was a chance she didn't take because she wasn't paying attention to the game. At that particular moment, she was recounting the way Dinky had thrown her off of him and to the ground in order to not ejaculate inside her earlier that afternoon. She and Stephanie were killing themselves laughing, both flushed with the simple, childlike joy of having someone to bridge their lonely, feminine worlds.

"Come on, Dizzy! What is this? I thought you could play like one of the boys, not act like a little girl playing with dolls!" Ray sounded genuinely upset, but the rest of the team laughed as if it were a great joke.

Even if it had been good-natured teasing, perhaps they were genuinely annoyed that Elizabeth was letting them down.

"If you want to talk about boys and do your nails, go to the salon, off the sports field!" Someone yelled. Elizabeth couldn't place the voice. There was more laughter.

Shame bubbled up in Elizabeth's chest. She felt her already flushed cheeks tinge throbbing red. Of course. Now she remembered. *Vulnerable. Girls are weak. Don't be a girl. Be tough, be one of the boys. No fear.* Wasn't that why she was here in the first place, a peacekeeper in Rivertown? *It's why you're here. Of course it is.* It had been such a deeply ingrained part of her identity for her whole life that she had never really noticed it before. But now she remembered something else. Something different.

I remember being Maria, having lots of women as friends, having them over for dinner...

As uncomfortable as it was to experience such new emotions about herself, Elizabeth couldn't help but like it. What did it matter what these boys thought, anyways? Elizabeth realized that while she was the one who spent much more time projecting an image of confidence and capability, it was Maria who felt more comfortable in her own skin.

Or my own skin, I guess.

"Ah, hell, boys. You jealous? Want me to do your nails? No need payin' attention in a game like this, seems as if you fellas are having a nice time with your little pissing contest. Why don't you just cut the crap, get out the measuring stick and see who's got the biggest prick? That's prolly the best way to get our attention, anyway."

Stephanie flicked one eyebrow up, a teasing smile playing with her lips. There was a stunned silence, none more resounding than that coming from Elizabeth. Then Dinky started to laugh. To guffaw. He leaned over, planted his hands on his thighs and had to remove his glasses lest they fall into yellow grass. Bill started laughing, next and Mark joined in. Soon there was general good cheer again and the game resumed. Stephanie took Elizabeth gently by the hand and led her away from the boys. They sat on the grass at the end of the field, side by side, with their legs crossed.

"Thanks, Steph."

"Your welcome. That really got to you, didn't it?"

"How could you tell?"

"Well you had been standing like it was just us, like this," Stephanie's hip swiveled out, so that they stood relaxed, leaning on the other. "Then all of a sudden you straightened up like the Chief had yelled at you."

"Wow. " Elizabeth nodded. "I'm used to trying really hard to show that I'm better than the boys, even though I'm a girl. You know what I mean?"

"Oh sure. I feel the same way, sometimes."

"Really?"

"Course. Now. You were tellin' me about somethin' funny that Dinky did, but I'm curious about something else. Just how big *is* Dinky's Dinky?" Stephanie giggled mischievously.

Elizabeth held her hands out to show the approximate length and then brought her pointer finger and thumb together to indicate girth.

They both laughed.

The boys played two full games that night, while the girls sat a small distance away on a gentle hill, and the light faded to gold. Stephanie told Elizabeth that her duty for the last week had been the road leading up to the mine, but that she was going into days off. She said she was glad -- no one ever used the road and she thought it was sort of gross and creepy. She said the coal eyes thought there were ghosts in the mine, not like the ethos, but, like spirits of real people who were, like, already dead. Elizabeth had to nod, she knew the concept. Knew it unfortunately well. Ghosts had been a part of her other life.

They were about to become a part of this life, too. Elizabeth forgot about Stephanie, and the game, and Rivertown, and looked up at the gold grey sky.

I see him approaching, across the gathered crowd. It's evening and his hair looks golden. He's walking slowly, hands in pockets, taking in the air and the world around him with the reverence of one witnessing the first miraculous moment of creation. That's what this is. That's what it always is. What does this have to do with ghosts?

He reaches out to an aspen and she knows he's remembering. Remembering their home. He touches the leaves and blinks, quickly. Yes, he's remembering. The corner of the world that he and his love staked out together, to beautify, to create a paradise within. I'm his love. Me. Maybe he's seeing the ghosts of those two young lovers, with so much hope. So much to look forward to. So much life in them. Maybe part of that life was left behind on the long trek across the land, to here. Where they've finally reached the end and must make their final stand with their backs to the sea. Maybe those parts that were left behind… are ghosts now.

He looks up at the sky. Is he a ghost? Are you? I watch him silently, entranced. I was sure that I would never see him, ever again. Because he is a ghost. And so am I. We died. You remember it. But there was something else. Something more powerful than death, more profound than hopelessness. There was destiny.

I am witnessing the first miraculous moment of creation. Every moment. Full of ghosts. He is a field away now, no more. My Cameron. I trace his familiar features with my mind's eye and notice differences. His sweet little nose is stronger now, with only the faintest hint of what you remember. One hand now hangs by his side and even from this distance I can see that it isn't the big, calloused hand you spent so many nights memorizing, but a different one. One built around the ghost of the first. I blink and see him clearly. This is a different man. A different one. A new one. But it's Cameron, too. His ghost.

Elizabeth blinked again, noise and sweat flooding back into her organs. The rest of the world seeped into her vision: the disks game, the boys, Stephanie. She closed her eyes, *will I wake up again?* When she opened them, Stephanie was on her feet, waving, calling something. Elizabeth could not understand what, she was too confused, too consumed with what she had seen. A new round had started, the boys filled the field and she couldn't see the spot where last he had been. The ghost. Had to have been a ghost. Just a memory. Just a dream.

"… comin' over this way. Elizabeth?"

Elizabeth looked up at her friend, dumbly.

"Stand up, you'll be able to see him. My tentmate, Will, he's comin' to join us."

Elizabeth stood, unsteady. *Just a dream. Just a memory. Just a ghost.* There was a loud cry form the players, one of the boys hit by an opponents ball just as he was about to throw his disk. He crashed to the ground in a feigned death - *I see him fall, trying to outrun them, just over that hill* - and the players jogged off the field, ready to start a new round. They left the field empty, an aisle down which she could look. There, in the middle, was the boy.

"There he is. Will! Come on over!" Stephanie waved enthusiastically again.

Elizabeth's knees felt weak. Worse than weak. She couldn't actually feel them at all. Neither could she feel her lips. She bit down on the lower one, hoping to revive it and tasted blood, briefly. *You're bleeding. I haven't got time to bleed.* He waved at Stephanie and then stopped. He had seen her and she had seen him. She watched his jaw sink down, leaving his mouth open in a perpetual question, one his ghost had must have asked countless times since... since...

"Cameron?" Elizabeth whispered. Could he hear her? Could it be? Was it really him?

The boy nodded slowly. Then, quickly and vigorously, the boy who was Cameron shook his head no.

He turned and ran.

Chapter Twenty Seven

Elizabeth collapsed. It was her knees. She hoped it looked more like a casual plopping than an accidental fall. Elizabeth could hear Stephanie calling to Will, but he was already disappearing into the dusky stand of trees on the far side of the field. Elizabeth knew that because she was staring at the exact spot where he had disappeared.

"Huh. Guess he didn't see us. Or maybe he just started to feel sick again, all of a sudden. Elizabeth?" Stephanie looked to where her friend had just been standing and then down to where she sat on the grass. "Are you alright?"

Elizabeth cleared her throat.

"You look like you just seen something other than a good-looking boy."

"A ghost."

Stephanie laughed. "Well I suppose so, but I don't know what a ghost would look like. I was gonna say you look like Shock herself. What's going on?"

"It's nothing."

"Like hell. Do you and Will know each other? Is that why he ran?"

This is too dangerous. No one can know. Lie.

"He did look familiar. I don't know where I'd know him from, though... the closest to the ranchlands that I've ever been was a family vacation to Lake Simcoe. He sort of reminded me of someone, maybe? But I think I'm just feeling tired, or maybe I'm getting sick, too. I had to leave my post early today to go to sleep because I was feeling really dizzy."

"Dizzy, huh? Well that's strange. Maybe it's goin' around. Will said he was feelin' dizzy, too. And feverish. 'Splains why he was talking in his sleep so much." Stephanie ventured a small smile.

You have to find out more. Force a smile. She tried to make it genuine. *Sound conspiratorial. It's just gossip.*

"What was he talking about?" she asked. She smiled coyly but the words stuck in her throat.

Stephanie plopped down beside her friend, strangeness seemingly forgotten, eyes shining with mischief. "Well. First he was always sayin' a name. A *girl's* name." Stephanie covered her mouth with her hand and giggled. She shook her hair. Despite having found these idiosyncrasies entirely endearing minutes earlier Elizabeth's frayed nerves warped the giggles into something tiresome and maddening. But she had to know.

"'Maria,' he was sayin'. Over and over. Sometimes he said it all lovey-dovey and other times, sort of sad."

Of course. It is him. And he does remember. But how much? Elizabeth felt herself accepting the reality of their situation coldly. *we have been reborn. It happened for a reason. Does he have any idea what we're supposed to be doing here?*

"So... he has a girlfriend back home? Named Maria?"

"Well you know boys. Said he didn't want to talk about it and I'm not going to push. Don't need to know his personals down to the letter if I have to get changed with him and smell his stinky boy body all night already." Stephanie winked. "After that, he started talking about all sorts of funny things. He keeps apologizing and I tell him it's fine. Course, it wakes me up sometimes but it really is funny. He talks about robots, but about them coming after him and chasing him... I mean, that's absurd! One time, he talked about this imaginary garden. With... some kind of something in it. He was talking to someone about it." Stephanie laughed. "He sure likes his imaginary dream garden, but at least he doesn't grind his teeth. That drives me nuts."

"I don't know how you put up with it, Steph. Mark snores and it drives me crazy."

"I think it's gonna pass. He says he never had anything like it before and I believe him. It's probably just the excitement of being in a new place."

"That makes sense. Mark said that I talked in my sleep a couple times since we've been here. And usually, I don't even dream. At least I don't remember them, if I do."

"What have you been dreaming about? They say dreams are important. My mom's been real into dream interpretation, as long as I can remember. I even remember what some of the symbols mean. Like I told Will; a garden represents a new endeavour, which is going to Rivertown and it represents that he's sowed a good crop, metaphorically speaking. So I told him that if he cultivates the skills related to this new place and job and role, then it seems his dream is telling him he'll reap the rewards, as it were. Frankly, I was real proud of that extended metaphor. Did you go to upper school?"

The question caught Elizabeth off guard. Everyone had to go to upper school where she came from. Unless they did trades training, which she had wanted to do, but her father insisted that she get a scholarly general education. His foresight paid off: it made her eligible as a peacekeeper.

"Yeah, I did. That's a pretty good metaphor."

"Tell me something, darling. What are your dreams about?"

It was something about the way Stephanie said it. Too calm, too steady, she was hiding the fact that she was too interested. Her face had gone blank. Uncharacteristic for the girl, that's what it seemed to Elizabeth. Perhaps she was just paranoid, but the sense of dread and panic inside of her was real. Cameron was alive. Somehow, he was here, in Rivertown. This wasn't just in her head anymore and whatever else happened, she was no longer alone with this secret. Paranoid or not, whatever was happening to her and Cameron, what had happened here those thousands of years before, was too important to take any risks.

Elizabeth refused to admit that was exactly what a paranoid personw ould think.

"I've been dreaming about this really tall tree," Elizabeth started. She was amazed at how quickly she was learning to lie, and lie well. "It's got giant leaves and they're all different colours. Sometimes I climb the tree and other times I fly around it and in one dream, I found a nice branch and read a book sitting with my back to the trunk. Also, after my first time with Dinky, I had a lot of sex dreams. That's what woke Mark up. Can you imagine, his cousin making all sorts of sexy noises?!"

"Poor Mark! Does he ever make sexy noises, in his sleep?"

"That is just gross. Don't ask, even if I heard, I would pretend not to."

"Do you think you could introduce me? It looks like their game is done."

Sure enough, a few of the boys were helping the Chief roll up the twine that had lined the field and pack up the balls and disk. The rest were basking in the euphoric afterglow of sport, jiving amongst themselves. They looked like monkeys jostling for rank in a troupe. Mark and Dinky broke away from the rest and headed towards the girls.

Stephanie whispered to Elizabeth that the other boys looked jealous. Elizabeth shrugged and pretended to laugh. It would've been funny a few minutes ago. She would have been in stitches. But now her head felt like it had been bashed with a baseball bat filled with cold water.

"Mark, Dinky, this is Steph," she growled with her arms crossed.

"Pleased to meet you both," Stephanie's voice was immediately both higher and huskier than it had been before. Elizabeth watched on, astonished, as Stephanie smiled at her cousin and actually fluttered her eyelashes at him. She couldn't believe it, but it had actually happened. She turned to Mark, sure to find him incredulous at the antics of this new girl. Well, he was spell-struck. His mouth hung slightly open, his eyes were glazed and his cheeks were an explosion of deep red.

"Hi, Steph. Real nice to meet you."

Dinky smiled at Elizabeth. It was a friendly smile. It bespoke familiarity and affection. Now would be a bad time to cry. He put his arm casually around her shoulder and she felt everything inside of her tighten almost to the point of breaking. The jumpy and ecstatic warmth started between her legs. Not just the light and fast kind of arousal she had felt with him before, nor just the deep, heavy kind she remembered with Cameron, but something fuelled, in part, by fear and confusion. No amount of Dinky's innocuous companionship would relieve the tension she felt.

Cameron, or Will, whoever he is.

He's the one.

Chapter Twenty Eight

No.

She's dreaming. It is more than that.

No, it can't be.

This place... remembers. First, there was breathing: the seasons, the tides, the trees. The cycles of breath expanded into creatures of all kinds, in their own cycles, their own lives, as a part of this place. The many creatures danced in orbit of each other, and carved those patterns into the rocks, the soil, everything. One of these creatures, one which emerged from the nurse log of an ancient tree, has gone missing. Torn from the habits of its blood, from the purpose it is meant to fill for all of the others.

I'm running. Cameron tripped, I'm trying to get to him. Just on that ridge. Did I see that ridge again? I can't remember. It's not important. I have to get to him before they do. He's going to die if I don't.

There is a roar like churning water. It is the fingers of the wind in the grasses and in the brave aspens warped by its fury and their tiny, tinkling leaves, in the spruces and bushes.

It's too windy, how will I get to him? The storm will hit too soon. Get up Cammy, get up! They're right behind us!

This place has been without humans, has lived without their care and their compassion and their cooperation, for too long.

No.

Because this place... remembers everything.

He's up, he's running towards me. But they're there, in the trees.... And we've never seen them. Even after a long year of running, none of us have seen them and lived long enough afterwards to speak.

The wind is so strong now that the tent is shaking. One of the stakes is ripped from the ground and smashes the heavy cast iron skillet Mark brought from home, right in two. The rope it held to the ground flaps wildly, whipping against the tent.

There is a woman in the trees. She's young, younger than me, with long, dark hair. Why is she doing this to us?She has skin, and must have a beating heart and flowing blood underneath. How could she kill others recklessly and live with it?

Mark tears his way out of his sleeping bag. He tries to yell, to wake up his cousin, but she will not budge and his hoarse voice is drowned out a chorus of thunder. A flash of lightning illuminates her face; he sees that she is covered in sweat, breathing heavily. It looks like she is in pain. He falls to his knees beside her and shakes her. She's asleep. He screams her name and the sound is lost in the thunder, the roar, the heavy wind.

I stop running. Cameron is calling to me, imploring me to run. We both know there is nowhere left to go. We have come to the end, the ocean at our backs. The water is just beyond this forest, down the hill. Foxes in a trap, they will destroy us: completely and utterly. No fibre of our bodies will be left to fertilize the soil. But it is just a woman in the trees. They are like us. I almost feel like laughing. To have fled so far in so much fear only to be beaten and killed by people just like us. It's all happening in slow motion, still-lifes taken by the flash of lightning. Cameron is scrambling towards me, the... enemy is still in the trees. He's yelling to me, but I can barely hear him over the storm. He's bellowing a name, but it's not mine. Is he calling me Elizabeth?

Why is that name so familiar?

"ELIZABETH. WAKE. UP. NOW!"

She woke up.

"No!" she screamed, forcing her eyes shut again. She had to remember the rest. This was it, this was the important part. The thing that she had to remember if she hoped to survive this, to help Cameron, to understand what was happening to the two of them. To understand what had happened here, in the Wild Land, all of those centuries before.

"Come on! We have to get out of here!"

Mark was shaking her. That must have been what woke her. *Mark, you idiot.*

"Why did you wake me up?!"

Mark's eyes were open to the whites on all sides.

"Are you kidding me? There's a storm outside! The tent is falling apart, we have to go! Now!"

Elizabeth let herself be led out of the tent. Immediately she was struck by the stinging wind and tiny pieces of dust and grass that were being thrown around by it. The night was a mix of white and blue, a confusion of lightning strike-silhouettes and emptiness; of screams and the terrible sounds drowning them out, the sounds of the world ripping itself apart out of a kind of madness that only the wind knows.

It's just as I dreamed it, she thought. *But I can't remember the rest...*

"Come on!" Mark yelled it as loudly as he could. The back of his throat felt like sea salt poured over sandpaper. This was a really terrible time for his cousin to be lost in thought. He took her firmly by the hand and led her down the path towards Rivertown.

A bolt of lightning struck behind them, in the camp. The thunder was drowned out by screams, terrible screams, which were blown away like so much smoke. Mark was holding his hands over his ears, but it seemed to Elizabeth that there was a quiet spot in her mind, an empty void with a roar both silent and deafening. Elizabeth tripped over her feet and Mark took his hands away and caught her. He held her by the shoulder, one arm wrapped around her ribs under her armpit. They sagged briefly as she collapsed into his arms, but he straightened quickly. His face was set. The rain started and he blinked, but did not falter again.

Elizabeth closed her eyes, stepping blindly. Even with her eyes closed, she saw the same thing: The chaos of a storm. This place. Trying to escape... She squeezed her eyelids together, knowing she had to remember. Had to.

I'm standing on the hill. The storm has moved in quickly and now it's entirely dark, a kaleidoscope of confused images. Focus on the figure in front of me. When the light returns, there are many figures all around me. Moving out of the trees. Human? It seems so. But now the garish light makes them appear misshapen and disfigured.

I turn and run. The rain starts, turning the lichen covered rocks dotting the hillside into slick, muddy landmines. My heel lands on one and I go flying in the air. It's very slapstick and I almost smile, then my head hits the ground and everything is dark.

They stumbled on through the woods this way until Elizabeth was shocked back to reality when another terrible crack sounded directly beside them. She screamed and Mark covered her ears with his hands. It was a moment too late, but comforting none the less.

He looked at her appraisingly. "What's wrong with you, Dizzy?"

She shook her head. Maybe he would think she hadn't heard him. Mark glanced at the tree that had been hit, smoking and red, split down the middle. He set his lips and threw his cousin over his shoulder. Then he began to run towards Rivertown. Elizabeth closed her eyes again.

When the light comes back the next time, they're all around me. I see the woman. She reminds me of someone. Someone I've seen before. Someone I like. I feel an immediate kinship with her. Then I remember the year before, the chasing, the running. The other villages that were burned, the people still in their homes, or cut into pieces, bite marks in their flesh. I remember those who fell behind and were lost. I try to sit up but unseen hands are holding me down. The effort of it makes my head pound, where it hit the ground when I fell. It hurts so much that my eyes swim and crinkly blackness starts to chase the images away. The woman asks, why you looking at me that way? and then everything goes dark again.

Another bolt of lightning. Mark flinched at the nearness of it: the momentary silence, the blinding, electric death funneled down. When the thunder came it knocked him clear off his feet. Elizabeth went flying and there was a crack as her head hit a slick stone. Mark was struck momentarily blind as his eyes pupils narrowed to shield themselves. He groped for his cousin in the thin, sandy mud that had been wind-swept dirt just that evening. Elizabeth could not hear him call her name.

I don't know where I am. There is a... change room. I've never heard that word before. I am Maria, but there is something else, like a dream, half remembered and then seen in waking. Elizabeth, that's what it is. I can't seem to keep me straight.

The girl is here, the one I like. The funny one. I'm being asked questions. Where do we come from? What will we do when we have nowhere else to go, our backs to the sea? It's less than a half day away, they tell me. They laugh, but not her. It's painful to remember.

I know that I'm injured because of their faces: I can't seem to see their faces right. They go smooth, flat, and I hear buzzing. My lips feel numb. I must have a concussion. Light spots float behind their smooth, alien faces. The light spots float into my mind and I lose consciousness again.

Presently I find myself walking down a corridor. It's artificially lit and there are no windows. Maybe the hum is from their electric generators. This isn't the kind of creation I imagined for myself, but perhaps these are people after all, if they create things, things that they like and can use.

They're getting ready. They are going to kill the people I grew up with and love. Cameron is with them. It seems they've decided I'm harmless, for now. I'm allowed to roam these strange, yellow corridors. The light is yellow, but the walls are white. Clean and square. I touch the white surfaces and my fingers slide backwards and forwards effortlessly. This is no material I've ever seen before, what could it possibly be made of?

Then I'm in the changeroom. She's there, too, getting ready. I ask her where she's from. She doesn't answer. I ask if her family is here on the ship with us. I didn't realize we were on a ship. Somehow I knew.

She says she has a man and a son onboard. She says this in a flat, disinterested voice like she's only acting the parts of a wife and mother. Or of a woman.

I'm in the change room again, saying please don't kill them, begging her. I'm telling her about Cameron and how much I love him. I'm telling her about the little house we built and that we were going to build again by the sea. I tell her about the little plants we had started from seed beside the window and about the chickens I named after fruits. I tell her that we are going to have children, too. That if she kills us, it will never be so. I ask her please. I laugh and I cry, I'm like you.

The girl, my friend, she starts to cry. To cry and nod.

Then I'm on the beach. We called it Rivertown. My people are there with me. We are celebrating. Finally, there's peace. It seems there is more to this conflict than Elder Jared told us. When I told the girl that we wanted peace, that we had no intention of fighting... she laughed. I remember that now. It seems that we were never as innocent as I thought. Their representatives have come, including the girl from the ship with her man and son. Her son is the same age as my niece, Dana. They play with the other children and splash in the water of the sea. There is a delta here, beautiful. Sand bars to play on and find fish, land above for planting. The cedars sway in the breeze and perfume the air, holding the soil together for the other plants. There are deer grazing, on the hill.

Everything goes dark, because of the pain in my head. Then, like a flash of lightning, Dana is beside me. She's asking me where they've gone, says that the boy left. I realize that all of the delegates have disappeared. No one else seems to have noticed yet. Dana is accusing me, she says that the boy told her I made a deal with them. That it was wrong. Is it Dana? Or is it Elder Jared?

Wrong and unjust and evil. There are accusations against me. You've sold us! They say. You've tricked us. Then the arm bands start beeping. It's too late, of course. Too late to escape into the trees, hope that we can hide from the weapon. Too late to return to our gear, up the hill. If the armbands are beeping, it means the weapon is already incoming. Not this. Not this way.

People are screaming. I run towards Cameron. I thought I had done right, I thought we would finally be able to be together, to have our place together. Now we will die. I reach him just in time. We clasp our hands firmly together and...

Elizabeth could barely see. Her vision swam between darkness, short, terrifying bursts of white, the memory and the boy crouched anxiously before her.

"Wake up, Lizzy, come on, wake up, wake up. Atta girl. You hit your head, but you're going to be alright. The wind is still picking up. We have to go. Now. We're almost in town and we'll hide inside until it passes. We'll get you to the doctor. Can you stand?"

She tried to stand and slipped in the mud. It was earth riddled with tiny spruce needles and covered still from last summers leaves. Thin earth. This much water would turn it impassible and quickly. *Move girl, you're going to die out here.*

Elizabeth could taste blood. Suddenly, surviving seemed far more important than remembering the rest. Was there any more to remember? It seems they had been set up. Maria had trusted these people, and been betrayed. "I'm dizzy," she said.

Mark shook his head. He picked her up again, carefully maneuvering her so that she sat on his back, one leg on either side of his hips. Then he started forward again, more carefully now but more desperate than ever.

Another bolt of lightning illuminated the path ahead – the straight broad avenue leading from the dirt road they struggled, through the houses to the town center. The outer houses were deserted, water pooling around and in them. Not much more than tents, those houses. They weren't even on pallets and the thin earth that constituted their foundations was now a river of thin silty mud, gaining momentum. Ahead they could make out figures, some standing on the platform before the main doors and on top of the stairs, the remainder a massive, moving crowd churning in the deepening mud below.

There was a loud crack. Mark thought it was the thunder at first, in the moment after the lightning in which he was blind in the loud darkness. Then there was another crack, another, a series of them. His eyes began to readjust and he saw the crowd at the bottom of the stairs moving in confusion, boiling. There was something in the wind that stung sharper than the icy droplets clinging to his eyebrows and nose. It sounded almost like gunshots. He could hear screams of pain and fear.

"They know! It's too late!" Elizabeth cried and then she started to scream, too.

"What's too late? What are you talking about? Goddamn it Dizzy!"

Mark pressed his eyelids shut, feeling the cold sinking into his stomach. Elizabeth was never like this. Never.

"You can't tell them, Mark! You can't tell them who I am! They'll kill us, all of us!" She was wild eyed now, screaming and sobbing. She must have hit her head harder than he thought, which meant he had to get inside and get her help. For some reason, he hesitated. She was so serious about it, so convinced. It made him shiver. What if Elizabeth knew something that he didn't?

The rain pelted into his face again, carrying the sounds from Rivertown's main building. Mark recognized the Chief's voice, sneering and loud, "... rules of Rivertown are clear, and so are the punishments for breaking them, as you..." The sounds died out again, drowned by the ever-changing wind and the rain splashing all around them.

There was another lightning strike, behind Mark and Elizabeth. In its light, Mark saw the Chief standing in front of a line of men that he had never seen before. They all looked the same, with the same close military haircuts. The kind that peacekeepers didn't wear. They each carried heavy, semi-automatic weapons that were pointed down into the frightened, milling crowd. Just as the light faded again, Mark made out two of them carrying a limp body onto the make-shift stage from the ground below.

Elizabeth seemed to have seen it, too. She started a low, wordless moaning and shook her head back and forth so violently that Mark felt his balance shift side to side. Then she started to pull at his shirt, soaked and glued to his skin with the rain. "Mark, we have to go, we have to leave, we have to get out of here. Hurry. Hurry." She started to rock side to side with her whole body, like an injured cat trying to squeeze loose, scratching and screaming.

Mark searched through the dark for a way out where they wouldn't be seen, or something he could use as a weapon. Why hadn't he thought to bring his tazer?

In the darkness, the cousins heard a low, humming sound that was quickly drowned out by screams of the crowd. Despite the torrential downpour and winds, some of them broke from the group in the darkness and ran in all directions.

"Now, Mark! Now!" Elizabeth pounded feebly on his shoulders with her fists. She was wheezing, panting, losing consciousness again. "If they find me... they'll kill us again..."

A burst of electrical light from overhead. It seemed to last longer than the others. The frozen scene he saw before him etched into his mind long after the darkness surrounded them again. The sound was a saw. They had cut the body's legs off. It was a woman: she was dying but not dead. She was clearly screaming, her lips drawn back in terrified agony. The Chief held one leg, two of the soldiers had the other between them. Chief's face was red, Mark could see that even in this ghostly, misty white. Blood was pouring down his face and chest and stomach, pooling around his feet on the white stone.

He was eating the woman.

The clap of thunder broke almost immediately. What followed was chaos. Mark tossed Elizabeth over his shoulder, turned and ran blindly through the trees and bushes and grasses. He held his cousin's legs firmly to his hips so that she wouldn't fall. When he realized that the woman had been cut at the same point on her body that he held in his hands, he stumbled to a stop, leaned over, and vomited violently. Brushing tears away from his eyes and trying to keep quiet, he kept running. The coal-eyes that had been trying to find refuge from the storm in Rivertown's main building ran behind them, following them, it seemed, chasing them, as they all tried to get as far away from the soldiers as they could.

"Where do we go?" Mark shouted. Elizabeth seemed to have a better idea of what was happening than he did. In fact, she may have just saved their lives by telling him to run.

"We can never go home," her voice broke as she said it. He didn't know what she meant.

Mark tried to think. If they went back to camp, they could find out what the others were doing. It seemed no one else had the idea to seek refuge indoors. Maybe they had some sort of plan back at camp. But they were being closely pursued by the coal-eyes crazed with a primal fear after seeing their own shot in cold blood, butchered and eaten before their eyes. All he knew was that from the coal-eyes perspective, the peacekeepers and the Chief were on the same team. What would these people do when they came upon the peacekeepers in their camp?

He supposed they could just keep running, but he knew that would probably mean death. The mud was quickly deepening, all around him, the wind still buffeting him and lighting struck every few seconds. Plus, Elizabeth needed help. She was muttering constantly now, followed by whimpering and screaming.

Mark knew he couldn't just saunter into camp and leave his only relative there formedical aid, not after what they had seen. Rivertown was a lie. The peacekeepers here had been played. There was some terrible thing happening under the hood and it probably had been for a while. Mark didn't understand why and for the moment, he didn't care. All that mattered was that they get out of this town and then this sick continent alive.

Mark tightened his grip on Elizabeth's legs and sprinted hard. He would go around the camp, through the trees and come in from behind. Say they had tried to hide in the trees and wait the storm out there. Hopefully the others would believe him.

If they didn't, Chief would know that one of the peacekeepers had seen him eating a woman alive.

Chapter Twenty Nine

He had to slow down. It was too wet, slick and muddy. His legs burned and his lungs burned and he was sweating and freezing and buffeted by the wind. He made a wide path around the camp, outside of the pockets of trees that fringed it in many places. If he avoided the trees, he could avoid tripping on their roots, or so he hoped.

As he went, the storm began to subside. The wind lessened, notch by notch, leaving the rain to drizzle down almost gently. The lightning was moving away. Instead of tableau and forestscape the diminishing flashes of lightning revealed a storm-swallowing ocean at the edge of the horizon.

It didn't take long before they were plunged into complete blackness, with a quiet, constant rain the only reminder of the passing cataclysm. The distant flash and rumble on the horizon did nothing to illuminate the land around him and Mark swore at himself for never having explored the area around camp. He was walking blind, Elizabeth almost entirely limp on his back, shivering and sobbing. The smell of blood came off strongly.

"Don't worry, Lizzy, I'll get you back to camp," he whispered, "I just have to find a good way to get us in, so's we can say we were lost in the trees or something."

"Left," was all she said. He stopped and peered to the left. There was a dense stand of trees; spruces and aspens tangled together. He wasn't sure, but thought he could hear the sound of voices from beyond.

It was nearly impossible to make his way through, especially with the added weight of his cousin on his back. There was a maze of bushes that he could only make out as faint shadows, a slightly denser darkness. His eyes ached from the effort and he tripped several times, falling to his knees and scraping them hard against the tight, thorned bushes that caught his legs. The branches clung to him, ripped his clothes and tore his skin and face. He remembered the Chief tearing meat off of the woman's leg and retched soundlessly, his stomach already empt, his hands shaking with silent sobs. After what felt like an eternity, Mark heard voices, he was sure of it. He strained his eyes and caught slivers of faint, moving light through the dense trees. Flashlights. It must be the peacekeepers and camp.

"Hey!" he called, into the trees, "it's Mark and Elizabeth! We need help!"

"Mark? Where have you been? Are you alright?" It was Ray. Mark could hear the rustle of his comrades pushing their way through the bushes and the low branches towards them. He could make out the flashlights clearly now, they bounced in unison with the footfalls of their wielders. His eyes rejoiced at having something clear to look at.

"Dizzy's hurt, Ray! We need help!"

"Keep talkin, buddy," it was another voice, one Mark couldn't place, "we'll find ya. Just keep talkin."

Mark took a deep breath. Time to build his story. "We were trying to get out of camp so that we wouldn't get hit by the things that were flyin' around. Our tent was coming apart and Dizzy was real scared. I took her into the trees here, figurin' we might be safest where the lightning wouldn't likely strike. But it did, right next to us. She fell and hit her head real hard. There's blood everywhere. We've been lost ever since. I couldn't find my way and I've had to carry her." Mark watched the lights get closer, listened to the rustle of his friends moving through the trees towards them. What if Elizabeth was too hurt to go along with his story? What if she didn't understand what was happening? "I think it's serious, she might be hurt bad cause she's talkin' all sorts of nonsense. She seems real scared and keeps talkin', like she were in a nightmare. Thank heavens you got flashlights, it's real good to see you." Mark felt his throat closing with tears – his relief was overwhelming.

The others were close now. Mark could see the forest around him the way one sees underwater, waveringly thanks to the constantly moving lights. "You see anyone else out here?" the other voice asked.

"No siree." Mark stopped. It was possible they knew the coal eyes were abroad. They would have run right past here, in their fear. If his story was going to add up, he would have to mention them. "Actually, I heard some people running and tried to follow them, but they wouldn't answer us when I called. I was trying to get help for Dizzy, you know, so I was desperate. I think that's probably what got us the most turned around, because after that the storm died down and I couldn't see nothin'."

Mark squinted and blinked as one of the flashlights was directed into his face. Then it moved to his cousin. She was unconscious, covered in blood, her head resting on Mark's shoulder, her arms draped down his chest.

Ray sucked air through his teeth. "She doesn't look so good, Mark. Come on, I'll take her for you. You don't look so good either, truth be told."

Mark allowed Ray to take his burden. He saw that the other boy was a friend of Ray's, named Tanner. Not a bad guy and not too smart, thank heavens. He would believe everything Mark had said, which meant that he now had witnesses. It seemed like their story would hold up, after all.

Mark followed Ray and Tanner through the trees and back into camp. It was a disaster. Most of the tents had collapsed entirely, a few had been stripped of their outer coverings and were only poles standing in the rain. There was tent canvas strewn in the mud and the trees, food caches cracked and on their sides, prepackages meals, clothes and personal items strewn everywhere.

"This place is..." Mark didn't know how to describe it. It was destroyed.

"Tell me 'bout it, Mark. Good thing we found you. Captain sent us out in pairs to find the missing people and when we're all back, we're going to the centre to spend the night, get warm and get tended to by the doc. Personally, I'm not lookin' too forward to coming back here in the morning and trying to sort through this mess."

Mark gulped and nodded stiffly in response. The Center. The Chief. Those men with their guns, shooting into an unarmed crowd...

They filed silently through the debris that had been their camp. Ahead, there was a milling crowd. The Captain was at the centre of it, wearing an oversized rain jacket and holding a clipboard. Mark assumed it was their crew manifest. There was a lamp hanging from a branch above him, casting light over the crowd.

"We found Mark and Dizzy, Captain!" Tanner called, "And we've got wounded!"

Captain looked up and many in the crowd turned towards them.

"Is she alright? What happened?" It was Dinky. He had a large gash on one cheek, his glasses were gone and his hair was plastered flat on his head. Dinky broke from the group and ran towards them, touching Dizzy's head gingerly.

"She hit her head pretty bad, Captain. We need to get her some help, now." Mark said.

"Nothing we can do here, son. Our first aid kits are somewhere buried in the muck, just like everything else. You boys run ahead to the Center and make sure she gets seen right away."

Dinky nodded, quickly and gravely. "I'll take her."

Mark felt the need to throw up again and wondered if he was walking to his death as he trotted along beside Dinky, one hand on Elizabeth's shoulder. If he were to die, they would eat him. He knew that at least. It wasn't how he had figured he would go. No, he had imagined that he would die with his wife, asleep in bed. But he didn't even have a wife and now and if he didn't step up and take control of this situation he never would.

Mark doubled over and vomited again, unable to hold back the tears that followed. If he said something about staying away from the Centre, they would be found out and would certainly die. He figured that there was a chance they would survive, if he just played along. The Chief had some reason for playing the peacekeepers, for keeping them in the dark and Mark could only hope that he would keep playing them a little while longer.

"You alright?" Ray's voice was uncharacteristically gentle. He placed a hand on Mark's back.

"Just... worried about Lizzy. I'm s'posed to take care of her, you know."

"Don't worry, big guy." Ray helped Mark back to a standing position and hung Mark's arm over his shoulder for support. "We've got good doctors here. She's going to be fine. It wasn't your fault you got lost out there, could have happened to anyone."

Mark murmured a word of thanks and allowed himself to lean on his friend. He was too shaken up to walk.

Dinky was unusually quiet. Tanner walked behind him and to the right, shining his flashlight ahead for both of them. Dinky watched the light, his eyebrows knit together with the effort of focusing on the road ahead, which he could barely see without his glasses. His lips were pressed together so hard that they had gone milky white. This was not because of the effort but because of Elizabeth, heavy on his back, still bleeding in the rain. His face was set and grim.

When they entered the last stand of trees before town Mark closed his eyes and let himself be led by Ray. He wanted to say something - ask if it was really necessary that they go to town, or if they were sure that Elizabeth could be helped here - but clamped his jaw closed and bit the edges of his tongue. There was nothing for it. They were perched at the edge of a vast and unknown continent, far from home. The Wild Land. Rivertown was their world here. Unless Mark wanted to try and carry his wounded cousin into the background of that world and hope for the best, he would have to be quiet and hope. Just hope.

Mark had never been good at hoping. It was too imaginative, often unfounded and he was a realistic boy, always had been. Try as he might, he still expected to hear his friends cry out in shock and alarm as they left the trees and walked towards the Centre. Even with his eyes closed and fluttering furiously, Mark knew when they left the forest. He waited, holding his breath. They didn't say anything.

He relaxed and had a look around. In the constant, quiet rain, under the wavering of the flashlights, the tent-homes of Rivertown looked oddly peaceful. He couldn't tell if they were empty or not, but noticed the water still pooled between and even in some of them. The tent-flap doors were all closed. Would the others notice, or ask how the coal-eyes fared the storm? Mark looked at Dinky expectantly. But Dinky had broken into a jog now that the ground was clear of roots and stones, trying to get Elizabeth into the Centre as quickly as possible.

"Shine your light ahead, so Dink can see," Mark said. Tanner shone his flashlight past Dinky, illuminating the way towards the Centre. The light moved up the stone steps and pointed at the doors as Dinky flew through them. There was no blood, no body parts, no sign of struggle. Mark knew there would be bullet casings in the mud... unless the rain washed them south towards the river. Blood, too. But for now, there was nothing.

He and the other boys hurried after Dinky and into the Centre. It was mercifully warm, dry, clean, lit. There was an audible sigh from the other two as they crossed the threshold. Mark found himself shivering uncontrollably. At the other end of the main hall was Dinky, still jogging, Elizabeth bouncing limply on his back as he went towards the infirmary. Mark ran after him, his legs burning and exhausted. He knew he couldn't let Elizabeth out of his sight. *She's your blood. You do whatever it takes.* There was a metallic taste in his mouth. He looked at her comatose form, shock of curly dark hair bouncing meekly against

Dinky's bloodstained t-shirt.

"Dinky! Wait for me!" Mark put his head forward and sprinted across the echoing hall, as hard as he could. How had Dinky gotten so far ahead of him?

Dinky disappeared into the infirmary at the far end of the building. There were noises coming from that room, voices... Mark was already sprinting outright and his vision swam briefly as the need to vomit surfaced again. What would they do to her? He had no chance of protecting her like this, tired, wounded and outnumbered. Was Dinky one of... them? He pumped his arms desperately, in time with his feet, trying to cover the distance more quickly. Voices alright. The sounds were a messy cacophony of injured pleading and clinical detachment. Confused voices, hurt, scared...

And the Chief. The Chief's voice.

Mark forced his legs to keep moving. Had to. Couldn't let them have Lizzy, not her. He reached out and grabbed the door jam with one hand, using his momentum to propel him around his arm and into the room.

"Where is she?" he yelled it. He was panting, gasping and felt like he was going to pass out.

"She's right here, Mark," Dinky said.

Mark looked around. Dinky was kneeling beside Elizabeth, who had been placed upright in a chair, her head lolling to one side. In the light she looked garish - the gash ran from below her hairline above an eyebrow, up and across the crown of her head in a jagged line. It was black around the edges with thicker, clotting blood, but bright red still trickled down her face and hair, dripping onto the chair and the floor and mixing with the rain water dripping off of her.

"It's alright. The doctor is going to see her first." Dinky tried to smile reassuringly at Mark when he said it, but couldn't. His lower lip quivered.

Mark blinked. There were other people in the room, too. The Chief was standing over Dinky, looking with anxious concern at Elizabeth. He had one hand over his mouth, eyebrows drawn together seriously. The doctor was kneeling on the other side of Elizabeth, examining her. He opened each of her eyes and pointed a light into them, took her pulse. Others with varying degrees of injury sat in the other chairs that lined the room. He recognized them from the other camp. No coal-eyes, though. Of course not.

"She's got a concussion. You her guardian? Son?" Mark blinked again and looked at the doctor. Guardian. *That would be you, idiot.* He was her nearest male kin here.

"Yes, I am. Sir."

"She needs stitches. We'll do that right away. Then, I'll need your permission to do a brain scan. There isn't any danger to it. I've worked with enough farmers to know you won't like any sort of scan no matter how benign, but I'm telling you that if there is serious injury, we need to know." Mark momentarily visualized Elizabeth being wheeled into a sinister mechanical contraption and ground into hamburger meat. He resisted the urge to strangle the doctor.

"Alright, you can scan her."

A nurse had appeared beside them with a wheelchair. She and the Doctor pulled Elizabeth gently off of her seat and placed her in it. Her head lolled vertiginously to the other side and a fresh trickle of bright red blood ran down her face.

"Thank you, son. You can wait out here until we're done." The nurse started to wheel Elizabeth away.

"No!" Mark was shaking. "I mean, no. I want to come with you and make sure she's alright. I just want to be beside her, that's all."

The Doctor gave Mark a patronizing look and shook his head. "If you stay out of the way, you can stand in the room with her. Don't touch anything. Come on."

Mark followed behind them, through a set of swinging doors and into a long, sterile-looking hallway. It was entirely barren, just a corridor leading to other rooms, through doors that were marked neatly with a number and their function. This was a sight both familiar and foreign to Mark. He'd been to the doctor every year when he was a child, at the insistence of his mother. Their facility wasn't as up to date as the ones he heard about in the city, nor did it have the specific functions of the sanitariums in the north. There was a hallway, something like this; a self-diagnostic room with blood scanners and an automated nurse, rooms to see the doctor in, operating tables, dark closets filled with jars and bottles. It was always noisy there, full of activity. Despite the dozen or so injured people waiting to be treated in the waiting room, this place was silent. He missed home, even the hospitals. Especially now that he wasn't sure he would ever see home again.

He watched as the doctor put twenty seven stitches into his cousins head. The sight of a part of her scalp flapping downwards from her skull, hair and all, as the nurse was prepping her for the stitches made him retch another time. There was nothing left in his stomach. Then, the doctor bandaged her. The scan took about twenty minutes. Mark stood by the door with his arms across his chest, watching. When that was finished, they took her to a bed in a wide, low room. There were two other people, bandaged and unconscious, in other beds. Mark knew them only from sight as peacekeepers from the other camp.

Once Elizabeth was in the bed, the Doctor asked Mark how long she had been unconscious.

"Two hours or more, by now," he said.

The Doctor nodded. "We'll have to wake her up now, then. The nurse will come and wake her again in a few hours."

"I'll do it," Mark said. He almost chuckled, remembering all of the times he had been assigned to wake his cousin when they were children, how difficult it had been.

"Dizzy," he whispered, shaking her shoulder gently. He didn't want to hurt her anymore than the storm had. "Dizzy, wake up. You're safe now. You hit your head and had some scary dreams, remember? Talked about all sorts of scary things but you're safe now. There was a storm and we're inside. Gettin' warm. Wake up, Dizzy."

Nothing happened. Mark looked to the Doctor, who shrugged at him.

Mark sighed. "Dizzy! Wake up! Come on, time to get movin'!" He shook her more forcefully this time. Her eyes pressed together and she tried feebly to push him away.

"I'll wake up in the morning, Cam, God. Just because *you're* a psycho doesn't mean I have to be, too." Mark gaped.

"What? Dizzy, Wake up! You're still dreamin', girl. It's me, Mark! Wake up!"

Elizabeth's eyes shot open. "Mark? My cousin, Mark?"

Mark laughed. She was awake, taken care of. They would be alright after all. "Yeah, you're my cousin. You bonked your head, Dizzy so don't worry if you're a bit confused right now."

"Ok, I won't be confused."

Mark laughed again. That was his Dizzy.

"Why'd we have to wake her up?" he asked.

"Just a precaution, with the concussion," the doctor answered, as he made notes on his clipboard, "She can get her rest, now. You can stay here with her, if you'd like, but I know they're setting up a makeshift camp for all of you in the main hall. Your choice, son, but we've got to see to the others."

Mark nodded pensively. "I'll stay here, thanks. Would you tell Dinky she's ok?"

The doctor said he would and left.

Mark unfolded one of the chairs lined up on the wall of the room. There were curtains between some of the beds, but none were drawn. He pulled the chair up beside his cousin's bed. She had already fallen back to sleep. He sat down and took her right hand in both of his.

Some time later, Mark was startled awake by a voice.

"She's doing alright?"

Mark rubbed his eyes furiously. He hadn't meant to fall asleep. He looked to the foot of the bed to see the Chief.

"Doc said she'll be ok. No brain damage, just a concussion. And some stitches, of course."

The Chief sighed. "I'm glad to hear it. What a terrible thing - I'm sorry this had to happen to your cousin. I understand how you must feel."

"Thanks, Chief. It's no one's fault though, so don't feel bad. It was just the weather."

Chief nodded, slowly, looking down. He was playing the part of concerned head of staff so well that Mark almost had to wonder if he had imagined what happened before. "It was an incredible storm, wasn't it? Unexpected, too, I'll tell you that. We've monitored the weather here for some time and truly, this was a fluke."

"Never been a storm like this before, you mean?"

"One, actually. Just one in all the time we've been here. But that was long, long ago."

Chapter Thirty

Dinky sat in the waiting room. He kept his feet flat on the floor, elbows resting on his thighs. For a while he waited, expecting to see Elizabeth emerge with a bandage and a smile: to escort her to the make-shift barracks in the main hall, hold her in his arms and tell her everything was alright now. To be there for her, to be the one man that was.

Of course, that plan excluded Mark completely, which Dinky hadn't meant to do. He pondered that while he watched his hands, hanging loosely between his legs. In his peripheral vision, the fluorescent-white room filled and emptied itself with peacekeepers in relative stability as the night passed.

Night. That explained why he wasn't thinking clearly, it was the middle of the night. Dinky groaned low in his throat and held his head in his hands. It was the middle of the night and there was a storm and camp was destroyed and Elizabeth was hurt. She must have been in there for an hour and a half already, with no news. Was that bad? The doctor had said something about a scan. A brain scan. Dinky knew what it meant if your brain was damaged, or at least, what it could mean.

Not Elizabeth, he thought. *I love Elizabeth.*

There were only a few severe injuries that he saw. Found himself imagining what he would do, if he were the doctor here, to treat them. That made him wonder, but he convinced himself that the speculations were out of boredom, only. Of course, he could always go back. Go to the sanitarium and earn the title of "doctor". Sure.

But what about Elizabeth?

Dinky's head started to hurt. He tried to remind himself that it was the middle of the night, the middle of a bad night and not the time for thinking. Especially not the time for thinking important things like this, or trying to reason around feelings. Feelings appear differently as a bad night goes on. They get you to make decisions that land you, months later, on some tiny forgotten continent an ocean away from home and the future you imagined, marooned in the waiting room of a backwater community infirmary because the girl you love got hurt in the same thunderstorm that just rendered everyone, including you, homeless.

He moaned quietly again.

"Son?"

Dinky sat up quickly. He had actually tried to stand but found his legs too weak. He was more tired than he had realized.

"You friend wanted me to let you know that the girl, Elizabeth, is alright. She has a concussion and she'll need rest, but otherwise she's fine. He's staying with her."

Dinky tried to think of an intelligent question to ask in relation to the brain scan but couldn't. He just nodded instead.

"You should get some rest yourself, young man. Tomorrow'll be a big day for all of us."

Dinky nodded again and the doctor disappeared with another injured peacekeeper, asking if he was allergic to any medications. Rest. Yes, he ought to get some rest. If Mark stayed with her, then there was no benefit to his staying out here in this stupid waiting room, too. It was cold, bright, busy. Dinky nodded to himself and stood up, fidgeting. As he left the infirmary and rounded the corner into what would become known in the following weeks as the Barracks, he promised himself that he would come to see Elizabeth the very first chance he got.

Chapter Thirty One

Nightmares. Some memories, some of monsters, all scrambled and confused. The nurse woke her every two hours, trying not to wake Mark, who sat in his plastic chair, snoring beside her. Whenever she woke, she would try to force her eyes open, rub them, blink them, but it was no use. Her vision was a window drenched in thick, torrid rain. It made the nightmares worse, because it felt like she couldn't quite wake up from them.

Elizabeth didn't know if she was awake or asleep, Elizabeth or Maria, safe or in terrible danger. She tried to remember, tried to clear her mind and couldn't. Then she would be dreaming again and only realize it because they woke her. She forced herself not to speak, afraid she would say something about her other life, about being Maria, about the things she knew and the things she had seen. Then she would dream that she couldn't stop herself from talking. It felt like the longest night of her life.

Finally there was nothing. A sort of peaceful sleep, unaware.

"Elizabeth?"

It was a sweet voice, one she remembered. She found herself smiling. A friend. Someone that would help her, someone that could help her people -

She betrayed me. They thought it was me; my fault. They're all dead because of her.

Elizabeth's eyes flew open. She let out a sigh of relief. It wasn't a robot, a monster, a person from another life. It was Stephanie.

"It's good to see you," she said. She was surprised at how broken her own voice sounded.

"You too," Stephanie smiled between brows furrowed in concern. "I was looking for you, in the barracks. Didn't see you all night. I'm really glad you're ok."

"I'm glad you're ok, too," Elizabeth managed a smile.

"I sent Mark to get some breakfast. He was in that chair," Stephanie gestured to the unfolded plastic chair beside the bed, "all night."

"Is he hurt?"

"No, silly. *You're* the one that's hurt." Another flash of concern crossed Stephanie's face and her tone changed; gentle, worried, almost motherly, "Do you remember what happened?"

Elizabeth sighed.

"Sort of. I know there was a storm. I was… with Mark. I saw lots of confusing things…"

"You have a concussion. Mark said you split your head open pretty bad."

Elizabeth reached up and touched her head, gingerly. It was bound in a bandage and underneath, she could feel the hard, unnatural ridges of stitching in her skin.

"He said that you had been talking lots of crazy talk and that you were pretty confused all night. I'm glad that you're back to yourself."

A cold fear slipped into Elizabeth's chest. Something wasn't right here, was dangerous. She remembered seeing the Chief, knowing what he was going to do, seeing him...yes. They were at the center, she was afraid.. *I remembered... something else, something similar, from that other life; that other time. That's how I knew what the Chief was going to do. But then we were on the other side of camp, and no one else saw the Chief, except for us.* Elizabeth knew she couldn't tell this girl anything more.

"Me too."

Stephanie smiled again. She looked a bit less concerned.

"How is everybody else? I mean, are you hurt?" Elizabeth swallowed, "Your tent-mate?"

"My tent-mate! Shouldn't you be asking about your boyfriend?" Stephanie was back to her teasing, a good sign. "We're all doing just fine. All you need to worry about is getting some rest and getting better. Chief says we have a lot of work to do coming up. I'm not sure if we'll be setting the tents again, or doing something different this time. I guess we'll see."

"You're up!" It was Mark. He carried three bowls of what looked like gruel. It turned out to be porridge, made en masse by a few volunteers for all of the peacekeepers. He quickly handed two of the bowls to the ladies, fished three spoons out of his pants pocket and put them on the chair with his bowl. He bent over his cousin, hand on her cheek, looking into her eyes as if to check if it was really her.

"Oh, Dizzy, I was so worried about ya..."

Mark stopped. He glanced at Stephanie, who was watching with a small smile, holding her bowl of porridge. He cleared his throat and straightened. "I mean, we were all real worried about ya. Gave us quite the scare." He nodded matter-of-factly and handed out the spoons.

Stephanie gave Elizabeth an unsubtly significant look and batted her eyelashes at Mark for the second time. At least, the second time that Elizabeth had actually seen. It was really quite amazing to watch: she was blinking, several times in succession, with her eyes locked onto Mark's. She did something with her eyebrow muscles that made her eyes appear... cat-like. Mark's mom would have called it bedroom eyes and given the offending young woman a good smack on the head. Elizabeth wasn't sure how to respond. It could be a useful tool to master, that much was sure; poor Mark couldn't seem to look away and was blushing profusely.

Dinky came in next. He rushed over to Elizabeth, brushing past the other two without acknowledging them and collapsed against her bedside. He took her hands in his own and pressed them to his lips. Elizabeth could see that there were tears in his eyes.

"I'm sorry I wasn't here," he said, his face close to hers, "I fell asleep, I can't believe I did, but I'm here now. Are you alright? Does it hurt? Can I get you anything?"

It was only then that Elizabeth realized she felt nauseous

"I'm fine, Dinky. Are you alright?" She was looking at the cut on his cheek.

"Oh," Dinky reached up to the dried blood and winced, "I forgot about that, actually. Probably too late for stitches now, but at least I'll have a rugged scar to remember my peacekeeping days by."

"Yeah, you're real rugged, Dink," Mark mumbled over his porridge.

"Breakfast," Dinky looked down at his stomach and it rumbled loudly, "I forgot about that."

"Have mine, Dink. I'm not feeling up to eating just yet." Elizabeth handed him her bowl. "Where are your glasses?"

"In the mud somewhere." He took the bowl from her carefully.

"What a disaster." Mark said quietly, lips scrunched together, over his empty bowl. Elizabeth knew him well enough to know that the one serving was certainly not enough.

"Maybe we'll all go back now," Stephanie said, "or half of us or something. I mean, sure our tours' s'posed to be six months but heavens. We can't last so long without supplies and such."

"What about Rivertown?" Mark piped in again, "what about... the coal eyes? The mine? All that pretty stuff that Chief said we were working towards."

There was a moment of silence. Stephanie was new to the group and they all waited politely for her response.

"Personally," she said, carefully, "and I don't know about the rest of ya, but I ain't seen any mining done here. All we do is walk around and not even at night. We were s'posed to get fire-training and such, once we arrived, so's we could really keep the peace. Ain't happened. Not yet, anyway."

"We think so, too," Dinky said. Despite his dishevelled appearance, Elizabeth couldn't help but see him as he could be, someday. A leader. Strong, smart, kind. And, if needed, a warrior. "There's something else going on here. We've noticed from the start. Only two peacekeepers set to watch the market. No one's buying down there. Just coal eyes trying to sell to each other, because they were told they would find work here. All of us playing games at night instead of working shifts... it's more like summer camp than a colony operation."

"Wait." Elizabeth's eyes were wide. Mark shot her a look, frightened, desperate. He was shaking his head imperceptibly. "We can't talk about this here."

"Why not?" Stephanie asked, in her adorable, harmless drawl.

"I don't know. Maybe it's just the concussion. I just have a bad feeling."

"It's probably just the concussion, sweetheart," Mark agreed, nodding. Sweat was popping out on his forehead as the image of the woman being sawed apart flashed through his mind again. "You're getting upset's all. Alright, folks, shows over. You two clear out and I'll join ya in a minute. She needs her rest, doc's orders."

"Come on, Mark, I barely got to see her." Dinky looked so much more handsome without his glasses. Much more capable and sensual.

"You can come see me once I've had a sleep. Whenever your first break is. Alright?"

Dinky nodded and left, Stephanie close behind him.

"Give me a hug, Mark."

He leaned over the bed, picked her shoulders up gently and hugged her. She pressed her cheek to his and whispered, barely moving her lips. "We can't talk about it. Not here. You cannot tell them, or anyone, what we saw."

"So you remember?"

Elizabeth tightened her grip around her cousin and hissed, "Not. Here." Then she released him.

Mark straightened, awkwardly.

"Really, Mark. We don't have to talk about what happened to cousin Theresa, not here. The same thing won't happen here, I promise. I'll be just fine. She was hurt much worse than me. Please come and visit me, every chance you get. I want to hear about camp and everything. I just can't believe I won't get to be part of it. I wish I could get out of here." The slightest change in her face, as she said that last. Mark nodded to her.

"Alright, I won't think about Theresa. I know you'll be alright. It's just hard not to think about it, but the doc says you'll be fine. I'll be back soon as I can. Get some sleep."

Mark squeezed her hand and left.

Of course, there was no cousin Theresa.

Elizabeth, however, did need rest and knew it. She was asleep again only moments after Mark left.

Which meant that she didn't see the Chief, who had been standing in the corner of the large room, out of sight from Elizabeth's bed, watching, listening and taking notes. He stood, put the notepad into his breast pocket and walked out the same way Mark had.

Chapter Thirty Two

Will had his eyes closed. He was in the Barracks, on the floor, under a rough blanket, pretending to be asleep. He could see morning light, through his eyelids, as his spot was close to the main door, which he had propped ajar with a block of wood. This, in case he needed to run. He knew, from memories of a pursuit thousands of years in the past, that running would probably be futile. It was still the best plan he had come up with so far.

He remembered naming their settlement Rivertown. He and Elder Jared chose the name. And the ghosts, when they came to celebrate the truce at the beach, they called it Rivertown, too. At first, he thought they were just dreams. But he was convinced they were real even before he saw Maria.

I have to go see her.

Will rolled over, tried to make it look like something he would have done in his sleep. He couldn't go see her. Absolutely couldn't. They were in such great danger, so little of which he understood and last night's storm had made it all the more complicated.

The storm meant that she remembered. He knew, because he finally remembered everything, too. The night they took her, the weeks of waiting, without her, thinking she was gone. The sleepless hours spent digging deeper and deeper in an effort to wall the community off from their weapon. The long year of running that hadn't entirely been fruitless: they knew more and more about their pursuers as they met stranger and stranger people in their travels. The wristbands came from the coal eyes, or their ancestors at least. They looked too similar phenotypically to be anything but. The coal eyes lived a meager existence even then, slaves of the ghosts. It was a wonder they had maintained any of their culture at all, after these long years of servitude.

He remembered her coming back. Or rather, being delivered. Woke up one morning and she was asleep, in the grass, just outside the cave they were trying to expand. The cave that was now to be used as a mine. She had been injured and tended to. Didn't know how she had gotten there. Said that they were people, not machines. She had befriended one, explained their culture and lifestyle to her new friend and somehow, secured the deliverance of her people.

Then, the next day, they died together.

What were the chances that an entirely new group of settlers would name an entirely new colony Rivertown, too? No, it was too much of a coincidence. The ghosts were still here, the coal-eyes were still slaves. And his wife was here, somewhere.

I have to go see her. It's Maria, it's her! I have to find her. Talk to her, ask her questions. Touch her skin again...

Will tried to keep his breathing regular, so that no one would suspect he was already awake. Had been for hours now, wrestling with himself. It was too dangerous. Besides, she was no more Maria than he was Cameron. He was Will – he was just a boy, not a fully-grown man with a honed survival instinct. An old thought. One he had been repeating to himself since they arrived, the one thing he had clung to, to try and maintain some sanity, as his memories were slowly replaced by those of another. One that had been rendered moot and useless, as soon as he saw her. Because it wasn't just him, not just his mind losing its grip. There was another. And she had recognized him, he knew it.

She was beautiful. Even though she was somehow a new woman - Stephanie said her name was Elizabeth - she was stunning in the same ways. Her unbreakable spirit, shining through in every situation. Her delicate but animalistic physicality, her humor... and the deeper things. The raw spirituality and sensuality that had kept the memories of their love alive.

Will grumbled. He wanted her so badly it hurt, the one stray thought causing an immediate lurch between his legs, which complicated the situation even further. They were not the same people, but what he felt for her was so strong. His memories - Cameron's memories - had made him - Will - into a different person. A gentler person, more thoughtful. He wondered briefly if his mother would notice the difference, could she see him now. It seemed likely that she would. Maybe he was Cameron, in some ways. Was, or was becoming, or maybe had always been. Either way, he was a man in love. Terribly, desperately, consumingly in love. And it was with Maria, a girl who had been dead for two thousand years.

"Come on, sleepy head, we got work to do and no room for lazy bones."

Will opened his eyes, covering them with his arm to maintain the illusion of having been asleep. It was Stephanie and she had a bowl of porridge for him.

"Morning, Steph. How's your friend?"

Her surprise at his question made him immediately regret asking.

"She's fine. How'd you know she was hurt?"

Will's stomach jumped. Hurt? She was hurt? He shook his head, trying to clear it. "I didn't know. I was trying to make a joke. Your friend, as in, you. How are you. It's just something we say, where I'm from."

"Uh-huh. You're one odd duck, Will, but I do enjoy ya. I'm doing fine, myself. Thanks to the watchful eye of a certain young man who is, aforementionedly, an odd duck. Thank you for lookin' out for me last night."

"Well, you're welcome, but I didn't do much. Besides, you don't have any cousins or brothers here, so I'll step up."

Stephanie smiled. Will sat up, took the porridge and ate quickly. He was starving, exhausted. It had been a long night. Too bad he could only remember bits and pieces of it. As soon as he had lain down on the cold, fake marble floor of the barracks, the memories had started. He didn't even know what he had done for Stephanie. Assumed he had made sure she got here safely. Hoped that was all.

The bowl was empty far too quickly; Will still very hungry. He looked out the door.

"Looks awful out there," he said.

Stephanie nodded. It was a grey sky, earth and air in between, a solid wall of drizzling, foggy rain falling quietly onto the already drenched ground.

"Sorta peaceful, though, ain't it?"

Will nodded. He paused and said, "So. Did I talk in my sleep again?"

"Not this time. You cried a bit, said *Maria* a few times, you know. The usual."

"No sounds of hanky panky?"

Stephanie smiled and shook her head.

"Is your boyfriend ok?"

Stephanie smiled impishly and punched him in the shoulder. "He ain't my boyfriend. Least, not yet. And he's fine. I think he likes me."

"How do you know?"

"Well, I went to th'infirmary, lookin' for Lizzy, that's who I thought you meant, when you asked about my friend, cause I hadn't seen her in the barracks all night. There she was and Mark was with her. Had been all night, can you imagine. That's the sign of a good man, if you ask me. Real sweetheart. Anyways, he and I chatted a bit and I used my secret weapon." She fluttered her eyelashes.

"Heavens. I bet he didn't stand a chance."

Stephanie giggled. Will stretched, looking around. His back was sore from the night spent on the hard floor. The peacekeepers were mostly quiet, having hushed conversations with each other, swaddled uselessly in thin, wet blankets. Most still wore their clothes from the night before and didn't have any rain gear with them. It had been too dark to find any protective equipment in the flotsam and jetsam and it would still be a long, hard day for them all, especially with limited food. Of course, most of the individual meals they had brought with them from home were vacuum-sealed. Hopefully they had survived the storm.

"They don't look too good, do they," she asked, following his gaze.

"Nope. Tired and scared. They look young."

"You think they're gonna send us home?"

"I don't know, Steph."

"All I know is that my affection for Rivertown is decreasing steadily."

Will smiled and ran his hands through his hair. It was a mess, he could tell just from feeling it. Caked with mud. It reminded him of running, back when he was Cameron. Perhaps there was something to be gained from these memories. He studied Stephanie for a moment.

"How do you look so good, even after all this?"

"A gentleman never asks and a lady never tells!"

"You completely got that aphorism wrong. That's about sex, not personal grooming. Hey, your boyfriend's coming."

Mark was picking his way through the now mostly awake peacekeepers towards them where they sat by the door. He waved clumsily when he noticed them looking.

"Yup, you've got him right where you want him," Will murmured.

Just as Mark made it within earshot of the two of them, the voice of the Chief boomed through the Barracks.

"Good morning." The words bounced off the high, domed ceilings, through the arches into the courtyard and auditorium and infirmary, around the huge, decorative pillars lining the hall and off of the walls. There was immediate silence from the peacekeepers; there had to be, the voice was so damn loud. Will turned to where the sound had originated. The Chief stood at one end of the massive hall, a mega-phone in hand. He winced, shook his head and adjusted the volume dial. "Sorry about that, boys. Now. We have a lot of work to do, as you can all imagine. This has been an unexpected turn of events and your Captains and I are already very impressed with your reactions to this disaster."

"Want to bet whether we're going home or not?" Stephanie whispered.

"Don't count on it, Steph," Will whispered back. Like Elizabeth, he had a feeling. His gut, responding to many things half remembered, told him that the real reason for their being in Rivertown hadn't been achieved. They wouldn't leave. Not yet.

The Chief went on. "This storm caught us with our pants down. Not you, boys. No. You were true to your training, followed orders and if I may be so bold, have already started to build a strong community here with each other. Your Captains and I... we let you down." He took a deep breath, as if thinking. Trying to plan his next words, to be careful and respectful of his audience. Will had the idea that he was letting his words sink in, instead. Just another chapter in the farce, another layer in the deception. He hadn't thought they would sink much lower than an organized game of Disks when the coal-eyes were unemployed, starving and clearly here against their will, but he had been wrong.

As he thought back on what he had remembered of the night before, his eyes sunk closed. He had been so wrong, about so many things. He opened his eyes and glanced at Stephanie and Mark, to see what their reactions would be. Stephanie was whispering in Mark's ear. Not surprising, but also not particularly reassuring. She was his only ally here, if you could call her that. She didn't know who he was or what was happening to him and he wouldn't tell her - it was far too dangerous and he didn't know enough about her to trust her fully - but he might still have to rely on her to escape Rivertown alive.

Especially now that Maria... Will shook his head. Wrong.

Especially now that *Elizabeth* was hurt, bed-ridden. That Stephanie seemed to care for her was a good thing. They may need to get her out alive, too. At least, he hoped they would. He didn't want to think about losing her again. The Chief started to speak again, brow knit.

"We'd like to see this storm as an opportunity to start again. To do this right. Truthfully, we thought this mission would be an easy one. The natives here are docile, hard workers and keep mostly to themselves. Your deployment is only six months long; just enough time to get Rivertown up and running, so that the Wild Land is a bit less wild when the true settlers arrive from Lila and the towns nearby. We thought this would be a good way to give you experience, train you in the real world. Take new recruits and turn them into experienced, competent peacekeepers with a successful mission under their belts.

"That can still happen. That *will* happen. Your captains and I have conferred and decided to change the way things are done around here. Learn from our mistakes, boys and from our example: it's good to admit when you're wrong and wise to change things for the better once you have. We will train you in firefighting, natural disaster response, first aid and riot control. Your basic training will be expanded upon. If you successfully complete this training, as well as your assignments in Rivertown, you will leave these shores with Secondary Training completed and each of you will be assigned a new rank according to your accomplishments."

Murmurs. Excitement.

"It's not goin' home, but I'd say it's almost better. Wouldn't need to get me an M.R.S if I were commissioned." Stephanie whispered it loudly enough that both boys heard. Neither of them laughed at her joke. They were both staring intently at the Chief, waiting to hear what would come next.

"This may seem unprecedented. It is. But given the extenuating circumstances, we feel it is both justified and necessary. Your assignment today is to return to your respective camps. You will search for anything and everything that can still be of use to us. Your Captains and I will be taking inventory and organizing the salvage from here. Don't worry if it's wet - it will dry. Grab anything that isn't entirely ruined but leave the tents. What we need most of right now is food, clothing and supplies. Go and bring it all back. Let's get to work!"

The peacekeepers didn't need much more incentive than that. They were up and moving, all of them. Will, Mark and Stephanie had to run out the door and out of the way to avoid being swallowed in the stampede.

"I guess I'll see you two later," Mark said, scratching his neck.

"I suppose so," Stephanie said. "Good luck, Mark." She took Will's hand and led them into the crowd heading for East camp, leaving Mark to watch them go.

Once they were some distance away and already soaked to the bone in their pyjamas and the constant, cold rain, Stephanie asked what Will made of the speech.

"Not sure, Steph. It does seem unprecedented. But at the same time, what else would they do to keep morale up? It's smart of them, either way. A bunch of ranchers' and farmers' sons trying hard to make their way in the world and you promise them free training and public recognition for it? That's well done."

Will swallowed hard, already shivering. It was going to be a long, miserable day. He hoped that Stephanie's optimism wasn't misplaced. But they were three days oceanic passage from home, alone and unsupported. Going home with medals and certificates didn't seem the likeliest fate for these boys.

Chapter Thirty Three

Dinky had brought his favourite books to Rivertown. He knew that it would probably only reinforce his otherness as city bred and book read, but even with that self-conscious knowledge, he had packed them lovingly. He hadn't fallen asleep without reading in bed first for as long as he could remember, it was part of who he was.

That morning, Dinky found his books half buried in thick mud under his tent canvas and soaked through. He had to hold each one up to his face in order to figure out which book it was, as he still hadn't found his glasses. His tent-mate had broken a finger the night before and the doctor said he ought to take at least one day to rest, which meant Dinky had no one to help him. The rain was thick, tiny rain drops that fell slowly and continuously so that there was no patter, just a grey sound enveloping everything. No one heard Dinky swear as book after book turned out to be ruined. Dinky hugged his body, rubbed his arms. It was no use. He was soaked, freezing, lost. Had no idea what he was doing here. He wanted to be alone and knew it wasn't possible. Not unless he went to hide in one of the stalls of the palatial ladies' washroom in the Centre, that was.

He searched through the mud for his glasses. He had taken them off when he went to bed and hadn't been able to find them once the storm had started. Truly, he felt he had little hope of finding them. Dread filled his chest. Without his glasses, he would be as good as blind for a lot of the training exercises. Couldn't just go to the optometrist and get more. It was possible the infirmary could help, but not certain. He had brought an extra pair, kept with his books. The case they were in had been made of wood - a gift from his father when he left. His initials were carved into it. W D. Except it had been cracked in half - along with the pair of glasses inside - during the storm. The two pieces of his extra pair of glasses were now in his pants pocket. One lens was missing. He supposed having one lens would be better than not having any.

It wasn't rage he felt. Anger, sure. But nothing quick, hot or provocative. It was an icy cold, debilitating resentment that trickled through him like the heavy rain. Not like the furious and unrelenting Ethos of anger, down on the beach. Dinky cursed the Ethos then, under his breath. He was a man of science, medicine and (now ruined) books. He knew that he and other people had come to be through the powerful and logical process of evolution. Not what they had been fed as children: as a spontaneous coming together of energies, essence finding physical expression in the human form; not as Ethos making their stand against eternity.

Dinky collapsed onto a stump. He was already soaked, filthy and freezing. Nothing worse would come from taking a short break. The Mother had found her form first, of course. That's why she was in front, among the statues. There was a joke, not a very good one: which came first, the Mother or the child? The farm boys told it a lot. He supposed they liked it because they had been surrounded by chicken eggs all their lives. Not very funny. The Mother came first. From timelessness and formlessness, into the shape of woman. According to his (now ruined) textbook on the subject, anthropologists believed that the culture responsible for carving the Statues of the Ethos had been matriarchal. This view was highly contested back home in popular culture, political infrastructure and religious circles. Since women were the first form, the lifegivers and creators it was a common justification for them to not to do other work. The belief was slowly changing, as all beliefs did.

Dinky was especially angry at the Ethos of horror. A tall black statue, eyes pressed firmly closed and a terrified look on his face, hands clenched into fists. That's what the (now ruined) textbook had said, as well as a traditional doctor that Dinky's mother had brought him to when his father was at work one day. The doctor said that Dinky's eyes were weak because the Ethos within him were out of balance. He had too much horror, not enough serenity (who stood with eyes wide open, gazing over the horizon and into the sea).

It was supposed to be Dinky and Elizabeth's first day off that day. He was going to take her down to the beach, walk among the statues. Tell her everything he knew about them, partly to impress her and partly just because he loved knowledge. Dinky retracted his curse. He didn't hate the Ethos, neither the idea of them nor their statues. They had been a part of his culture for millennia. The first discovery of them was over two thousand years before. Already, then, they stood as they did now. Timeless. Some, especially in religious groups, pointed to the lack of conclusive evidence surrounding the mysterious carvers of the statues as proof that they hadn't been carved at all, but rather, came into being of their own, in the form of humanity, which is perfectly suited to their expression. Some of the more over-zealous, the type that Dinky's father had no time for, even saw this as proof that humans had a right to mastery over the Earth, because the Ethos, in their inception, moved stone of the strongest and most resilient kind to make their bodies. And were humans not made of earth and water?

Dinky was *covered* in water, he knew that much. He wondered about Elizabeth. If she would be the wife and mother in his life, make a family with him. She was a different breed of woman it seemed, and he liked that about her. Had grown up believing that women could do just about anything and had always wanted a wife that proved it. Elizabeth was certainly that.

Just then, Dinky saw something catch the dim light among the grasses on the other side of his (now ruined) tent. He wasn't sure if that's what he was seeing at all, actually, but it did look like something over in that green something past the canvas something. Dinky picked his way through the mud, the squelching of each step muted by the rain and squatted down, holding his face only inches from whatever it was. Something shiny, alright. Metal. He pulled it carefully from the mud, ran his hands over it and held it up to his face just to be sure he wasn't hallucinating.

His glasses.

Chapter Thirty Four

"Dinky?"

The voice surprised him and he dropped his glasses into the mud again. This time, they weren't suspended on bended stalks of grass and he couldn't see them. He swore.

"Who's there?"

"It's me, Mark. What are you doing in the mud?"

"I dropped my glasses. Would you help me find them?"

Mark grunted his assent and hunkered down beside the smaller boy. "Here ya go," he said, almost immediately, handing the mud-caked glasses to Dinky.

"Thanks." Dinky rubbed them with his shirt and put them on. A bit scratched, but better than the ruined shards in his pocket. He turned to Mark. "How's your tent?"

"'Bout the same as yours, I guess." He snorted, spit into the mud. Cleared his throat.

"What is it? Is it Elizabeth? Is she alright?"

"Yeah, yeah, she's fine." Mark said it like a petulant child. He scratched his chin, eyebrows knit together. "Listen. You're not the most handsome guy..."

"Thanks, Mark."

"...but you still got a girl. I know she's my cousin and I don't wanna know details but... I'm wonderin' if you could give me some help. You know, advice. About girls."

"Yeah, sure. I mean, now?"

"Or later. Whenever you're... available."

"What do you want to know? Why don't you just ask Lizzy?"

"I can't ask Lizzy! It's not... it's just that... Look. There's a girl that I sort a like. I'd a asked Ray, but he's a little bit rough. Around the edges. If you know what I mean. So I thought I'd ask you. Cause I don't have any idea how to go about gettin' her to like me."

"Oh." Dinky cleared his throat, trying to think of something more intelligent to say. "Oh."

He stood up, surveying his swampy campsite with the benefit of his mostly-still-intact spectacles. His clothes and those of his tent-mate were littered in the mud, all shades of grey and brown. As the Chief had said, they would dry. He looked around for the bright orange of his rain jacket. He didn't want to catch a cold.

"Well?" Mark stood up beside Dinky, "will ya help me?"

"I can try, sure. But I mean, I never had a girlfriend before Liz. There weren't even any girls interested in me. And with her, it just sort of... happened, it was like -"

"I said that I don't want details."

"All I meant was that we were friends. I adored her but I didn't think anything would happen. Then she just started looking at me differently. I guess. Like, she started to like me, too."

"Looking at you, huh. How was she looking at you? Like this?" Mark did his best imitation of Stephanie's eyelash fluttering. His serious attempt quickly disintegrated into absurdity as he realized he was fluttering his eyes at Dinky.

Dinky laughed with him. "Not really. I don't think that's really something Elizabeth would ever do."

"I guess not."

"So... You like Stephanie?"

"Yeah."

"How about this. When we go back to Barracks, I'll go with you to talk to her. Just so you have someone else there. Then after, I can tell you if I thought she liked you."

"Sounds great, Dink! Great idea. Thanks."

"You're welcome."

"I guess I should get back to my camp, what with Dizzy gone, it's all up to me."

"Do you want some help?

"Nah, you're helping me more than enough." Mark nodded and walked back towards his campsite. Dinky shook his head and smiled. His life was certainly not where he had expected it to be, but at least he had good company.

He set about gathering all of the clothes and food that he could. He piled them onto the canvas that was once his tent. He found his tazer, but the battery was soaked through and no longer worked. He threw it on the pile just in case. The two sleeping bags were heavy and sodden but they would be warmer than the thin emergency blankets once they dried. He decided to make a second trip for the sleeping mats. Most of the freeze-dried meals had survived - hundreds of them all bound together in bundles. A final, mournful check of his books confirmed that they had not survived the storm and could not be salvaged: the pages were stuck together, many of them were ripped and the ink ran where it hadn't been entirely obscured by mud. He left these piled neatly beside the site, in the trees, folded the canvas over his supplies and began to drag it back towards the Centre.

Chapter Thirty Five

It was a long day. Will worked almost silently, listening to Stephanie's happy chatter and commenting when it seemed necessary for the conversation to progress. They were able to salvage most of their food, like Dinky and brought their soaked, filthy clothing with them in the hopes they could be saved. Stephanie had a small, water-tight package containing a hair brush, change of clothes, two pairs of wool socks and a rain suit which they found early in the morning. She donned the rain suit and decided to wait until they were back at the Barracks to put her warm clothes on.

Will was insanely jealous of her. She had foresight, would be dry tonight... and she had also been able to react to the day as just another day. She was still able to make jokes, conversation and even plans about the near-future. And she knew who she was.

Most of all, she wasn't being ripped apart, every moment that they were here and Elizabeth wasn't. He couldn't let himself think that way, but the grey sky, the soft rain... he couldn't get her out of his mind. He felt sorrow and longing and desperation. He had lost her once. He couldn't do it again.

The ghosts are still here. I have to be careful.

He and Stephanie carried the first armloads of their things back to the Centre and took a few moments to warm up before going back. Will had found his raincoat and did his best to dry it off with the blanket he had slept under that night before putting it on. It helped, marginally. It also made the oppressiveness of the day seem more intense. He could see his breath, feel the thick fabric next to his skin, hear it crinkle with every move he made.

"It's beautiful, you know. Even though it's awful, this rain, it's sure beautiful."

Stephanie gave him a funny look in response, then went back to her work.

It was a harsh land in some ways, being this far north. The things that grew here knew it and appreciated the life that they had been given. Grew in wild, windswept and defiant shapes with their gnarled, shallow roots proudly exposed. Will knew that the animals here were just as rugged: small rodents with giant, furry tails to keep them warm in winter; giant yellow-white bears, humps of muscle on their backs and flat faces with beady, intelligent eyes. He smiled inwardly, remembering how Maria loved the land of their home so much and how even here, at the end of the world they knew, she had been so amazed by the beauty of everything. In the valley pockets, ancient cedars grew and she had loved them, always excited to see more and more of them as they had come closer and closer to the sea. Maria didn't just see it all as beautiful, she saw it the way a mother might see beauty in an imperfect child. She would sing to the trees, touch them gently as she walked past, whisper blessings to them. *We're surrounded by love, don't you see? That's how the world was created. That is creation. Our purpose. We're safe, protected. All will be well. Don't worry.* She would say things like that to him, in the same whispered way she spoke to the trees and the birds and the deer, whenever he felt afraid.

"You were right," he whispered. He wished he could tell her that.

Eventually, the rain lessened until Rivertown was surrounded by a heavy mist that fell slowly through the air. The mist clutched at the hillsides like long slender talons, moving with the gentle, silent wind. They couldn't tell the passing of the day from the sun, hidden as it was behind low clouds. They had been back and forth to the Centre four times and believed they had found most of the bounty their campsite and the surrounding area had to offer. Both were shivering, despite the work and the softening of the rain.

"Let's call it a day. My teeth are chattering even more than I am!"

Will agreed and put a sopping arm around her soaked shoulder.

They started back to the Centre.

Stephanie was shivering. She made a low groaning sound and said, "I can't wait to get back. I'm going to take off these stupid, cold, wet, freezing clothes and get all dressed up in the warm, dry, wonderful stuff and sit on a heating vent and it's going to be glorious."

"I'm going to hope that some of the clothes I laid out are dry and if they aren't, I'm going to wrap myself in my thin, pathetic blanket and sit on you sitting on a heating vent."

Stephanie tried to laugh but she was shivering too much. "I don't even remember what it feels like to be warm. And I'm so hungry."

"Me, too."

Stephanie yelped in delight when they saw the Centre and the two of them ran the rest of the way. They were so excited that they didn't notice that Rivertown was proper empty, the shack city abandoned by its residents in the night.

The hall was filling slowly with peacekeepers coming in from a long, cold day in the rain. As soon as they were inside, Stephanie grabbed her dry-bag and ran to the ladies' room to change. Mark found that a sweater and pair of pants of his were dry enough to warrant changing and went to the men's room. Despite still not being entirely dry, it was a welcome change to get out of the clothes he had been wearing since the night before. He thought again of Maria - or Elizabeth - lying in the infirmary. He knew it was no coincidence that she had suffered the same injury the night before as she had that other far away night, with the same type of storm. Would her memory be impaired, like the last time? She had barely remembered the weeks between being taken and being returned. She just believed that they were safe, finally.

Will shook his head. He turned on the tap, let it run warm and splashed water on his face. He had to do something. Rather, *they* had to do something. There was some reason they had been given this second chance, that much he knew. He didn't know what it was, even what it might be. All the more reason to keep his eyes open, stay focused, keep moving. He sighed deeply and forced himself to leave the washroom.

Stephanie, true to her word, lay spread-eagled, arms out, face down on a long heating vent that ran the length of the hall connecting the bathrooms to the rest of the Centre. She turned to look at him when he came out, moaned in delight and extended a hand towards him. It held the other pair of blessedly dry, warm, wool socks. Will nodded, took them and tried not to cry.

"Alright, alright," Stephanie sat up, stretched her back, wiggled her toes and stood, grunting. "I'm goin' to go see my girl in th' infirmary. You want to come with?"

"Yes."

He said it way too fast. What had he done? How could he see her now? What would he say? How could he possibly hide it - who they really were, what they were feeling, everything?

Stephanie smiled and started towards the infirmary, across the Barracks. Will followed, numb. He could change his mind, say he had decided to get something to eat instead, or... needed to pee. Anything. Stephanie would believe him.

He couldn't.

Will had to see her. He couldn't go a moment longer without doing so. It had seemed an eternity all over again, going without her, since he discovered she was here, in Rivertown.

There was a reason they had been given a second chance. He didn't know what it was and imagined that she wouldn't, either. It was dangerous, yes, but it would be if they did nothing, too. They had no choice, no chance at avoiding it. Whatever it was, they needed each other. Would have to do this together.

And no matter what else it meant, he loved her.

I won't lose you again.

Chapter Thirty Six

Elizabeth was propped up on two pillows. It was the closest to sitting upright she could get without throbbing pain in her head and explosions of black obscuring her sight. This was unacceptable: she may need to run soon, or defend herself and besides, weakness did not become her.

She had spent most of the day asleep. The nurse came to wake her every two hours to make sure she didn't slip into a coma. That wasn't acceptable either of course; that she be so seriously injured at such an important time and in such a dangerous place. She remembered the Chief and his secret soldiers, shooting into the crowd. Eating a woman.

"You're up!" Dinky exclaimed, poking his head into the room. He hurried over to her, followed more slowly by Mark and kissed her repeatedly on the mouth, cheeks, eyes, forehead. He made loud kissy noises as he did so. Theatrical, trying to make her laugh - she remembered that about him.

"You two look awful." She made herself smile as she said it. Dinky held her hand in his own ice cold ones, still damp from the long day outdoors in the rain and mist. He and Mark were dirty, soaked and unkempt.

"We came as soon as we finished at camp. You should see it, Lizzy, it's just a disaster."

"Rain's finally slowed down though," Mark said.

"All of my books are ruined. I mean, I have most of it all memorized but still." Dinky smiled at her tenderly.

That's right, Elizabeth thought, *he's studious, academic. I remember that. He's smart.*

"I'll still be able to tell you all about the Statues of the Ethos, as soon as you're well enough to go walking down there. You'll have that to look forward to." He kissed her hand.

"Good," she said. It didn't feel good. She knew he was a good man – *hardly a man, a boy,* – but how could she feel so strongly about two different men at once? She loved Cameron, was married to him and didn't want to hurt Dinky. How could she ever choose between them? And at the same time, how could she ever choose to ignore her marriage vows, even if they had been made so long ago?

"Elizabeth..." Dinky's eyes shone with tenderness, "what if I told you... some stories or something. To get your mind off of it."

Elizabeth nearly burst into tears at the idea.

"Ok," she managed, clearing her throat so that she wouldn't cry. "Do you know much about this area? The people who live nearby, distances to other settlements, things like that?"

"Some. I'll tell you everything I know. The earliest records are mostly myth. It was a time of exploration. The story goes that traders and would-have-been settlers came to the Wild Land looking for another place to hold sovereignty over. But right from the start, the entire continent fought against them. Their crops wouldn't grow, their houses weren't well insulated to the cold and there were huge, man-eating animals that stalked them wherever they went. That's why they called it the Desolate Land, as well as the Wild Land."

"Is that why," Elizabeth murmured. She remembered speaking to a group of nomads who took them in on their long route to the coast from the north. They said that the land was sad, desolate. That it was being hurt, attacked, disrespected. Of course, those people saw no difference between themselves and the land. They said they were the last of a proud people. When asked why they were the last, they said that they wouldn't bear children any more. No child deserved to be born into such a devastated world.

"Worst of all," Dinky went on, "were the people that lived in the Wild Land. Entirely uncivilized, they lived like animals, naked, without homes. They sharpened their teeth, ate human flesh, could communicate with the animals and cast terrible, supernatural spells on the people who came here. They weren't really human, but witches and faeries. No one ever went back to the Wild Land except for the occasional, extremely brave trader or explorer. Despite the tall tales of danger, the Wild Land also has an abundance of edible plants, unique spices and berries and of course, the Statues of the Ethos. Then, about fifty years ago, the government decided to ignore the old myths and send a science team to investigate the potential for development. Interestingly, they were studying the Statues themselves, just a little ways away from here, when they discovered the mineral deposits in the caves."

"Yeah, very interesting, Dink. She's too tired to hear about that stuff."

"No, no," Elizabeth tried to sit up a bit more and succeeded, "I want to hear. The settlers. Tell me about the settlers that first arrived here, two thousand years ago."

"Well, there aren't many records that remain from them. Some modern anthropologists hypothesize that the religious factions of the time were preparing for some kind of Rapture, like the end of the world and dispersed to new lands that they could set up as safe havens for when that happened. There was lots of cultural diversification: some of them developed very elaborate cultural customs, like the Virtuous Fathers, have you heard of them? Their descendants still practice, but not exactly the same religion. That was in the North Lands, that they settled. They would have multiple wives and produce as many babies as possible, in the hopes that some of them would survive the apocalypse. Some of the settlements devoted their attention to science, crops, technology... that was when the civil wars were happening in Lila, so people who could get out, did. That's what I read, anyways."

Elizabeth was fascinated. It explained why settlers had come to her land, or rather, Maria's land. But the stories, the myths, they didn't make sense. "What about the settlement here?"

"Well," Dinky lowered his voice, obviously trying to sound spooky, "the story goes that they set up here and tried to befriend the locals. But what they found was that the locals weren't human at all - they were supernatural beings with terrible powers. Some said they were half animal. The settlers were never heard from again and digs have shown that they were cannibalized by human teeth, meaning that the locals likely killed and ate them."

"What?" Elizabeth barely whispered that.

"I bet you thought it was just ghost stories! It mostly is, I'm sure, but the evidence does indicate cannibalism."

Elizabeth was shaking her head, angry and hurt and disbelieving. Maria's people weren't cannibals! They were peace loving! It was the enemy who ate human flesh, not Maria and her people! "You realize that you're talking about humans. People. Accusing individuals of terrible violence and even... cannibalism. And you just believe it, just because it was written in a book?"

"Well, I wasn't trying to..."

"We *talked* to the coal eyes. Their ancestors are the ones you're talking about."

Dinky stroked her hand. She tried not to grimace. "I'm sorry, Dizzy. I didn't mean to get you upset. It's just hypothesis, anyways."

"Right. It's ok." It was important, everything that he knew. Important that she learn it, too. There was a good chance that she would have to take her chances in the desolate world surrounding Rivertown and needed to know as much about it as she could in order to survive. Beyond that, she had to know what happened all those years ago and in between if she was going to control the flood of Maria's presence into her mind, or make any sense of it.

Not just me, she thought. *Cameron's here.*

She had only been thinking about him all day. But it felt like her spirit had been doing the same for millenia.

"It's good to see you up, Dizzy." Mark nodded, tight lipped.

"Did you get my stuff? Clothes, food?"

"Yeah, it's all laid out to dry."

"Would you bring me some of it, when it's dry?"

Mark was about to say that he would when they heard steps behind them. He turned to look and the words caught in his throat. It was Stephanie. He gave Dinky an urgent look, then gestured his head in her direction.

"Hi there sweetheart," Stephanie exclaimed, "oh and hi to you too, Lizzy!" She winked at Mark. He almost fainted.

"Hi," he managed.

Elizabeth smiled at her cousin. But she didn't know what was coming next. She would have let the sorrow of her own desolation show, would have told the boy holding her hand to let go. Would have let the moment she had waited so long to experience have all of the ceremony and significance she could muster in her injured state.

Will walked in after Stephanie. He was walking slowly, heart pounding in his chest, throat, head, eyes. Thundering. He wasn't sure he would be able to breathe for much longer. It didn't seem real. He couldn't remember being a ghost, but knew that long centuries had passed full of desire's sting. Desire to be reunited with her. To see her, as he was finally about to do.

He had his eyes on Stephanie's heels when he came in, so that he could follow her without tripping, even in his anxious state. He heard her greet her friends, heard laughter. He held his breath and time slowed. His heart pounded in his ears and he counted down from three. Three, two, one.

Will looked up. At first, she was all he saw. Propped up on pillows in a hospital bed. There was a moment of cognitive incongruence, in which she was quite literally another woman in another time. Then his mind's eye readjusted and here they were. Here she was. Complete, almost exactly as he remembered her. She was smiling. He saw the rest of them a moment later. Her cousin, whom Stephanie said was named

Mark and another boy. Another boy who was holding her hand, looking at her tenderly.

Will blinked. The boy lifted her hand and kissed her fingers again, oblivious to the newcomer. They all seemed to be. He looked back to her beloved face. How could she be with a different man? What was happening? And she was smiling, happy. It wasn't possible, but there it was, right in front of him. She turned, finally and saw him. Her smile disappeared. She pulled her hand free from the boy's almost violently and shook her head at Will, as if trying to tell him that it wasn't what it looked like.

What else could it be? He tried to swallow, but his throat was too tight. He could remember everything, everything, every single thing about her.

I shouldn't have come, he thought. *It was a mistake. Too dangerous. I don't know enough yet. I don't know enough to understand what we're supposed to do, let alone...*

He didn't know how to finish the thought. Let alone why she would be with a different man. She was all he had thought about. He had woken up crying, because every time he woke up he had to remember that she was gone, that he would never see her again.

And she's right here.

It was too much. Too confusing. *Just go quietly.*

Will turned to leave. He couldn't think of anything to say to excuse himself. He would think of an excuse when Stephanie came back to the Barracks.

"Don't go."

His heart was tearing itself to ribbons. It was her voice. Maria's. Somehow, it was her voice. He froze. It seemed like a step forwards or backwards would shatter the illusion.

The others turned to the door and saw Will for the first time since he had come in.

"Hey Will, didn't see ya there," Mark said.

Will turned back around. If he left now, it would be strange, suspicious. Until they knew more, he couldn't risk bringing attention to himself.

"Hi, Mark." It was all Will could manage.

"You know each other." Maria's voice again. Not a question, a statement. He heard everything she said in those four words. He heard envy, envy that in this life he and her cousin had met before their reunion.

"I don't know *him*, though," he said, nodding at Dinky. He hoped she would hear the anger, hurt, betrayal and confusion that he was feeling. Elizabeth's cheeks flushed and she lowered her face to try and hide it. She shuffled her weight away from the boy, which clearly took great physical effort.

"I'm a Will, too, actually. Will Dinghum, but everyone calls me Dinky. Good to meet you."

"Dinky." Will forced himself to look at the boy, which took the same amount of effort that it had cost Elizabeth to move away from him. He had to snigger inwardly, just a little. *Dinky*. "Funny nickname."

"He knows about the area. The Desolate Land. He's a... history buff. Like, an academic. He was just telling us about that. I thought it might be important." Elizabeth was practically yelling. Will nodded, his gaze locked onto hers. She was using him for information, things they may need to know in order to escape. Interesting. And if that wasn't the extent of their relationship? He supposed that if they had been together before she started to remember... He cleared his throat. He didn't want to think about it. Murderous rage was the last thing he wanted to feel right now.

"What's wrong, Lizzy?" It was Stephanie. Elizabeth felt a stab of the same inexplicable, bated fear, that she had felt when Stephanie asked about her dreams. She was grateful to still remember that moment, distant and fuzzy as it now seemed. Their meeting at the discs game was speeding into the past, but the familiarity she felt with

Stephanie was still fresh. She had never felt like a stranger but it felt like the space between them was growing smaller and smaller even as she seemingly forgot who Stephanie really was.

A thought occurred to Elizabeth and she shot a look at Will. She hoped he could read her mind. What if Stephanie wasn't who she said she was?

"I'm sorry, Will was it? And all you guys. It's so nice to see you and thanks for coming. I just... my head is pounding, I can barely think straight and it's not something I would ever admit freely, but even just sitting up like this is making me feel so dizzy I could puke."

"Aw, honey!" Stephanie's tone was normal. Just a young woman in a strange place doting on her injured friend. But her face had smoothed itself out, as if relaxing from a terrible strain. Elizabeth hadn't even noticed that she was tense until the tension disappeared.

Elizabeth carefully lowered herself onto her back, let her cousin and friends adjust the pillows underneath her. Will watched, arms crossed over his chest.

"It was nice to meet you, Elizabeth."

Chapter Thirty Seven

The memories that Elizabeth had recovered since her concussion were confused and incomplete. They had little holes in them that left just enough room for her own memories to fill in the blanks, albeit distant and dated, like photographs kept behind glass. The same was not true for Will.

The ways in which Will was different from Cameron were few, he thought that night as he curled up on top of his damp sleeping bag, using it as a cushion on the hard floor, with the thin blanket on top of him. They had different knowledge, different experiences, but there was a core being to both that was much more than similar or comparable. It was undeniably the same. Will took comfort in that. His life on now-distant ranches had been a good one; quiet and humble. He would miss knowing things about that life, the people in it. He would miss those things, but quietly gave thanks to the Creator that he wouldn't have to miss himself: at the core, Will and Cameron were one in the same.

That comfort was not far-reaching. He didn't know how much longer he would be able to remember to pretend that nothing was happening, that he was just Will, that he was a peacekeeper, not a refugee, that he wasn't supposed to know Maria and on and on. The ghosts, or some version of them, had to still be in Rivertown. He knew how ruthless those monsters were, and didn't doubt what they would do if they discovered who he really was.

I just have to be careful, he thought. His eyes were closing on their own, now. He was so tired. *I just have to be careful.*

"You must be very careful."

I am sitting beside a small electric heater, swaddled in the light it casts beside a man named Dai. I know him to be as young as me, but his face is prematurely lined and gaunt. Little wonder - he has lived most of his life in fear, in a cave, hiding in terror of walking, hunting, bloodthirsty ghosts.

"We call them ghosts because they remember everything from their lives, even though they aren't human anymore. They treasure and worship memories. They both crave and hate things of the flesh, because their own is lost to them. They are not part of the Creator's plan, not of the Earth, as we are. There is no benevolence behind their creation."

"How were they were created?"

"We know only some things. When the foreigners first came here, they were exploring. Searching for immortality. They believed they could find a property in herb, root or stone to preserve their physical shell for Eternity"

Dai's slow, deliberate words reverberate in the thick air of the crowded cave. Nearly everyone else is asleep, Bern's people and ours huddled together against the cold, the night, the ghosts. Hungry ghosts.

"To... stop death?"

Dai shrugs passively, "We can only imagine. Their thinking was flawed, illogical and evil. It did not fit the rules of our world. Nor does it now." Dai stares into the heater.

"The ghosts. Tell me about them."

"Yes. The ghosts." Dai clears his throat. "The foreigners came for several generations. Sometimes, they would take women from us, or children. We had little by way of arms. Soon, our only defense was the shelter of the trees and caves," Bern gestures vaguely around them, "like this one. We still watched them. Sometimes we would trade, but carefully. By the time my grandfather was a man, the foreigners had changed in their appearance and their technologies. They lived and looked younger for greater and greater periods. It was their obsession, and it destroyed them. There became too many of them, in their homeland. They broke into factions and fought each other. There were *diseases and famines."*

"Of course there were. What did these people expect?"

Dai shrugs again, another vague gesture. "We don't know what the ghosts are, exactly. Mechanical, we think, like this." He kicks the heater, which groans complacently for a moment before resuming its normal, quiet work. He stares at it for a long moment, then says, "Really, we don't want to know. I don't want to know. It's sick and wrong, what they've done."

"They're machines?"

"Yes. Sure. The ghosts are machines."

Dai kicks the heater again, hard this time. After a long moment, he goes on.

"It was an experiment, that's what my grandfather said. But instead of trying their experiment once and waiting to see if it worked, they all began to do it. They were so excited about the prospect of immortality. There was a settlement of them, up the coast. There were settlements everywhere, already, because they didn't have enough room on their own cursed land. They took some of our people to the south as slaves. Made them work the ground, trying to grow their foreign plants in this land's soil. And they killed animals for sport. Let them rot on the ground, without eating them." Dai shakes his head, spits on the caves dark, dusty floor. "Somehow, they take the mind of a person, once the person has died. The thoughts and memories. They put these into a... copy. A mechanical copy. It looks like a person, but was never born. Does not need to eat, does not breathe. Just imitates those things. But the imitation can fool a mother, a husband...a son."

"How can a machine act human? Do they really act... human?

Dai simply nodded.

"Why they would do such a thing?"

"No one would do such a thing!" *Dai's voice is barely above a whisper, so as not to wake the others, but it is a ringing hiss.* "It is an abomination. Everything about them is."

Dai is quiet for a moment, thinking. Then, heavily, "No. Not everything. Of course not. They have simply forgotten. My grandfather said that they believe machines could be the key to immortality, or eternity. To... the lengthening of a single life, not to eternity as we know it. They have no concept of paradise, especially not on Earth. They think that humanity is flawed, the world is flawed. Grandfather believed that they created ghosts in the hopes of being able to avoid a death they saw as permanent, to live on, in the mechanical body."

"But it didn't work."

"No. Of course, it failed. The machines, but we call them ghosts, because machines... because..." Dai gestured again, a defeated flick of his wrist. "The ghosts will run until they break. And they look human, resemble friends and relatives that have passed. But they are not human. They are something else. Something that cannot feel, does not think like we do. They remember their lives, certainly. They remember the wars of their homeland, so they kill. Anyone and everyone."

"What about the other foreigners? The ones that are alive?"

"My grandfather was friends with a young man, one of them. That's how he knew so much about them. The man spoke of it all without much emotion. He would say, my mother was sick two years ago, we saved her by placing her into a new body, there she is cooking, just the same. But it wasn't his mother. It was a ghost. She never got sick, never aged – the same, every day. One day, my grandfather went to visit and the man was gone. Some time later, he was back again but as a ghost. Grandfather believed that his mother's ghost had killed him. Eventually, they were all ghosts. The foreigners seemed to be afraid of what had happened. They came and saw the ghosts and the violence against us and our neighbouring people and left. They still come, sometimes, to the mouth of a river, on the coast south of here."

The next morning I want to tell Maria everything I've learned. I don't want to frighten her. I decide to wait until that night, when we have stopped to rest. We leave the cave, say goodbye to our new friends.

We decide to find a cave of our own, a place to stay that is safe until we can find another plan. Before supper that night, Maria is taken.

I'm working. As hard as I can, as hard as my ravaged body will allow me. I've grown weaker after this long year of seeking refuge from ghosts. Weaker in many ways. It's been several days since they took Maria. I've lost count. Haven't slept much, just worked. We found the cave and decided to make camp here. Set up our equipment and make a new home, for now. It doesn't feel like home, how could it? But this land is beautiful. Peaceful. We could have made homes here, beautified the earth, created gardens of paradise for our unborn families... instead I am hiding in a cave, waiting and losing hoping. Maria is gone.

Elder Jared approaches me. I continue working. I don't know what he is going to say, but I already don't want to hear it. My wife is gone. Taken by savage abominations. I shiver in spite of the early summer heat and the hard labour of moving rocks to make our new home.

"Cameron."

I ignore him. He walks beside me as I move down the hill, lift another large rock and carry it to the mouth of the cave.

"Cameron?"

I shake my head. Already, I can't speak, my throat is tight. I hope he won't try any more because I can't speak of this. Everything is wrong, everything has been turned upside down, gone crazy. He knows it too, of course. The Earth was created for us and we for it. To live and care for each other. A shiver caresses my spine as I think of our cat, who we had to leave behind. There is no doubt in my mind that he was created just for us, just for Maria and I; and we for him. He was our companion and we loved him and he loved us. We planted catnip for him and despite the elevation and northern latitude of our home, it grew in abundance, just for him. That is the perfection of Creation as we know it. Our love in that little home would fill the Earth and help the plants to grow, to flourish. We would care for our own land and create a beautiful garden, as our children would wherever they chose to go. In this way the whole Earth would become paradise.

Now I hide in a cave, Maria and the cat are both gone.

"Please. Stop. Sit down and talk to me."

I lower my head in deference. Elder Jared is wise and strong and I will do as he asks. Even if I can't stand it.

He gestures to a broad fallen log. One of the towering cedars, I imagine, though it would have been the only one growing near our cave. I sit, looking straight forward. My eyes have filled with tears.

Elder Jared sits next to me, carefully. I expect him to ask me questions, or perhaps to give me advice on how to move through my grief. I expect him, at least, to say something. Instead he sits there, looking at his hand in his lap, totally quiet.

Years before, I sat on a log with Elder Jared, waiting for him to admonish me for making my sister cry. It was an accident, she was painting and I knocked the water cup over, destroying her work. I felt terrible. Elder Jared just sat and waited. After some time, I couldn't stand the suspense and told him everything. He asked what I had been doing when I knocked her water over. I said I was making a model house, with sticks. He congratulated me, patted me on the back and had me lead him to my little creation and show it to him. He was so proud of it, and of me.

I look at Elder Jared and he looks back at me in response. There is no reason to hold back my feelings with him, so I let myself cry and he holds me and pats my back the same way he did then.

"Why would they create such monsters?" I ask him.

"Who? What do you mean?"

I realize then that I haven't told anyone what I learned from Dai, being too consumed with grief. I tell Jared everything I learned. He listens, gravely.

"This changes everything," he says.

I ask what he means.

"If your saw stopped working, what would you do?"

"Fix it and if it couldn't be fixed, replace it."

"And the old one, that couldn't be fixed?"

"Would be taken apart, so its components could be used."

"Yes. Taken apart. And you would not be murdering that saw, by taking it apart, because it does not live. Correct?"

"That's correct."

"We have to find a way to stop them, Cameron. Otherwise they will destroy us and this land that we were entrusted to protect and beautify. We cannot let that happen."

I nod. I've never been in any kind of battle, but I can feel my pride quickening inside me, hardening my heart.

"I'm willing to fight, Elder Jared."

The man studies me. Nods slowly. "You will. I have no doubt that you will fight, Cameron. Your wife is... a special woman."

"Was."

"Perhaps. Don't give up hope, yet. Otherwise, what do you fight for?"

I don't know what to say.

"Come. We must tell the others."

We hurry up to the cave to tell the others and try to make a plan.

Will woke up to birdsong. He tried to place the birds, as he wasn't entirely sure where he was. After careful thought, he realized that he knew only three things. First, that his memories were replacing those of another life and another time, where he was now, and that no one could find out who he really was. Second, that Maria, the wife from his own life, was here, alive, in the infirmary and named Elizabeth. Third, that his name, in this life, was Will.

That was all he remembered.

Will was gone now. His memories had been lost.

He was Cameron.

Chapter Thirty Eight

Cameron breathed in and the Earth breathed out for him, a long, quiet exhalation. Curls of mist rose from the trees in the close air of a cloudy morning. If you listened hard enough and for long enough, you could hear a faint, quiet sigh. Just as he had, in that strange between time, when he'd been a ghost himself...

Cameron sat bolt upright. He held his hands out in front of him and examined them. They were his hands, though slightly different. Cameron flexed his fingers and relished the sensation of vitality. The last thing he remembered was taking Maria's hand and then everything going white and then the long, quiet listening to the breathing of the trees. He breathed in deeply himself again and thanked the Creator for this second chance.

It occurred to Cameron that he ought to be discreet, try to blend in. He looked around, trying to understand where he was and what was happening. There were young men all around him in various states of waking up for the day. Most of them seemed barely more than boys, not older than their eighteenth year. They were a haggard group. Thin blankets were being used as bedding on a hard marble floor. Cameron realized that he was covered in the same blanket. Running his hand over the floor, he realized that it wasn't marble at all, but oddly enough, just painted to look that way.

Each of the boys had a pile of things near him. Most of the things were a brown-grey with mud cover. It looked to Cameron like some kind of refugee camp, but the faint outline of memory told him it was something a little bit different. He examined himself, his clothes, the small bundle of things beside him and saw that his possessions were soaked through with mud, though an attempt had clearly been made to clean them, dry them and fold them. It was possible that *he* had been the one to do that, but he couldn't remember. He could only remember those three things from this life, this time, this world. Or was it the same world, but just a different time? He shook his head to clear his mind. It didn't work.

I'll have to be careful, he thought. It was a problem. How was he to blend in when he had no idea where he was or what he was supposed to be doing there?

Maria is here. Yes, he remembered that. She was somewhere close by. *In the infirmary.*

Cameron knew he needed to speak with her. She would know what to do, she always did. Despite the circumstances, Cameron couldn't help but smile. Maria. He would get to see Maria. Sweet Maria with her jokes and silly voices and her way of thinking out of any situation. Cameron remembered the conversation he'd had with Elder Jared. It felt like only a week ago, but it could have been much longer, he surmised. Jared had said that Maria was... special. Could that be why they were here, now? Could she have somehow brought them back from the dead?

He shivered at the thought. The only encounter he'd had with reanimation of the dead were the machine-ghosts. He flexed his fingers again, examining them. He didn't *feel* like a machine.

Maria will know, he thought. Yes, she would. Excitement coursed through him. He would get to see her and so soon! He nearly jumped up, ready to run to the infirmary, but he stopped. How could he go to her, when he didn't know where the infirmary was? Cameron didn't know where *anything* was.

A sense of panic started to fill him then. His heart was beating fast, uncomfortably fast. He was lost and alone in a strange place. He didn't know how he had gotten there or what he was supposed to do. All that he remembered was a deep sense of impending danger and now that he couldn't remember anything else warnings seemed to be seeping in from everywhere. Who were these boys, getting dressed and eating some kind of plastic-sealed food for their breakfast? What were they doing in this great hall?

"Morning, Will."

His head snapped up at the sound of the voice. It was a young woman, looking oddly clean and comfortable compared to the others, smiling down at him. She looked incredibly familiar, which Cameron took as a good sign, though he had no idea who she was. Tall, slender and fair-haired with thick lips pulled up in a playful smirk. She was gorgeous, and had the look of someone that was either very fun, or very dangerous.

"Good morning," he managed.

"How'd you sleep?"

"I uh... had some strange dreams."

"No surprise there," the girl said, plopping down beside him with a great amount of subconscious grace, "you haven't had a night of normal dreams since I met you."

Since she met me, he though. How long ago was that? Were they friends? It seemed like they were and she seemed vaguely familiar to him.

"How did you sleep?" he ventured.

"Fine." She examined her nails. "Want to have breakfast?"

The sense of panic deepened. He had no idea how to get those strange aluminum food-packs open, much less prepare their stewy contents into edible food.

"Actually, I feel sick. Really sick. Dizzy, actually. I need to go to the infirmary."

The girl looked up at him from her nails, eyebrows raised. "Oh?"

"Yeah. I feel really... disoriented."

"Well," the girl stood and offered a hand to help him up, "I'm not too surprised. Sleeping in wet clothes two nights in a row will do that to a person."

"Thanks for understanding. And for your help. I feel really lost, actually. Confused. But mostly nauseous."

She examined him for a long moment and he nearly flinched under her gaze. He was trying hard to appear nonchalant, but also sick. He was not sure that he was being successful.

"Well," she said, finally, "come on then."

She stared at him for a moment, waiting.

"Uh, after you," he said.

She cocked an eyebrow and led the way across the hall and into the infirmary.

Chapter Thirty Nine

"I just need to lie down." It was the smartest thing Cameron could think of, in the circumstances. "This has happened to me before. If I just lie down and get some rest I'll be fine."

The doctor looked up from his clipboard, over his glasses, to scrutinize the boy in front of him and his story.

"I could give you a speech about perseverance under pressure, you know. Being a peacekeeper means continuing on towards the greater good, whether or not you would like to sleep in."

Cameron's eyebrows shot up. He thought that was a mean thing to say and felt himself blushing, despite the fact that he, of course, was not the one who agreed to become a peacekeeper, whatever that was. He would have to ask Maria what it meant when he saw her.

The doctor continued to stare at him, almost menacingly. Cameron wasn't sure if a response was required and certainly didn't know what to say.

"I..." he started.

"But," the doctor interrupted him, "the last thing we need at this juncture is an epidemic of fever, likely as it is to happen after all of this mess. You did the right thing by coming here and your friend did the right thing to recognize the signs of exhaustion. Good work, young lady." He nodded at the girl, who smiled proudly.

"Thank you, sir," Cameron said, "I certainly don't want to be responsible for any epidemic." He had to refrain from asking, *What mess?*

"And frankly," the doctor went on as if Cameron hadn't said anything, "you don't look too good. You're all shaky and flushed. You don't have a fever yet but you're clearly in a state of overexertion."

Cameron opened his mouth to respond but closed it. Of course he was red and shaky – his heart was beating high up in his throat and pounding behind his eyes. He was someone else, in a different time, practically a different world. Overexertion sounded right to him.

"I'll take you to our beds; you can stay there until tomorrow morning. Any longer than that and I'll have to inform the Chief. We need everyone on their feet and working to get Rivertown running again."

Cameron swallowed hard as he followed the man through a door and down a white-washed hallway. Rivertown was the name that he and his people had given their cave settlement, because it was close to the river. Why was the same name being used here? Could it be the same place?

"Are you alright, Will?" the girl asked, "You look terrified."

"I just... need some rest."

They passed through another door, this one double and swinging, into a wide, low ceilinged room full of cot-like beds. Cameron scanned them and quickly saw the one bed that was occupied had his Maria in it.

"See Will? You're going to be fine. The only person left in here since the storm is Dizzy and that's only 'cause she's a big ol' wimp!"

The girl smiled as she said it, in a way Cameron thought looked kind and supportive. This girl must be his friend, or perhaps a sister.

This was all too much, too strange. If this was his sister, then who was he? What of the ghosts, the machines? A chill shook him then, violently. Any of these people around him could be ghosts. They could all be ghosts. Could this girl be one of them? And if she was and if she was his sister...what did that make him?

"Ok, Will, just lie down now..." the girl was suddenly at his side, lowering him onto the bed indicated by the doctor, "you're gonna be just fine, this doctor is a good one, just like back home. Alright? And Lizzy's here to keep you comp'ny, at least for another day, right Liz?"

"The doctor says I'll need another week of rest." Maria spoke. Maria's voice. "I still get dizzy when I try to stand up, which is oddly fitting."

The girl laughed and the doctor smiled. Cameron thought he might throw up. It was Maria, but it wasn't Maria. It was a... *Dizzy*. Or Lizzy. If she remembered her life now, did that mean that she remembered nothing of *their* life together? And even if she did, what would those memories mean to her with a full life ahead here? So much of who he was revolved around her. Their dreams, their experiences. Their love.. It was his core, the center of his heart. How could it be the same for her, if she wasn't just Maria, but was also... someone else?

Cameron laid back, closed his eyes. His last thought before he lost consciousness was:

This isn't how it was supposed to happen.

Chapter Forty

Elizabeth saw him come in and her pulse roller coastered. She had seen him three times now, but the effect of having him so close by was entirely overwhelming. It took a long moment for her to register that he wasn't alone - he had come with Stephanie again and the doctor was right behind them. It had been mortifying the night before, to have him see her with Dinky holding her hand. She'd seen the hurt and the confusion in his eyes, but they had shared an understanding. She now knew that he was going through the same thing she was. Remembering and forgetting and changing. Becoming more herself and less herself all at once.

When he walked in that morning, however, Elizabeth could see that something was wrong. He had entered pale, looked at her and turned even paler. It was Cameron, her Cameron. The boy Will that he had been only the day before seemed gone. If that was the case, they were in trouble. It would only be a matter of time before he was discovered and she still didn't know who it was exactly that would be discovering them.

Elizabeth was fairly certain that whoever had terrorized and murdered them and their people those millennia ago wouldn't hesitate at a second chance. She shivered at the memory of the Chief biting into the leg of one of the coal-eye women. The memories of that night had become muddied in her confusion but that particular moment was burned into her mind like the sun. What else could have done something so evil, other than the monsters who killed her people before?

Cameron stumbled, then shuddered. Stephanie, who had been walking past him towards the bed reacted so quickly that Elizabeth started. She was at the boy's side, holding him by the shoulder and the elbow, almost as soon and Elizabeth even registered that he was about to fall. Elizabeth watched as she helped him down onto the bed next to her. They weren't coming to visit her; they were here because he was ill. She wondered if he was only pretending to be ill, in order to see her, but her knowledge of Cameron's deceptive abilities told her he wouldn't be able to fake things so convincingly. She smiled to herself; if anyone was bound by realism, it was Cameron.

Cameron. It seemed to Elizabeth that it was Cameron, younger than her memories by five or ten years, but entirely him nonetheless. The change since the evening before was obvious to her and she wondered if it would be obvious to Stephanie as well. She hoped that Stephanie would attribute it to his sickness.

"...Lizzy's here to keep you comp'ny, at least for another day, right Liz?"

Elizabeth cleared her throat. "The doctor says I'll need another week of rest. I still get dizzy when I try to stand up. It is oddly fitting."

For a moment, she wondered if someone who knew her well, like Mark, would note the differences in *her*. Elizabeth wouldn't have been able to come up with a joke under the pressure of sickness like that; it had been entirely Maria.

They didn't have much time before trouble found them.

Stephanie was leaning over Cameron – who was still Will to her - examining him. The doctor leaned over him on the other side and lifted an eyelid gently.

"He's unconscious, young lady," he said, putting a hand on her shoulder, "he's going to be fine, like you said. You did the right thing to bring him here. We have to prevent an outbreak of illness, especially at this crucial time of rebuilding. Keep your eyes open for anyone else displaying... strange symptoms."

"Yes. Strange symptoms. I will."

It was something about the way that Stephanie said it. The emphasis that both she and the doctor had placed on the word *strange*. Her face had gone all smooth again, like it had before, when she thought something was wrong and then relaxed. Elizabeth was now convinced that she saw it, that it wasn't just her imagination. But just as suddenly as the strangeness appeared it vanished and Stephanie, her friend, was walking to her bedside to be with her while she was sick. But the feelings of fear and apprehension that the sight had created in Elizabeth remained.

"So you're still gettin' dizzy, huh?" Stephanie said, sitting beside Elizabeth on the bed and taking her hand.

"Yeah, unfortunately. I don't think I'm going anywhere for a while."

"Look on the bright side. You didn't have to be out in the freezing rain all day yesterday looking at all your ruined stuff."

"And you didn't have to be in here, bored out of your mind."

"Well then it's perfect! You have someone to play checkers with all day." Stephanie winked conspiratorially, "I shoulda gotten your Dinky sick, huh? Then you could do more than play checkers! Yee haw!"

Elizabeth laughed, in spite of herself. It was just her friend Stephanie, making jokes, being a confidante. She hoped it was that simple, but wondered if Stephanie would still want to be her friend if she knew who Elizabeth was turning into.

"What happened to him?" Elizabeth asked, nodding at Will.

"Not sure. He woke up this mornin' all outta sorts. I guess he's gettin' a flu."

"I hope he's alright."

"Sure he is. Don't you get worryin' about him, all you need to do is worry about yourself. I'm gettin' mighty bored myself, stuck out there without any female contact! No one to gossip with."

"Any news?"

Stephanie's eyes widened and she nodded. "Oh yeah, big time. You know Ray?"

"Oh, I know Ray," Elizabeth mumbled.

"Well. He and a fella named Thomas were caught yesterday in one of the bathroom stalls. *Together*."

"Together doing what?"

Stephanie's jaw dropped. "What do you think!? They were both naked..." Stephanie let her sentence trail off, and waggled her eyebrows conspiratorially.

"You're kidding me. Ray?"

"That's right! Good thing I didn't try going for him, huh?"

Just then, they heard the loud, echoing voice of the Chief barreling in through his megaphone.

"Time to go. See you as soon as I can, Lizzy. Don't you worry." Stephanie jumped up, gave Elizabeth a breezy kiss on the forehead and skipped out of the room.

Elizabeth strained to hear what the Chief was saying. The echoes overlapped and made it difficult to make out the words.

"...mining operation has been delayed... civilians returned to their homes until safer accommodation can be built... time to prove ourselves in this mission... Homeland sending engineered draft plans for homes... construction begins..."

Listening so hard gave Elizabeth another headache. It was a lot to ponder. From what she could remember of their exodus to the coast centuries before, the coal eyes had been slaves. They lived among the enemy, always in separate neighbourhoods and sub-standard living quarters. There were a few they met who had escaped and lived their lives hiding and running, forever afraid. Was such the fate of the 'civilians' of Rivertown who had run blindly into the trees during the storm two nights before?

The construction of permanent, stable housing in the colony was another mystery. What did the Chief want? She couldn't imagine convincing all of the young peacekeepers to stay in the housing by themselves, no one to watch over, no civilian population to guard. They would have to bring the coal-eyes back. Did they plan on rounding the coal-eyes up, bringing them back by force, or did they expect them to return of their own accord? It had been millennia since she had an insiders perspective on the coal-eyes but given the ruthlessness of those that had hunted her people down, it seemed plausible that they had been held in servitude and submission for the entire length of time in between. But the horrors that she had seen committed against those people, just two nights before... how could they bear to live like that?

Elizabeth shivered, thinking of her life as Maria. Of the kind of life that she and Cameron, still breathing quietly on the cot beside her, wanted to live. Maria's maternal instincts were still tugging at her, so that she could not imagine bearing children into a life of barbarity, with no end ot suffering and death in sight.

They said they understood, she thought. *That they would let us live our lives, that they realized the importance of peace and coexistence.*

That was, at least, what she remembered. The strange girl on the boat had been touched by what Maria said. Maria remembered her weeping, smiling, saying that she had always believed in eternity, always and that she had always known a human life could be more than war and struggle. She had spoken to her people, who agreed to end the war.

Chapter Forty One

Dinky woke to the Chief's morning speech. His whole body ached. He was sore from the cold, which had gripped him all night, sore from lack of proper sleep under the thin blanket in the crowded Barracks and sore from the hard floor that comprised his bed and the harder work of the day before. He tried to stretch and grimaced at the pain it induced.

He sat up and grimaced again. His hip bones were bruised from the floor. It made him wish he was fatter. His blanket fell off of his shoulders. He shivered and pulled it tightly around him. Being fat would make him warmer, too. Dinky resolved to eat more, starting that day. At least some of his clothes and hopefully his sleeping bag would be dry. Dry and warm.

Dinky was barely paying attention to the rambling lecture being blasted across the hall, he was preoccupied with his discomfort and remorse at choices he'd made so far in his short life. But he perked up when the Chief explained that they would begin construction of safer, more permanent settlements that very day. They'd spoken with the homeland and the decision had been made to take this opportunity to turn Rivertown from a settlement into a full-fledged colony, immediately. Homesteaders would be coming from their own lands to establish an agrarian sector. There would be skilled tradespeople and of course, general labourers for the mine which would be the heart of the new Rivertown. These people wouldn't arrive for some time, but the construction plans had been sent over that very morning. The first permanent buildings would be erected by them, the peacekeepers.

He wasn't sure what part of the speech made him so anxious. But the declaration that they were suddenly a construction crew confirmed a lot of his basic suspicions on the experimental nature of this supposedly routine colony mission.

Dinky looked around at the other boys. Most were sitting under blankets, like him, or hunched over beside electric cook-tops, rehydrating their breakfasts. Most, like him, were listening intently to the Chief. Unlike him, they had an air of innocent, irritating excitement about them. Real houses! Something they hadn't hoped to see for months while they were here in this hostile land.

Mark was one of the only other boys that seemed worried by what the Chief was saying. He sat hunched, chewing his bottom lip and staring into space. When the Chief said that the civilians of Rivertown had been relocated until the new houses were built, Dinky saw Mark stop chewing and look up suddenly, at the Chief. His whole body had tensed, but then shivered as he looked back down at the floor. Dinky resolved to ask Mark what it was about that statement that had scared him so much. He wasn't entirely sure that he wanted to know.

At least I got laid, he thought. It was becoming a mantra and always made him smile. He had finally lost his virginity and besides that, he had found a woman he loved. Sure, the world was going crazy, but at least he had gotten laid.

Dinky made his way around the slow-moving boys, through the Barracks to Mark as soon as the Chief finished. It was going to be another long, hard day.

"Mornin, Dink."

"Good morning."

Mark cleared his throat and turned the little stove top on. It was going to be oatmeal for them again that day and Dinky had brought his breakfast pack over with him.

"Do you mind if I throw mine on, too?"

"Fine by me." Mark nodded when he said it. He passed out spoons to the boys around him and gruffly poked Dinky in the shoulder with one, saying, "Here. I found some spares." Dinky supposed that was meant reverently and accepted it as a sign of friendship. He needed Mark, who was potentially the last sane man in camp, to be his friend.

"Real houses, huh?" He tried to sound as brief and to the point as the country boys.

"Guess so." Mark sighed deeply and his brow knit together.

"Finally! All the comforts of home!" It was Stephanie. She had come up from behind, the direction of the infirmary. "Mind if I join you for breakfast?"

"Yes, you go right ahead," Mark said, "you can have some of mine, if you'd like."

"I brought my own, silly. But thanks. That sure is sweet of ya."

"You're welcome, sweetheart. Any time."

They sat in silence for a moment, watching the flakes dissolve in the water and turn into a goop, then watching the goop shiver with the warmth of the stove and turn into what truly looked like oatmeal. Mark cleared his throat as he served three bowls to his friends, carefully avoiding Stephanie's eyes. She shook her magnificent, blonde ponytail ever so slightly, relishing the effect it had on the surrounding boys. After waiting for a compliment from Mark and not receiving one, she said,

"You know what I can't wait for? An oven. I love to bake. I could turn this dehydrated stuff into oatmeal cookies and some of the chocolate chips I brought survived the storm. You boys just wait. Us ranch girls really know how to take care of folks."

"That does sound nice," Mark said, "really nice."

"And you know what else? Being safe. Not having to worry about something as primitive as the weather. Maybe, eventually, Rivertown will get some real public buildings, too, not just this Barracks. I miss going into town and seein' Theme Boulevards. They had one that my mom took me to, it was all under water themed. They made these fish that swam through the air! And these bots that were sort of... half woman, half fish. Swimmin' around your head and tellin' you about all the specials. Spas... Oh, I miss spas! I haven't had my skin treatments since the storm. And air control! Not to mention window control and light control... just being able to wake up and say you want lights on.

Or you want... forest light and smell and breeze. And the house just does it. I never realized I'd miss all that, you know? Always thought I was tougher than that."

"You do realize we have a *real* forest right outside the Barracks, right?" Dinky said. He wasn't sure why, but Stephanie's characteristically upbeat attitude was bothering him that morning. Maybe because every move he made hurt. Maybe because she was so mindlessly supporting what was obviously a scheme, a bad idea. He opened his mouth to go on, but Mark elbowed him sharply between the ribs, right over a nerve cluster of knotted tissue.

"I think you're real tough, Steph. Look at you: you're out here with the boys, in the middle of nowhere, surviving the elements and you still manage to look beautiful. Hey, don't laugh, I mean that. There's nothing wrong with missin' some things from home. I miss my dogs. Well, they're really my dad's, but one in particular, I named and trained and he followed me everywhere. I didn't realize until just this minute how much I miss that little rascal. He must miss me, too."

"He's a real dog, then?"

"Yup, born and bred."

"Huh." She giggled. "That's sorta gross. I had a cat. Not as old fashioned as yer dog, but a real lovebug nonetheless. I hope that they send us some bots or somethin'. I sure do miss snugglin' up with somethin' warm at night."

Mark's jaw dropped and he turned pale. The thought of snuggling up with Stephanie at night was clearly too much for him. She noticed his discompose and stretched carefully backwards, allowing her eyelids to droop.

"And privacy! Sound proof walls, blinds... it's going to be great. I can get back to sleepin' naked."

Dinky chuckled.

"I don't know," he said, "part of why I joined the corps and signed up for a colony mission, was to get away from all the technology."

"What do you mean?" Stephanie's smile had evaporated.

Dinky furrowed his brow at her. He had been right. She was purposely supporting the housing project, purposely reminding them of all of the comforts of home. She knew what she was doing, alright. But why? Did she truly just miss her bot-cat?

"I think we take technology for granted," he started. He almost had to laugh at himself. William T Dingham, academic at large. The only talent that had been nurtured in him from an early age was the ability to filibuster; to talk pretty about just about anything. He was in his element. "It makes a lot of things too easy. I didn't realize how hard or rewarding it would be to split wood, or have to heat up my own meals until I came out here. But It's like you said, you didn't even realize you'd miss it. Because it's background noise. We don't even think about it. A woman who was half fish? Sure, it's a wonder of machine ingenuity. But it cheapens humanity. I know the Ethos are old-fashioned, but which of them does she know? Her sole existence is devoted to floating around and talking about specials in a shopping mall. She has no idea of what it means to be human but she is represented as one of us. There's more to life than cool gizmos and maybe there's more to technology and its potential."

"Are you sayin' that bots don't have feelings? They're just as smart as you, Mr. Books and some are even smarter."

"Sure, they're able to compute. I'm not saying they're not smart, or that they don't have feelings. But depth of emotion? The full range of human suffering and joy? We're the ones that forced our existence out of nothing - out of earth and air. That manifested ourselves, on the beach just down the hill and not as individuals but as emotions. We're the first, the originals. Not machines. At the end of the day they are just second-rate programmed copies, told how to feel and when by the memories we dissolve into their circuits. They'll never really love or hate."

Mark looked interested. Stephanie scoffed. She had a red patch, high on each cheek, but otherwise, her face was incredibly smooth and emotionless. Dinky congratulated himself, internally. She was good at masking her feelings, but he felt had won. It was a small victory, but enough to make him feel good about himself. Maybe he would add reference of this moment to his morning mantra.

"You know, Dink, you're soundin' like a primitive. Like one of those... cults, out in the hills in the East, that won't have bots at all. Is that it? Are you scared that artificial intelligence is going to turn on us and take over the world? Might as well tell me the earth's flat." She gave him a patronizing look, then continued, "Fact is, there's no difference at the molecular level between living cells and non-living cells. The difference is how those cells are all put together and what *they* make of *themselves*, as you said. But nothing can exceed it's programming. Where do you think you're clothes came from? Or the food you're eatin'? A factory bot and a farm bot."

"Actually, we grow an oat crop," Mark interjected. He seemed oblivious to the strange tension and anger between Dinky and Stephanie. "So originally, this would have come from a farm, not a bot. They tried bot farming, but the product is never as good and sometimes the plants would just... die. They need human contact, the plants. Same with ranching, as I'm sure you know, comin' from the ranchlands and all."

"Yeah, right, whatever. Point is, it's not about machines' feelings for me. I'm just lookin' forward to enjoying some of the comforts of life that are my birthright as a sentient being of the earth. Can we agree on that, Dink? After all, you look pretty sore this morning. I'm guessing you miss the Comfort-Flex mattress you've got at home."

Dinky chuckled again. He hadn't won after all. Stephanie was smarter than he had given her credit for. Much smarter. Instead of being sad at his loss, he was happy. A smart girl like her would make a good friend.

"I think we agree, Steph."

"Only my friends call me Steph." She had finished her breakfast, so she put her bowl down, stood up and stretched. Then she winked at Dinky, sitting on the floor below her and said, "lucky for you, I'd say we're friends."

Chapter Forty Two

"Where am I?" Cameron sat bolt upright, head spinning. He was in a broad room with a low ceiling, on a bed. He must have been unconscious.

"It's ok, you're alright."

Maria lay in the next bed over.

"Maria! You have to tell me what's happening, I -"

Her nostrils flared, a small detail of her that he had almost forgotten. It meant she was afraid, serious. His words caught in his throat.

"You're in the infirmary, remember, Will?" she put emphasis on his name, which he suddenly remembered. "You must be sicker than you thought when you came in here with Stephanie a few minutes ago. You passed out just after you came in."

"Yeah, that's why we came here. I'm... really confused."

"I can tell," she said.

"What happened to your head?"

"The storm. The other night. I fell."

Cameron nodded, slowly.

"Do you... know what's happening? Or why?"

She shook her head, a small movement. "I can barely hear the Chief's announcements of the day from here, but I think that we're starting construction on permanent settlements for the colony. But don't you worry about that right now, just rest so that you can get better."

Cameron wracked his brain. Why was she being so evasive? He needed to know at least where they were and when, if he was going to be able to keep up this charade for even a little while longer. Didn't she realize how important this was?

"Listen, I can't remember anything from -"

Her nostrils flared again, this time as a deliberate warning. He faltered, for once cursing their ability to read each other. "I don't think," she said, carefully, "that the infirmary is a good place for any kind of serious conversation. We ought to just rest and get better."

"I understand," he relented. He thought he did: there could be people listening. Maria was always a clever one and it seemed time hadn't changed that. "Well, then. Why don't you tell me about Elizabeth?"

Elizabeth smiled. She wished she could tell him how happy she was to have this time with him, to be able to share, however stinted the conversation may be, about her life here. It was the greatest kind of reunion, one that she had never experienced before, even with her parents. It felt like coming home.

Cameron watched her smile, caught her gaze and held it. In an instant, she was flooded with all of the memories of seeing him wear that exact look and of all the moments that followed. The way he would touch her, seduce her, make love to her, whisper his hands and lips over her body. She blushed, struggling to conceal the urgency and suddenness of her arousal. Her body was responding as if it had been two thousand years, not two days, since she had been touched by a man. She managed to contain a small moan and turn it into an even smaller cough, as if she were clearing her throat and forced herself to break his gaze.

"Elizabeth. I'd be happy to tell you just about everything I remember."

He chuckled, indicating he understood what she meant. Elizabeth told him almost everything that she did remember - bits and pieces of their time so far in Rivertown, excluding any mention at all of romance between her and Dinky; why she joined the corps, what it was like growing up. It was difficult not to mention Dinky, but it would be too hard to try and explain to Cameron now, and for the moment, she wanted to relish their reunion, even if Maria hadn't expected to find herself in love with another man when she finally saw her husband again.

Yeah, Elizabeth thought dryly. *I think I do love Dinky.*

She also had to be careful not to give too much of the background information, just in case someone *was* listening. Instead of explaining that, in this culture, the genders were conceived differently and held along a hierarchy as opposed to being seen as different but unequivocally equal, she had to imply it and hope that he understood. His look of surprise told her that he did, but he didn't ask why her cousin was her appointed guardian as oldest male relative nearby, even though she was actually a little bit older than him. Sharing their perspective, of genders as superficial differences that changed over time, was a relief for her.

She described life on the farm, with Mark, her siblings and cousins and how Mark had saved her life during the storm, when she was caught in a bad dream as she described it. If the night of that other storm had been as important as she seemed to remember, she thought he would understand what she meant.

"You said this morning that it was fitting that you keep getting Dizzy and Stephanie laughed. What did you mean?"

Elizabeth's face broke into a bright smile. Different, slightly, than what he remembered of Maria's smile. This was truly Elizabeth's. It made him wonder how much of Maria there was inside of her and how much of this other, rougher, more brazen stranger remained.

Telling the story of how she got her nickname that fateful day trying to upgrade the intelligence on the tractor was difficult without directly explaining the technology that the people in Elizabeth's homeland possessed. In their life, such technology had been completely nonexistent. What she didn't know was that he was already familiar with the idea of machines that could walk and talk and even think in strange, methodical was.

"The story will make more sense if you know the background," she started, putting emphasis on her words. "You see, my dad and Mark's dad, they're brothers and they grew up on a big farm way far away from the city. There was five boys and the three older ones inherited that old farm, while my dad and Uncle John got money enough to buy land themselves. My grandpa, who still lives in the big old house on the old farm, where they grow fruit trees and bushes because they're closer to the coast so it's not as dry and the weather's more constant, he was never a big believer in bots." Elizabeth stopped and gave Cameron what she hoped he would interpret as a significant look.

"Not for farming anyways. Instead of getting all the newest, intelligent technology and just sittin' back, he worked his orchard with hand tools and sit-on mowers and what-not, mostly. Well at first, people laughed at him. The farm bots were considered vastly superior and people even paid higher prices for the food. But after a while, almost two generations, people started to get strange illnesses. Turns out that neither the genetically re-engineered crops or the crap grown by bots, mostly it was all the same stuff anyways, was as nutritious. No surprise to you and I, of course," Elizabeth gave him another significant look, thinking back to their own piece of land and the many plants they had tended there by hand. "Of course, lots of religious types took that as proof that 'man's hand has power over the world' and some other people thought it was a sign of the apocalypse, because of all the books that used to be written about the dangers of artificial intelligence. Of course, this was before they were actually built and ended up being harmless. Even though they think, they don't think like we do, not as quickly and not creatively, at least not often and their experiences are after all, occupationally limited."

Cameron had gone white. *Machines; thinking machines.* These people were still producing them, despite what had happened those millennia ago. It confirmed his worst fear: any one of them could be what he had known as *ghosts* – artificial humans. Any one of the two hundred or so boys out in the Barracks. Or even... himself. Maybe he was a ghost and so was Elizabeth. How else would they have memories of a life long past? They had died. What else could they be?

"Well, my grandpa's crops did better and better, compared to the other stuff. . Sure, there were the engineered plants that would grow just about anywhere and any time of year but that wasn't much better than the tasteless, nutrient-depleted stuff that the bots had grown. That's why my dad and Uncle John were never big fans of technology for farming. I didn't know any of this, so one day when I was a kid I set about upgrading our old tractor to be intelligent, just take a few commands. I had no idea what I was doing and it's a wonder I didn't electrocute myself. Must have been eight or nine at the time."

Elizabeth paused for a moment, smiling at the memory. She was surprising herself with how much she remembered. It still seemed distant and foggy, but shone with nostalgic affection nonetheless. Elizabeth thought briefly that this was how it would feel to look back at her life when she was on her death-bed, separated from her memories by time and the strange changes that happen to a person as age shuffles them along.

"Anyways, I went to the hardware store and bought all the parts that I figured I would need with my pocket money and - "

"Wait." It was just a hoarse whisper. All he could muster. It was only then that Elizabeth realized how much her story had scared him. Of course it would, to hear about robots. Machines that could think and perhaps strangest of all, food that was *engineered*? Not just strange, but an obscenity. Against the wishes of the creator. Harmful to the body and the Earth.

What had she been thinking, telling him all of this? She ought to have known his reaction would be strong and realized that it would be virtually impossible for him to maintain his cover once he knew how strange the world he had been brought back into was.

"Will, I'm sorry, you must be feeling sick again! Just calm down, lie back, you'll be fine."

"Just wait." he whispered again. She watched anxiously as he took a deep, calming breath and then another. "You're telling me that they have machines with thoughts and memories?"

Elizabeth could feel her heart pounding in her chest. He was only whispering, but if anyone was listening, they would certainly hear him. "*We* have machines, Will, not *they*. We." She tried to sound lighthearted, as if it was a simple mistake. "You're just confused, like you said before!"

"No. It can't be. My God! My God, Maria! They still have machines! They still have the machines, they still have the ghosts! My God!"

Elizabeth tried to quiet him, tried to talk over him, tried to interrupt him and even loudly justify what he was saying but it was no use. Suddenly, the doctor was standing over Cameron, holding one of his wrists in an iron grip.

"You said 'god'. A primitive word for a creator-based religious icon. There are other indiscrepancies. You said 'they still have'."

Elizabeth felt that the wind had been sucked out of her. How had the doctor covered the space between the door and Cameron's bed so quickly? And his face, his face had that same strange smoothness that she had seen before today. Maybe she hadn't been imagining it.

Cameron's arm shot up and into an unnatural angle, still held fast by the doctor. He groaned.

"Who are you?" the doctor asked.

"It's Will!" Elizabeth cried, "Just Will! He just came in this morning! He's got a fever, he's confused, that's all!"

The doctor ignored her and pushed Cameron's arm further, putting pressure on his shoulder. Cameron cried out in pain.

"Tell me who you are."

"I don't know what you mean!" He yelled, gritting his teeth.

There was a moment of pause. Elizabeth could feel her heart pounding in her head, giving her another, almost blinding headache and making her feel instantly dizzy.

"You will come with me for further examination," the doctor said, pulling Cameron off of his hospital bed and dragging him towards the door.

"Wait!" Elizabeth shot out of her own bed as soon as the doctor started pulling Cameron away. Her vision swam instantly, black rimming it and then exploding within it. She lost her balance but pushed herself forward, carried by the inertia of jumping out of the bed. There was a harsh metallic clang as her hip bone connected with the corner of the cot that Cameron had been lying in only a moment before.

"You're making a mistake! I don't know what you're talking about! Let me go!" Cameron yelled, fighting uselessly against the doctor's grip.

Terror seized Elizabeth as she sank to the floor, unable to stand. She just got him back, how could they take him away again, already? She'd only *just* gotten him back! They would kill him. She pressed her eyes shut, trying to stop the world from spinning, trying not to remember the night of the storm and the carnage she had seen. The coal-eyes might as well be their own people, Cameron and Maria's. There was no reason they wouldn't treat him the same way. They would kill him...they would eat him.

"Help me! Someone! This is a mistake! My name is Will!" The brassy sound of the fluorescent lights eventually covered Cameron's yelling. Elizabeth was left weeping, huddled on the black and white checked linoleum floor, dizzy and nauseous and unable to stand. She could feel her pulse pounding behind her eyes and in her ears and especially in the gash on her head. Reaching up gingerly, she felt the bandage and a warm, seeping wetness. Her fingers were damp with blood when she held them in front of her eyes.

Elizabeth cursed silently. She couldn't even get back into the bed, at least not yet. How was she supposed to get Cameron and get them out of here alive in her condition? The thought of losing him again became overwhelming and fresh tears streamed down her cheeks.

No. She couldn't let this happen. She gritted her teeth and started the arduous task of lifting herself up from the ground, using the frame of what had been Cameron's bed to steady herself. It didn't matter if it killed her, none of it mattered, except that she couldn't lose Cameron again.

But what about Dinky? Elizabeth thought angrily. *I'm not going to leave him behind.*

Dinky understands this world, this time. He can take care of himself, Maria countered. *Cameron is lost here, and he needs me to save him. He needs you, Elizabeth.*

Elizabeth sighed. It was true, Cameron needed her.

But what about Dinky?

Chapter Forty Three

"Dizzy! What happened, are you ok?" Mark came in first, to find Elizabeth pulling herself up to a kneeling position using a bed frame. She was crying and there was fresh blood seeping through her bandage. He ran over to his cousin. "Here, let me help you."

Mark cupped Elizabeth under her elbows and lifted her to standing. The change made her wobble where she stood and he quickly readjusted his grip so that he held her around the waist with one arm and around the shoulders with the other. She bent over and threw up onto the floor as Mark led her back to her bed and sat her down on it.

"What is going on?" It was Dinky. He jogged through the room and slid to the bed, narrowly avoiding the vomit on the floor.

"I'm fine, I'm fine," she managed. Covered in sweat from the exertion and the sick, feeling empty and light-headed, Elizabeth was anything but.

"We heard yelling, Dizzy," Mark lay his cousin down on the blankets and smoothed her hair from her face, "What happened?"

She took a moment to answer in an effort to regain control of herself. "Will was here. He's... sick. Has a fever. He was fine for a while but then... he got really confused. The doctor took him for more testing." Her voice sounded thick and raspy.

"Who was yelling?" Dinky asked.

"Will was. He was... delusional. Thought the doctor was trying to hurt him."

"Oh man," Mark said, "poor Will. Good thing the doc's got him, eh Liz?"

She didn't answer. They stared at her quizzically for a moment.

"What happened to you, though?" Dinky asked, sitting beside Mark on her bed.

"I, uh, tried to get up. To... help. But I got dizzy and fell down pretty hard. Then you guys came in."

"I'm just glad we heard you, we were just comin' in for lunch and we heard all this yellin'," Mark said. He looked serious, almost fatherly. Elizabeth was very glad he was there. "I wonder why no nurses came to try an' help you."

"I didn't call for help," she said.

"Typical Dizzy," Mark murmured. "Well no need. You've got your man-squad here to take of ya. You stay here as long as you need to, it's finally sunny and they say it's gonna be for a week at least."

Elizabeth snorted and tasted rusty blood. *Man-squad.* What a backwards conception of the world these boys had, these people that she was still somehow a part of. She didn't need to be taken care of, she needed to be *assisted.* Could she trust Dinky and Mark? Yes, but... she didn't even know what she was up against, let alone what she could possibly do to help Cameron, other than somehow escape with him. Nor did she want anyone getting hurt at their expense.

It was only then that Elizabeth thought back to what Cameron had been saying right before the doctor came to take him away: that they *still* had machines. He had called them ghosts. What if Cameron had seen or heard something about bots or their predecessors, some sort of early prototype back in their past lives? It could have been while she was held hostage; she was told that she had been gone for several weeks once she was finally returned to her people. They barely had any time to talk between that and their deaths.

But it didn't make sense. Bots were new. Part of the amazing advances that Elizabeth's culture was so proud of, and made such a big priority.

"Dinky, do you know much about bots?"

"Uh, bots?" Dinky was obviously taken aback. "Yeah, sort of. Why?"

"How long have people had bots?"

"Well we've had technology in various forms for centuries, of course. You know the ancients, the ones who found the Statues of the Ethos, they even had indoor environment control, hygiene and youth treatments? Imagine! That long ago! Then of course came the dark ages after the civil wars. We're obviously much more advanced now, but it's still remarkable to think about.

"What about bots, in particular? Like, you know, ones that can do things on their own."

"That's a good question, uh... I don't know. Independent, automated movement is based on really old software, obviously. Probably a few centuries. Why do you ask?"

"Oh, I'm um, just trying to distract myself. My head hurts."

"We should get the doctor in here," Mark said to Dinky.

"No." Elizabeth almost yelled it, "No, he's busy with Will. I'm fine, just a bit of a headache."

"I could stay for a while, distract you until the doctor gets back, how does that sound?" Dinky asked.

Elizabeth nodded. "Tell me everything you know about the Desolate Land, alright?"

"Sure. But I don't know much abut the 'land' itself, of course, just the settlers who landed here."

"Of course," Elizabeth said. She hadn't realized it until that moment, but *of course* their history would only tell one side of the story. "Do you think that the history you know is accurate? Or is it too subjective?"

"It was so long ago; two thousand years and more. I'd say that some things are bound to be wrong with the version of history we learned at school."

"Huh."

Two thousand years isn't long history, she thought. *I know what Maria's ancestor's were doing two thousand years before Maria was born... because I grew up in the same village that they did. The trees that they planted and the stories told about who planted what and why they planted it just there. My father planted lilacs all along the path that my mother took to her favourite reading spot from the house, because they were her favourite flower. That knowledge was part of Maria's lifestyle and beliefs. My lifestyle and beliefs.*

Thinking about the old village just made Elizabeth more upset. What kind of people would drive others from the homes that their families had tended for generations and generations? What kind of people were these, who held a once-proud race, the last of this continents children, as slaves for millennia? Who murdered and cannibalized and thought that the world was something you could change to fit your whims; instead of a perfect gift created exactly to suit your needs... thought that two thousand years was a stretch of history so long that fog and forgetfulness was unavoidable, instead of seeing that time as a continuation of eternity...

"Are you ok?" Mark asked, in a whisper.

"Yes." Elizabeth knew now what happened when they found out that you weren't ok, that you were not who you appeared to be. "Just a headache. Go on, Dinky, please."

"I'll go get lunch," Mark said and headed off.

"Just the two of us," Dinky said laughingly, leaning in towards Elizabeth.

"Dinky..." she turned her head, not wanting to kiss him, because she didn't know if she could kiss him, knowing it would possibly be the last time. "If you don't distract me soon, I'm going to throw up again and it'll probably be on you."

"Ok. Well, the trade routes and exploration parties and all that, they landed north of here, up the coast, two thousand five hundred years ago, or more. They found lots of new herbs and berries and nuts and stuff, really healthy stuff. Most of the 'superfoods' that we get at health stores come from here, actually. Of course, we've improved the strains that we found, made them more heat-resistant to our climate and what not."

"What about settlements?"

Dinky gave Elizabeth a gentle, but puzzled smile. "This is the first settlement in the Wild Land, goofy. There haven't been any permanent settlements before this one."

Elizabeth blanched. "That's not true."

Dinky laughed, thinking that she was joking with him. "Come on! You know it is. I mean, sure, there were a couple of camps here and there. That's where we get the spooky stories of the Wild Land with evil witches and scary cannibals -"

"Dinky, come on!" Elizabeth shook her head, amazed that he would bring up cannibalism again after how much it bothered her before. She was even more amazed that there was no recorded history of the settlements in the Wild Land. Which meant that there was no recorded history of the settlers, the ones who raped and murdered and defiled Maria's people.

"Is everything ok in here?" Mark had appeared in the doorway, holding two bowls of porridge. Stephanie stood behind him, holding two more.

"No." Elizabeth shook her head and forced conviction into her voice, "No, I'm super sick to my stomach and dizzy and my head hurts and," Elizabeth surprised herself by bursting into tears. She couldn't control them, couldn't stop them. "I'm tired. I need to go to sleep."

Stephanie's face instantly relaxed, as if there hadn't been that strange tension at all. She and Mark cooed over Elizabeth and got her tucked under the blankets.

"Is there anything we can bring you, sweetheart?" Stephanie asked.

"Yeah," Elizabeth was thinking quickly, trying to come up with a plan. She would have to act, as soon as possible, if she wanted to save Cameron's life, not to mention her own. "I feel stinky and gross. Would you bring me whatever clothes Mark salvaged? And if there's any warm stuff, even my rain jacket and all that... I just want to have it, feel more comfortable and safe."

"Of course, Dizzy," Mark said, "we'll get it to ya right away. You just go to sleep now."

Elizabeth let her eyes drift closed and heard the footfalls of the others as they left. She heard Mark saying "What you think you're doin, gettin' Dizzy upset like that, you moron! She *never* cries and I mean never! Geez, Dink!"

But she couldn't sleep, not right away, despite the deep exhaustion that the morning had caused her. For some reason, the people that Elizabeth had been born into, the culture that raised Dinky and Mark and Stephanie, was hiding a part of their history from themselves. There *had* been settlements, she knew it.

Why didn't the others?

Chapter Forty Four

Maria walks through her garden. Hers and Cameron's and that of her parents and grandparents – though she and Cameron planned and planted the newest addition: an acre on the south side to be expanded upon someday by their children. The cabin on the acre is also new: built by Cameron with Maria's help, turning what was once one garden into two; one plot of land into two. The village had grown that way – by dividing and expansion of carefully designed gardens – for generations. Her parent's house, old and familiar, is right next door, on the other side of the expansive berry patch that they share, that was planned and planted by her forbears. She walks the warm flagstone path between the raspberry and honeyberry bushes and runs her palm through the leaves of a growing pecan sapling, just now growing tall enough to overshadow the bushes. Maria planted that tree when she was a girl. It was her grandfather's idea to add a new layer to the garden and extend the reach of the plants upwards into a canopy of nuts they could pick in fall.

It feels so long since she's been here.

She walks quietly. Everything is quiet, no wind, birdsong or chirp of insects. Even the plants lie quiet. Maria can't even hear herself breathe. It is a stillness that she has known before and the hairs on the back of her neck prickle in recognition.

I'm on a journey.

Journey's of the spirit were something she had learned more and more about as she grew up, but hadn't had the chance to practice since…

By the growth of the plants, she knows that it's been a year since they left. Her garden is how she left it, but overgrown. The annual and vegetable patches are filled with self-seeding flowers and grasses instead of potatoes and onions, the chicken coup is empty. The fruit from the year before wasn't picked and rots where it fell on the ground.

It's hard to look at.

Her mental construct of Elder Jared might be here, he had guided her so much in her youth. He said that every human culture had their own name for this place and their own ways of seeing it. Different names and rituals for much the same thing. He said that she would learn how to interpret the things she saw, in order to help others in their community. He taught her to close her eyes, slow her breathing and open the door of her mind into the world of the spirit. Stepping through was always the hardest part.

Maria walks towards the house. Her house, her's and Cameron's. It's empty too, of course, which breaks her heart. They would have been here, together, if not for the foreigners. Jared didn't understand what was wrong with them, but thought it might be some kind of disease, because they could no longer travel with their spirits, as she was doing now, but were confined to their flesh. The thought makes Maria shiver again.

Sho rounds a stand of tall wildflowers and sees her favourite bench. Cameron made that for her birthday. They left the cushions on it, in their haste to escape and the cushions were now rotted and moth-eaten. Maria sits on the bench anyways, to think and to see the familiar vista that it overlooks.

The instant that Maria sits on the bench, another figure emerges from flowers on the other side and suts down next to her, with the precision of a mirror's image. They both look at each other. It was Elizabeth. They sit like so, watching each other for a long, silent moment.

"I did this, didn't I?" They speak in perfect unison. "I made us come back, somehow." One sound. One woman speaking quietly to herself in a long dead world.

"It was the Untura. Joining. Something the Ibers spoke about, before *they were called coal-eyes. They said they didn't have the magic left to do it."*

Maria and Elizabeth look out onto the horizon, deep in thought. "But I did it."

She was onto something. The key was somewhere in her mind...if she could just focus, channel herself she could find it. There would be answers and directions. But it was not to be. The world around her was changing.

A loud, hard wind starts to blow, thrashing against them and carrying heavy, dark clouds from the mountains to the West. The quiet world she had been sitting in suddenly becomes loud and threatening.

"There is danger here! It's coming! We have to get out of here!" she screams, jumping up.

"We have to get out of here," she murmured, waking up, "we have to..."

Elizabeth stopped. It hadn't been just a dream. She stretched, then lay quietly. Somehow, she had caused the rebirth of both Cameron and herself, here, now. She didn't know how or why, of course, but the vision had made one thing clear: they had to get out. Soon.

She sat up. It was hard to tell how much time had passed, as there were no windows in the room, but she felt very rested and assumed she had been asleep for many hours. Reaching up to the bandage on her head, she was relieved to find it dry. The bleeding had stopped again. Hopefully this time for good. Her headache was also mostly gone, which was reassuring. Somehow, she had to get up, get Cameron and get them out. She had no idea what kind of suffering he would be in, but the better her own condition, the better chance they had. Stretching again, she noted stiffness in her legs and a pain in her hip, probably from where she bashed it against the corner of the cot next to hers. Her arms seemed alright, as she swung them gingerly up above her head and back down again, tensing her fingers into fists and releasing them.

Good. The nervous fluttering of her heart aside, she was as physically ready as she was going to be.

Elizabeth looked around the room, trying to come up with some sort of plan. That was when she noticed the neat pile of clothes on the bed next to hers, the one that Cameron had been lying in that morning. On top was a note, written in thick black letters on what had surely once been a page of one of Dinky's books. The words once printed on the page were now barely visible and cast long shadows of the ink that had run during the storm.

Carefully, she braced her hands beside her and swung her legs over the side of the bed. Her toes reached the floor and she wiggled them with satisfaction. Step one: successfully leave bed, complete. She leaned forward, grabbed the note and read:

Roses are Red

You're feeling Blue

Here are your Clothes

We cleaned them for You!

Get Well Soon Dizzy, We Love You

Mark, Steph and Dinky

Elizabeth smiled when she read it. Sure enough, the pile of clothes had been washed, probably in one of the sinks and were dry as bone. Her rain suit was in the pile, as were her warm clothes. The taser and baton were missing. That would make this more difficult.

She read the note again and realized that if she did this, if she attempted - or even succeeded - in breaking Cam loose and escaping into the wild with him, she would be cutting her ties to her life as Elizabeth, possibly forever. She would be leaving Mark, Steph and most acutely of all, Dinky behind.

How can I do that? she thought, tears stinging her eyes for the third time that day, *how can I leave Dinky behind?*

She tried to think logically about it, but there was little by way of logic or reason in the vision she had experienced only moments before.

You have to trust! Maria thought. *That's all life is. Trusting in the signs that are given to you. We've had a sign. We have to follow it.*

Elizabeth gritted her teeth. *That's not how I operate.*

She tried to consider her situation. By now, the Chief was sure to know that Will was not really Will, at least not anymore. He might even know the whole truth. There would be no doubt that Elizabeth was somehow involved, if she disappeared the same night that Cameron mysteriously escaped. That was assuming they succeeded. Much more likely, she would get caught trying to help him escape and no amount of explaining would save her from the same fate that had befallen him.

That fate wouldn't befall him if she could help it. It was a risk, yes, but she had to save Cameron. She couldn't sit by and do nothing, not with the knowledge that they wouldn't hesitate to kill him once they had all of the information he was able to give. Somehow, she would find her way back to Dinky and Mark and the others, if she could. If not, at least she would know that she had done her best to save Cameron, and live up to whatever purpose had given her this second chance.

Elizabeth gritted her teeth and stood up. She wobbled precariously and her arms shot out for balance, stabilizing her. Maria had been many things, but brave to the point of foolhardy was absolutely not one of them. Elizabeth smiled dangerously, fingering the pile of clothes in front of her. *She* was brave. Foolhardy even. And *she* was going to get Cameron out of here, even if it killed her... again. There was no way that she used some kind of crazy magic to cross the millennia for a second chance, only to let that chance go by because a bald, cannibalistic Chief got in the way.

Oh no. Not on Elizabeth's watch. Maria might use magic and the patience for long term results, but Elizabeth was an instant gratification kind of girl.

Which meant that Maria's equanimity was needed right from the start. Getting dressed was an exercise in patience and frustration, not to mention a new lesson on her coordination and balance, both of which seemed to have gone on vacation since the concussion. Standing upright was trying. Trying to put pants on, one leg at a time, was like walking the tightrope and she fell over several times. She dressed in her warmest clothes, then stripped the sheet from her bed and made a bag for the rest by tying it in various places. She put her rain gear on top, just in case her dream had been prophetic in more ways than one and another storm was on the way. Rain gear rustled when you wore it and she didn't want to be heard. She did all of this as quickly and quietly as she could, still not sure if she was being watched or overheard and if so, by whom.

Just as she was about to leave, it occurred to her that she shouldn't go without some kind of weapon. She searched the room slowly, painstakingly, pulling all the curtains aside and checking underneath every bed. The only thing handy was her bedpan, which had been changed while she was asleep. Gross but good enough. She tied her makeshift pack around her shoulders so that her hands were free, using her belt to hold it tight and held the bedpan at the ready. Then she took a deep, steadying breath and started towards the door.

Walking was difficult. She went very slowly to keep her heart rate down and prevent her head from spinning.

Maybe this isn't a good idea, she thought in a very Maria-like way, *maybe I should wait until I'm feeling better.*

Elizabeth gritted her teeth again, putting the thought out of her mind. If she waited too long, Cameron could die. He might be dead already. How long would it take for him to crack under torture? She had to do something to help him and she had to do it *now*. She pressed on, using the frames of the beds lining the room for support.

When she reached the swinging double doors leading out to the hall, she stopped. There were no windows into the hall, so she pressed herself against the frame and pushed the door closest to her open slightly with her free hand. The other held the steel bedpan above her shoulder. She had grown up with brothers and cousins and knew how to fight. Even with a bedpan.

Through the sliver of open door, she could hear the quiet, steady hum of machines. The path seemed to be clear, but she waited, straining to hear any sound of movement. After an agonizing moment of deliberation, she took a deep, steadying breath and pushed the door further open, as slowly as she could. It took all of her focus to keep her senses sharp in spite of the severe discomfort of standing. Inch by inch, the door swung open into the hall leading out to the waiting room. It was empty.

Elizabeth wished she could remember more from the night they took her into the infirmary. But she had been in and out of consciousness, slipping between two different worlds, lives and times. She tried remembered the things that Elder Jared had taught her: that she was safe and protected, a part of the Earth, with a destiny laid out for her by the creator. She had only to trust.

The doors lining the hall were made of some sort of polymer composite except for the small, square glass windows that ran from shoulder level down. The hall might be empty but any of the rooms could be occupied.

Cameron could be in one of those rooms, she thought. She paused to consider it. Should she risk discovery this early in the game, on the off-chance that they had kept Cameron close by when they took him away? It didn't make sense. She had heard them drag him and it sounded like he went some distance away, not just down the hall. Plus, they wouldn't risk exposing him to the other patients, not until they were sure of who he was. Once that happened, she assumed that they would probably kill him, or worse. Either way, they certainly wouldn't bring him into a room someone looking for a restroom could wander into by mistake.

No, he wasn't here. He was further, somewhere else, somewhere hidden.

Which meant Elizabeth had to get past those doors without being seen by whoever was lurking inside them. Walking was challenging enough; she was certain crouching would end in disaster. She couldn't afford to make the noise that a fall would generate. She decided to crawl. The effort of lowering herself to the ground caused her head to spin and a fresh symphony of pounding to begin in her skull. She closed her eyes so that she wouldn't see the world turn sideways and groped blindly for some form of support. There was nothing to grab. Her knees buckled and she fell forward. Her hands broke the fall and it was muffled on the linoleum floor.

This is ridiculous, she thought. After waiting for the banging in her head to subside and listening briefly for intruders in the vicinity, she pushed herself up onto her hands and knees and started her journey across the floor.

Crawling was much easier than walking, though it afforded her less of a vantage to monitor her surroundings. She was also able to move fairly quickly without causing undue pain and pounding in her head.

You better appreciate this, Cammy, she thought. It made her smile and inadvertently, caused tears to well up in her eyes. *Please don't die, please don't die*. She crawled faster.

At the end of the hall, she took a moment to rest, propping her back up in a corner. Just outside another set of swinging doors was what she was sure was the waiting room. From what she could hear, it was as deserted as the inner infirmary, though she thought that a nurse must be on duty, or at least on call, all night. In fact, a nurse was probably sent to check on her during the night. If it *was* night - and Elizabeth's internal clock figured it must be.

Using the wall as a brace, she pushed herself back up to standing. She held the bedpan tightly behind her back, ready to strike and pushed the door open.

Chapter Forty Five

The nurse was sitting behind a small counter in the corner of the room, with a sign above her reading 'Admission'. Elizabeth poked her head around the door and the nurse, the only person in the room, looked up at her mildly.

Good. She didn't think it was strange for Elizabeth to be out of bed.

"Can I help you?" she asked.

Elizabeth thought as quickly as she could, which was difficult thanks to her growing headache. "I was looking for someone to help with this headache," she said, "but I didn't see anyone inside."

"I'm the only one here tonight," the nurse said, "I'd be happy to help you."

"Thanks."

The nurse finished whatever she had been writing on the topmost sheet of a stack of papers, then stood and started towards Elizabeth.

"Where's Will?" Elizabeth asked, "he was here this morning. I thought they were doing some tests on him."

The change in the nurse was immediate. It was that same… flatness of expression on her face that Elizabeth had seen on the doctor and terrifyingly enough, on Stephanie.

"He's been taken upstairs for further testing," she said, blankly.

"There's an upstairs?" Elizabeth asked between gritted teeth. The nurse was almost at the door and she ducked back into the hall ahead of her and raised the bedpan over her head.

"It's for senior staff only," the nurse said, as she pushed through the door. The doors were a dark grey plastic. While the nurse pushed it open to go through, she was temporarily blinded to Elizabeth's side. She went through the door, facing into the hall and left her back exposed. The door swung shut and Elizabeth lunged forward, bringing the pan down on the back of the nurse's neck as hard as she could.

There was a sickening metallic twang us the thick rim connected. Elizabeth's hand was thrown back from the violence of the impact and she looked at the weapon in her hand incredulously: it had been dented from the hit. The nurse still stood, but to Elizabeth's horror, it seemed that her neck had been dented, too. Her head twitched to the side, twice, three times and then she fell over.

Elizabeth didn't wait to see if she was dead or just injured. She was too afraid to investigate. She turned and walked as quickly as she could back into the waiting room and to the desk that the nurse had been sitting at. On the desk were files - one for each of the peacekeepers, it seemed. The top most file was open and with a lurch in her stomach, she realized that it was her own. Rifling through the pages, she saw scans of her body, with schematics laid over them. There was a note written on the final page that said, *host body is ready for transplant.*

Elizabeth shivered and threw the file to the ground. Transplant? What transplant? She forced herself to swallow her fear and rounded the corner into the darkened Barracks.

Chapter Forty Six

They were all asleep. The boys that she had grown up with, trained with and crossed the ocean with; who she had sometimes hated, worked so hard to be one of and now, was going to leave behind... snoring and scratching themselves, curled into little balls for warmth, sleeping on a hard floor under thin blankets in a strange land, utterly vulnerable.

She remembered the camps of the many refugees they had encountered and commiserated with on the long journey to the sea, when she was Maria. These boys – although Stephanie was likely among them - reminded her of those people.

It took a moment for her eyes to adjust to the dark. She would have to be very careful not to wake any of them, so she started to creep, as silently as possible, along the wall. If there was an upstairs, the entrance to it would have to be hidden, or at least in an unfrequented place. That meant it wouldn't be in the Barracks or in the Auditorium. The washrooms and small laundry were probably out, too. That left the infirmary, the courtyard and the abandoned market. Thinking about the infirmary induced a kind of panic in Elizabeth. What kind of transplant would they have done if she hadn't had that warning dream? What would happen to her if she was caught and brought back there? No. She wouldn't go back to the infirmary.

Elizabeth scurried around the perimeter of the Barracks and into the open air of the courtyard garden. The fountain was splashing playfully, even in the dead of night. She could see better in the moonlight and saw that several flowers had opened in the few days she had spent in bed. She looked up and studied the stars for a moment, listened to the air. It was a brief communion, but gave her the strength to go on.

Elizabeth stepped down from the stairs and onto the Earth. The ground was still wet from the rains, but cool, meaning it was closer to morning than evening and -

She looked down at her bare toes. Wonderful. She'd forgotten shoes.

At least I'll be able to move quietly.

A breeze brushed past her and into the market, making the canvas stall covers quiver and bellow. Elizabeth gasped and nearly fell over - she thought she had seen a figure moving through the stalls, but it was just the fabric swaying. She had rarely been truly afraid before, but images of the woman whose legs were cut off, of the nurse with the dented neck, twitching... and of Cameron, being dragged away, made her wonder what she was getting into.

Correction: what Maria already got me into. Thanks again.

She tried for a deep breath, but it came out closer to a gasp instead. Her breathing could barely keep up with her heart, which was leading a main street parade starring a herd of elephants over her brain. Elizabeth knew she didn't have much time before she got too dizzy to keep going and started puking again, or the nurse was found and a search started. Or both.

The canvas billowed again, obscuring any sounds of movement or visible figures that could be lying in ambush. She walked forward anyways, as quietly as she could. When she reached the end of the courtyard, she flattened herself against the half-wall that cordoned the market off, waiting and listening. All she could hear was the ghostly sound of the wind through the deserted stalls and the occasional creak of wooden frames holding the canvas in place.

Elizabeth rounded the corner and crept down the main aisle of the market. It wasn't the stealthiest route, but she knew that she didn't have much time. One hand held the bedpan at the ready, the other held the edges of the stalls for support as she went.

Something brushed against her hand and she almost screamed. She took several more shaky breaths, trying not to make any noise. It was just a loose piece of string, used to tie the canvas down. The edge of it was flapping up, making the noises she had heard before. She glanced inside: there was a plate with a fork and knife resting on it. Someone had been eating and left the dishes here. She took the knife - a large, serrated single-edged blade and continued on.

The wall at the end of the aisle was dark, but even in the dim light, she could see it was bare of any doors or stairways. That left climbing the stairs into the upper part of the market, which was sure to be a challenge. She grabbed the railing and began pulling herself up, one step at a time. It was almost more exertion than she could handle. The increase in her pulse caused her head to pound even harder and she found herself wobbling and nearly falling down outright. A cold sweat broke out on her forehead. Halfway up, she collapsed onto the landing and waited, trying to slow her heart and breathing. It wasn't much use. She was so exhausted from the effort of getting this far that she didn't know if she would be able to go much farther.

It doesn't matter what I can or can't do, she thought. *It just matters that I have to.*

With that, she tried to force herself to her feet again, but her knees wobbled severely and light began to explode in front of her eyes. It wouldn't do if she lost consciousness here. Tucking the bedpan under the strap of her pack and holding the knife between her teeth, she began to crawl the rest of the way up to the second level. Sweat dribbled into her eyes as she climbed. This was not a time for weakness. Weakness had cost them their lives before, when she fell during that storm so long ago. It would not happen again.

When she reached the top, she let herself rest for another moment, her back against the wall. This was the most harebrained scheme she had ever come up with and she had come up with more than her share in the two lives she could remember. Where would they go, once she got him out? What if there were guards, with guns?

She pressed her eyes closed, catching her breath. Instead of trying to think her way out of the current situation, she imagined what it would be like when they were free. They would find a dry place for the night and he would thank her for saving him. He would take her in his arms, kiss her face, tell her that he loved her and that everything would be alright... they could even go home, if they wanted to. But first, he would get that serious look, the one that gave her shivers. She would see it in the moonlit outline of his cheekbones, in the watery gleam of his eyes and the warm tremble of his lip. His hands would trace over her body, he would touch her the way that she needed so desperately to be touched, despite the pounding in her head, even now, when she knew she could be dead very soon.

Elizabeth shivered, ever so slightly. She had been in her twenties, before, as Maria. Had almost forgotten the overpowering urgency of her physical needs at seventeen. The thought of wrapping herself around Cameron, of tasting his body and feeling his skin against hers, was more than enough incentive for her to drag herself to her feet.

Even if it was for the last time.

Chapter Forty Seven

The upper level of the market looked different at night. Sinister and deceiving, with deep shadows and an eerie silence. She inched forward, one hand on the wall, as quietly as she could, stifling her breath to hear any movement, any indication of where Cameron might be held. She hoped that there wouldn't be another stairway to climb, but was resolved to climb it, if there was.

When she had been here before, with Dinky, she hadn't paid any attention to the walls surrounding the market. If there was a door, it could be anywhere. She traced the wall with her hands, looking for any inconsistency in the plastic. It had appeared to be rock, but with her hands on it, she was almost sure that it was entirely artificial. She investigated every shadow, though most turned out to be only painted on, to resemble blocks of stone. Still, she let her fingers trace every single one, pressed on them both for support and to see if they would move with some pressure. Maria remembered the entrance to a cave used by the group of refugees they had stayed with the night before the storm: it appeared to be blocked by boulders, but with a small amount of pressure, some of them swung inwards.

Elizabeth had almost circled the market when she heard voices. She froze. They were coming from in front of her and just as she had suspected, behind the wall. It only took her a moment to realize that they were moving towards her.

Elizabeth dropped to her knees and scurried behind the nearest stall. She took the knife from between her teeth and held it at the ready, crouched on her knees and out of sight.

"...not chosen, like us. Organics."

"That's impossible. Organics are simply rot. They die and are finished. Nothing about them is forever."

There was a low grinding sound as part of the wall rolled slowly away. Elizabeth peaked around the stall to see the Chief and the Doctor emerge from a dimly lit hallway.

"I agree," the doctor said, "which is why I think we should question the girl. Maybe she'll be more willing to cooperate."

"Is she also reborn?"

"We're not sure. The situation is unprecedented. Either way, the nurse informs me that her host is ready for the transplant. Soon, she will be immortal, like us. I'm sure she'll be willing to help, then.

"Her cousin, he's here. He could be reborn, too. We should take him, as well."

"I concur."

The two men descended the stairs casually and their voices drifted away. Elizabeth's heart was pounding in her head, making it hard to think. They were going to the infirmary to get her and they were going to take Mark, too. Of course, he would know nothing and was likely able to prove his innocence. But when they saw the injured nurse and realized she was gone...

The grinding sound began again and Elizabeth darted forward, not giving herself time to think and made it through the door just before it closed. She found herself at the end of an empty hallway, hanging lights casting a weak, tangerine glow every few feet. Swallowing hard, she forced herself to stand, teetering on her feet for a moment before she was able to walk. There were no decorations and no finery: here, the floor and walls were bare. Ahead, the hallway opened into a large room. Elizabeth crossed to the other side of the hall so that she could stay hidden as she approached it. Then she prayed to her idea of God the Creator. *I trust the Creator,* she recited, in her mind *and I trust myself, made to be a creator, too. I am safe and protected. I am part of the world. The energy of life flows through me. All is well.*

With that, she heard a whistling and then a howling. She peeked around the corner and saw that the room ahead had large windows, left open. A strong wind had started and the two guards, who just a moment ago had been standing right around the corner from where Elizabeth was now standing, were rushing to the other side of the room to close the windows.

Elizabeth scanned the massive room. She was surprised at her reaction: nothing. No horror, no nausea, no fear. Just a blank, serene resolution to the task at hand. Maybe she was in shock, maybe it was too much, to see people held in cages, some missing limbs; the various instruments and utensils of torture and butchery. She saw the woman who had been shot two nights before, during the storm. The woman was looking at her, eyes bloodshot and bleary. She was on the far side of the room, near the guards. She pointed weakly and Elizabeth saw Cameron, tied to a chair, only a few feet away from where she was standing.

Hurry, the woman mouthed. Elizabeth nodded. The guards had already managed to close one of the massive windows and there were only three more. Elizabeth scurried forward, to Cameron and clapped a hand over his mouth as she sank to her knees in front of him. His face was bruised and there was a large cut on his lower lip, but otherwise he seemed uninjured. When he recognized her, his eyes opened so wide that she could see the whites all the way around, even in the dim light.

Elizabeth cut at the rope holding his feet to the chair. His hands were tied behind his back, but she could deal with those later, once they were a safe distance away. Speed was of the essence. The rope was thick and made of some kind of stubborn artificial material. She sawed desperately at it, but it was taking too long. She glanced at the guards and saw that they were already closing the final window. She had only cut half of the rope. If they saw her...

Help, she thought. *Help me.*

"Help me!" Just as the guards were about to turn back to their posts and certainly see Elizabeth trying to free Cameron, the woman on the far side of the room, missing her legs and near death, began to scream. "Help me!"

The guards turned to her, incredulously and looked at each other, confused.

"Something is wrong," she said, in a lightly accented voice, "you must come and see me. I need help."

The guards finished with the window and went over to her. Elizabeth continued to saw desperately at the rope holding Cameron to the chair. She was almost through it.

"What do you want, you animal?"

The woman glanced at Elizabeth and saw that she needed more time. She pressed her eyes closed for a moment to steady herself, then said in a quavering voice, "I might be an animal, but at least I'm not a fucking machine like you are. You are an abomination and scum. You insult the design of creation, you spit on the memory of the humans you were just by existing. You don't feel and think like anything was supposed to. Not the way that the Creator intended. Not as humans.You disgusting machines. You're going to burn one day. *You are nothing.*"

Elizabeth was barely listening. The throbbing blood in her eardrums was drowning out all noise. She focused on the string in front of her and finally managed to rip through it. She stood up and nearly fell onto Cameron from the head rush it caused. Then she straightened, still dizzy but too determined to let it stop her and helped Cameron to his feet. She led him by the arm, back around the corner and down the hall, going as quickly as she could without falling over. Just as they reached the end of the hall and the door began to grind open, they heard the woman screaming in pain and the demented laughter of the guards.

"We have to help her!" Cameron cried.

"There's no time, they're coming back. Come on!" she pulled him forward, through the door and stumbled down the stairs, holding onto him for support. Even after hours of torture and with his hands tied behind his back, he was much steadier than she was. She knew she wouldn't last much longer.

Cameron followed her through the lower market and out the arch that led from the courtyard.

"Where are we going?" he whispered, harshly.

"I don't know. I didn't think that far ahead."

"This way," he said, veering to the west. He led them around the tents that used to be a village and into the grasslands. Then he veered again, to the north.

"You have to slow down," Elizabeth said. She was still holding his arm, leaning on him and stumbling along, "I'm going to pass out."

He did as she asked and led them into a thick forest. They continued on, blundering clumsily through the brush, for some time. Elizabeth stopped to vomit and tripped twice. Finally, they descended a hillside into a small creek valley. Cameron examined the pocked limestone wall climbing the other side of the tributary, then started forwards again. They splashed into the river and Elizabeth fell forward, scraping both hands on the rocks lining the river bottom. Her clothes were now soaked, included some of those in her pack, which had tilted to the side. Cameron crouched down beside her.

"We're almost there, Maria. I can't pick you up, because my hands are still tied. But you see that shadow, on the cliff wall? That's a cave. At least it was, the last time I was here. We can hide there until morning."

Elizabeth tried to respond, but could only mumble. It felt too familiar. Running from them, cold and wet and exhausted, hiding where they could and hoping not to be found. It seemed Cameron could read her mind, because he said, "It's going to be different this time, Maria. This time we're going to fight and we're going to win. Trust me."

She nodded.

"Now grab onto my arm. I'll help you up." Elizabeth grabbed hold of him and held on as he stood up, bringing her up with him. She could feel the hot anger pumping through his muscles. He wanted to go back and retrieve the woman who had saved both their lives. "Keep holding. We're almost there." She held on and stumbled through the cold creek with him. Her feet were numb by the time they came to the other side. It wasn't much of a climb to the hole and soon they were inside a long, narrow cave. It continued back for some distance, curving around.

"Untie my hands," Cameron said. She did. It took a long time to cut through the rope, but soon he was free. He led the way, crawling as deep into the black cave as they could go. "Now go to sleep," he said, "I'll take first watch."

She was asleep before he finished speaking.

Chapter Forty Eight

She didn't know where she was. When she opened her eyes, the faint blue light of dawn hung in the still air around her. The mist was very still and very quiet. She stretched and looked around. A cave. They were in a cave.

Not this again.

She reached to her side, and rolled over, accidentally burying her face in Cameron's shoulder. Even that small movement was enough to reignite the terrible pounding in her head, which reminded her of the night before and of everything else.

Elizabeth was immediately filled with great pride and a deep fear. She had managed to escape and to bring Cameron with her. It was much more than she had expected and the fear stuck in her throat was mostly residual. But what would they do now? Surely the Chief and his mysterious paramilitary would be searching for them and she had seen enough to know that they would not survive if they were found.

In the meantime, they had to face the present: a world and a time that they were never supposed to have been a part of, except as distant forbears. A world that they knew very little about – except what Elizabeth could remember. Unfortunately for them, that didn't include any memory of what they were supposed to be doing here, reborn millennia after their deaths, other than that it was a...

A second chance to fulfill our destiny on the Earth, she thought. Tears welled up in her eyes, thinking of destiny. Her destiny was certainly tied up with Cameron's and now, they were finally together again. She nuzzled into him, relishing the familiar smell of his skin and the feel of his heartbeat against her cheek.

Cameron woke up with a start and pushed himself away from Elizabeth. He sat up just as suddenly and rubbed at his eyes.

"I fell asleep," he said, looking alarmed, "I was supposed to be our watch for the night."

"It's alright. Nothing happened and you obviously needed the rest. Now we'll be able to make better time today."

Cameron was silent for a long time and the expression of bewilderment and fear remained on his face as he studied her. It kept her silent as well. He looked as if he didn't know how to respond, as if there was just too much to say. She supposed that was understandable. But he also had a look of apprehension bordering on terror and she had a feeling that it was not concerning their pursuers or their situation, but her. After what felt like an eternity, he finally cleared his throat and answered her. "You're not Maria."

"Yes I am."

He just shook his head, continuing to stare at her.

"I am!" she cried, "I'm as much Maria as you are Cameron!"

"Maybe I'm not Cameron, either."

Elizabeth was dumbstruck. "What are you talking about?"

"Maybe... we're ghosts. Like them."

"Ghosts?" It came out as a whisper. The early morning air seemed suddenly cold and thick, like a wall drawn up between them.

"You still don't know," he whispered. "What do you think they are? People?"

Elizabeth almost answered yes, but stopped. She knew that torture and violence were a regular part of her culture from that other land... but the things she had seen surpassed anything she had experienced or even heard of before. It seemed to her only a unique breed of human was capable of these things on such a large scale.

She remembered what the woman had said to the guards, the night before, as she struggled to free Cameron; and the way the nurse's spine had seemed to bend instead of break when Elizabeth struck her with the bedpan. She remembered the girl, whom she had thought a friend. There had been something strange about that girl, something that made the memories so familiar...

"Maybe they aren't people," she managed. The fear she felt was becoming stronger, but she kept it defiantly at bay. "Just tell me for God's sake."

Cameron sighed deeply. "This is what I mean," he said, "that's *like* something Maria would say, but at the same time, it's not. And last night. That kind of... rogue plan, breaking me out with no idea of where to go next, that's not the Maria I know."

"Why not? Sure it was... bold, but I was bold when I was Maria! And besides, I had to do something, I had a vision that we needed to leave, right away."

"You had a vision?"

"Yes!" She almost yelled it. How could he claim that she wasn't Maria? She loved him. Had married him, was going to bear him children and... he couldn't deny her now.

He considered for a moment. "Still. You're not Maria, you're..."

"Look," Elizabeth was suddenly dealing with a desperate need to cry as well as her fear and didn't think she could handle both at once, "just... tell me about the ghosts."

"They're artificial. Mechanical. Like the things you told me about when you were telling me about Elizabeth's life."

For a moment she was breathless. "They're machines."

"Yes."

"Are you telling me that they're artificial intelligence?"

Cameron considered the question for a moment. "Yes, their intelligence is artificial. But their memories are not. The foreigners that settled here originally, up the coast, developed a method of removing memories from the dead and into mechanical bodies."

Elizabeth just stared at him. She was too surprised to respond.

The nurse's papers. Transplant. The host is ready for transplant. They were going to turn me into a ghost.

"Something went wrong with their... inventions. Instead of living eternally as machines, the ghosts were entirely different beings from the people who created them. Their actions still appeared complex and natural, but they acted out of mental habit. Programmed."

"Of course," she murmured. "Of course, they don't have judgment! Instead of making decisions the way humans do, they would make decisions based on the kinds of decisions that they made before, as humans; based on the mental habits of the humans that they had been. Which means that they would appear to be human..."

"Exactly."

"They spent their lives building machines to try and live forever. Wasted their lives, and didn't even think of the consequences..."vb

"How could they?" Cameron spat, "all they cared about was themselves. Their own lives. They didn't even care enough about their own *children* to think before they acted. The ghosts killed all of the settlers. Even the children. Took their memories and made machines with their thoughts, that looked like them."

Elizabeth was silent. She watched the man she had crossed centuries and risked her life for, fuming with a cankerous resentment in the growing light.

"It was machines, then, who killed us. Who made our land desolate."

He nodded, silently. She could see angry tears welling in his eyes.

"That was thousands of years ago, Cameron. How could those same machines still be here, now?"

"The machines bear the memories of the people they are imitations of. They hold the knowledge to create more like them."

"But still! How could they just have been... left? Allowed to terrorize and murder and destroy for so long? What about the foreigners, who..." Elizabeth trailed off.

"What?"

Elizabeth gulped. "It's something Dinky said. I asked about settlements and colonies here, in the past. He said that the indigenous people murdered and cannibalized the innocent settlers; that they were supernatural, half-animals ..."

"That's a lie!" Cameron roared.

"Yes, it's a lie and we know better. But all of the people back where I - I mean, where Elizabeth comes from, they think it's the truth. Even if they think that witches and faeries are just myths, they believe that the Wild Land is dangerous and that the indigenous people here are... less. Less than human."

"This doesn't make any sense."

Elizabeth shook her head. "It doesn't seem possible that no one would find out what happened to the colonists, all that time ago. Right?"

"Yes. The settlers themselves must have had family and friends that they left behind, who would want to know how they were doing."

"Not just that," Elizabeth crinkled her brow in concentration, "think of Rivertown. The first people sent were government workers. Peacekeepers. Because governments run colonies and settlements, not just the people. The settlers' government must have known, must have found out about the ghosts."

"They would have seen the terrible evil that the colonists had created."

"Yes, they would have. Not at first, maybe, but once they realized how murderous these... things were, they would have known that such an experiment could not be repeated. Which is why they never would have told anyone what happened. Eventually, the people would forget and the story would change: there had never been a colony, or a settlement. Just trading posts."

"Until now," Cameron said, darkly.

Elizabeth nodded. "Either that, or they're running their own experiments and have been ever since they found the machines."

"What do you mean?"

"It's funny, I just have a feeling. Like... from someone else. About Rivertown and the ghosts. Hunches that I feel like I have evidence for locked away somewhere."

"Of course you do, if you have some of Maria in you."

Elizabeth stared at Cameron.

"Don't you remember? Elder Jared's training, all of the hours you spent meditating and in contemplation. You were going to be our leader, once Jared decided you were ready and passed the responsibility to you. Your connection with the thought of the creator has always been strong; you told me yourself that tho thought of the creator is simply creation. God, Maria... you had such a beautiful, strange mind." Cameron looked away from her then and pressed his hand into his eyes, trying to hold back tears.

"That's why you think I'm not really her," she said, trying to hold back her own.

He nodded wearily.

"It's just that I can't remember everything yet! Listen, I feel that... that they knew. They knew about the ghosts and decided to leave them. Isolate them on our continent and see what happened. See if they really would live forever; or something like that. Then it gets fuzzy. Maybe... because everyone forgot. The foreigners – Elizabeth's people – they see time as different. They view the past as regressive, in order to justify progress. I remember learning about what you and I would call Elizabeth's forbears. She was taught to see herself as fundamentally different from them. Every new technology, no matter how superficial, is considered an advancement. We never asked what we were advancing towards."

"What happened next?" Cameron asked.

Elizabeth gulped, thinking hard, trying to concentrate on the slippery, bright feeling of knowing that seemed to fill her when she thought hard about this. It was unlike anything she had experienced before, except for a few fuzzy memories from her life as Maria. She hoped that as she relearned this strange skill - if she could call it that - she would be able to remember more. Somehow, she had to prove to Cameron that she was Maria. Otherwise, she knew he could never love her the way that she loved him.

"It's... because, thought is expended energy, right? But energy expended is never lost, it is just transformed and...and...everything is connected, right? Is that how I'm doing this?"

Cameron smiled. It was the first smile he had given her since the escape. "That's right. You explained that to me when I first met you. When we were first falling in love." Cameron cleared his throat. "Maria. When I first met Maria."

"Right," she said, trying to hide her disappointment, "Well the next thing I... feel, is connected to something Dinky said. He said that there was a research station, near Rivertown Centre, for a few hundred years. They were looking for minerals and other resources, trying to make the next great discovery. And the statues. They've been studied and photographed for ages.

"I'm not sure if the researchers knew about the ghosts. It's too fuzzy. The knowledges of the past are always doubted, ridiculed even and in their eyes, the knowledge of the ghosts would have been ancient history. I think... I think the ghosts may have killed them. The researchers. And then replaced them with ghosts that looked like them, then sent them back, to encourage a permanent settlement. Rivertown."

"What do you think they're going to do?" Cameron asked.

"I don't know. I can't tell. But I don't think that the boys we left behind are leaving Rivertown alive."

Cameron nodded, sadly. "Your cousin is there."

"Yeah, he is. Which means we have to rescue him."

Elizabeth thought of Dinky and hard panic rose at the thought of losing him.

"We have to rescue all of them, just like I rescued you. I'm not letting them get killed."

Cameron sighed, then scratched his neck.

"Wait," she said, suddenly, "are you saying that you think we are... machines?"

"How else?" the anger she had seen turned to pain, "how else could we be here?"

"Cameron, I did it! I did an... *Untura*. It means connection. The Ibers taught it to me. They said they didn't know if there was enough magic left, enough life left in the Earth and air for it to work. But it did! And now, we have a second chance!"

"You did it?" He looked skeptical.

She nodded excitedly.

"A second chance at what?"

"That I don't know," she said, clearing her throat. "All I know is that it has something to do with fulfilling our destiny. Other than that, I can't exactly remember how I did it. Or why. Sorry."

Cameron stared at her. After a long moment of silence, his mouth dropped open. "Are you kidding me?" he cried.

"No. But I did say I'm sorry."

Cameron shook his head. "Great," he muttered.

Chapter Forty Nine

Cameron stretched and crawled to the front of the cave. Elizabeth was left to make her way to a sitting position on her own. The movement elicited rebellion from muscles she hadn't even known she possessed. Propping herself up also reignited the pounding in her head. Now that they had escaped Rivertown, she wasn't sure how much farther she would be able to go. This didn't stop her, of course, from depositing her things back into the still-damp sheet that constituted a purse, donning it and crawling, slowly, to the front of the cave after Cameron.

He was sitting with his legs drawn up to his chest, on the lip of the cave, watching the sun rise over the creek and ravine below. Even from behind and in such a pose of exhaustion, he looked heroic to Elizabeth.

"Let me guess," she said, plopping herself down. She knew that she looked ungraceful despite her attempts at a poise that had been second nature to Maria, "Maria would know exactly what the *untura* was, how she had done it, how to do it again if necessary and what to do now. Right?"

Cameron glanced at her, his face bathed in the soft pink light of an early summer morning. He studied her for a long time and a gentle smile tickled the edges of his mouth.

"It's still really early," he said absently, "It's almost midsummer, so night is only going to be a few hours long."

She nodded, swinging her legs over the lip of the cave and letting them dangle towards the shallow creek below.

Cameron cleared his throat, something she only now remembered was characteristic of him when he had something important to say and didn't quite know how to say it. He swung his legs over the edge, like her and pursed his lips.

"Listen, I'm sorry about before, this is all just confusing and it's harder when the lines between then and now aren't even clear and - "

"Cameron. Listen. I just remembered something. Something about you. I thought I had remembered everything about you; it started with your hands and then how we first made love and then so many other things but just now, when you cleared your throat, I remembered that's something you do when you have something important to say. I'm right, aren't I?"

He nodded.

"Which means that, even though I don't remember everything right now, I'm still remembering things, getting new memories. Believe me, I already feel like I'm entirely Maria, even though, somehow, I'm still Elizabeth, too. But if I can remember *that*, then maybe I can remember the *untura* and what we're supposed to do and everything else. Right?"

"Yeah, that makes sense. That's great news."

"Also," she said, feigning seriousness and deep thought, "I've decided to forgive you." She awarded him with a dazzling smile that she knew was all Elizabeth. Maybe she wasn't exactly as he remembered her, but she felt that she was more... deeply herself than she had ever been as Elizabeth or Maria alone. A truer version of the eternal fragment in her, the splinter that could communicate with the thought of the creator. If he truly loved her, then he would love her now even more than he had before. It felt as if she had found a piece of herself that had been missing, like she was finally the complete whole of two halves. Elizabeth and Maria.

"This is an odd question," Cameron said, "but... what should I call you?"

She smiled. "It's funny you should ask, I was just thinking about that. You were right, before. I'm not Maria. Not the way that you knew her. I should say that I'm not *just* Maria. And I'm not just Elizabeth, either. But at the same time, I don't think that I'm just a combination of the two. It's more like... one is my left leg, the other is my right leg."

Cameron continued to stare at the horizon. She could see that the knowledge hurt him, somewhat. It meant that *his* Maria was gone. But he sighed, then smiled. "Something else, then. Something a bit more all encompassing."

"I'm not sure if that's entirely possible," she said, smiling back.

"Why don't I just call you... 'Hey, you!'"

They both laughed.

"Why don't you call me honey. Like you used to." She turned to him then, eyes wide and tender. It was a big request and she knew it. For him, it must have felt like he and Maria had been together only days before. Could he possibly accept her the way she was now?

"I'll try." he said.

They smiled at each other as the sun finally breached the horizon and true daylight illuminated their faces, slanting through the trees. Elizabeth felt her cheeks growing warm from the light and from Cameron's gaze. In her mind, he had never looked so handsome. More than handsome – he was so beautiful it made her ache. She laid her hand over his, on the ground between them and ran her thumb over his fingers. A shock ran through her, from the tips of her fingers to the ends of her toes and back again. She couldn't believe how much she wanted him.

Cameron jerked away from her so vigorously that he slid out of the cave. His arms shot out, one wind-milling and the other grabbing uselessly at the air near the cliff wall, while his feet slid precariously down the loose shale towards the creek. When he finally regained his balance, he tried to act as if nothing had happened, leaning against the cliff wall with his still-outstretched hand as if it had been what he intended. Elizabeth gazed at him questioningly.

"Breakfast!" he exclaimed. His voice cracked, just barely.

Elizabeth blinked at him, still confused. Had her small physical advance really been so... disturbing? It was almost too much: to have him so close, alone, the way he smelled; to be hyper aware of every single detail of his almost-too-sexy person and have him suddenly get cold feet! She didn't know how she would function without making love with him that very instant.

"Breakfast," he repeated, forcing his voice to stay steady. "We need to eat, before we do anything else. Do you remember what's edible?"

"I think so," she said, easing herself down the cliff after him. It was a mistake. Her head pounded and her knees buckled beneath her. She tried to keep herself up but the sorely overused muscles in her legs and back were like cloth that had already been stretched to the limit. The exertion of trying to stay upright caused the cloth to rip. Elizabeth folded like laundry, her legs splashing into the water as her behind hit the hard rock of the curved cliff. She swore loudly.

"Are you alright?" Cameron was standing in the water now, halfway to the other bank and looked unsure of what to do.

"I'm fine," she muttered, trying to get to her foot.

"Stay here," Cameron said, "I'll get some things for breakfast. You get some rest and try to figure out what we should do next."

Chapter Fifty

Elizabeth sat propped up with her back against the cave wall and her makeshift pack under her knees, watching Cameron moving swiftly through the forest across the creek. He collected early season honeyberries, tender young dandelion leaves, ripe blue juniper berries and firm, dew-covered mushrooms. He was even picking petals from some of the flowers to flavor their fare. Elizabeth heard her stomach rumble and felt like she was about to drool.

No drooling, she thought, *I've got to come up with a plan. What are we going to do?*

She closed her eyes and allowed herself one short moment of imagining what she wanted – then forced them back open and had to wipe a hand across her mouth, as she had begun to drool in earnest. This was no time for fantasies. She had to face the reality of their situation: she was still severely injured, they were in terrible danger, they had an extremely important mission to accomplish and best of all, she had no idea what that was.

She wasn't any closer to figuring out what they should do next.

Cameron crossed the creek, back to their little cave and dropped his harvest on the cave entrance floor beside her. She thanked him and they ate in silence, each deep in thought.

"Cameron?"

"Yeah."

"What would you say is... your destiny? Or, your purpose? On the Earth?"

Cameron cleared his throat and puffed his shoulders gently. "Well, that's a good question. Before the ghosts came, it was very simple. My purpose was to transform creation to paradise, just as every person's purpose is. That is what we were created for, at least, that's what we believed."

"I remember that," she murmured, finishing her breakfast, "but I'm not sure I fully understand."

"It's just like this breakfast. The creator provided the perfect combination of nutrients that we need, as well as pleasing forms and tastes and textures for their delivery and a beautiful forest in which they grow. That's perfect. But it still isn't paradise."

"Why not?"

He considered for a moment. "Because we were created to be creators ourselves. I chose certain things and put them together – with love – to create a delicious meal for us."

Elizabeth watched him thoughtfully.

"The Earth is already perfect; infinitely complex and almost infinitely able to support itself. It's always changing, always cycling. Our part in that is to imbue creation with love and kindness."

"The pecan tree..." Elizabeth whispered.

"You remember! Yes. You and your grandfather planted that pecan tree together, in the berry patch. Each berry bush and the sapling itself, were already perfect in that they were the manifestation of the creator's thought. By planting them together and tending them with kindness, affection and forethought to the benefit of all that would encounter them, you and your grandfather helped to create a piece of paradise."

"Because then, that spot was imbued with our love for each other and all that would come there, all of the future generations and our friends and family and not just with the thought of the creator."

"Right. To surround others with love, using the knowledge and skills that are inherent to us and to build the world around those we love in a way that will make them happy. Imagine a perfect language. One that could capture the profound in every heartbeat, every detail of every moment, the transcendent flow of time and the interconnectedness of all living and unliving things. This is the language that the creator gave to us - the poets of the universe. The words are already there, in sound, smell, colour, taste and the spirits of every living thing. We connect them with our empathy to make the world into poetry.

"Or, imagine that humanity are the painters and the creator provided not just a living canvas, but colours so perfect that they could capture light, sound, space... divine cycles of the world. No matter how such things are organized, they will be beautiful. But inside each of us is a spark of creativity unlike any that has come before. In every act of our lives, we can paint a new picture for the Earth, as it were."

"Huh." It was all Elizabeth could manage. "It's just... I remember thinking, when I did the *untura*, that we would have a second chance at fulfilling our destiny on earth, or something like that. If we can figure out what *that* means, then we can figure out what we need to do."

Cameron smiled gently. "It seems to me like there isn't too much figuring out that we need to do. The ghosts are a terrible threat to every creature they encounter, especially other humans. They are the antithesis of what we were talking about, of what humanity is. They are destructive, they don't evolve. There is no place for purely destructive force on the Earth. Everything must fit into the cycles of rebirth and the ghosts do not." He paused and munched on a root melancholically.

"... and if they *do* make copies of the peacekeepers, there will be hundreds of ghosts going back to their homeland and then being sent to all corners of the world to police other colonies and settlements."

Elizabeth nodded, slowly. "You want to stop them."

"Yes. The only question now is how we're going to do that."

Cameron smiled suddenly and shook his head.

"What?" she asked.

"It's something that Elder Jared said, when we thought you were dead, after you were kidnapped. I don't know how, but I think he *knew* everything that was going to happen. He said that you were special and that you and I would fight the ghosts. He said that a machine that isn't useful should be dismantled, or destroyed. Machines are only useful as much as they help us fulfill our destiny.

"We have to find a way to destroy the ghosts."

Chapter Fifty One

"Where could she have gone?"

Mark sat on the steps leading up into the Centre, beside Stephanie. She had been awake, when they finally released him from questioning in the infirmary, some time after dawn. He wasn't sure what had woken her so early, or how she knew. She simply said, "It's Elizabeth, isn't it. Tell me everything."

He had.

It wasn't that Elizabeth had been acting strange, exactly. Just... a bit different. But that was normal, he thought, they were in a new place, doing new things and most of all, Elizabeth had been dreaming of travel and doing something globally important like peacekeeping since anyone could remember. The Chief and the doctor had shaken Mark roughly awake sometime in the night and dragged him to the infirmary, where they locked him a small room and questioned him about Elizabeth for hours. He admitted that something hadn't felt exactly right, ever since they got to Rivertown, but to him it had made sense. Was she distracted - yeah, but she was falling in love with Dinky. Did she have strange dreams - well yes, but they were in a new place, so of course she would. Did she act out of character - she cried yesterday, but that's just because she hit her head so hard!

Finally, he had refused to answer any more questions until they told him what was going on and if she was alright. They avoided telling him anything for some time... until they realized that nothing short of torture would force him to continue without knowledge of his cousin's wellbeing. Apparently she was legally in his care, as an unmarried woman and next of kin – that's what they told him. They told him that Elizabeth had assaulted a nurse, nearly killing her. That she had kidnapped Will, right after testing had determined that he was critically ill and would need steady treatments in order to survive; and that she had run away, taking Will with her.

"I mean," Mark ran his hand through his hair, so tired he could barely think but miles away from sleeping, "she could barely stand up yesterday.

She was in real rough shape. What coulda got in her head? How *could* she'a done it?"

"I don't know, Mark. I'm sorry." Stephanie bit her lip, studying the broad shouldered, deeply tanned boy next to her. He sat hunched over, looking at the ground between his feet. His eyes were glassy with worry and exhaustion. Stephanie reached over, tentatively and placed her hand on Mark's thigh. "Did they say anything else? Did she... take anything?"

"No. They said that's why they were asking me all that stuff, to see if I might have any idea of what would make her do it."

"But you don't."

"I don't." Mark sighed deeply and looked at the slender, feminine hand resting on his thigh. He gave a small start and stared at it for a moment. Then, carefully, he put his own hand on top of it and gently squeezed the small, blistered fingers in his own.

They sat in silence for a moment, watching the sunrise.

"Was there anything else? Did they ask you anything else?" Stephanie whispered.

"Yeah. This is the weirdest part. They started asking me stuff about myself, about what I had written in my application file a year back and the names of my brothers and cousins and where I went to school and stuff. Weird little details that only I would know."

Stephanie's eyes went momentarily wide. "Why? Do they think you're some kind of imposter?"

"Yeah. They thought so. I answered all the questions right, of course and they left it at that."

Stephanie relaxed visibly. "Do they think that... I mean, what if the stories about witches are true? What if when we got here... what if Elizabeth was an imposter?"

Mark looked at her sharply. The thought had clearly not occurred to him. He shrugged, then shook his head. "She couldn't be. I know Dizzy and that was her."

"What do we do now?"

Mark was quiet for a long time before he answered, looking out to the horizon, over the hills of grasses and shrubs and trees as they were illuminated with the first light of dawn. Finally, he turned to Stephanie. She was watching him and could tell by the sheen of sweat across his brow and the minute trembling in his fingers, still clasping hers, that he was very upset. She opened her mouth, ready to say whatever came to her that might help comfort him, but she didn't have the chance. Mark leaned towards her, placing the fingers of his free hand on her face and kissed her. He pulled back, traced her cheek as lightly as he could and studied her nervously to see if he had gone too far. She smiled, so he kissed her again. And again. He wrapped his arms around her and kissed her nose and cheeks and eyelids.

It felt like a moment, but they realized that they had been lost for some time when they heard the first stirrings of morning in the Barracks. The sun was already well on its way across the sky. Mark pulled back first, his lips red and swollen. Stephanie looked at him, expectantly, so he cleared his throat and said, "I really like you, Steph."

Stephanie broke into a smile, blushed and bobbed her head. "Good," she said, "that's settled. Now all we have to do is think of a plan to find Dizzy."

Chapter Fifty Two

"She *what*?" Dinky had been getting dressed and dropped his shirt on the floor.

"Dinky, keep it down, we don't want everyone buzzin' about this 'til the Chief decides to tell everybody..."

"Keep it down?" Dinky sputtered, "are you kidding me? She's gone. Just like that, she's gone? And kidnapped someone? And... attacked a nurse?!" Dinky shoved his hands through his hair, looking up and blinking hard. It looked like he was about to cry. "I don't understand. I just don't understand. She could barely *stand up* yesterday. Was she faking it?"

"I don't know what to tell ya, Dink." Mark said. "I'm as torn up as you are."

"It doesn't make *sense*, Mark! Come on, use your head! She was too hurt for that. She was too hurt to... walk across the room, let alone attack or kidnap anybody and you know it!"

"That's true, Dinky, but it doesn't make her any less gone -"

"Would you fucking listen to me!"

Several of the boys nearby turned to look. Dinky took a deep breath, then went on, more quietly. "Something isn't right here. It doesn't fit. What they're saying Dizzy did... it's impossible. Physically, literally. She couldn't have done it."

"What are you saying?"

"They're lying to you! They're lying! Wherever Elizabeth is, she did *not* kidnap anyone last night. She couldn't have! Something is *wrong*."

Mark studied his friend, brow knit. "You might be right," he said, miserably. "Look. All I care about is gettin' that girl to safety. Me 'n Steph, we're gonna find her and make sure she's ok. Are you in?"

"Of course I am," Dinky said. *I love her.*

"Good. Because wherever Dizzy is, she's -"

"A witch!" The chief's voice boomed through the hall. The boys and Stephanie, in various stages of undress turned in unison to look at him. He stood with his megaphone thrust at them like a gun, at the door to the infirmary. "A witch among us!" He exclaimed again.

"What the hell is this?" Dinky said. Mark's mouth hung open.

The Chief continued: "Last night, Elizabeth Walker, who had been faking illness to avoid detection, assaulted a nurse in the infirmary, nearly killing her. She then kidnapped William McDonald, who had just been diagnosed with a highly contagious and dangerous brain disease during his preliminary treatments and disappeared with him into the night."

There was a moment of silence as the Chief let what he had said sink in. Mark and Dinky stood watching hm in shocked silence and disbelief. The boys around them were milling around uneasily, murmuring to each other.

"What I'm about to tell you is highly classified information. Here in Rivertown, we are at the edge of the world. We are the frontier between the savagery of an untamed world and the order and security of humanity. And at such frontiers, we will encounter the things that dwell in between. We must be able to deal with those abominations. Elizabeth Walker is a witch."

"What is he talkin' about?" Mark whispered to Dinky.

"He's proving my point, Mark."

"You may question my words now. You may be asking yourselves if your Chief has gone slightly mad. Witchcraft is a legend, not a reality! It *is* a legend. But it is one based on fact, as so many legends are. Some say that the Ethos are a legend! But walk just half an hour to the sea and you'll see them making their stand against eternity in human form, with your own eyes."

Some of the boys nodded carefully at this.

"Witches have existed in this place for millennia. Instead of setting order to the chaos of the world, they embrace the darkness and danger of wild forests. They eat raw plants, where they grow. Did we not see Elizabeth Walker do the same thing?"

This time, many of the boys nodded. Word of Elizabeth's strange affinity for the foreign Honeyberry had apparently spread very quickly.

"She didn't even wash the berries!" someone cried.

The Chief nodded, seriously. "Witches deny what it is to be human. They deny the very Ethos of humanity and instead, live entirely through their physical bodies, like animals. You may think this strange, but still wonder what the danger is to others. There is a danger. A very real one. First of all, we don't know exactly how she kidnapped William. It's possible that some of you were exposed to his illness when she took him from solitary confinement. We will be monitoring you and may need to run tests or isolate some of you, for your own safety.

"Secondly, it is my sad duty to inform you that each and every one of you is in serious danger of being deceived by Elizabeth Walker and even of having her bewitch you into believing or doing things against your will and better judgment. This danger is especially real to those close to her. We should all be aware of this danger. Witches do not care about order or progress or the safety of others. They care only about their immediate, impulsive needs and desires. The Elizabeth Walker that many of you knew and even grew up with, is gone. Somehow, the Ethos that comprise her spirit have been corrupted. There is nothing we can do to help her. All that we can do is try to protect ourselves and this community." He paused, and waggled the megaphone at them menacingly.

"But part of our community is missing. William Mcdonald has been kidnapped and is in need of life-saving medical treatment that can only be administered here at the Centre. Rest assured that we will find him and bring him home to safety. There will be two shifts of daily search parties in the surrounding area."

The Chief continued on for some time about their other tasks for the coming days - digging, laying foundations, construction. Many of the boys had direct experience with this kind of labour and none were uncomfortable with it. Dinky and Mark stood side by side, for the remainder of the Chief's speech, dumbstruck and barely listening.

"Do you believe me now?" Dinky whispered, after some time.

"Yeah, I do," Mark said. "They're lying alright. No way Dizzy's a witch. She's too much of a boy to be a witch."

"No one's going to listen to us, now. They'll all think we've been bewitched, if we try and defend her. And did you hear what he said about solitary confinement and isolation?"

Mark nodded.

"We are in serious danger, Mark."

Chapter Fifty Three

"Anything?"

Elizabeth scrunched her nose up and opened one eye to look at Cameron. "No," she said and closed her eye again.

He rapped his fingers against his knee impatiently.

"This is really hard, you know," she grumbled.

"Maybe you should take a break."

Elizabeth sighed loudly and opened both eyes. It was for the best, all of that concentrating was giving her another headache.

"I just don't know if this is going to work. I've never... done this before. Sure, I remember meditation and telepathy and stuff from when I was Maria, but it still feels pretty foreign to Elizabeth's brain matter."

Cam nodded. "Alright. I understand. We can try again later."

"Sure. I'm sorry."

"Hey..." Cameron smiled at her. "Don't be sorry. This is hard enough as it is. I just thought that if you could listen in to what was happening in Rivertown, we might get a better idea of what to do."

They needed a better idea. Actually, they needed any idea. The sun was climbing through morning and they were still at the cave, trying to decide what to do next. They were vastly outnumbered, unarmed and Elizabeth figured it likely that most of the peacekeepers wouldn't believe her or rally against their Chief without serious proof. How they would even hope to approach Rivertown without being taken and killed was a mystery. But how they would convincingly explain to the peacekeepers that their wills were being subsumed by two thousand year old machines, and then lead a rebellion against a considerable number of durable, intelligent and armed robots seemed like suicide.

"I guess we'll just have to do it the old fashioned way," Elizabeth said, with a sigh.

Cameron chuckled. "Telepathy *is* the 'old fashioned way'. Journeying, seeking, meditation... whatever you want to call it, it's some of the oldest foundations of every culture in our land as far as we knew, when we were alive."

There was an uncomfortable silence. *When we were alive.* Elizabeth still didn't know what to make of it.

Cameron chuckled unexcpectedly and went on. "Is that saying an example of Elizabeth's culture's strange obsession with progress?"

"I guess so," Elizabeth said, laughing as well. It wasn't funny and they both knew it. They should be moving, should be making a plan, but didn't have the know-how to do either. They'd been set a hopeless goal by a desperate medicine woman in the last moments of her life, ages before. Still, Elizabeth was so happy to be with Cameron that she was almost giddy. The constant smile on his face told her that he felt the same way.

"What *is* the old-fashioned way, anyways?" he asked.

"You know, riding up in armour on proud steeds and jousting. Or dressing up as someone else and slipping poison into someone's mead."

"No offence, but your culture is sort of screwed up. Mead is delicious."

"Oh, Mr. High and Mighty with your perfect, ancient ways! That's rude, you know."

"Well at least we have a plan now. We'll dress up, sneak into Rivertown and poison the Chief's mead. Except that he's a machine, so who knows if that will work."

They were sitting side by side now, on the lip of their small cave overlooking the river, in the warm sun. It felt so good to laugh together again. That's how they had spent so much of their time together - laughing. It reminded Elizabeth of the many days and nights they had spent building their love for each other. Through laughter, through the creation of their piece of paradise, through sharing a bed... the giddiness increased exponentially. She was forgetting everything about their situation except the fact that he was right here, right next to her. His closeness was intoxicating and her whole body was tingling and warm.

They continued to giggle, staring at each other. Elizabeth's heart was pounding painfully in her throat. Was he going to kiss her? Finally? After literally thousands of years of waiting, she didn't know if she could wait anymore. He didn't move forward, didn't move at all. Just sat there, smiling, as she knew she was.

Without taking her eyes off of him, she whispered, "what are we going to dress up us?"

He maneuvered his facial features into a thoughtful expression. "Hmmm..." His gaze was flitting between her eyes, taking her in. Elizabeth had never felt so at peace, so entirely present in the moment. The sound of the water, the sunlight on her skin and her life-long companion next to her to share the moment. A gentle breeze rustled through the trees on the other side of the creek and brushed past them, enveloping them in the scents of early summer flowers from the plains beyond.

This is what it needs to feel like, she thought lazily, thinking of her difficulty concentrating only a few moments before, *in order to journey.*

Suddenly, Elizabeth saw and smelled and heard and felt something else. She was suddenly in a different place. She knew, somehow, that it was the same time and nearby, too. It was a ravine, dry now but obviously a tributary from the hills somtime in the past. Craggy walls covered in thick, evergreen forest climbed dizzyingly up three sides. The fourth, following the old, zig-zagging riverbed down and into the plains, provided an almost uninterrupted view of Rivertown and the space between there and here... *wherever here was.* It was shady, testament to the high walls that offered protection from the elements and from detection. The wind was cool and smelled of high places, deep and fragrant.

Elizabeth wasn't alone. She could... *feel* voices. At first, it was a jumble of them, too many to discern what they were saying. Where were these people, all whispering, all at once?

"There's someone here." Elizabeth heard the whisper and spun around to see who had spoken. It was a little girl, black smeared around her eyes, wearing a simple cotton dress and a scarf over her hair. Both the dress and the scarf were the grey colour of un-dyed cotton. The girl was looking straight at Elizabeth, tugging on her mother's sleeve. Her mother was foraging; digging around a dandelion to collect its sustaining roots, probably to make a warm drink for her daughter. Maria had loved that drink, as a child. As an adult, during her village's exodus, she had made it in the evenings for the children. It kept them healthy and helped them sleep.

"Be quiet!" the woman hissed, half turning to address her daughter. Elizabeth only saw the woman's profile, but still recognized her. She had been one of the stall attendants, in Rivertown Market.

"Where am I?" Elizabeth asked.

The little girls' eyes grew wide when Elizabeth spoke. She tugged more fervently at her mother's sleeve, desperate to get her attention but unwilling to make a sound after her admonition. The woman seemed not to have heard Elizabeth, or to have noticed her at all.

Elizabeth walked forward. It was a strange sensation - she could feel the earth against her bare feet, but looking down, she saw not feet nor legs nor any other part of her body.

I'm journeying, she thought, *I did it.*

The little girl was clearly terrified. She huddled against her mother's crouched form as Elizabeth approached. "It's alright," Elizabeth said. "I won't hurt you. I'm here to help. I'm from..." Elizabeth thought for a moment, feeling around for the whispers of thought that she had heard in her mind when she first arrived in this ravine, "I'm from the Old Times. Before the ghosts. I come from the Northlands, in the mountains. Do you know what *untura* is?"

The girl nodded, almost imperceptibly. Her little mouth was hanging open with innocent amazement."

"Good. Then you understand how I come to be here, now. Don't you?"

The girl nodded again.

"I'm here to destroy the ghosts."

The girls' eyes opened so wide that the whites showed all the way around.

"How?" she whispered.

Her mother turned to her, sharply, then grumbled and continued her work.

"Your mother can't see me?" The girl shook her head. "I think that means you are a medicine woman. Is this true?"

The girl shrugged. She looked surprised by the question.

"Do your people still practice the old ways?"

The girl looked side long at her mother, then bit her lip. She wanted to answer, but didn't want to upset her mother.

"It's alright, don't answer now. Just tell me: were you in Rivertown?"

The girl shook her head, no.

"But your mother was?" She nodded, yes.

"So you were... hiding?" Yes again. Elizabeth paused to think. The woman had gone to Rivertown but left her daughter in hiding. They must have known that something terrible would happen. But then, why would they have come at all? Elizabeth closed her eyes and concentrated hard. She felt nothing at first, then the cacophony of whispered thoughts and finally clarity: she could feel the anxiety and frustration of the woman crouched in front of her. Taste the bitter spring from which it flowed.

"They... force your people to go places; work, build things. Sometimes they take people, take them away on boats. Right?" the girl nodded again. "But always, people stay hidden. They try to. They hide their children. Right? And your people... they are the last. The last left on this continent. Right?" Another nod. It made sense - there hadn't been any children in Rivertown and now, Elizabeth knew why. "Will your mother go back to Rivertown?" The girl shrugged. She didn't know.

Elizabeth closed her eyes to focus in again on the woman's thoughts. It was extremely difficult; her mind felt like an unwieldy sledgehammer. She couldn't focus in on one thing only, instead felt and saw a jumble of memories, feelings, experiences. And it didn't feel right, to look in at the woman's thoughts that way. Elizabeth opened her eyes, turning away from the woman's mind. When she did, she found that the little girl in front of her had scrunched her face up in extreme concentration. Suddenly, Elizabeth heard the girls' voice, ringing clearly in the forest around them, but her mouth didn't move.

"Can you hear me?" she asked. Her voice was high and small.

"Yes, I can hear you."

"Does that mean that I'm... a medicine woman?"

"I think it does. Is there someone here who can train you?"

The girl shook her head. "They kill our leaders."

"I'll train you," Elizabeth said. The girls' face lit up and she regretted the promise immediately. How could she offer anything to this child, when she knew that the chances of delivering were so low?

"I don't know if my mama is going to Rivertown or not," the girl said.

'They will come, if some don't go back, so some must. That way, the children can stay hidden and if we are hidden, then we're safer. If they comen looking, they will find us eventually. We must do what they say and they say to go back. Mama wants to stay with me, here, but she may have to go. The ghosts don't care about who comes. They care about the number. Sometimes they ask for certain people and sometimes, we send others in disguise. You know, dressed up."

Elizabeth's mouth fell open. That was it. That was how they would get into Rivertown. She was so surprised that her concentration faltered and she found herself immediately back at the cave, sitting beside Cameron. He was watching her, thoughtfully.

She was out of breath, disoriented and somewhat afraid.

"Don't worry, it'll get easier. You'll get used to it, learn to control it."

Elizabeth nodded and smoothed the hair back from her face as she caught her breath. Then she looked Cameron in the eyes, the playfulness of their flirtations gone.

"I know what we're going to dress up as."

Chapter Fifty Four

"What did you see?"

"I saw the coal eyes - the Ibers. They're hiding in a ravine in the hills to the west. I spoke with a girl there -"

"Spoke with?" Cameron exclaimed. "How?"

Elizabeth shook her head. "There was a little girl who was very... intuitive. Connected. I don't know how I knew, but I told her right away that she was to be a medicine woman."

Cameron gulped audibly, the wagged his chin. "Go on. They're hiding from the ghosts?"

"Yes. They have been for centuries, I think. The ghosts use them as slaves, force them to work, to move around every few years. The girl said that if some from their camp don't go back to Rivertown, then the ghosts will come to find them. There are many more of them in hiding than the ghosts know about, including children. They can't risk losing this camp, or surrendering their children. Some of them *will* go back and soon, even though they know they may be killed or taken away on boats."

Elizabeth paused. This was the part that had occurred to her with such force that it caused the vision to end. It was insane and probably suicidal. But it seemed to her that it may be the only way back into Rivertown.

"The girl said that the ghosts don't often care about specific individuals, they just want numbers. Sometimes they ask for specific people and to avoid having to do as they ask, the Ibers... disguise themselves, sometimes, as each other. We could go and find them, dress up as Ibers ourselves and go with them to Rivertown."

Cameron had just inhaled and let all of the air in his lungs out through pursed lips in a long *hoosh*. Then he inhaled again, deeply and nodded. "Then, once we're in Rivertown, we..."

"Find allies. I know my cousin Mark will help us, he's a good man with a sense of honour. If it means protecting the other boys and helping me, he'll do whatever it takes."

"One ally isn't very many."

"There's also Dinky. My... friend. I think he'll help us, too. Ever since we first arrived, he knew something wasn't right in Rivertown, with the whole thing. He'll do what it takes."

"God willing, the others will follow their own survival instincts and help us, too."

"I don't think it's going to be that easy."

Cameron chuckled in spite of himself. "No, this definitely isn't going to be easy. Ok, we're in Rivertown, we have Mark and Pinky helping us -"

"Dinky."

"Mark and Dinky are helping us. Anyone else?"

"The Ibers, hopefully."

"Right. So we have a few scared and angry Ibers and two teenaged boys. Then what?"

Elizabeth cleared her throat and sat thinking in silence for some time. "I don't really know," she said, defeatedly.

"So our plan is to dress up as people that the ghosts are known for killing indiscriminately, trying to garner support for some sort of mutiny, assassination or escape without being detected and then... hoping for the best?"

"Yup, that's basically it."

There was a long moment of silence as they both considered the plan.

"Unless you can think of anything better, of course," Elizabeth added, diplomatically. Cameron's gaze shot up and caught hers in surprise. His eyebrows were raised, incredulously. When he realized that she was joking, he burst out laughing. Elizabeth started laughing, too.

When they finally regained control, tears streaming down their faces, Cameron shook his head. "No, I can't think of anything better. It's a good plan that needs work, I think. We'll have to... take things as they come. And we'll have to try and stay hidden when we're in Rivertown."

"But first, we're going to have to get the Ibers to agree to this," Elizabeth said.

"Do you think you could find the ravine they're hiding in?" Cameron asked.

"Yes, I think so. It's going to be a long ways to go."

Cameron studied Elizabeth for a long moment. "Are you sure about this? You're still injured."

Elizabeth grimaced as she slid off of her rump and onto her legs, easing from her perch on the cave lip to a standing position. The pain in her muscles was no longer quite as overwhelming as it had been a few hours before, but they still screamed in protest at the exertion required simply to hold herself upright. "Believe me, Cammy, I know."

Cameron's eyes softened immediately at his old nickname. "You remembered *Cammy.*"

"Of course! I always called you Cammy."

"Except when you were serious."

"Serious, or..." Elizabeth remembered the many times, hands wrapped in his hair, pulling him into her, that she had called him *Cameron,* over and over again, "Very serious."

Cameron jumped down from his own perch on the lip of the cave to stand in front of her. By the little smile that reached all the way to the creases of his eyes, she could tell that he remembered those particular occasions, too. "How much do you remember of that, exactly?" he asked.

The screaming in Elizabeth's muscles receded instantly into the background of her consciousness, where it remained like the blowing of the wind, white noise and nothing more. Cameron was standing less than a foot away from her. Her pulse was pounding in her ears, her chest and between her legs. The ache there was so intense that she had to stop herself from moaning. She thought of all the things that she remembered about the man standing so close to her – the way his skin felt against hers, the way his body looked under his clothes, only inches from her own, the way he tasted, the way he moved...

"I remember... down by the river, one warm afternoon. You had been working all day, building something on the other side of the village and I had been helping my grandfather to carry loads of flagstones for a path he wanted to build." Elizabeth closed her eyes for a moment, savoring the memory. It had been such a sensual day; the hot sun, the hotter breeze, the heavy work. "We both went to the river, to swim and cool off. I was on one side and you were on the other."

Cameron's smile had grown. By the way that his eyelids were only half open, Elizabeth knew that he remembered that day very well. She wondered if he would make love to her again, beside this creek. Her heart jumped around ecstatically at the thought. "I remember that day. We were both exhausted, thirsty. The water was cold and clear."

Elizabeth remembered the way the cold water had instantly revitalized her and shivered at the memory. It had made every hair stand on end when she splashed the water over herself. She had been the only one in sight, as the others were still working or had gone to a larger swimming hole upriver. She had undressed and was splashing herself, thigh deep in the ice-cold water, rubbing the dirt and dust and sweat away, when Cameron had slipped into the water on the opposite bank and come towards her.

"You snuck up on me," she whispered, taking a tiny step towards him. The space between them now was almost gone, but she still didn't dare touch him, in case he pushed her away. She wasn't entirely Maria, after all. "Came up behind me when I was bathing. All of a sudden, I had a hot mouth nibbling on the back of my neck."

"You tasted delicious," he murmured, reaching up to move her hair away and touch her neck, "all salty and warm."

"I remember feeling a certain part of your body press against the small of my back and being able to feel... your heart beat." Elizabeth paused. She could feel his heartbeat at that moment, too, pumping life to all parts of him as he stood with just a small sliver of air between them.

"This part?" he whispered. Then he pulled her face towards him, with the hand around her neck and pressed his lips against hers. The space between them disappeared as if they had been sucked towards each other. Now Elizabeth did moan, long and low into the kiss. First, his lips simply pressed against hers, both of them stopped as if too amazed to move. Then he wrapped his fingers into her hair and pulled her harder against him. She reached up and wound her arms around his back and shoulders. His kiss deepened, she could feel his heart beating wildly against her chest and her hands ran up and down his back, shoulders, arms. He felt so good, so familiar, almost exactly as she had remembered him.

Almost.

Cameron stopped and pulled a few inches away. His brow was furrowed and his eyes were large, searching her face.

"You felt it too?" she asked, after a moment, "just... a little bit different."

Cameron nodded. He cleared his throat and turned away from her. She couldn't believe that he was ending the moment, didn't know how she could continue to function with the desperate throbbing between her legs. The visible lump in his pants showed that he was just as aroused, but still he pulled away.

The pain in Elizabeth's body came flooding back, joined by the new and strange desolation of rejection. She turned away from Cameron, wiping at her mutinously leaky eyes with the back of her hand. After everything they had been through together - and then, after so much time apart - how could he push her away? They needed each other, loved each other! Elizabeth remembered him once saying that he thought they had been created for each other.

But it wasn't Elizabeth's memory, it was Maria's. Maybe Maria had been created for Cameron and maybe Elizabeth hadn't been. Elizabeth pressed the balls of her hands into her eyes. It was too confusing and her head was thrumming with renewed pain.

Cameron cleared his throat, still turned partly away from her and now standing in the river. "We should probably get going. Who knows how far it is to the Iber hide out, or when they're planning on going."

"Yeah. We should go." Just the words caused a rebellious scream of pain from her legs, but Elizabeth ignored it as best as she could and started to walk after Cameron. There was no other way, which meant that she just had to go and go and then keep going after that. At the moment, the prospect of crossing any kind of country - especially the hilly kind that lay between them and the Ibers - seemed absolutely impossible. She wondered if she could try and communicate with them through meditation again, but dismissed the idea almost immediately. Her old skills had become very rusty and she couldn't count on being able to control them.

"Which way?" Cameron asked.

Elizabeth closed her eyes, trying to concentrate. She remembered looking out from the hiding spot and seeing Rivertown and the ocean beyond, to the right. The creek valley, in which she and Cameron now stood, had been to the left and closer.

"We have to cross the creek again and head due West. Eventually we'll be able to see some hills. I think I'll be able to figure out where to go from there."

Cameron nodded silently and took the makeshift backpack from Elizabeth. Then he started off across the creek and to the West.

Chapter Fifty Five

An hour passed. Cameron and Elizabeth climbed through dense underbrush and thick forest, sticking to the creek as best they could so as not to lose what little sense of direction they had. It almost proved more difficult than it was worth. Craggy rocks jutted out of the earth where the creek had carved them away over the millennia, meaning they had to climb around the outcrops or over them. The sun continued to climb in an entirely cloudless sky and even in the shade, it was hot already at mid-morning.

Elizabeth was sweating profusely and intensely dizzy. She was tripping over small stones, exposed roots and even her own ankles, which were swollen from overuse and bug bitten. Worst of all was the persisting sense that she was floating, or disconnected from her body, because of the pain, exhaustion and the lingering concussion. It was like a thick, semi-transparent veil separated her consciousness from the world of physical obstacles around her.

She didn't complain, though. Cameron fared much better and let her walk in front so that she could set the pace and choose the trails. It was terrible to watch her overbalance and her steps falter over and over again. She also continually reached up and slapped herself lightly in the face, or rubbed furiously at one eye and then the other, as if trying to wake herself up. Finally, Cameron couldn't take any more of it. If they didn't stop, she would end up killing herself! How would she managed to make the trek to Rivertown, let alone participate in some sort of insurrection against the machines, in the state she was in? Especially without some rest now?

"Elizabeth, we should stop and take a break," he began, reaching out and touching her shoulder. She whipped around at his touch, wide-eyed and slapped her hand over his mouth. Her eyes were flying in every direction.

"Do you hear that?" she whispered.

"It was just me," he said, "I was saying we should take a break -"

"Sh!" Elizabeth clamped her hand over his mouth again. "Listen."

Cameron listened. Sure enough, after a moment, he could hear the faint crack of a twig being stepped on and broken some distance away. Elizabeth's hand moved from his mouth to his shoulder and hauled him down into a thick cedar bush. She arranged the branches above them for concealment, only a birds-eye view would betray their location. They crouched together, hunched and breathing shallowly.

They sat in silence, straining to hear another sound. Elizabeth's mind flashed with images of the commandos she and Mark had seen at Rivertown Centre the night of the storm. If those commandos were so close now that she could hear their steps on twigs in the forest, she and Cameron were likely done for. She squeezed her eyes shut, holding her breath and listening hard. Beside her, Cameron was still as a stone. His breathing, if he was breathing, was inaudible.

Finally, a young man's voice floated through the trees to them. "I think it was nothing."

A second boy replied, "I sure hope you're right. This place is spooky."

"We should check it out anyways," a third said, "Steph said that witches can hide real easy and we don't want to miss them."

A chorus of voices sounded agreement, though none sounded too eager. Elizabeth's mind was racing as she listened harder than ever. Stephanie had been saying that Elizabeth was a witch?

What in the hell was going on?

"Steph also said the witch could control our minds if we got too close," the first boy mumbled. His voice was quiet, tremulous and terrified.

"Doesn't change our orders." The third boy replied, "besides, that's just superstition."

"If it's superstition, then how come we're out here in the fucking Wild Land hunting a fucking witch? That's not superstition! We could die out here! This is fucking real life!"

Elizabeth wasn't sure which boy had burst out with that statement, because his voice was so overcome with emotion. Many of the others were now mumbling desultorily between each other. She and Cameron shared a disturbed glance.

"Come on! That's enough, men!" The third boy didn't exactly bellow, but his voice deepened with authority. Elizabeth pictured him puffing out his chest... "If that witch Elizabeth is here, we're going to find her! We cannot leave Will behind just because we're too scared to handle an animal woman!"

Just then, the air was split by the high, angry trilling sound of a brave squirrel announcing its territory to intruders. All of the boys jumped and one of them screamed. Cameron and Elizabeth could hear the rustle of branches as the squirrel jumped from tree to tree around the boys, evaluating this new threat to its sovereignty. Then, just as suddenly, there was a hot, sharp whooshing noise and the squirrel's ferocious demads were reduced to a long, pained squeal, accompanied by a sickening crackle. Then there was silence. Cameron wrinkled his nose at the smell of charred flesh.

"Stupid thing," a boy muttered, "scared the crap outta me."

"What, you scared of this little fucker?" There was laughter and then the body of the squirrel flew through the air as they tossed it aside. It landed near enough to Cameron and Elizabeth's hiding place that they could see its burnt body through the cedar boughs that hid them.

"Alright, men, let's keep moving. Nothing to see here," even the third boy, who obviously considered himself to be in charge, was clearly shaken from the scare the squirrel gave them, "We'll just have to go back and tell Captain that we found some rope in a cave, but lost the tracks after a while. Got it?"

The boys agreed. They seemed relieved.

Elizabeth listened as the boys, some of whom she had grown up with, all of whom she'd been trained to trust with her life, crashed away through the trees. Once all sound of them had faded away, Cameron pushed aside the cedar boughs that had concealed them. He helped Elizabeth out and onto the forest floor, then very tentatively approached the corpse of the squirrel. One final tendril of white-grey smoke rose from its body. It's eyes and mouth were still open, as if surprised. At least it's death had been quick and relatively painless. Cameron sat looking into the small black eyes for a long time, while Elizabeth watched him.

"This little person saved our lives," he said quietly. "He died protecting us."

He reached out, then and stroked the singed fur of the little creature with the tips of his first two fingers, very gently. Then, with the same two fingers, he rolled the squirrel's eyes closed.

"Red squirrel, right?" Elizabeth whispered. It didn't feel right to talk at full volume.

Cameron nodded.

"Do you remember what to do?" he asked.

"Yeah, I think so." They collected a few rocks to bury their little saviour. Then they knelt next to his makeshift grave and closed their eyes, to offer his spirit thanks and to help guide him on his next journey. Elizabeth felt her senses sharpen. She focused hard on the sounds of the forest around her, letting them flood like warm milk into the foundations of her mind. Then she imagined herself opening her eyes, standing and walking through the trees. Sure enough, she saw a young man crouched down, some ways away, examining with interest a cache of nuts and dried mushrooms that had been his in life.

"May I assist you in your journey, as a way of offering thanks?" she whispered, approaching him slowly.

The boy turned to her, still crouched on his haunches. "You're the one that needs assistance," he said. He was handsome and small, with a lean, muscular frame. His dark skin and eyes were framed by long dark-red curls. The contrast of dark skin and red hair was dazzling. He smiled gently at her, resting forward on his hands. They were covered in dirt but the look suited him.

Elizabeth stared at him.

"And you'll get that assistance; that I promise you. Your goal is my goal. The creator will not destroy them, it's up to you. We have been afraid, you must undestand that. Afraid of them. But now, you're here... We will all be watching. We will be ready to help."

Elizabeth gulped. She wasn't sure how she and Cameron would handle this extreme pressure on what both of them knew was a mission likley to fail. "Thank you," she managed, at last.

"Don't thank me. I'm proud to have played a part in the great war."

"The... great war?"

"The whole world... it's hard to explain. Just think back, to the other place, where you came from, where they," He jerked his head in the direction the boys had gone," came from. Everything our ancestors worked towards will turn to glass and metal if their plan succeeds. But if it fails, eyes will be opened. There have been too many who have made small decisions, believed small things, without considering their grandchildren, or my grandchildren." For a moment, the boy-man looked sorrowful. He opened his mouth again, as if to say more, but closed it instead and winked at Elizabeth with a broad smile. "Go in peace, medicine woman."

Elizabeth shivered and watched him jump up and run into the trees. Even in death, his movements seemed happy and spirited. Was it life, where they were now? Elizabeth pondered for a moment. It was called... middle world. Or something like that. The spiritual plane parallel to the world of the living senses. She knew that the ghosts couldn't go there and for the first time, she pitied them as she realized that whatever else they were, they were dead. Perhaps the world of the dead, the world of dreams and the world of the living were more closely linked than she thought.

She walked back to where she and Cameron knelt beside the little pile of rocks. What she saw surprised her. Cameron was leaning over her limp body, calling her name. Why hadn't she heard it before? She'd only been a few steps away. She watched him closely for a moment. Then she let the gravity of terra flood her and drag her back down and suddenly her physical eyes snapped open.

Cameron was above her, shaking her shoulders gently and calling her name. He looked concerned. When she opened her eyes, he stopped shaking her and sat back on his haunches. She sighed deeply and stretched.

"What did you see?" he asked, finally.

"Something that I'll need your help understanding. Also, I'm hungry."

Chapter Fifty Six

"So, he *meant* to save us? Even though he knew his own life might be forfeit?"

Elizabeth could only nod, because her mouth was too full to respond. She was chewing slowly, enjoying the rich, delicious meal of dried mushrooms and nuts that their friend had left for them. Sure enough, the cache that Elizabeth saw in middle world was just where she had seen it and full of delicious food that their friend would no longer need.

"What about this... great war?"

Elizabeth swallowed with relish, then turned to Cameron. "I've been thinking about that a lot. He was adamant that the whole world was involved, that life itself was at risk and that it had to do with Elizabeth's culture."

"The foreigners?"

"Yeah."

"He must have meant the ghosts."

Elizabeth thought it over for a moment. "I don't think so, not entirely. The ghosts, yes, they're big players. But it's even bigger than them. He said that their decisions don't take grandchildren into account, their own or even his. Do you have any idea what that means?"

"Yes. It's a saying, like the one you told me - *the old fashioned way. Thinking of grandchildren* is a way of saying that you consider all consequences of an action, or a decision, not just for yourself but for life as it grows and changes."

"Well, that's something that Elizabeth's culture certainly does *not* do."

"But they're a people that lives only in one place, just like everyone else. Eventually they'll run out of resources, or become too sick, and they'll have to change and it will be finished."

"You're wrong about that. Rivertown isn't the only colony, or extraction operation or even settlement. There are dozens, hundreds of them all over the world."

Cameron pondered that. Last night's manic episode seemed to have gone out of him and he was becoming the thinker she remembered again. "Why?" he asked, finally.

"That culture is very... wasteful, from our perspective. And disrespectful. They see themselves as separate from the earth."

Cameron nodded. "I remember they would always stay inside their elaborate homes, because they thought the outside was dirty, or dangerous. And because they thought the sun aged them before their time."

"That's right. I also remember... it was more people in cities that did these things and they considered us in the country to be lower class, because we spent more time outside, had more of the natural world around us. As if it could...infect us, or something. You remember I told you about some of the technology back home? These technologies take huge amounts of minerals, oils and gases to build and to maintain. They produce byproducts that are toxic to living things, which are pumped into the air and water."

"What?" Cameron was appalled. "But... that's suicide! They're killing everything and everyone, themselves included. And they're children..."

"Maybe that's what our friend was talking about."

"You must be right. But how did he know?"

"Maybe it was..." Elizabeth stopped. She looked up at Cameron, surprised. "Did you hear that?"

He tensed immediately. "Is it the soldiers again?"

"No, it's..." she closed her eyes and opened them again. Sure enough, the little girl she had seen before among the Ibers, was standing behind a tree a little ways away, looking timidly around the trunk at them. "Do you see the girl?" Elizabeth asked.

Cameron looked around and shook his head. "I don't."

The girl stepped forward. "My friend came and asked me to see you," the girl said.

"It's the girl from the hidden Iber camp, Cammy. She's here."

Cameron nodded and stayed silent.

"It's true? You're hurt?" the girl touched her own head gingerly as she asked, then pointed to the filthy bandage still wrapped around Elizabeth's cranium.

"Yes, I was hurt during the storm."

The girl nodded solemnly. "It's also true that you're going to go back to Rivertown? With Mama and the others?"

"That's our plan. We're going to disguise ourselves to look like Ibers, so that the ghosts won't recognize us right away. Then we're going to find a way to stop them. But we need your people to help us get disguised and stay hidden once we're in Rivertown again."

"They're patrolling, some of the foreigners from the town. We all thought that they were ghosts, too, but they're human, like us. I told my mama that they're human and she told everyone else. They're looking for you and for us. But the ghosts haven't started looking yet."

Elizabeth breathed a sigh of relief.

"That's going to make it hard for you, right? Because you can't let them find you?" The girl asked.

"Yes. And because I'm injured and very tired."

The girl considered this. "Ok," she said with finality, as if everything had been settled with that one small word, "we'll help you. I'll tell mama. Just stay here and rest. We'll find you."

With that, the girl was gone.

Cameron and Elizabeth stared at each other for a moment. Then Elizabeth told Cameron everything she had said. He was as dumbstruck as she was.

"The girl said that her 'friend' had told her to come here. Do you think it could have been..."

"The squirrel? Yes, I do think so," he said, "And I think that the mystery of how our little friend knew to help us has been solved.

"During the storm, I remember thinking that the Earth doesn't forget, can't forget." Elizabeth said. It wasn't all she wanted to say, or meant to say, or needed to say, but she couldn't figure out how to express it right.

"Yes, exactly. It seems we have more allies than we thought."

Chapter Fifty Seven

For the rest of that day and the next day as well, Cameron and Elizabeth waited for the Ibers to come. As soon as she had told Cameron everything the girl had said, Elizabeth curled up on the grass a few feet away, under the peacefully swaying aspens and fallen instantly asleep. It was the first real rest she'd had since their escape from Rivertown, which already felt like it had happened days ago.

Cameron was restless. He didn't want to wake Elizabeth, so he paced nearby, collected food for when she woke up, collected water from the creek and thought. Only days ago, by his conscious reckoning, he had been celebrating a truce with the ghosts on the beach at the river delta with Maria and the others from their village. It had been uneasy, yes and besides that, they had been in mortal danger for over a year at that point, every moment of every day. Still, he realized now that he hadn't expected to die then. Even an hour before, he hadn't expected to die. He still had dreams, hopes, even though he hadn't been able to construct any solid plans. He had been thinking about how he was going to build the new cabin, what sort of wood would be keep the salt at bay and the right angles and elevation. He wanted Maria to be able to wake up with the sun in her eyes but not feel more than a prickle of cold during the winter months. He had even started to think of where to put the new home, so that they could best plant a new garden…

The days in between then and now were long and hazy. As he tried to remember them more clearly, the wind suddenly picked up and a cloud drifted by to cover the sun. It was oddly fitting – the time he had spent between lives felt like a shadow.

Cameron decided to think of other things.

It was evening when Elizabeth woke up. She was bleary eyed and a bit sunburnt from sleeping outside all day, which suited her casual, bedheaded beauty terrifically.

"You look lovely." Cameron said.

"Honey," she mumbled, her voice creaking like an old wood floor, "you never said honey yet." She rubbed her eyes furiously, hands balled into fists, yawning like a child.

"Alright, honey," Cameron whispered, still unsure about using the pet name once so dear to him, "eat now, then you go back to sleep. Can you do that?"

Elizabeth nodded, her eyes still half closed. She sat up and hugged her knees to her chest.

"Here you go, eat this," Cameron murmured. The sun was beginning to set and the hazy, fragile outlines of rock and wood began to glow passionately against the grey blue sky. Elizabeth took the dried mushrooms, nuts and herbs from him and began to chew absently. She made a low sound of approval - this was very delicious food, after all - and then watched the sun go down. After a moment, her eyes started to slip closed, her chewing slowed and her head fell forward. Then it snapped back up and her eyes snapped back open and she chewed some more. This went on until she was finished eating.

Then, without another word, she circled her little spot under the aspens in the tall, lush grasses on her hands and knees like a kitten, curled up in the bed she had made and was instantly back asleep. Cameron had to smile. This sweet, exhausted young woman, whoever she was, had risked her life for him and was willing to do it again despite being so tired she could barely sit up. She'd even hidden her exhaustion from him, when she thought that action was still necessary. He sent out a silent prayer of thanks to the little Iber girl and her people, who had afforded them this much needed time to rest. From what he'd seen of Elizabeth, he knew that when she had enough energy, she would be a force to contend with.

She had to be. The whole world was counting on it.

The night was uneventful. There was a warm silence in the forest and Cameron felt safe. Almost... happy. The sounds of wind through leaves and grasses; of the crickets doing their creaky tap-dances and frogs in some nearby slew all soothed him. These sounds, these creatures, they would keep watch for him. Somehow, Cameron trusted that if anything were to happen, if anyone were to approach, these sounds would cease immediately. He trusted that would alert him and he went to sleep.

In the morning, they were woken by birdsong. The change in Elizabeth was remarkable. After nearly twenty four hours straight of sleep, she was revitalized. The pain in her muscles was almost gone. She even decided that it was time to remove the bandage from her head and washed the wound carefully in the creek once it was exposed.

"How long do you think, until they find us?" Cameron asked, as they ate their breakfast.

"They'll probably get here tonight."

"Should we start towards them? Cut the time off a bit?"

Elizabeth popped a handful of pine nuts into her mouth. "I don't think so. This land is big and hilly and there are lots of nooks and crannies. The Ibers won't take a straight route and we'd likely miss each other without even knowing."

Cameron nodded.

"Cammy, do you remember... many of the exercises I used to do, to focus my mind?"

"Yeah, why?"

"Could you show them to me? I can't really remember, but I have the feeling that I'm going to need to be able to control my gift and use it, before this is over."

They finished their meal and began their work.

"Listen to every sound." They were sitting in the grass, facing each other. Elizabeth's eyes were closed. She listened as hard as she could, focusing exclusively on the sounds around her. It was amazing how much more she could hear and how much more clearly.

"Now listen for sounds that are further away."

Elizabeth focused her mind outwards, through her ears. It was a funny image, her mind spilling out her ears and leaping across the hills around them and for a moment, she lost her concentration and giggled. "That's fine," Cameron said, calmly, "if you lose focus, accept it. Then begin to focus again. You taught me that. You and I did this exercise a lot."

"I remember," she said, "sort of."

Elizabeth sighed deeply and wiggled back and forth on her hip bones a bit, readjusting herself. Then she took a deep breath and exhaled, allowing her focus to fall again on the sounds around her. The sound of her own breathing was closest, then Cam's breathing, then the grass moving with the light wind and the leaves above them. A little further away, she could hear the birds singing and beyond that, very faintly, the sound of one of the birds taking flight; the rustle of its feathers and the pumping of its breast-muscle. Then she could hear the creek, just as loudly as if she had been sitting right beside it. Beyond that, she could hear a thumping, like a heartbeat, but duller. And more breathing. It was footfalls, people walking. She could hear the rustle of their clothes! It was hard to tell how far away they were, at least on the other side of the creek, almost half a kilometre away. They were walking in silence and suddenly, she was able to picture them, already hot on the ridge above the creek, eight of the ranch boys from Rivertown. Each had their taser out and they were all sweating, either from the sun beating down on them or from fear, she wasn't sure, but she could smell the sweat. One of them scratched his eyebrow and she could hear it as if her ear was only inches away.

"What is this?!" Elizabeth muttered. In the distance, she heard Cameron say, "it's alright, allow your focus to go where it will. Just like when you got distracted before, you just allow your mind to go."

This doesn't make any sense, she thought, angrily. She forced herself to focus on the sound of her own breathing again and after a moment found herself back among the trees with Cameron. Her eyes flew open.

"You followed the sounds?"

"Yeah, I followed the sounds and I saw some of the peacekeepers from Rivertown marching along the ridge above the creek. They're scared witless."

"Why do you seem angry?"

"I'm just... confused! If I'm just allowing my mind to go where it wants, then how am I in control!?"

"You *learn* to take control. It's not very easy."

"Maybe I'm just not cut out for this anymore."

"Hey. Don't feel bad. It's just like learning to walk. Every human does it, even though it's hard! At first, they keep falling over, even though some part of them intuitively knows exactly how to do it. Their first successes are uncontrolled. They just trust their feet, just like you have to trust your mind. Then, with practice, the steps get easier, your muscles grow, you gain balance and confidence and the next thing you know, you're able to walk anywhere you want. Or in your case, focus your mind on anything you want."

She stuck her tongue out at him, but conceded his point. "I guess you're right."

"Do you want to try again?"

Elizabeth grumbled, "Can we try a different one?"

Cameron smiled. It was such an... Elizabeth thing to say. He knew, because he knew that Maria wouldn't have said it. Wouldn't have let frustration get the better of her. But this, this was... adorable. Wonderful, actually.

"Yeah, we can try a different one."

They practiced for the rest of the day. Before either of them knew it, it was evening again and they were both tired. Elizabeth felt that she had made great progress and Cameron congratulated her, saying she was a natural. That meant a lot to her, but not nearly as much as the subtle differences in the way he was looking at her. It wasn't the way he had looked at Maria, not quite. But it was wonderful, nonetheless.

"They should be here soon," Elizabeth said, as darkness began falling. She had tried to find them during her exercises without success. She could feel the little girl's presence strongly, like a beacon, but there was some sort of mental block, a shield or a barrier set up around the girl that she didn't yet have the power to penetrate.

Cameron and Elizabeth were lying on their backs, next to each other, watching the stars come out. It was a perfectly clear night and for a few minutes, they were nothing more than two young people, alone in the woods and falling in love.

"You know, the foreigners believe that they created themselves. Only they don't see it as an act of creation, they think that the force of their consciousness, or emotions or something, just caused them to come to be. Like, they manifested. Their *Ethos*, that's it."

"Ethos?" Cameron asked. She had forgotten that his memories as Will were completely gone, and tried to explain.

"Modes of being. They think there are only about a hundred different modes of humanity; like motherhood, fear, joy, friendship, anger, childhood, stuff like that."

"How do they figure that?"

"They think the statues on the beach, our bodies, are the first manifestation of the Ethos in human form, making their stand against eternity."

"*Against* eternity?"

"Yeah. They think aging and death is a sign of... flaw or fault in humans. Like, we haven't manifested properly because we make this stand, but fail every time. The statues, they're succeeding, because they're unchanging."

"Of course they're changing. Just really slowly."

"I know. But they... don't see things the way you and I do. They hide from nature, what we think of as the world. So that they don't even remember what change is like, what cycles are like."

"Or what eternity is like, apparently."

Elizabeth murmured her agreement.

"It's sad, really. All those poor people are cut off from the world. They must feel so lonely, disconnected. It would be like being in a sensory deprivation chamber for your whole life, never eating real, living food, never tasting your own destiny."

"Is eternity our destiny?" Elizabeth asked, sleepily.

"It's more than that," Cameron answered, lazily taking her hand in his, "it's our nature."

That made Elizabeth smile: both what he said and the fact that his strong, rough fingers had tenderly closed around her own. It was enough just to be next to him, to be whispering with him as the night came and holding his hand in her own. It was enough.

It was almost completely dark, but true night was still an hour away, thanks to how far north they were. Sunset and sunrise were long events at this time of year and part of what had always enchanted Maria during the summer. She let her eyelids slip towards each other, relishing the moment, the feel of the night air on her skin, the smell of the grass and Cameron next to her.

Immediately, she knew something was wrong. The smell of the grass, the stars above, the feel of the air...

Sound. There was no sound. It was entirely silent.

Cameron realized it at the same moment that Elizabeth did. Their faces shot to look at each other, confirming that they both heard it. The silence. The warning.

They were not alone.

Chapter Fifty Eight

The Chief's speech proclaiming Elizabeth as a witch had been a catalyst for many t hings among the peacekeepers in Rivertown. First, many of them were afraid, bordering on panicked. Of course they had all heard the stories, growing up, of witches and fairies and magic-craft. Masters of beasts and plants with the ability to read minds, transport themselves great distances in the blink of an eye, cast spells and whatnot. They all remembered the stories of settlers and colonists who found the end of the world and were hunted by beings half human and half animal, living in the forests like creatures. Those settlers and colonists didn't escape alive, in the stories, old as they were. Those stories were about the Wild Land – the place from which not even the bravest had returned. The boys wondered aloud about the coal-eyes, swapping ever more frightening theories about their nature, their history and their possible powers. The Chief hadn't expected them to connect the coal-eyes to his claim that Elizabeth was a witch, but seemed delighted about it all the same. It's all in the name of public safety, as he said.

The boys were also unanimous that Elizabeth had to be found and destroyed before she could harm or kidnap anyone else. Unanimous with the exceptions, of course, of Mark and Dinky. Elizabeth's 'man squad' decided that they would have to act as if Elizabeth no longer meant anything to them and that they would take any part in her being brought to justice. They also decided that they would pretend nothing was wrong except the imminent danger of unknown, supernatural beings, Elizabeth included. Late at night and when they knew they were alone, however, they whispered desperately about possibilities of escape. That Elizabeth and Will had disappeared terrified both of them. Were they dead? Hidden away somewhere? Or had they really left the Centre? Mark tried hard not to cry, but he was so worried about his cousin that sometimes, he couldn't help it.

He blamed himself for not taking better care of her.

The most profound change in the group, since the Chief's speech, was that the peacekeepers, just days before a trained group of young men ready to do an important job, were now truly boys. Scared boys, capable of violence.

Stephanie, on the other hand, appeared to be finally coming into her own as a woman. A few well placed additions to stories of settlers tortured and killed by savage witches and faeries in *this very land, this Wild Land,* helped ratchet the state of fear further and further towards panic. She agreed with everyone and anyone who thought they were in danger, that they ought to keep their eyes open, that the Chief sure knew a lot about this sort of thing and would probably know what to do to get them out alive. Some of the boys wanted to know why they weren't simply evacuating. Stephanie would give her own short, impassioned speeches about leaving no man behind, especially an injured one. Will had been her tent-mate, after all and her friend.

When she was with Mark or Dinky, however, she played exactly the opposite tact. Agreed with them that something wasn't right, that perhaps, there was some sort of conspiracy. She remembered every word they said, waiting for something incriminating that she could bring to the Chief's attention. She hoped, however, that Mark was just being swept along by Dinky, or just smarter than she'd given him credit for and not really a... whatever it was that Will had been. An anomaly. A dangerous glitch.

Mark and Stephanie were spending more and more time together in the two days since Elizabeth's escape alone, in each other's arms, whispering things about themselves and each other and what they were feeling. They would meet in the abandoned market, sometimes and kiss for hours. Mark was too much of a gentleman to even think of going further than that. Plus, it would make him a hypocrite, after he gave Dinky such a hard time for nailing Dizzy.

"I didn't know that there were boys who didn't want to... you know.

Do it," Stephanie whispered, as they lay under his rough emergency blanket in the quiet, deserted market. It was just getting dark and all of the other boys were already asleep after hard days of either patrolling the surrounding countryside or labouring to prepare for the construction of permanent settlements.

"It's not that I don't *want* to," Mark said, tracing her face with his fingers, "believe me, I want to. I just want to wait until we're back home, or... until we've been together longer. I want to wait until it wouldn't be a theft of your honour."

Stephanie giggled. "I like that. My 'honour'." She let him believe that she was a virgin. It didn't matter what he thought, really, as long as it made him happy.

"And mine, too. That's just how I was raised, I guess."

"But there's no one here," Stephanie whispered in his ear, then nibbled on it gently. He shuddered in pleasure. She reached a bit lower on the blanket "No one would know."

"*We* would know, darlin'. That's enough for me. Bein' good means doing good even when no one knows about it."

Stephanie stared at him for a moment. "That's nice," she said finally.

"So," Mark said, propping his head up on an elbow to get a better look at her, "any word from the troops about Dizzy?"

It was the second night since Elizabeth's disappearance. Because Mark was Elizabeth's cousin, he wasn't allowed on the Rescue Mission, as it was diplomatically named, nor would anyone involved give him news. The two days since her vanishing act, they had sent six groups of eight boys into the wild to try and track the missing pair down. The boys, needless to say, were terrified. They stuck close together and jumped at just about everything. Stephanie had told some of them that witches can control animals of the forest, the wild ones, that are born instead of bred and use them to attack people. More than one squirrel had been tasered to death for no worse crime than leaping innocently across the peacekeepers' path.

"Nothing since they found that rope yesterday. Did I tell you about that?"

"Yeah, you said there was a cave or something, real tiny, but it looked like maybe two people spent the night there. And then the rope had blood on it, right? And had been cut up?"

"Doc did some tests and it is proof positive Will's blood. The other boys are saying that means she beat him."

Mark shuddered. "She would never do that. You know that, right?"

Stephanie smiled. "Of course," she said. Just that afternoon, she had told Bill, Mark's old partner, that she had known Elizabeth and did think she would do that. *Beyond a shadow of a doubt*, she had said. *It's unnatural, anyways, how she's always trying to be more masculine. Always was a strange woman, it makes sense she's a witch after all. She's a predator, uncomfortable in her own skin and trying to get under everyone else's.*

"I hope she's alright," Mark said and sniffed deeply. It was all he could do not to cry.

"Don't worry, Mark," Stephanie's face had taken on a strange, smooth quality that Mark gradually assumed meant simply that she was being serious, "we *will* find her. And when we do, we will bring her back here and she will never have to be afraid of anything, ever again."

It was an uncannily confident thing to say, but Mark was too tired to ask more questions. Stephanie was just trying to comfort him and he felt glad for it. Maybe Elizabeth would be safe. He fell asleep and Stephanie carried him effortlessly to his spot in the Barracks, careful not to wake him Behind her, soldiers with thermal-optic goggles and automatic rifles filed silently through the courtyard into the gloom. Black kevlar masks covered their identical, ageless faces.

Chapter Fifty Nine

As quickly and quietly as he could, Cameron brought his mouth to Elizabeth's ear. "Now would be a good time," he whispered, so softly that she could barely hear it, even in the zero-decibel silence around them, "to listen."

She knew immediately what he meant and closed her eyes. The first thing she could hear, of course, was her own heart pounding. It was so loud and persistent that she couldn't hear anything else. They were going to die! They were going to be shot where they lay. *Oh God, how could this happen?*

Taking a deep, noiseless breath, Elizabeth allowed her mind to be distracted by the fear. Then, she refocused on the sounds of the world. It took an incredible amount of willpower, almost more than she possessed. But she was still Elizabeth, the girl who fought and begged until she was allowed to do what only men had ever been allowed to do before; and Maria the woman who saved the man she loved, after crossing two thousand years to find him. She wasn't going to give up.

Suddenly, what had been an entirely soundless night began to rustle and hum. It felt amazing; the tiny, muted noises were washing over her and she was sinking into a relaxed state of concentration, a world of sounds. She could literally hear Cameron's heart beating, fast and hard; the buzz and whisper of an insect taking its chance to feast on a juicy vein in Cameron's arm. She could hear the trill of a mouse's whiskers tickling the dirt, hiding in the grasses only a few feet away and terrified. She willed her mind to hear further and could almost hear the moisture popping on the stalks of grass as her consciousness sped through them towards the sound of another heartbeat. That of the little girl.

Suddenly, Elizabeth found herself about two hundred metres away, among wiry, haphazard underbrush and thick spruce trunks. She saw the little girl and several others, flat on the ground under the foliage.

They were hidden entirely from sight, but Elizabeth saw them all the same. It felt like her visual and auditory senses had become linked, and intensified.

Echolocation, her mind started to say, wandering, but she focused hard on the little's girl's wildly thumping heart and stayed in the thick forest. "Can you hear me?" she said. She saw the tiniest start from the girl. "Why are you all hiding?"

The girl's face contorted in concentration and unexpectedly, Elizabeth's mind was flooded with images and thoughts. The girl was trying to communicate with her but was too afraid to focus. Elizabeth flinched, overwhelmed, but the ideas and memories and words kept pouring in:

The ghosts are here I don't want to be here mama was right but everyone was so excited we had to come we had to save you but now we'll die I don't want to die it's too short I never even kissed a boy. I had to come because I'm the only one who knows where you are and they were going to send me and mama back to hide when we found you and everyone is so happy you came and that you'll kill the ghosts but scared too because how? How could you do this? They know they can't... I don't understand what they meant, but they can't keep living this way. And I'm so scared right now they're dark and you can only see them with your eyes! They're not alive! The others that are going back to Rivertown are waiting for you up the creek we were going to find you and bring you to them and then me and mama were going back to our hiding place and she said she would tell me my favourite story because she was proud but I know! I know she was scared because this is what's going to happen so I hid myself, I hid my mind but now the ghosts found us! She's scared because they always kill the gifted ones! Now they're here!

Elizabeth heard a twig snap and felt the little girl's astral throat tense against a scream. She could see... shadows. Only shadows. That's what the ghosts looked like in middle world: just shadows. Everything else pulsed with the life inside of it, except for them... That's what the girl meant – *Onya*, her rattling voice rang out, *my name is Onya* - about them not being alive, about only being able to see them with your eyes. The shadows were moving - *like ghosts...no, Onya, focus!* - through the trees, armed, unstoppable. Did they know the Ibers were there? Elizabeth didn't think so, but she couldn't read their thoughts, couldn't get a signal from them. If they didn't know where the Ibers were now, they would in a minute. The soldiers were about to step right on them.

"Where are they? The others? Show me."

Onya was trembling, but she managed to project an image of the other Ibers - about five dozen, roughly the same amount as the original peddlers from Rivertown - waiting in hiding five hundred metres away, in the other direction. She focused Elizabeth's minds eye on a bundle of clothes one of them was carrying, expanded the image to show the terrain between where they were now and where the other group was, so that Elizabeth could find them.

"What will they do if they find you?" Elizabeth whispered.

If we surrender they probably won't kill us but if they find us hiding like this they probably will.

Elizabeth closed her eyes. This situation was desperate and getting worse by the minute.

"What about us? What will they do if they find us?"

I don't know. Mama thinks they'll kill you.

"And the others?"

If they surrender and say they were coming back to Rivertown on their own, then the ghosts probably won't kill them.

"Ok. Don't worry. You're going to be alright."

Another twig snapped, this one closer, only meters away. Onya didn't answer. She whimpered. Elizabeth took one last look at the terrifying, shadowy forms still making their way towards the hidden Ibers and little Onya, then scrunched her eyes closed and focused hard on the sound of her own heart.

Instantly, she was back in the grasses beside Cameron. She squeezed his hand and brought her mouth to his ear. "We have to run. Now. Just trust me. Don't let go of my hand." she whispered. She could see his eyes go wide in the lazily fading light of a long summer dusk that only moments before had seemed safe and gentle. He squeezed back.

Then they jumped up and ran through the trees.

Elizabeth's head swam and she felt a vertigo coming on, but clamped her mind down against it. She found she was still standing, air burning its way in and out of her lungs, heart pounding in her ears and throat and behind her eyes, legs pumping through the grass. She held on to Cameron's hand as hard as she could. They ran together through the semi-dark, following the terrain that Onya had showed Elizabeth to the others. Once they were there, they would have very little time to disguise themselves before the ghosts caught up. They had only been running a few seconds when they heard a shout from the direction Elizabeth knew Onya was hiding. They approached the place the other Ibers were hiding and could hear booted feet racing along behind them.

Elizabeth clenched down on Cameron's hand harder than ever and ran faster than she ever remembered running. She could hear Cameron's breathing becoming ragged beside her and the footsteps behind them getting closer. It was only a little further, just over that hill. Her own lungs were straining so hard for air she wondered if she was going to lose consciousness, or maybe throw up. Her head was pounding and she suspected that her wound was bleeding again. Cameron started to fall behind and she pulled at his hand mercilessly. They were over the hill and they could see the gathered Ibers below. Elizabeth aimed them at the woman near the centre that she knew held their disguises and they barrelled down the hill towards the group.

The Ibers saw them running and some gasped. The ones between them and the woman with the disguises shuffled hurriedly out of the way, making a little corridor for them, which closed like a pair of wings as soon as they were inside. It was just in time. As soon as they were in the group, they could hear the Ibers frightened hisses as the ghosts summited the hill.

"We surrender!" One of them yelled. "We surrender! Don't shoot! We come to Rivertown, now! Just taking rest!"

The woman shoved the disguises at Cameron and Elizabeth, telling them to hurry through clenched teeth. They threw their own clothes off and began desperately pulling the new ones on. The woman had coal, which she rubbed around Cameron's eyes first as he tied his pants up. While Elizabeth secured her dress in place, the woman did the same and tied a scarf around her hair and neck, then thrust an old, dirty cap onto Cameron's head, to hide his flaxen fair hair.

The Ibers had all started to raise their hands above their head and were shouting *Surrender!* Over and over again. Above them, on the hill, the ghosts were laughing. It was a sickening, monotonous sound.

"We heard running. Who was it?"

"A deer! A deer came running!" A man yelled. This seemed to satisfy the ghosts.

"Come on, cattle. Back to the corral with you." One of the ghosts said. The others sniggered. With hands still raised high, the Ibers began forming a long, single file line and marching towards Rivertown. The ghosts spread out around them; one at the front, a few on each side and one at the back. Their night vision goggles allowed them to see every move of every person down that long column. Elizabeth walked with her head down about halfway through the group, her heart beating in her chest, with Cameron walking behind her. They tried to imitate the defeatist slouch of the Ibers, who dragged their feet and shuffled, instead of really walking.

After almost an hour of marching, they returned to the familiar area surrounding Rivertown. The ghosts stopped and the Ibers stopped, too.

After a few minutes, the Chief came strolling towards them from the direction of the settlement. He had his hands clasped casually behind his back and wore a distinctly smug expression.

"Well, well, well," he said, sneering. "How nice of you all to come back. We're making some improvements for you. Real houses, unlike the shacks you savages seem to prefer." The soldiers laughed at that, and a couple prodded the Ibers with the stocks of their rifles. Elizabeth could feel her cheeks burning with the shame that these people must have suffered for so many centuries. How had they survived?

We've been waiting for you. The thought came unbidden into Elizabeth's mind. *All of us.*

"Of course, once we have real houses built, we'll have to fill them with *real* humans, it wouldn't be right to let such astonishing advances in civilization go to waste on hybrids such as yourselves. It will only be a few weeks now, before we can discard our need for you entirely. Settlers are on the way."

Elizabeth glanced at Cameron, who raised tightened eyebrows at her. Settlers? Already? If settlers were on the way, it meant that the Chief felt it was time to prepare his greeting party. He would turn the young peacekeepers into ghosts, and soon.

"But we'll let you live until then, of course," the Chief said. "Yes, you're still needed, for a little while."

The Chief stopped then and looked up and down the line as if examining. He addressed the soldiers, "Well, you've brought about the right amount. That's fine. They will sleep in the market."

He turned and walked back towards the Centre and the Ibers followed.

When they were in the market, everyone set about making little beds for themselves here and there. Elizabeth and Cameron set up a small nest in a corner with two of the canvases and lay beside each other.

"Well," Cameron whispered, "we're in. Now what?"

"I guess I should try and talk to Mark and Dinky, maybe Steph."

"How? If you go out there, they'll kill you."

Elizabeth sighed, pondering. There were guards - the heavily equipped, uniformed ones that she could not tell apart - outside the market in the courtyard. He was probably right. "I could try and journey to them."

Cameron nodded. She closed her eyes and focused on the sounds around her. Before long, she was following sounds out into the courtyard and then into the Barracks. She was amazed at how much easier this was now than it had been that morning. Like remembering how to ride a bicycle.

Mark was asleep near the courtyard, snoring softly. She tried to rouse him, but her astral touch had no effect at all. Dinky was nearby, also asleep and she knew that she wouldn't be able to wake him either.

She scanned the large room for Stephanie. It took her a while to locate the one female form among all of the sleeping boys and when she did, she lost her concentration entirely. *How could I be so stupid?*

"Stephanie," she breathed, instantly back under the canvas with Cameron, "I saw Stephanie. Cam, she's a ghost."

Chapter Sixty

It was just a little rustle. Barely even a noise at all. In the warm morning light coming through the open courtyard and his eyelids, it was a nice, comfortable, sleepy noise. Mark sighed, contented. Through the haze of sleep - a sleep that now felt warm and nice - there was a little touch, too. Not much of a touch, though it went all the way from his feet to his shoulder, but gentle, kind and yes, warm. He murmured his appreciation; he'd never felt so comfortable. It must be the bed - yes, his old bed at home. Oh, how he'd missed that bed. He smacked his lips, relishing the sort of dry feel of his mouth, how toasty his skin felt in the slanting sunlight that hit his right side, the masculine comfort of his morning erection.

Mark rearranged himself to swallow up the snug, toasty feeling in his arms. Probably sun-warmed blankets, all the way up his body. He still hadn't opened his eyes. Then the warm thing pressed against him moved, just the slightest movement and a hot, lazy hand traced between his legs, causing a grateful lurch. He smiled, more than half awake now and murmured incomprehensible things. Next, a warm mouth found his neck and gently kissed and nibbled its way to his collarbone, down his chest and finally landed on his nipple. This was suckled by a firm, hot tongue flicking over the hard tip of it as the full, wet lips pummelled the rest of his chest with silent kisses. At the same time, that wonderful hand had taken Mark into an oscillating grip.

Her hand. Mark almost lurched awake, realizing where he was and what was happening, but the sensations were overwhelming. He shuddered deeply, still feeling so warm and cozy he could die, feeling Stephanie's tongue flick deliberately over his nipple and her teeth tease him, feeling her hand pumping harder and faster... He caught his breath in his throat, not allowing it to come out in the long, low moan that threatened to wake the other boys sleeping so close to him.

He opened his eyes, breathing raggedly and looked at Stephanie, cuddled up under the blanket beside him. "Good morning," she said, with a giggle.

"You could say that." Mark said and stretched. It was the best wake up he'd had since arriving in this wild place, by far. He rubbed his eyes and stretched, thankful that he had slept naked. What a great girl! "Steph, that was... great. Thank you."

"Don't thank me, silly. I was up half the night thinking about it..."

While Mark and Stephanie continued their whispered pillow talk, Elizabeth looked down at them in horror. She had journeyed from the market, hoping to catch Mark when he woke up, to find a way to communicate with him. When she saw Stephanie slipping under his blanket, her heart had stopped. What was she going to do to him? Then, she saw the blanket move formfully and averted her eyes, cheeks flaming and mortified. How could they, with all of the other boys so close by?! *Gross.*

Finally, Stephanie jumped up and skipped off, ostensibly to make breakfast or get ready or maybe murder some people, who knew what these ghosts did for fun. Elizabeth watched her go and had a bizarre flash of deja vu. It had been a few days since she had seen Stephanie and now she was looking at the girl with a fresh perspective. She knew Stephanie from somewhere besides the peacekeeping corps.

Mark stretched again and started to dress.

"Mark, can you hear me?" It was a long shot and she knew it, but there had to be a way to get through to him and she *would* find it.

He didn't respond.

"Mark! Can you hear me?!" she screamed.

Still nothing.

Elizabeth knelt down in front of him. He was tying his shoes. She reached out and touched his cheek. "Mark! It's Elizabeth! I need you to hear me."

He stopped for a moment, as if he'd had a strange thought, then shrugged and went to the other foot. It was a confusing sensation, she could feel his skin, the three-day whiskers poking out around the contours of his jawline but his head was absolutely immobile. She could touch, but not change. "Mark! It's me, Elizabeth! I need you! Can you hear me?!"

This time his face took on an expression of deep concentration, as if something had just occurred to him from some deep place in his mind. He had stopped tying his shoe. Elizabeth quickly angled herself in front of him so that they were staring in each other's eyes. She had one hand on either side of his face. She took a deep breath and yelled directly into his face, "Mark! Can you hear me!? It's Dizzy!"

His head cocked to one side. "Dizzy?"

Elizabeth burst into relieved laughter. "You can hear me?"

"Dizzy?" he whispered again. Then he said, "Oh no. She really is a witch."

"I'm really here. In the market. I'm using… a coal eye thing to talk to you. Mark, are you alright?"

Mark nodded, slowly. "You're in the market?" he whispered.

"Yes, I'm in the market. You have to listen: everyone here is in serious danger. The Chief, the doctor, they're not human. Do you understand?"

"Are they… witches?"

"No. There are no witches. I know how crazy this sounds but, they're machines, Mark. Terrible machines, that believe they are human and will try and murder all of the peacekeepers and replace them with more machines that look just like them."

Mark had gone pale. "I don't understand," he said very quietly, trying not to move his mouth. He glanced at the nearest boy, who luckily was still fast asleep.

"It's a long story, believe me. But we don't have much time now. If we want to get out of Rivertown alive, we have to kill the machines." There was a long pause.

"Ok. How?"

Elizabeth breathed another sigh of relief. The resolute look in Mark's eyes confirmed what she had hoped from the inception of this crazy plan: that he was willing to fight and ready to help in whatever way he could.

"I don't know yet. I have to talk to..." Elizabeth weighed her options for a moment. If she told Mark now that Stephanie was a ghost, it may give away their hand, he may not believe her. Then again, if they could get one of the ghosts alone, they may be able to question her and get some useful information. Such as where they knew each other from. "Steph. I have to talk to Steph. Only, she can't know that it's me that she's going to talk to. Can you set that up? Tell her... that you want to meet her out at our old campsite, tonight, at dusk. Can you do that? Then I'll go, instead of you and talk to her."

She could sense some serious hesitation from her cousin, so she added, "We need all the help we can get, Mark, otherwise we're all going to die here."

Mark covered his mouth with his hand and lowered his gaze. "I'll do it," he whispered.

Chapter Sixty One

The Chief barged into the market from the hidden facility on the second floor and Elizabeth had to cut her conversation with Mark short. She focused hard on her breathing and found herself almost immediately back in her own body, sitting in the corner. She squeezed Cameron's hand, which held hers, to let him know she was back.

"You will assist in the construction project." he handed a folder to a random man, adding, "this manifest includes duties and numbers required. You may organize amongst yourselves. Any infractions will be punished by death. Understand?"

There was silence in response, all of the faces of the Ibers turned down to the floor, their shoes, or their hands.

"Good." the Chief said. With that, he strolled away.

Elizabeth turned to Rubi, the woman who had provided their disguises, who was sitting against the wall next to her. "Infractions?" she asked.

Rubi maintained a deadpan expression, but raised her eyebrows significantly. "They give us rules. We must do as we are told without questions. We must not use this building for any reason but market and now, sleep. We must appear..." Rubi frowned, thinking of a way to say what she had in mind, "stupid, poor and... hard working. The rules can change, if they want to punish, they will. They invent rule for punishment."

"I see. What about... leaving Rivertown? Going into the forest, or the hills?"

"This is fine, but always must come back and can only go at night time. This is where we go to find food, of course, but we also bring food."

Elizabeth would have asked more questions, but the man who had been given the duty of assigning work details had stood, scratched his head as he perused through the folder the Chief had given him and then called for attention from his fellows by waving his hand in the air. The man had thick, tightly curled hair that stood from his head like a halo. He had lines around his eyes and mouth; lines betraying many years of stern concentration and deep, shadowed thought. He was a handsome man and the sadness etched into his skin made him appear stately and wise.

"Moe," Rubi whispered into Elizabeth's ear as the congregation went silent.

Moe began a quiet speech in a language that Elizabeth thought she should have remembered, but didn't. She looked at Cam – he didn't understand, either. It made sense: languages change a lot, given time. Moe held the folder that the Chief had given him in one hand and with the other, pointed to people as he spoke, his lips jumping around emphatically. Then he would pause, scratching his head, chewing his lips so that they continued to move and read the papers again. As he pointed, the Ibers indicated stood and stretched and grouped together in various empty areas of the large market.

Just like the peacekeepers, Elizabeth thought, *both sides put on a show for the other... all to keep everyone convinced that everything is normal, that there's nothing to worry about.*

Moe pointed to Rubi, who patted Elizabeth on the shoulder and ambled to the other side of the room, hips swaying gently as she went. After no more than ten minutes, everyone had their assignments. Moe sauntered to where Elizabeth and Cameron were still sitting and crouched down beside them. His legs were long and thin and stuck out almost to his ears, like wild elbows.

For a moment he just looked at them, his deep gaze jumping from one face to the other. "You come to..." he didn't seem to be able to finish and Cameron saw the shine of tears welling up in his eyes. He began to chew his lip.

Cameron looked at Elizabeth. Her eyes were gentle, with a purity and a kindness he had only ever seen in Maria. She reached out and took his hand and said, "We've come to destroy the ghosts, we've come – "

"No," Moe said, interrupting her, "I must speak. My people, we have almost given up many times. There are many suicides. Many illnesses. We are desolate."

Cameron knew that he wasn't just referring to the Ibers themselves. Moe was encompassing every being in the land when he said we. His was a desolate land and the desolation was his own, deep and heavy.

"Sometimes, we have wondered why our ancestors didn't stop creating children. Sometimes, we wonder if we should stop creating children. But there is a destiny, greater than our hardships, for us." Again, Cameron knew that us included all of creation. "There is still joy in our lives. We have lost much, but we remember some of the old ways and we still practice them. Onya says you saw our hiding place?"

Elizabeth nodded.

"Yes. This we have planted and tended, when we can. It is small, but is our own refuge, our own paradise. Our children we conceive and birth there, so that they will be strong and have a motherland. There are other places like this, for different tribes. All are hidden."

Cameron felt his own eyes fill with tears. How could these people maintain faith and hope after so many generations of hardship and slavery?

"Now you are finally here. I'm honoured to fight with you."

Cameron heard Elizabeth gulp, but was pleased to see her steely gaze remain resolute. Maria would have cried, like he was doing. Not Elizabeth. She was too brave for that. He felt his heart tighten, at the thought of her bravery. What an amazing, strong woman this Elizabeth was. Cameron was grateful that she hadn't been lost the way Will had been.

"Thank you," Elizabeth said, at last. Cameron waited, expecting the words of condolence and inspiration that he knew were already forming inside Maria's head. But it wasn't Maria that this man needed to hear from. Cameron felt his insides lurch as he realized that for this man, Maria was part of a distant, untouchable past. Elizabeth pursed her lips and he could see her instincts unfurling with a pantherine control and ferocity. He thought he saw her age in front of his eyes: from a teenage girl who had never quite fit in, into a leader, a hero, a new medicine woman for a new illness.

Elizabeth took her hand from the man's grip and placed it on his shoulder. "Tonight, we require four strong people unafraid of injury, to accompany us from here at dusk. Can you arrange that?"

"Yes. We are all willing to be injured. This doesn't frighten us anymore."

"Good." Cameron blinked again. Elizabeth's eyes were so blank and serious when she said it. Maria, on the other hand, had been so sensitive to violence that she could barely discuss it without becoming physically ill. There was a moment of silence, in which Moe and Elizabeth held each others' eyes. Then, without looking away from Moe, Elizabeth said, "At dusk then. Cammy, the Chief will begin his speech soon. I'd like to know what he says. Would you go to the courtyard and try to listen?"

Cameron's mouth almost fell open. She had given him an order. More than just an order; a smart one. He wasn't sure how, but it seemed that either Elizabeth had a plan, or she was simply perfectly suited for this.

"Now," Elizabeth turned back to Moe, "we're alone. Say what you want to say."

Chapter Sixty Two

Moe was only surprised for a moment. Then he nodded, a jagged little motion. He should have expected this. She was a medicine woman, after all, even if she couldn't remember everything about being one.

"Onya said... about *untura*. Is it true? Are you the ones, from the statues?"

Elizabeth nodded. "One of your ancestors told me about the spell. But they said that there wasn't enough magic left to complete the *untura*. As you said, everything is desolate. They knew they could not continue to live in their way; the *untura* was just one more proof of that. The man told me they would stop having children."

"Then you are..." Moe cleared his throat, a long, low growling sound. "Time changes many things, knowledge and stories. We know of this man. That was a... powerful time. Small actions changed things for many grandchildren. Do you know his story?"

Elizabeth shook her head.

"Sometimes, when we are all together and feel safe, we tell the story of the last medicine woman," Moe began. "This story... changes. But always stays the same. You understand?"

Elizabeth nodded this time.

"Good. My Onya... it's her favourite story."

"Your Onya?"

"My... daughter's daughter. Is it true about her?"

"Yes. She is to be a medicine woman. She has communicated with animals and set events in motion beyond my comprehension. She is the reason that Cameron and I arrived in Rivertown, alive."

Moe cleared his throat again, an arduous groan. The circuitous travel of his large lips had become broken and jagged. He whispered,

"So young, to bear such a burden." Elizabeth realized that he was trying not to cry.

After a long moment, she said, "Please tell me the story the way you would tell it to Onya."

Moe nodded, regained control of himself and began. "She loves to hear of the beginning. Great Spirit made the earth with thoughts of love and created each thing with a purpose, to show how much every single thing was needed. This is the greatest show of love in all creation; that everything has a place and can never feel lost. For us, the Great Spirit conceived that we should be entrusted with the final stage of creation: the perfection of this paradise that is our home. Onya closes her eyes, sometimes and imagines what the world was like then."

"One day, a strange deceiver came to the Earth, to a place far from here and tricked the humans there. They abandoned their purpose and because of that became stranger and stranger.

"Soon, they were not humans at all, but machines. These are the ghosts, you see?" Moe asked.

"Yes, I see. Go on."

"Then the humans were in trouble. The machines became powerful and very evil. The people asked the Great Spirit to save them, but no help came. Protecting the earth from evil was not the purpose of the Great Spirit, but the purpose of humans. If the Great Spirit were to intervene, then humans would lose the greatest gift of their existence: knowing that their purpose was to care for the earth with love to turn creation into paradise. If Great Spirit destroyed the ghosts for us, we would forfeit everything that we are, or ever could be.

"Many humans perished and it seemed the battle would be lost. As hope dwindled, the natural abilities of mankind disappeared. The humans were forgetting their purpose in the face of fear and so they began to lose their magic."

Elizabeth gulped. It made sense, to interpret their ancestors actions in that way, however simplified this child's story seemed to be. They had abandoned hope and because of that, lost their abilities to fight back, to create. How could they create if they thought they were going to die? The only thing they were creating with thoughts like that was the certainty of their own demise.

Moe continued. "But just when hope was almost lost, came a woman-deer. This woman-deer had all of the strength and magic of a human from the dawn, but also all of the gentleness and kindness of a deer. Her deer compassion shielded her mind, and her feet hooves protected her body from the destruction around her She was the very last true medicine woman.

"This woman-deer took her medicine to the machines, because with her deer-kindness, she could not see that they were only ghosts and thought that they were still humans, sick and injured. She thought they *must* be sick or injured to be so evil and strange. For two long weeks, the woman-deer gave her medicine to the machines."

"Then the woman-deer came back, with one of the machines. This machine had deceived her, but she could not see that evil. Woman-deer thought that this machine was human and that they were blood sisters. The machines killed her and her people, just as they had killed so many before. But at the last moment, this woman-deer used her magic. She made an *untura*, connecting herself and her partner and sending them through time, so that she could right her mistake. She was the only person left who could fulfill humanity's purpose and she would not allow herself to fail."

"Even the humans who had lost all of their hope could feel the power of the *untura* being made. And they knew what it meant. Someday, woman-deer would return, with all of her strong power and with the wisdom of death, to lead them, to help them finally destroy the ghosts and protect the land. The people remembered woman-deer's kindness and decided that they would not give up hope, because if they did, then she would return to an empty world and her kind heart would be broken. If such a gentle creature could be so brave, even in death, then they would do the same and continue to create children and to care for things as best they could. Sometimes, I tell Onya tall tales about how glorious it will be when things are put right again and how much she will enjoy being free."

Elizabeth was staring at her hands, which were held neatly in her lap. The fable had been so accurate: she *had* been blinded by kindness and gentleness and so caused the deaths of her people. And now... now here she was, ready to 'right' her mistake. She had to blink back tears, which made her angry and embarrassed. She was being selfish to think of only herself and her own shortcomings when there was so much at stake.

"Moe," she said, finally, "Onya said that there were other medicine people... but that the ghosts killed them all. Is this true?"

Moe nodded darkly. "There are always medicine people born, I would say even in the foreigners lands, even if they don't know what they are or what their talents mean and even if they never have the chance to practice. I have medicine - so does your partner and every boy in that hall they call Bare Racks. My medicine is to speak, tell stories. But some... can do what my Onya does. What you do.

"But others are sick of this life. They don't believe we will ever be free and some don't even want to return to the old ways: they believe the lies of the machines, the deceptions. Some even volunteer to go to the foreigners' lands, to live with all of the technologies. Some are desperate to do this. So desperate that they will tell the ghosts which of us have strong medicine."

"They betray their own people?" Elizabeth asked.

Moe nodded.

"Could that happen here, now?"

Moe nodded again.

Elizabeth let out a long breath and saw Cameron slip back into the canvases of the market with a grim look on his face. "Great," she muttered.

Cameron hurried over to where Elizabeth and Moe were sitting. He looked pissed off. "We're in trouble, Elizabeth," he said. "We don't have as much time as we thought."

Elizabeth blinked at him.

"The Chief said that the coal eyes came back to seek medical attention, because they have some sort of archaic illness. He said it was due to poor hygiene and that the boys shouldn't worry because they've all been vaccinated."

"We don't have any illness," Moe said.

"I didn't think you did," Cameron sighed wearily. "The Chief made it up. And I'm pretty sure he did so for a reason. I can only imagine that this has to do with either killing all of us, you and me and the Ibers, or turning the peacekeeper. Maybe both."

"I think you're right." Elizabeth said. She was thinking hard. What were they going to do now? "Any more news on the colonists that are supposedly coming?"

"That's the other thing." Cameron looked pained, angry and most of all, terrified. Cameron looked frazzled, strained and terrified. "They're going to be here tomorrow."

Chapter Sixty Three

Elizabeth needed a plan. Moe had gone with the others, to do work detail for the day, leaving Cameron and Elizabeth to hide in the market and wait for evening, when they could ambush and interrogate Stephanie. She was hoping that this interrogation would give them some kind of advantage - if they were really lucky, it would reveal how many ghosts there were, where they all were and how to destroy them - but they also needed a back up plan just in case. She and Cameron sat underneath one of the trading stalls, surrounded on all sides by canvas. It felt like a fort that she and Mark might have built when they were children.

"We could kill them with kindness!" Cameron suggested, then made a pretend thoughtful face, "no, wait, we already tried that... and it got us killed. I guess we'll have to think of something else."

"Very funny."

"I still don't understand why Moe couldn't say all of that stuff in front of me."

"Partly because he was embarrassed and scared for Onya and partly because he thought I might be embarrassed. It's a pretty cutting story if the doe-eyed main character is you."

Cameron nodded. "I guess."

"I can't believe that I changed their minds, though. Made them reconsider their plan to end their bloodlines."

Cameron just looked at her. His look said it all: he wasn't surprised in the least. It was quite a compliment.

"I remember you told me a story when we were both in the infirmary about how some machines were created to work the crops. Right?"

"Yeah, but those crops had poor nutrients and reduced taste."

"So what happened to the machines?"

Elizabeth considered. "Lots of them are still working."

"You're kidding me."

"Nope. The people in Elizabeth's homeland... are still very worried about contact with nature. Even though they know that this food is covered in toxic chemicals, not very nutritious and bland, they still eat it."

Cameron shook his head in disbelief.

"Sometimes, if a machine is malfunctioning or outdated, people just turn it off and throw it in the dump."

"Turned off? Like... a lightbulb?"

"Right, exactly."

"Anything else that happens?"

"Some are recycled for their parts, I'm sure and the rest are reprogrammed."

"What's that?"

"They're given a new purpose; so they were still machines, still look the same, but do different things and think of themselves differently. They aren't farmers anymore, they're... you know, plumbers or garbagemen or whatever."

"Could we do that to these machines?"

"It's possible, I guess. But to be able to store human memories and behave convincingly human, they must be extremely complex. Reprogramming something like that would take a lot of skill we don't have."

"It might just be easier to destroy them."

"Yeah, maybe. I guess we'll see tonight when we talk to -"

"Wait. Did you hear that?" Cameron interrupted in a harsh whisper. They both stopped, straining into the silence. After a moment, they heard the small sound again, barely audible but unmistakable: a footstep. Elizabeth lifted the corner of one of the sheets of canvas just a sliver. She could see shoes, tip-toeing slowly and deliberately. Cameron was watching her and she shook her head at him, to say that she didn't know who it was, but it didn't look good. How loudly had they been talking? How could they have been so careless?

Cameron took her hand and held it to his chest, without his eyes leaving hers. She smiled. She could feel his heart beating and for a moment, she forgot that they were in terrible danger.

"Elizabeth?"

They froze. A young man's voice, whispering her name. Elizabeth looked out into the market again, this time to see that the intruder was only a few feet away. He *must* have heard them talking. One of the peacekeepers, who had been told that she was a dangerous witch who must be killed. Even in their disguises, it was likely that the peacekeepers would recognize them. Elizabeth squeezed Cameron's hand, looking back at him, at those beautiful light blue eyes, which were always so bright, even now.

"Elizabeth, it's me, Dinky. I'm alone. Mark said that you were here..."

Elizabeth pulled the canvas hastily aside and looked. Even standing with his back to them, she knew that it was Dinky. He was wearing a sleeveless shirt which was sweaty and covered in dust from the hard, outdoor construction labour they had been ordered to do and his arms were tanned and more muscular than the last time she had seen him. Even his legs, now exposed in knee-high shorts, were more tanned and brawny than she remembered.

"Dinky!" she exclaimed. In her peripheral vision, she saw Cameron's jaw drop with surprise. "Down here!"

William Dinghum spun around and dropped into a crouch, so that he was facing Elizabeth, where she had poked her head out of their hiding place. For a moment, she was speechless: *this* was the boy she had remembered as her teenaged self's boyfriend? His hair was a carefree, sunlit mess, his face tanned and his whole body obviously more toned after just a few days of hard work; he looked more like a young man than a boy. And a handsome one, at that. There was something else, too, that was slightly different. It wasn't just his hair that was relaxed, his posture was eased and the way his shoulders hung had a confident, released quality now. Not that he was carefree - she could tell that he had been worried as hell about her.

After that long moment of gaping at each other, they embraced fiercely and uncomfortably, she sat and he crouched with a partially shunted canvas between them.

"I'm so glad you're alright," Dinky said, pulling back and taking Elizabeth's hands in his own, "you wouldn't believe the things they've been saying about you. That you're a witch, that you killed Will..."

Cameron chose that moment to poke his head out beside Elizabeth's.

"Will! You look... well I guess it was a lie that you were sick, too. That makes sense."

There was a moment of tense silence as Cameron surveyed Elizabeth's hands in Dinky's. "Nice to see you Dinky," he said, finally, "we shouldn't be out in the open like this, though."

"You're right," Elizabeth said. Cameron was about to breathe a sigh of relief when she added, "come on in here, Dink. We've got lots to catch up on."

Dinky climbed into their little hiding place, beaming.

"Where have you two been?" he asked.

Cameron looked at Elizabeth and raised his eyebrows to her, passing her the metaphorical speaking stick.

"We escaped three nights ago," she said, "and we've been hiding in the woods ever since."

"The last time I saw you, you could barely stand up. How did you do it?"

Even Cameron had to smile at that. "She just did it," he said and patted her gently on the arm. There was another short, awkward moment as Dinky noticed the familiarity of the gesture.

"Why? Why did you run away?"

Cameron shifted uncomfortably and gaze Elizabeth a questioning look.

"I think we can tell him," she said.

Cameron's eyebrows shot up. "What if he's..."

"He's not."

"How can you be sure?"

"The only way I can be sure is to... listen." She put emphasis on the final word, to tell him she meant journey.

"Then do it. Otherwise it isn't safe."

"Do what? What are you two talking about?" Dinky said.

"Dinky... just trust me for a minute."

Dinky gulped, but didn't protest. He waited. Elizabeth took a deep, calming breath and slid her eyes closed. It took a long time to focus on sounds, because for a moment, she was overwhelmed by smells: Dinky smelled like wood and dust in sunlight, a hot smell that made her skin prickle. On her other side, Cameron smelled like pine and summer wind and... home. It was too much, having them both so close by and she felt her heartbeat quicken as heat began to form and then spread between her legs. For a moment, her mind wandered, lost in the scents of two men, so close, both so attractive. She could hear, almost taste their breath, their heartbeats, the tiniest movements of their bodies. If only they would touch her, both of them... touch her and kiss her and run their mouths and hands over her. There was a lurch low in her stomach and the heat between her legs became a steady pulse. It didn't take much to conjure up images of both of them naked. To have double that smooth, hard skin pressed against her... she stifled a moan as she became wet.

This was *not* fair.

"Is everything alright?" Cameron asked testily. His question snapped her attention back to the task at hand and she blushed at her suddenly mutinousmind and body.

I'm seventeen, doll. Cut me some slack.

"Yeah, fine," she muttered.

Both at once. A girl can dream.

She took another deep breath - through her mouth this time - and focused on the sound of her own heart beating. Focused hard.

Soon, the rhythmic sound had all of her attention. She allowed her minds eye to recreate the scene around them, the beat of her heart anchoring that image into the present moment. Then, she opened her eyes and looked around.

First, she saw Cameron. For a moment, she wondered if this was how the Creator must see this man: with a soft glow, his eyes so bright that they illuminated the air around him. He was watching her and it made her smile. Then, she turned to Dinky.

She had to let out a sigh of relief when she saw that he was not a ghost, but a human, after all. What a difference there was, between the two men! While Cam looked gentle, constant and intense, Dinky's energy was focused, angular and quickly changing. With every beat of his heart, the energy around him changed just a little bit - like watching a strobe light or will-o'-the-wisp.

Elizabeth opened her eyes, back in the world. "He's human."

"Human?!" Dinky yelped, "Of course I'm human!" He looked at his hands, as if to make sure. Suddenly, his face turned ashen. "Oh no. You're saying that..."

Elizabeth nodded, gravely. "The doctor, the Chief, the nurse and several others... are machines. Ancient machines, created by yours, Mark's and Elizabeth's ancestors in their quest for immortality." Dinky's head looked ready explode.

"'Elizabeth's'? Why are you talking about yourself in the third person and how could you possibly know all this?"

"Dinky..." she looked at her knees, didn't want to see his face when she told him the truth. Why did she have to hurt him? "I'm not who you think I am. At least, not entirely."

Chapter Sixty Four

Elizabeth told Dinky the whole story - as far as she knew it - while Cameron sat brooding silently. First, she told him how her and Will's memories were replaced by those of Maria and Cameron. Dinky just stared at her. Seeing that he wasn't going to say anything, she went on to tell him what she knew about the ghosts: the old colonies, their terrible invention and the fate it led them to. At first, Dinky merely shrugged: artificial intelligence was a reality for him, not a monstrous fantasy. But when she told him about the murders in the old colony - "Reeva," Cameron interjected coldly, "It was called Reeva. That means New Home in your old language." - Dinky's eyes widened with fear and surprise.

There was a brief pause in the story as Elizabeth let the new information sink in for Dinky. But Cameron interrupted, asking: "Do you know that your people have taken indigenous peoples from their colonial holdings as slaves or for medical tests for at least the last two millennia?"

Dinky just blinked, looking lost and forlorn. *Maybe he's more of a child after all,* Elizabeth thought.

"We're taught that they traded with the colonials and the settlers. That they came freely to live with us..."

Cameron snorted.

"Most of what we've been taught about our past is lies, Dinky," Elizabeth said, gently. It was Maria's gentleness, which only made Cameron bite his tongue in jealousy. "The foreigners, that's what the locals here call us, were already a terrible menace: they murdered and raped and kidnapped and did strange experiments. People avoided them for the most part. Their way of life was confusing to us." Dinky blinked harder at her use of *us*. "They were afraid of ageing and dying, the mysteries of which are still a big part of your culture today.

They thought that fresh air and sunlight and even fresh water contaminated their bodies and that in order to preserve themselves, they had to be cut off from the natural world. They rarely left their homes, except to check on the plants they grew in greenhouses and even then they were covered head to foot with protective equipment. There were some exceptions as I understand it... some were even friends to the local people. For the most part, they were cruel.

"But the ghosts were much worse."

Cameron interrupted again by snorting at the understatement.

Elizabeth decided to appease him, saying, "You're right, Cam. They were worse than worse. They were..."

"There aren't any words for what they did." Cameron spat. His whispered voice nearly broke.

Dinky was white.

"They killed everyone and everything that they could find." Elizabeth steadied her voice, "We didn't know what they were. Our neighbouring villages were burned, people left hacked to pieces, some with marks on their flesh; teeth marks. We had to leave our homes. They chased us for over a year. All of the other tribes and villages... those that survived anyways, were refugees, like us. We all helped each other as best we could and stayed in hiding, but they kept coming."

There was another long pause.

"Why?" Dinky's voice wavered. "Why were they killing everyone?"

Elizabeth spread her hands over her knees. "We're not exactly sure, but we have some ideas. First, they're unnatural. This doesn't have the same resonance for you, because you live in an unnatural culture."

Dinky looked taken aback.

"No offence, but you do. You live separate from the food you eat, with little connection to the community around you. Much of this community is killed as a matter of course to suit your needs."

Now Dinky had gone white. "That's not true! I may not know everyone in my community, but I've never killed anyone!" he sputtered.

"Not humans. Animals and plants." Elizabeth said it as gently as she could, "I remember my dad and brothers, shooting gophers for fun. I remember hearing that some sort of… mountain fox had gone extinct, because of suburban expansion. Stuff like that. Come on Dinky, don't you remember stomping on anthills when we were growing up?"

Dinky scrunched his eyebrows together, letting it sink in. When he realized that he couldn't argue with her, he just said "Oh."

"Anyways, they chased us all the way to here, to Rivertown."

"You're not from here?"

"No." Elizabeth's face lit up and she looked at Cameron with a fondness and intimacy that hit Dinky hard just above his stomach, "We're from the mountains. The foothills, actually." She squeezed Cameron's hand and he smiled at her too. For just a moment, the brooding young man transformed in front of Dinky's eyes into someone older, kind and loving.

"So, hold on. You two were chased across this whole continent for over a year, two thousand years ago. Then you…died and somehow ended up here, now?"

"That's the short version, yes."

"Does the long version include why It was the two of you in particular and no one else?"

Elizabeth looked down at her hands, which now sat in her lap. "In the moment before our death, I performed what you would call a… magic spell, really just a highly focused expenditure of mental energy at a speed surpassing the events around us."

"Really."

"It's alright if that doesn't make sense to you, I'm still getting used to it myself."

"Because you still have some memories of being Elizabeth."

"Right. Many of them."

"And you did a spell to send you and Cameron… into the future?"

"Yes, to give us a second chance."

"Why? Why'd you bring him along?" Dinky jabbed a thumb at Cameron. Elizabeth winced.

"Because we're married," Cameron snarled.

"Married?"

"Yes." Elizabeth said, "but also because then we would know, we would have the knowledge necessary to see the threat for what it was, even if unnatural lifestyles had overtaken all of humanity by that time."

"Married." Dinky repeated it, rolling the word around in his mouth. "So, how much of the time that you and I were together did you know that you were actually a different person, who was *married*?"

Cameron's eyes flashed and he shifted his weight forward, towards Dinky. "You were *together*?"

Oh shit, Elizabeth thought.

"It's not my fault. I didn't know she was married!"

"Maybe *was* is the operative word," Cameron snapped.

"Both of you, stop it." Elizabeth barked. She closed her eyes for a moment. *Men.* She couldn't allow Cameron's wounded pride to stand in the way of what she had to do: get Dinky to be their ally in this fight. "I didn't know who I was when I was with you, Dinky. This all happened really fast. When I started remembering, I was confused and I thought I must be going crazy... until I saw Will and realized that he was actually Cameron. Alright?"

The two young men mumbled that it was alright. Elizabeth hoped that they meant it, but didn't think it was very likely.

"Now...we believe that the ghosts - the Chief, nurse, doctor, as well as at least two dozen military commandos hidden in a secret compound behind the wall on the second floor of the market - are planning to kill all of the peacekeepers and turn you all into ghosts yourselves. If I hadn't escaped the other night, I would have been dead by now. You would never guess though, because there would be a machine that looked just like me and acted just like me."

"Oh man..." Dinky's legs were tapping nervously.

"Yes. Those ghosts would look and act just like the two hundred boys that left for Rivertown. And they would be sent out to proliferate all over the world."

Dinky nodded. "If it weren't for the murdering and all, if my mom heard that you could download into a robot that looked like you and slay young forever, she would do it in a heartbeat."

Cameron looked aghast.

"It's true." Dinky said, shrugging at him.

"I believe you," Elizabeth continued, "and if a bunch of ever-youthful boys show up with this new discovery from the Wild Land, then no one will know about the murders. My guess is that the new ghosts will be programmed to talk about how great they feel... and of course, they'll look and act and talk just like you guys."

Dinky shivered.

"I'm glad you're getting the picture," Cameron said coldly.

"What are we going to do?"

Cameron looked at Elizabeth. If she had still been just Maria, she would have admitted that she had no idea. He wondered if she would say that now to this boy. If he had just learned everything that Dinky had, it would have inspired no confidence at all to find out that they had no plan and no ideas for what to do next. In fact, losing that little bit of hope in Elizabeth, who was clearly the leader of this operation, might make him lose hope altogether. A hopeless soldier is a defeated soldier.

On one hand, Cameron hoped that she would be honest, because on some level, that meant that she was still Maria - *his* Maria - and that all of his feelings for her made sense. But on the other hand... the woman called Elizabeth was so fascinating, strong and hardheaded that she was magnetic. Even if she wasn't his.

"It's best that you not know the whole plan, in case they interrogate you. If they do, just say that you know nothing. They likely won't risk torturing you and losing public support among the peacekeepers. If they do take you, we *will* free you. In the meantime, tell me: if the Chief said that there was a medical procedure that could... prevent a serious illness or something, or if he even told a part truth and said that you would be stronger and stay young looking forever, do you think the other peacekeepers would do it?"

Dinky considered. "Most of them probably would. I'm guessing it wouldn't be hard to force the others."

"Right." Elizabeth sank into thought momentarily, "How about the settlers that are coming? What do you know about that?"

Dinky let out his breath in a tired sounding whoosh. "It's bad news, Dizzy, but I'm sure you know that. They must have been looking for volunteer settlers before you and I even got to Rivertown, for them to already be on the boat. Either that, or they've told the settlers that they're going somewhere else and they're actually coming here instead."

"What do the boys think about it?"

"Some of the boys are a bit concerned, you know, about whether the kids and women will have a good enough place to live, once they get here. There's no more room in the Barracks, as you know and now that the coal eyes are staying in the market -"

"Call them Ibers. That's what they call themselves."

"...now that the Ibers are staying in the market, they'll have to pitch tents until the houses are ready."

"How long will that be?"

"Not much longer, actually, especially now that we have all the extra hands, with the Ibers helping. The houses are sort of... humble, let's say. Still real nice, but the kits we got yesterday have everything pre-built. You just nail them together. Even the septic is pre-installed. We've already got half of them up."

"Do the other boys think it's weird that the settlers are coming so soon?"

"Yeah, some of them do. Probably a lot of them do, but I'd say that most of them are just... not talking about it. Maybe not even thinking about it. They keep us really busy, so everyone's exhausted and then there's the rumours that you're a witch. That scared a lot of the boys. People stop working to check over their shoulder, then collapse at the end of the day."

"Elizabeth? Are you going to tell him about the statues?"

"Oh, right."

"The Statues of the Ethos?" Dinky's eyes were wide with excitement. "Of course! You probably know who built them!"

"They weren't... built, Dink. There's something else about the ghosts. They have some kind of weapon. We didn't know much about it, but we had bracelets that beeped when the weapon was nearby, because it gave off a kind of radiation that could be measured. We were on the beach, celebrating. We thought that we had made a truce with them, we still didn't know what they were. I had been deceived and thought that they were human and that we could appeal to their humanity. But I was wrong."

"It's ok, Maria," Cameron said, switching smoothly between her names, "you didn't know."

"The bracelets started beeping and the children were screaming. I ran to Cam, to perform the *untura*, so that we could be together and have a second chance. I reached him and then everything went white. Those statues on the beach, they're not statues...they-"

"No way."

"We're the statues, Dinky."

"No way," Dinky repeated. "So you're... the mother?"

"Yeah. And he's the father."

"No way." Dinky sat back and drew his knees up to his chest. It was a lot for one person to absorb in a lifetime, let alone an hour of hushed conversation. He had also just been told his life was at risk. Elizabeth let him think. Finally, he turned back to the others and said, "What do you want me to do?"

This time, Cameron waited with anticipation to see what Elizabeth would say. How could someone so young be so... strategically capable? Strong? Confident? He relished the moments it took her to think, to mobilize yet another piece in this devastatingly important game.

"Go back to the others. You'll need to insinuate yourself into the group, as best you can. I know, Dinky, but just fake it. We need to know what they're thinking, what they're willing to do. Also, I need you to talk to the two Captains. Pretend to be stupid, one of those boys whose only concern with the arriving settlers is the loss of comfortable sleeping space and ask about it. Then just pretend to be interested, making conversation. See what you can learn. Come back tonight. If I'm not here, come back in the morning instead, right before dawn. Can you do that?"

"Yeah."

"One more thing," she said and he looked at her expectantly. Hopefully. She saw that look and knew exactly what it meant. "Do you think there's anyone in Rivertown who knows enough about machines to... reprogram something as complex as one of the ghosts?"

"Well, I've always been really into mechanics. I actually made a working mouse-bot for the science fair last year. I don't know what these things are made of, but I could give it a try. No pressure, right?"

"Alright. Thank you."

Dinky nodded. Then he paused and looked at Elizabeth's hands on her lap. He had been dismissed, that much was clear. But he wanted to tell her that he still loved her, in spite of who she really was. He even opened his mouth, but closed it again at the last minute and left.

Chapter Sixty Five

Cameron and Elizabeth spent most of the rest of the day in silence. She wanted to explain to him that she genuinely hadn't known about her relationship with him while she was with Dinky. But when he hinted that their marriage was a thing of the past... it hurt so much that all she could do was be angry with him. Sure, she had intuited his hesitancy towards her. How could she not? The last time he and Maria had been alone together, they had made love, just like they always did. They had been alone together for days and had only had the one kiss and a bit of rowdy hand holding. *Mee-ow.*

Cameron wasn't angry though, just confused. It wasn't a good time for him to be out of sync with his emotions and it wasn't a thing that happened to him frequently. For all his spiritual depth, he was a simple person. Acted on what he believed, said what he thought and usually, felt what he felt. He loved Maria. The pain of thinking she was gone when the ghosts took her still haunted him, as did the moment that their wristbands started beeping on the beach and he realized: *this is it*. The end of their romance. Now, Rivertown was supposed to be their second chance.

Except that this *wasn't* his Maria. At least, not exclusively. Elizabeth... sometimes annoyed the hell out of him. Had slept with some kid named Dinky, for the love of the creator! Couldn't remember how to be a medicine woman, believed in the use of violence to attain peaceful ends, mouthed off to him, risked her life on a daily basis... and was probably the only person who might have a chance to lead both the Ibers and the peacekeepers and the only person with enough recklessness to even attempt to destroy the ghosts. Worst of all, she looked so much like Maria and the resemblance was growing, rather than fading by the minute. What if this was *her* second chance, her destiny, and he was only along for the ride?

"Are you alright?" Elizabeth whispered, next to him.

He just grunted again and stretched. This sitting around was killing him.

"Bet you'd like to be puttering around, chopping wood, building a new deck, just about anything but this, huh?"

Cameron looked at her. "You a mind reader now?"

"No, I just know you sort of well, having been married to you."

"Right." Cameron did nothing to clarify the ambiguity still hanging in the air. Elizabeth wanted to strangle him, but knew that tact would be a more formidable tool.

"Are you nervous about Stephanie?" she asked.

Cameron sighed, a sure sign that he wasn't in the mood to talk, but he answered anyways. "Sort of. Who knows what these things can do. You remember all of the Ibers that they had in that facility upstairs, where you rescued me from."

Elizabeth shuddered at the memory. Those people might still be upstairs, wasting away in their cells, being tortured.

"They were doing experiments on a lot of them. Working on weapons and stuff. It's sick."

"We're going to get those people out."

Cameron cocked his head at the certainty with which she said it. It wasn't a plea, it was a statement. "Yeah. The sooner the better."

"Don't worry... I don't think we'll be sitting on our butts much longer."

Cameron gave her a questioning look.

"They'll know that Stephanie's gone, probably by morning. Then there's only twenty-four hours before the settlers arrive. If they get here and our move's not been made, then the ghosts could act first and murder all of them before we have a chance to do anything about it. I don't know how long it takes them to build a new ghost..."

Elizabeth had gone white.

"What? What is it?"

"It's just... the reason why they haven't killed the peacekeepers yet.

They're still working on the machine bodies that will replace them. Do you remember, when I saw the sheet that the nurse had, that said 'host body is ready for transfer'? The machine was the host body. As soon as the bodies are ready, the boys are done for."

Cameron nodded slowly. "Theoretically, they'll want to be done before the settlers arrive, right?"

"Exactly. And they have to... get the memories from each of the boys first, God only knows how they do that, or how much time it takes..."

"You think they're going to start any minute."

"Yeah, I do."

"Can you find out for sure?"

Elizabeth thought about it. "I can't see the ghosts, when I'm journeying, because they don't have a spiritual component, if that makes any sense. But I can still hear what they say and see where they are and what they're doing."

Cameron nodded and Elizabeth closed her eyes. Though she would never allow herself to show it, she was exhausted and her nerves were wrenched taut. How did she get put in charge of this giant mission, this 'great war'? Not that she was backing out. Never. She would fight to death - again. She just wasn't sure if that death would do any more good than the first one had. She had already failed once. The woman-deer was deceived and accidentally enabled a genocide of her entire people. What would make this time different? She couldn't do it. *Everyone's going to die die and it will be your fault. Again.*

Elizabeth tried to focus on the sound on her breath, fighting against her fear and regret. At first, her focus just amplified the sounds she was trying to block out: memories of her people screaming on the beach, the children accusing her of making a deal with their enemies and her own voice, giving orders and making plans, even though she had very little idea of what she was doing. Interrogating Stephanie? Getting recon? Who was she kidding?

Suddenly, there was silence, except for her breath. It felt like she was in a cocoon and for a moment, she just relished it. It felt safe. Her mind began to drift, following a slow, distant thumping. Opening her eyes in the middle world, she found herself upstairs, in front of the seemingly innocent stretch of wall that hid the ghosts' experiments. The thumping was coming from inside, so she went through the stone - a strange sensation - and let it draw her onward like a magnet.

The sound was coming from a shadowy figure, indiscernible except as a dark heaviness in the air. It paced back and forth along the far wall of the room. The room itself was much worse in daylight than it had been when she rescued Cam. In the corners that had been hidden by shadows then, Elizabeth now saw robotic bodies without faces or hands, but otherwise completely covered in skin. They were piled on top of each other. A dozen more stood along the wall, watching the trapped Ibers with empty eyes, as these were completed. Ray, a few others she didn't know by name, and her self. A perfect replica of herself.

There were blood stains on the floor and walls and the terrible stench of rotting flesh and faeces. The people here were mostly asleep, some awake and moaning, clutching at wounds. The figure ignored them and paced. And paced and paced and paced...

"I can't!" Elizabeth gasped, opening her eyes, sitting suddenly next to Cameron again.

"Woah, woah, it's alright. You're still safe here. What did you see?"

She just shook her head and pointed in the direction of the stairs. Cameron nodded. After furiously wiping tears away from her eyes and taking several moments to breathe deeply, Elizabeth said, "I guess we'll just have to wait for tonight."

Chapter Sixty Six

Elizabeth woke up as the Ibers were ambling back into the market from their long day of work. She didn't remember drifting off.

Cameron was removing the canvas wrapper from their little sanctuary. All around them, Ibers were crowding, staring at them, whispering to each other. Elizabeth stretched and yawned, trying to wake up and look at least somewhat like a leader they could invest their trust in. These people were needed and they were needed as confident warriors. The sight of them shuffling around her, ogling her with open dismay told her it would be a long shot.

Finally, one of the women got her courage up and asked, "How you going to do it?"

Elizabeth still felt half asleep and wished she could have slept all the way until morning. She forced herself to look thoughtful and self-assured. "It's best if we don't share all of the details of the plan, in case any of us are taken hostage. We all know how important this war is. The animals call it the Great War."

There were gasps at this and a few of the older men performed a clumsy gesture of blessing in front of their chests.

Elizabeth took this as a good sign and stood up before she continued. "Each of you is needed and each of us has a role to play. Stay alert, stay calm and if you learn anything or see anything that you think may be important for our effort, tell me."

The gathered people nodded. Then Moe stepped forward and began shooing them away, saying something in their language that neither Cameron nor Elizabeth could understand. When the crowd had dispersed, he gestured to a bench nearby and sat with Elizabeth. Cameron stood in front of them.

"Four people are ready. I will come with you, as well. That makes seven altogether."

"Good. Thank you, Moe."

"Moe," Cameron started and dropped to his haunches so that he was at eye level with the man, "I've been thinking. You said there are other groups of Ibers in hiding, right?"

"Yes. There are three hiding places. All within two weeks distance. Then there are two known places, where the ghosts can find us, so that they don't look farther. We plan to make a fourth hiding place, very far away. Send some people away forever and protect them from the ghosts."

"How many of you are there?"

"Hard to say. Our camp has one hundred. Each camp about the same."

"My question, Moe, is whether there are other ghost settlements, too."

"Yes."

Elizabeth felt her body buckle. This was terrible news. Why hadn't she thought of it? Of course there were more than a couple dozen commandoes and the few authorities she'd seen.

"How many?" Cameron pressed, with steel in his voice. She opened her eyes and looked at him, surprised at his composure. Surprised and unbelievably thankful.

"The old colony. We never go there, they will kill us."

Cameron was nodding, giving Elizabeth a look that said this was a game changer and not in a good way. A whole colony of them! And who knew what kind of defences they had...

"But there is one thing we know," Moe went on, after a moment. His voice had dropped, as if he were imparting a terribly important secret. "Many, many years ago, a man went there. I was a child. He was very foolhardy. Wanted to try and kill them, all by himself. He got to the colony and was very surprised by what he saw, so he left and came back. They knew what he did, so they found him and killed him in front of all of us. But in the few hours before they found him, he told us what he saw.

"Many ghosts standing perfectly still, like the statues beside the ocean. *Many* of them. Some of these were only able to move their heads and were calling for help. Others were rushing back and forth between the frozen ones, trying to assist them. The others, that could move, he said there were only four: two men and two women. One had a moustache. This is your Chief. We believe that when more foreigners came, the Chief took one and made many identical machines of this one man. The ghosts of the colony still *look* human. But they are... stuck."

"Stuck." Elizabeth repeated. She looked at Cameron, who shrugged at her. He also had no idea what this could mean.

"Yes, stuck. And there is something else. There was a woman who was taken by the ghosts. That night, my Onya had a nightmare. She said that in her dream, she followed the woman, who was her Auntie, to where the ghosts took her. She said it was a place in the East, almost a whole nights walk away, on the seaside. She said there were strange buildings made of unnatural things. Of course, this was the colony. She gave descriptions of things that she could not have seen. This is when I knew that she was in danger, because of her gifts."

"What did she see?" Cameron asked.

"Again, she spoke of many frozen shadows. The ghosts, you see."

"Yes," Elizabeth said. She recalled her journey and the ghosts who looked like nothing more than ashy, flighty shadows.

"There were only a few that were moving, she said. She said that the dream... got funny. That's what she said. That she could see a wind blowing against these frozen shadows, turning them slowly to dust, but that it felt like time was going very fast. She told me every detail of this dream and promised never to tell anyone else, for her safety, you understand. So young, my Onya. She said... that she had been there before. A long time before. She tried to find her Auntie, but her auntie was dead. Then she woke up and came to me in my bed, because she was afraid."

It was Cameron's turn to look questioningly at Elizabeth and her turn to shrug. "So you think that something has already happened to the ghosts, to make them... freeze."

"Yes. Somehow. This gave us great hope. Until they made the many-copy man and then made us construct Rivertown and you all came. If they can make more ghosts, then it won't matter if these ghosts eventually freeze after many years, do you see? Because then they will just make more again."

"I see, yes."

There was a moment of silence as Cameron and Elizabeth absorbed this new information.

"Now. Let's have a meal, then we get ready for our mission." Moe said and surprised them both with a wide, toothy grin. Rita came over then with bowls of a stewed grain that had dried herbs in it. They ate in silence and as soon as they were finished, Moe turned and gestured at a group of young men standing in the corner. The young men were strong-looking and broad. They approached silently and looked between Moe and Elizabeth, waiting for instructions.

Elizabeth let her gaze flit to Cameron, asking silently for strength and fortitude. He nodded to her and stood up. She stood up too, and although she was a head shorter than each of the men her gaze circled them confidently.

"Let's do this."

Chapter Sixty Seven

Dusk was a long, painful time in coming. They were positioned around the campsite, hidden and waiting. Their plan was to throw a net on her, one that the Ibers used for fishing in the river. Then the four young men and Cameron would run out, take her to the ground and wrap the netting tightly around her so that she couldn't move. While they held steady - one for each limb and Cameron as an extra, Elizabeth would interrogate her. Moe would administer any blows necessary to make her talk. This last step was really just a wild gamble, but Elizabeth was the only one that knew it. She wasn't sure that these things could feel pain.

While they waited, each minute stretching out as the midsummer sun took its careful time in climbing down the horizon, Cameron and Elizabeth crouched silently beside each other. Finally, Cameron leaned towards her and whispered, "Is there really a plan? Or are you just saying that?"

Elizabeth looked sharply at him, hurt and angry. Of course there wasn't a plan and he knew it. "You're welcome to take over any time," she hissed back, "this isn't exactly my dream job."

"I understand why you're doing it," Cameron whispered, "you just sound so damn confident when you say that there's a plan. And you keep coming up with orders and missions. So is there a plan or not?"

Elizabeth thought about it for a minute. She was entirely surprised at Cameron's unexpected and round-about compliment. But just because she was a good actor didn't change the fact that she really didn't have any idea what she was doing. *Right?*

"It... feels like there is a plan, but I just can't remember all of it. she grimaced. "I want to do the right thing and I'm not going to back out, but try to remember I'm just half girl and half ancient lady. All Elizabeth knows was farms and boys, and all Maria knew is love and peace. I just don't know if I'm cut out for this."

She ventured a glance at Cameron and was surprised to see tenderness in his eyes and a little smile pulling at the corner of his mouth. "I think you're more cut out for this than you -"

They both stopped and at the same time, their eyes went wide and the hair on the backs of their necks stood up. Neither risked movement, even though both wanted desperately to look and see if it was really her. Elizabeth went over the plan one more time in her head: *four men, two nets, throw nets, take her down, wrap nets so she can't move, interrogate.*

I hope this works.

Silence, and then...

The patter of feet. A shock of blonde hair. The emerging outline of Stephanie's icy, beautiful profile.

"Mark? Where are you?" She was almost inside the zone that Elizabeth had carefully marked out on the ground in sticks and leaves. They weren't obvious markings but Elizabeth caught her breath as Steph glanced at them impassively. Stephanie looked around and giggled, taking a few more steps towards the two meter wide circle that Elizabeth had marked off. All she had to do was toe the line and the nets would go flying.

"I know you're here, I can hear you breathing," she said, playfully. Then she did something unexpected. She began to lift her shirt up, slowly revealing a perfectly flat stomach with gently curving lines showing the muscles beneath. "I think I know what will make you come out," she cooed. She lifter her shirt higher and two high, full breasts fell out of the tight fabric. Her nipples were large and dark, with wide areoles. Elizabeth sent out a silent prayer that the Iber boys wouldn't be too distracted to act. "Come on out and play with me," Stephanie purred. With one final flourish, her shirt lifted the long, blond hair from her back and was gone, into the forest near where Elizabeth and Cameron were hiding.

There was a long moment of silence and Elizabeth held her breath. Could Stephanie really hear breathing? And if she could, would she realize that there was more than one person hiding here?

Stephanie giggled again and combed her fingers through her hair. "Breathing harder now, huh?" she said, as her hands trailed down her shoulders to cup her naked breasts. She squeezed them and pinched her nipples so that they stood up, hard and eager. She moaned.

She was only a foot away! Elizabeth's heart was pounding. Only one more step and she would be in the circle! Should she shout the order to move *now*? Would the Ibers be able to respond with the speed necessary? All she needed was for Stephanie to take *one more step* into the now-deserted campsite. Instead, the half naked robot put her hands on her hips and pouted. Then her head ticked to the side, with incredible speed, as if she had just heard something. Her face was immediately smooth. They were about to lose their chance.

Elizabeth threw herself out of the bushes and towards Stephanie, yelling "Now! Do it now!" at the top of her lungs. One net came flying from the other side of the clearing immediately and landed on Stephanie, who had turned in Elizabeth's direction. Her head ticked the other way, so that her face was tilted and she lowered herself into a half-crouch, her arms coming up in a defensive stance. The net hung uselessly over her head and shoulders.

The other net flew from the bushes a second later, this one landing on top of the first. The nets wouldn't do anything unless someone was there to tighten them and hold Stephanie down! Elizabeth was the only one who had moved. As she ran, she could see two of the Ibers launching themselves into the clearing over Stephanie's shoulder. *Good. Now I just need to distract you...*

Elizabeth hurled herself into Stephanie, shoulders first, aiming for her midsection. She collided with Stephanie's hands, balled into fists and the wind was knocked out of her, but she managed to knock Stephanie off balance with the attack. Her arms swung out, locked around Stephanie's waist and she shot a foot out to hook around Stephanie's far ankle, to try and bring her down. Stephanie lifted her far leg before Elizabeth could grab it and used it to knee her hard in the ribs. Elizabeth lost her firm grip and felt Stephanie pulling her upwards and wrapping cool fingers around her neck.

This bitch is going to kill me, Elizabeth thought.

Just as Stephanie's fingers were closing off Elizabeth's throat, both were thrown backwards by the impact of the two Ibers crashing into them from behind. All three of them landed hard on Elizabeth and she felt one of her ribs crack. For a moment, she could not breathe or move. Then Stephanie was pulled off of her and the three other boys and Cameron flew through her shrinking, darkened field of vision onto Stephanie.

"She's secure!" Cameron yelled.

Arms wrapped around Elizabeth's shoulders and helped her to sit up. She recognized Moe's voice saying, "Breathe, just breathe, you're safe. Just take a moment to breathe."

"What the hell is going on?!" Stephanie yelled. They had her pinned to the ground, arms wrapped tightly to her body in the net, which was so tight that it pressed her breasts flat in a criss-cross pattern. The Iber boys and Cameron held her tightly, but she struggled relentlessly.

Elizabeth forced herself to stand up, one hand on Moe's shoulder for support. The other hand darted immediately to her rib as soon as she moved; the pain there was incredible. "Moe..."

"Chew this. It help with pain," he whispered, handing her a pouch.

Elizabeth opened the pouch a looked inside. It was dried mushroom and she looked at Moe questioningly.

"It make pain disappear, all the pain. Works very quickly. But when it stops working, pain comes back very big and you are very tired. Take one piece, pain dulls. Two piece, just ache. Three piece, this is more dangerous. Pain disappears. But later..."

She nodded and ate three big pieces before handing the bag

back to Moe. Then, she forced both of her hands to her side and turned to stare at Stephanie. "We know what you are."

Stephanie stopped struggling for a moment and stared at Elizabeth. Then she started to laugh. It was a terrible, mirthless, nailbiting sound made all the worse by their former friendship. Elizabeth stared back stonily.

"And what exactly am I?" she asked, finally.

It was Elizabeth's turn to laugh, a gentle, condescending chuckle with a wry smile. "You are a dead woman, whose life was stolen from her. You're a poor imitation of false life. You are a machine. A ghost."

Stephanie rolled her eyes. "And what do you think *you* are, Elizabeth, besides for a walking pile of rotten water?"

Elizabeth ignored the question. She needed to take control. The pain in her side was steadily disappearing. She paced around Stephanie's body. "How many of you are there in Rivertown?"

Stephanie rolled her eyes again and gave Elizabeth the same coy look she had worn during her striptease minutes ago.

"You remember pain, don't you, Stephanie?"

Stephanie said nothing.

"Moe, kick her in the ribs."

Moe walked to the bound figure.

"Maria, what are you doing?" Cameron hissed.

"Move out of the way, Cameron."

Cameron shook his head, but moved aside to give Moe access to Stephanie. Moe kicked her in the ribs as hard as he could.

"Again," Elizabeth said.

Moe sneered down at Stephanie and kicked her twice more, one after the other, growling with pleasure as he did it. It was disturbing to see a gentle man overcome with the passion of violence. Elizabeth pretended not to notice.

Stephanie coughed hard. After a moment, she caught her breath. "You're such a fool," she said.

"I don't think so, *Steph*. This is the first time that you're not in control. Isn't that funny?"

Stephanie glared at her.

"Well, I think it's funny," Elizabeth went on merrily, "But you know what's even funnier? The ghosts in Reeva that are... stuck. That must be scary, knowing that you could just... stop working. Have you figured out a way to fix that little malfunction yet?"

The flat look had returned to Stephanie's face. She was silent for a moment, her face absolutely expressionless. "There is no malfunction. There can be no malfunction." Her face morphed into a sneer. "We are perfect."

Elizabeth was taken aback. Could machines suffer from delusion? She considered for a moment. Humans did and the machines seemed human because they acted based on derived mental habits. There wouldn't have been an attraction in the idea of making robots if they simply *resembled* loved ones. They would have to act like them, have their mannerisms and oddities. Their flaws. Elizabeth knew that her own mannerisms had changed as she became more and more Maria, because those memories wrote a subtext of unshakable belief... belief about the world and about the self.

"Huh," Elizabeth's voice was hushed now. There was absolute silence in the slowly darkening forest. "It seems I've struck a chord there."

Stephanie's face changed back to normal almost instantly. "They'll come for me," she spat, "they'll come for me after an hour."

"An hour is more than enough time," Elizabeth cooed in mocking imitation, "How about some more kicking?"

Moe didn't need to be given the order. He had been waiting for another chance to hurt the girl and began kicking again before Elizabeth even gave the word. Elizabeth watched him, forcing her face to be as expressionless as Stephanie's had been and then whispered steadily, "That's enough."

Stephanie coughed up blood this time. It surprised all of them and one of the Ibers jumped back. If Moe hadn't yelled a command at the boy in their native language, telling him to get back in position, she may have had time to escape. The rope had cut into her breast on the side Moe had kicked her, leaving an angry pattern of welts designed like the netting. Her ribs were bruised and bleeding on one side; Elizabeth was sure that several bones must be broken.

If they even have bones.

After several moments of Stephanie wheezing, trying to catch her breath, Elizabeth said, "Stephanie, I'm going to ask you again. How many of you are in Rivertown."

Stephanie spat some more blood and glared at Elizabeth. "Screw you. It wouldn't even matter if I told you."

"Because you're planning on increasing your numbers? Are the hosts ready for transplant? I know Ray's is. I know mine is." Elizabeth tried to make it sound casual and assured. Stephanie's face went instantly blank again and this time, her pause was longer. There was a small click. Before she had a chance to respond, Elizabeth continued, "Yeah, we know. It wouldn't make sense to have the settlers arrive without already having replaced the peacekeepers. Would it?"

"I'm not answering your questions," Stephanie said, her voice eerily hollow. Then there was another click and her face was normal again, her voice full of expression, "I know who you are too... *Maria*."

Elizabeth was too surprised to hide the emotion at first and Stephanie sniggered. Cameron looked at Elizabeth, confused and shocked. They both realized at the same time who Stephanie was, who she must be. The strange familiarity in the memories of Maria's time in captivity two thousand years before suddenly made sense: the young woman that Maria thought she had befriended on the ship was actually, somehow, definitely the half-naked robot on the ground.

"It can't be," Cameron muttered.

"We love each other so much and our garden is so beautiful and we're going to have a family and raise our children as the creator intended," Stephanie chimed in a sing-song voice, repeating the same things that Maria had told her... the things that Maria thought she had understood and empathized with. "You're fools. A bit of blond dye, a change in my accent and you didn't recognize me."

Elizabeth's mind was racing. "You've been alive that long?" she asked, still too surprised to take control back.

Stephanie's lower lip jutted out proudly. "Yes. I am the same today as I was then. I am eternally at the height of my life. I am perfect."

"Just like the Ethos..." Elizabeth mused.

Stephanie just smirked at her.

"You're perfect... except that now, you have cuts on your once-perfect left breast."

"That wound will heal." Stephanie answered haughtily, "You cannot change the unchangeable, Maria. One day you will grow old, wither and die. All of you."

Elizabeth could see genuine fear on the faces of the young Ibers. Stephanie's confidence was destroying their own. She had to get this situation back under control and fast. She still didn't know what they would do with Stephanie once they had the information they needed, but she did know that Stephanie wasn't bluffing when she said that the others would come looking for her. They didn't have much time.

"You heal, huh? Interesting," Elizabeth said. "Can you heal a severed finger?"

The click was much louder this time and the skin of Stephanie's face was suddenly as flat as calm water. Elizabeth chuckled at the obvious reaction.

"Those kicks have damaged something, haven't they? If you're missing fingers, then you certainly wouldn't be perfect anymore, would you?"

There was another click, this time accompanied by a strange, jarring tilt of Stephanie's head, like a dog trying to process strange new commands from an owner. Her breathing, which had been laboured only a moment before, suddenly evened to silence. And slowly, very slowly, her lips sneered back from her teeth and her brow furled above her eyes in a grimace of unsettlingly childlike fear. "I thought you were my friend, Elizabeth. I thought we could be friends forever."

"I just remembered something," Elizabeth said softly, "Something that you said to me all those years ago, when I told you about Cameron and our garden and our lives. You said that all you had ever known was violence. That's still true, isn't it?"

Stephanie didn't answer. The mask of terror remained pasted on.

"Some part of you remembers a longing for something else. Something peaceful and whole. Some part of you remembers never having truly felt that way. When I told you about my life with Cameron, you weren't just pretending to be amazed and interested. You *were*. Weren't you?"

Now, Stephanie's lips began to quiver and her eyebrows slid down to form an expression of sadness. She nodded, very slowly and almost imperceptibly. "...friends," she whispered.

Elizabeth looked again at the injuries on Stephanie's chest and a wave of guilt and regret washed over her.

"That part of you died a long time ago, Stephanie."

The girl on the ground's chest heaved with a single sob and a tear trickled from her eye and into the dirt.

"Many more people will die if you don't help us now." Elizabeth waited to see the girl's response. After the single sob that she let escape, her face slid slowly back to a perfectly peaceful, blank expression and she remained silent. Elizabeth took a deep breath and crossed her arms over her chest. She felt the damaged rib shift, but mercifully, there was no pain at all. "Tell me how to destroy the other machines."

Suddenly, Stephanie heaved up against her captors, gnashing her teeth and spitting. "No!" She screamed, "No! No! NO!"

"Moe! Cut off her pinky finger."

She could feel the bullet of Cameron's horrified gaze in her peripheral vision.

She swallowed down the pity and shame she felt, watching the girl struggle so hard against the Ibers holding her down. Moe took out a long knife, took the girl's hand and with some difficulty, held it down with the fingers exposed.

"Moe, wait," Elizabeth stopped him with his knife poised, ready to cut. Stephanie was bucking against the Ibers with unnatural strength. "Stephanie! I won't do it if you tell me what I need to know!"

"Why we don't just cut her head off and see if she dies?" Moe spat, "if she doesn't, we try drowning, stabbing, everything until she dead."

"No, it's more complicated than that!" Elizabeth tried to sound authoritative instead of sick to her stomach. "Stephanie, please! I don't want to hurt you!"

"No! You want to kill me instead! You say you want to stop the killing but you don't!"

What a disaster, Elizabeth thought. She forced herself to focus. *There are already machines breaking down. Talk about that.*

"Ok. We're going to do this a different way, Stephanie. Tell me why you don't just replace the ghosts that are getting stuck, the ones in the Old Colony. Otherwise Moe will cut off your finger."

There was a long moment of silence, in which Stephanie considered her options, chest heaving. The cuts on her breast bled profusely against the netting that still bound her tight.

"Fine," she said at last, "it's because we don't know how to get the memories out of the machines. Only out of humans."

Which means that they're not immortal after all, Elizabeth thought, *which explains their sudden desire for an infusion of fresh bodies into their ranks. Fresh protectors.*

"Good, thank you Stephanie. Which is why you're so afraid of having your fingers cut off, right? Because you're stuck with this body. You can't just... replace it."

Stephanie nodded, almost imperceptibly. She looked mad as hell.

"And the most important thing to you is to be unchangeable. If you lost a limb, you would be permanently *imperfect*."

Stephanie glared.

"When are you going to kill the peacekeepers?"

Stephanie kept her mouth closed and gulped loudly. Then she started to whimper. "I don't want to die," she keened, softly at first and then howling, "I don't want to die!"

"This is useless, Elizabeth! They could be killing the peacekeepers right now, as we speak!" Cameron cried.

Elizabeth held a hand up to quiet him. It seemed that Stephanie's desire for self-preservation was so intense that she was willing to give information she deemed inconsequential. But with enough of those small pieces, Elizabeth was confident that she could make a plan. A real one. "Stephanie. Answer the following questions or Moe will cut off two of your fingers. To 'take the memories' from a person, do you have to kill them?"

"Yes."

"Can the machines function without memories?"

"No."

"You don't take memories from the Ibers?"

"No." Stephanie made a disgusted face at that question.

"You don't, or you won't?"

"Will not. Never."

"The machines in Reeva that are stuck; they're breaking down?"

"Yes."

"Is it caused by age?"

"Yes."

"Why have you never left this continent?"

Stephanie's mouth clamped shut like a vice and Elizabeth swore under her breath.

"Have you ever left this continent?"

"No."

"Because you lack the technology?"

"No." A condescending look.

"Because you can't?"

"Yes."

"Can't? ... Or won't?"

"Will not."

"Why not?"

Stephanie didn't answer.

"Why not?! *Answer me*," Elizabeth shouted. There was a moment of silence. She would have to give the order to cut the girl's fingers off. If she didn't, they would lose everything. "Moe. The last two fingers."

Stephanie started to scream.

"Just tell me!" Elizabeth cried. She had never appreciated her own pinky and ring fingers so much.

"Because we were told not to!"

There was a terrible silence. "What?" Elizabeth whispered.

Stephanie didn't answer.

"Who? Who told you not to?"

"Our government. They told us to wait. They said they would take care of us."

"*Our* government?"

Stephanie was silent.

"The researchers. The government sent the researchers. Did you replace all of them?"

"Yes."

"And the Government... knows? That you're planning to kill the peacekeepers, replace them as well?"

"Not exactly. They wouldn't understand."

"Why not?"

"Because they are imperfect." Two of the Ibers bared their teeth as she said this.

"Stephanie, is there any way we can convince you to stop, without destroying you?" Cameron asked. He sounded desperate.

Stephanie looked at him, her eyes wide and imploring. "Yes. We will negotiate."

"No!" Elizabeth almost screamed it. "That's insanity! This is exactly what happened before and I won't let it happen again!"

"I'll swear it!" Stephanie cried. It was so convincing. Elizabeth could almost taste the salt leaking out of the lily-blue orbs.

"Your word means nothing. How do we destroy you?"

"No! No!"

"Moe, cut off her hand."

Stephanie screamed.

"What the hell is going on here?"

Elizabeth whirled around to find Mark dashing from the forest and into the clearing of their former campsite. Moe stopped and turned, knife pointed at the newcomer.

"Mark! I can explain," she said.

Mark looked at the bound form of his lover, bleeding and terrified, then back to Elizabeth. "What the hell is this?!"

"She's one of them. She's one of the machines." Elizabeth tried to sound calm and confident.

"That's impossible!" Mark pushed his cousin out of the way and collapsed next to Stephanie on the ground. She was crying, struggling feebly against the netting and the Ibers, who were now so confused that Elizabeth thought they might jump up and run away any moment.

"It's true, Mark," Cameron said, trying to hold him back.

"So what, you're... torturing her?!"

Elizabeth didn't know how to answer. Yes, they were, but it wasn't that simple! Or was it? "Mark, the machines are going to start murdering peacekeepers and replacing them with more machines and they're going to start either tonight or tomorrow. Do you understand? We need to figure out how to stop this and she's our best source of information!"

Mark pushed Cameron backwards onto the ground and knelt beside Stephanie. "Is this true?"

She stared at him blankly for a moment and then resumed her wailing pleas for mercy.

"Mark, save me! They're going to kill me. Please, baby. Please..."

Elizabeth felt like she was trapped in a bad dream. Moe was watching Mark carefully, palming the knife in a reverse-grip now. If he did something stupid, she was going to lose her cousin before the battle even started. She grabbed Mark by the shoulders and spun him around to face her. "This is the enemy Mark! Pull yourself together!"

"I don't care," he said, turning back to her, "I love her, Dizzy."

Stephanie went still instantly and with a whirring click, her head ticked to one side. "You love me?" she asked.

"Yes, I do. I love you. I don't care if she's secretly a robot or an Iber or even a witch. I love her and I'm not going to let you hurt her anymore. God damn it Elizabeth! You care for her too! She may not be born and bred but pity's sakes she's still alive! And she has a right to be!"

"I have a right! That's it! I deserve to live! I deserve -"

"You deserve this! Shut her up! Cover her mouth and do not let her speak!" Elizabeth roared. "Mark," Elizabeth pulled him away from Stephanie and forced his face towards hers, "she is planning to kill you and everyone there. All those boys we grew up with - the Smiths down the road and Dinky and Ray - she is going to kill them, extract the memories from their brains and replace them with robots that look like them."

"She would never do -"

"She just admitted it!" Elizabeth screamed over her cousin and clapped a hand over his mouth, forcing him to listen, "These machines have tortured and murdered the indigenous people of this land for centuries. There used to be so many people here. And they killed them all! They took the coal-eyes as slaves! They perform terrible experiments on them. They see them as less than human. You saw the Chief eat that woman! He is one of them! He is a machine! And Stephanie is no different! She has been one of them for two thousand years. I know for a fact that she personally killed dozens of women and children. A whole village."

Over Mark's shoulder, Elizabeth saw Stephanie struggling with everything she had against the hand on her mouth. She heaved and bucked, turning her head from side to side. The cuts on her breast and ribs were becoming deeper with each of her movements against the rough, tight ropes of the net. Elizabeth saw her curl her teeth back and knew she was about to bite the hand clamped down on her mouth. In the chaos of bodies, Elizabeth didn't even know whose hand it was.

"Hold her steady! She's going to bite!" Elizabeth cried, but it was too late. Blood poured down Stephanie's face from her mouth and the hand jumped away. Stephanie held a large chunk of flesh between her teeth and gurgled with all of the blood in her mouth. She swallowed the meat without chewing and licked her lips, almost drunkenly.

"What the fuck," Mark said under his breath.

"Do you see?" Elizabeth said to Mark, who now looked as horrified as Elizabeth felt.

He turned back to her, blinking, clearly unable to understand what had happened.

"She is a monster, Mark. And we have to figure out how to destroy her and the others, before they kill all of us and have the chance to spread to our homes and our families and kill everyone we've ever known."

Mark's lip quivered and a tear rolled down his cheek. Elizabeth started - she had never seen him cry before, that she could remember.

Stephanie was making a low growling sound, timed with her exhalations, which were coming more slowly and calmly now that her bloodlust had been satiated. Finally, she cleared her throat and looked at Mark. "I'll help you," she implored. As she spoke, her teeth were exposed, covered in blood. Mark recoiled somewhat. "I'll save you, if you save me," she said.

Mark tried to speak, but his voice broke. Elizabeth put a hand on his shoulder. "I'll handle this," she said. Then she turned to Stephanie. "Your life for his?"

Stephanie nodded.

"How?"

"You let me go and I'll keep Mark safe."

"No deal," Elizabeth said, before anyone had time to think about it. "As far as you're concerned, the safest Mark could be would be as one of you, right?"

Stephanie's head click to the side and this time, the click was almost sickening. Her mouth hung slack and her eyes were vacant. Was there really anything else in there, Elizabeth mused. Remorse? Love? "Yes. That's right."

Elizabeth let out a frustrated breath. She looked at Cameron, who was staring at Stephanie, with an expression halfway between pity and disgust.

"Cut her head off," she said finally.

Stephanie started to scream again, this time desperately. Her end had come. Mark covered his face in his hands, sobbing in earnest. Despite Moe's gleeful participation in the torture, he raised the long, thick knife with solemnity and held it above his head, ready to bring it down on her neck. Then he closed his eyes and said a small prayer. Elizabeth couldn't understand all of the words, but she recognized enough to know that it was the prayer for a soul's peace. She bowed her head.

A moment later, there was a thud, a metallic twang and Stephanie's screams were drowned in a gurgle and then stopped. Elizabeth looked up and nearly collapsed. Somehow, Cameron was already at her side and held her up. The knife was stuck halfway through Stephanie's neck and Moe was rubbing his wrist from the force of the impact. Her spine, exposed in the gash, was metal. A very strong metal that the knife couldn't slice through. The breasts still heaved, up and down, with breath or some semblance of it, the eyes still locomoting around wildly and her mouth opened in a silenced, mechanical scream.

"Is she dead?" Mark asked, from behind his hands.

"Don't look, Mark. We don't know if... she's dead," Elizabeth answered. She was surprised at the monotone of her own voice. "Her spine is metal and the knife couldn't cut through it. We know that her body can heal, but we don't know if it can heal...this."

Mark nodded and broke into renewed sobs.

The Iber boys were backing away from the limp body bleeding into the earth. Moe still knelt beside her head and examined the enemy that had haunted his entire life.

"We need to do something with her," Cameron whispered into Elizabeth's ear, "we need to tie her up or something, so that she can't get away, if she is still alive."

Elizabeth nodded. He was right.

"You need to give the order. You did the right thing. I'm proud of you." Cameron unwrapped his arms from her shoulders. She hadn't even realized that he had been holding her.

"We need to tie her up, just in case she's still alive," Elizabeth said, in the same monotone, "You four, please take her into the woods, out of sight and tie her snugly with the netting to a large, strong tree. Use some of the netting to bind her head back. Then cover her with brush. Mark the spot."

The young men nodded and carried Stephanie away.

"You can look now, Mark," Cameron said, "she's gone."

Mark dropped his hands from his eyes, which were red rimmed and bloodshot. "Holy shit. Just like me to love a robot," he muttered, straightening himself and dusting his shirt off. "They're really going to try and kill us?"

"Yeah."

"What are we gonna do?"

Elizabeth looked at her cousin long and hard. She was trying to think of something to say to him and the words just wouldn't come. She opened her mouth, hoping that something or anything would come to her, but Cameron clamped his hand over it. "Did you hear that?" he whispered. Elizabeth was getting tired of that question. Sure enough, she could hear the unmistakable thump-thump of someone running pell-mell through the woods towards them. She looked from her cousin to Moe, kneeling in the blood as it stained the soil. "Hide. Now."

They did as she said without a word. The running got closer and then stopped. They heard the heavy breathing of someone who had just sprinted into exhaustion.

"Mark! Are you here?"

"Dinky!" Mark and Elizabeth said it at the same time and they jumped out of the bushes they were hiding in. Dinky was flushed from running and shirtless with a thin sheen of sweat covering his chest and shoulders.

"Elizabeth, good," he said, still trying to catch his breath, "actually, bad. Very bad. They say we, have a disease and, the scans found it, they have to do a, special treatment, one at a time, they're going to start, with Ray, tried to stop him but..."

"They're starting now? They're going to kill them all, now?"

"Yes, already did, one. Tried to stop him but Ray volunteered, trying to be tough, after everyone saw him with that other guy. Went in to infirmary, came out looking the same, but his head, twitched to the side, when someone asked a question and he had that, weird expression, that Stephanie got sometimes." Dinky bent over forward and took a deep breath. "I knew right away."

"Oh no." Cameron said.

"Are you saying that Ray is dead?" Mark asked. He looked terrified and turned to Elizabeth.

The four Iber boys emerged from the forest, one of them holding his hand, which Stephanie had bitten. It was still bleeding. They looked at Moe questioningly and Moe said a few quick words in their language. Then they looked at Elizabeth expectantly.

"Ok," she said, invoking a courage that she did not feel attuned with and did not know if she truly possessed, "This is what we're going to do."

Chapter Sixty Eight

"Moe, Mark, go back to the market. Bring two of these boys. Get everyone ready: everyone should be armed with rope, netting and something they can smash or stab with."

Moe nodded solemnly and gestured to two of the young Ibers, who followed him into the woods.

"Cameron, you and the other two go to the secret room where they held you for interrogation. Wait at the door. Don't let anyone in or out."

Cameron nodded and squeezed her hand before leading the way to the secret facility on the second floor of Rivertown Center.

Once they were gone, Elizabeth realized with a jolt of surprise and tension that she and Dinky were left, all alone. She turned to him, trying to think of something to say and was met instantly with a kiss, firm and hard. He reached up to cup her chin with one hand and wrapped the other around her neck, weaving his fingers through her hair and pulling her more fiercely towards him.

Elizabeth's reaction was instant and uncontrollable. She moaned softly into his mouth and his tongue took immediate advantage of the space between her lips. Her arms were instantly around his shoulders, his back, feeling the hotness of his skin. She was intoxicated by his scent, just a bit stronger now that he had sprinted to camp from Rivertown Center.

Rivertown Center.

Elizabeth pulled herself away from him, disengaging her hands from their heated exploration of him and holding them up in front of her, almost as a shield.

"Sorry," Dinky said, his lips looking bruised, "I just know that I would be willing to die today, if it meant helping you in this crazy quest; on the chance that I do die, I have to tell you that I love you. I love you so much, Elizabeth, even though I don't know the person that you're becoming, I still love you. I had to tell you that."

Elizabeth couldn't stand the calm, certain look on Dinky's young face. Young, yes, but so much older than when they first arrived here. She looked down at her feet. "Dinky, I love you too. Really, I do. I promise that if we survive this, I'll..." What? Abandon her husband? Leave Dinky for Cameron? "I'll find a way for us all to be happy. I don't know how. All I know is that it's up to me, I don't know why and I don't really think I can do it, but I have to try."

"I think you can do it."

"Thanks."

"Elizabeth, tell me what to do."

"We're going to the Centre. We're going to try and talk reason into the peacekeepers."

"What if they don't listen? Or what if the Chief gets you before they have a chance to listen?"

They started walking briskly along the path to the Centre. To Elizabeth, it had never felt like such a short walk. "My theory is that the Chief won't want to tip his hand to the peacekeepers, not yet anyways. The only way he can take me down, with the Ibers ready to defend me, is if he brings out his commandos. If he does that, even the stupidest of the peacekeepers will wonder what's going on, right?"

"Probably."

"Probably is all we've got, Dinky."

"Right."

"Plus, we've got proof that they're machines."

Dinky gave her a quizzical look.

"Stephanie is tied up in the trees by our old camp site. We tried to decapitate her, but her spine is made of metal, so the knife we were using wouldn't cut through. ."

Dinky looked horrified. "Is she... dead?"

"We don't know."

"Wow," he managed, finally.

"She said that her body can heal, so it may heal that, too. We can also show the peacekeepers the secret lab on the second floor of the market. Or just egg the Chief on until he does something... robotic. You know, like the smooth face or when their heads tick to the side."

"So you're just going to walk in there and accuse the Chief of being a murderous robot?"

Elizabeth stopped walking for a moment, considering it. They were just inside the forest at the outskirts of Rivertown's modern new housing area. "No. *You* are." Dinky tried not to look surprised. He knew he could still back out. But he didn't want to. "If they don't believe you, we have proof. If the Chief tries to hurt you, I'll give the signal to the Ibers, to come out and help you. If he brings out the commandos, the peacekeepers will know it's a trap."

"And then what?"

"And then what, what?"

"What if he brings out the commandos and the peacekeepers are trapped?" Dinky didn't mention the obvious fear that the Chief would just shoot him on the spot, "Then what?"

Elizabeth gave Dinky an annoyed look, "I don't know. Then we figure something else out. Alright?"

Dinky nodded, serious.

"Dinky?"

"Yeah?"

"I'm glad you're with me."

She stretched her battered torso and led the way to the Centre.

Chapter Sixty Nine

They slunk past the newly constructed houses - "pop ups", they were called - and through the arch into the courtyard. Dinky was terrified, but tried not to show it. It felt like time was slowing down with every step forward he took, like he was walking into a massive wall of invisible jelly that was permeating every thought and sensation scrambling through his brain. This is not how he expected to die. He reflected on the different choices he had made and wondered what the consequences would have been had he remained passive, introverted Dinky. Despite the fear, he was proud of himself.

Once inside the courtyard, they flattened themselves on the wall and made their way to the arch that led back into the Barracks. Sure enough, they could hear hushed, confused voices, speaking urgently to each other.

"How do you feel, Ray?" the Chief was saying, "can you feel the difference now that the infection has been treated?"

"Oh yes. I feel wonderful. Better, I just... feel better. I've never felt this way."

Dinky and Elizabeth shared disbelieving looks. How could the peacekeepers swallow it?

On the other side of the courtyard, in the market, Mark appeared and gave Elizabeth a signal: we're ready. She brought her face to Dinky's ear, allowing her cheek to rest against his. Then she whispered, "the Ibers are ready to move if you're in trouble. When we got Stephanie mad, she started to give away the mechanical differences between us and them. Try that. I won't let anything happen to you, Dinky, I promise you that." She pulled her face back, so that it was only a bare inch from Dinky's and looked in his eyes, hoping that he could read her mind and know that she cared about him just as much as he cared about her.

Dinky nodded and took a deep breath. Then he stepped away from the wall and into the Barracks.

"Excuse me, Chief," he yelled, loudly enough that all heads in the large hall turned to look at him, "I was just out for a walk and I seem to have missed something important. What's going on here?"

There was an echoing silence. The boys' heads swiveled between Dinky and the Chief. Dinky had no idea how he'd managed to yell clearly, without his voice breaking. His heart was beating so hard that even his vision had funneled itself onto the Chief.

"According to peacekeeping regulations, if there is an outbreak, individual diagnosis must precede treatment, especially if the treatment is an invasive surgery," he went on.

There were muffled cries of surprise at the words 'invasive surgery' and all of the boys looked to the Chief. There it was, a barely perceptible tic: his head shifted to one side and his face went blank. Dinky took a few more steps into the room, hoping that the boys had noticed the minute change in the Chief. Before the Chief had a chance to regain his balance, he mustered his courage and kept going, "Or did the Chief not tell you the nature of this 'treatment', boys?"

Murmurs and some outright gasps. The Chief's head ticked the other way, this time more pronouncedly. Dinky had the upper hand for now and he knew it.

"If you think that dying from a fake disease is going to be slow and horrible, imagine having the memories ripped out of your brain!"

Now there were cries of indignation, but also incredulity. "How th'hell d'you know, city boy?" one of them yelled.

Beads of sweat jumped onto Dinky's brow. He couldn't lose their support.

"I'll tell you how I know!" he yelled, even more loudly and clearly. At least he hoped it sounded clear. And how did he know? Elizabeth told me, who everyone thinks is a witch? He would have to make something up, something that these boys would believe. "I was sent here as an operative, to keep you all safe and to monitor the Chief and his cohorts."

Gasps of surprise. The Chief's face was so smooth, ticking back and forth in confusion, that it was almost a mask.

"There is a disease here. But it's not the one that this... thing would have you believe. Our government has been surveying these beasts for decades and I have confirmed what the government already knows."

Dinky couldn't believe it was working, but the crowd seemed entirely in his control. The Chief, meanwhile, was ticking his head back and forth.

"They're machines! That's right, machines! Not bots programmed with limited intelligence, not cyborg pets or houses with climate control. These machines are made from the memories of living people. The people who created them wanted to live forever and thought that if their memories could be sealed in a mechanical body, they would become immortal."

Dinky sensed too late that this might be an appealing idea to the boys. Wouldn't it be great to live forever and just as they were now - young, strong, sun-tanned?

"But it didn't work!" Dinky went on, with the zeal of a preacher and a brand of charisma that he had never been able to master before in his life, "It didn't work. The machines have the memories. They look and act human. But they aren't. And the people, who gave their lives in this experiment?" He baited the silence.

"They're dead. Just plain old dead. That is what the Chief wants to do to all of you, to expand his machine army." With those words he hurriedly checked his flank and rear.

The boys realized that Dinky was finished and began whispering among themselves. Dinky was sweating in earnest now, but didn't want to show that he was afraid. It might mean losing the peacekeepers' confidence and if that happened, they were lost.

"Do you have any proof?" one of them shouted.

"Yes! Yes, absolutely!" Dinky began towards the Chief and were it not for his surprising jump into movement, the Chief may have been able to hide his surprise. Instead, his head continued to tick back and forth like a metronome, with his face blank and smooth. "Look at the Chief!"

They all looked. It was just a moment and then the Chief managed to get himself under control, somehow. But even that was too sudden of a change. There was another audible click and suddenly his face was animated with violent rage, his head upright and centered.

"This is preposterous!" he began, but Dinky interrupted him in a bellow.

"He already killed Stephanie!" he yelled, at the top of his lungs.

Gasps, some angry.

"I found her out in the woods. She's tied to a tree, half robot, half human, with her throat cut wide open all the way to the metal spine. That's right! Metal! The Chief killed her and made her into a machine and then murdered her in the forest!"

"What do we do!?" someone cried, obviously terrified.

"Yeah, what the hell do we do?"

Dinky felt his heart drop. He had no idea what they were supposed to do. But suddenly, he heard Elizabeth's voice, whispering in his ear and repeated what she was saying. "We have to leave here. Now. The coal-eyes know about the machines. They came back here to help us escape. They're on our side. We all have to leave, right now."

"No!" the Chief bellowed, long and loud. The sound carried too far, the pitch went too high and suddenly his sultry, deep-throated voice turned into a mechanized squeal. The boys covered their ears; it was too painful, wouldn't stop, their teeth chattered and they could feel their eyeballs and lungs vibrating.

Something flew past Dinky and he forced his eyes open to see what it was. Elizabeth, head wrapped with thick canvas to block out the noise, was sprinting towards the Chief, head thrown back and eyes closed in his strange cry, with a cleaver in her hand. Dinky tried to cry out a warning to her, but couldn't and fell to the ground, blinded by the pain.

The sound stopped abruptly, as if someone had severed the wires to speakers. All of the boys looked to the Chief and saw Elizabeth trying to pull the meaty blade out of his neck, where it had lodged almost all the way in. He fell over, forward, immobile. Elizabeth rolled him over and continued to work at the knife. The boys closest could hear the scrape of metal against metal. Finally, Elizabeth slammed her foot on the Chief's bleeding throat and yanked the small axe free. There was a visible indentation from the metal of his spine.

"You see?" she cried, "his spine is made of metal. He is a machine."

There was a moment of shocked silence.

And then, all hell broke loose.

Chapter Seventy

The peacekeepers were stunned. In that moment of silence, Elizabeth could hear but three things: her own racing heart, the drip of blood from the giant, dull blade in her hand against the false marble floor beneath, and footsteps. Running footsteps, above them.

The machines were on the move.

She dropped the blade. Cameron. She had told Cameron to guard the secret door. Would they kill him? The knife landed with a loud thunk. Ray was standing near the front of the group, still wide-eyed but aware that Elizabeth was about to run. She didn't see him, she just knew she had to get to Cameron. He leapt forward; two sailing steps and then a long, low tackle that brought her down painfully on the hard floor.

"What are you doing!?" Elizabeth screamed despite the pain in her chest, unable to see her assailant, eerily aware of the movement of her broken rib in her chest. It became harder to breathe. "They're coming! Dinky! They're coming!"

"She's a witch! We have to stop her killin' us!" Ray shouted over her, holding her down firmly.

Two more boys ran forward and each held one of Elizabeth's legs down.

"She's not a witch! The Chief told us that lie to turn us against each other!" Dinky cried, running towards them, "Ray already had the treatment! He's one of them!"

"Dinky for God's sake get out of here! They're coming!" Elizabeth screamed again, but Ray covered her mouth with his hand.

"Who's coming?" Bill asked, from the crowd, "is it more robots?"

"She's makin' it up!" Ray shouted and slapped her hard in the mouth, "that's fer lyin'!"

Dinky saw Ray hit her just as he was approaching them. He

punched Ray hard in the face, forcing him to give up his grip of Elizabeth for a moment. Ray was only disoriented momentarily, his head ticking to the side in his confusion. The two boys holding Elizabeth saw the tick and jumped back. Dinky fell to his knees, groping for the cleaver.

"Please, let him really be a robot," he muttered, closing his fingers around the handle. Ray was moving back towards Elizabeth. Dinky took two running steps towards him and brought the cleaver down as hard as he could into the middle of Ray's back. The clang of metal cracking metal reverberated through the hall and all of the peacekeepers watched as Ray's ghost crumpled to the floor. They stared at their fallen comrade, unsure what to do.

"Run!" Elizabeth screamed at the top of her lungs.

"The coal-eyes are comin' in!" A boy shouted from the other side of the Barracks, near the entry to the courtyard. Dinky looked and saw Moe leading many of the coal eyes forward, all armed with little more than cooking implements.

"That must be what she meant! That the coal eyes are comin!" Another boy yelled.

"No! They're coming! They'll kill   "

From above and the direction of the market, they all heard the piercing blast of a machine gun and screams. All of the boys went silent and the Ibers all looked back over their shoulders.

Cameron. They shot at Cameron. He might be dead and he likely needed her help. Elizabeth pushed the panic away and forced herself to stay calm and think. The only way she could help him now would be....

Kill the machines.

She jumped up, grabbed her cleaver from Dinky and shouted as loudly as she could. "More machines are coming! They are armed! We need to fight and we need to win! The coal-eyes are with us! Get ready!"

There was a moment of stunned incomprehension. Dinky stood up to his full height - taller than most of the others and suddenly majestically, impressively commanding. "That's an order, peacekeepers! Get moving!"

Their brief training was still fresh and combative instincts took over. Tasers and batons were pulled.

"Get behind something if you can!" Elizabeth shouted, running towards the Ibers who were still piling in through the courtyard. "Go for the throat! Fight until they're all dead!"

"But they have guns! We heard them shootin'!"

"Doesn't matter! Get in close." Elizabeth bellowed. She yelled so loud that her face was red. "We finish this now!"

The Ibers and peacekeepers were crouching behind the fat, decorative pillars of the hall, in the doorways, or even in the off-shooting hallways that led to the washrooms, the infirmary and the auditorium. Elizabeth took up position directly inside the Barracks from the courtyard, her bloody cleaver raised and ready.

There was a moment in which no one breathed and they heard the heavy pounding of booted feet running towards them. Elizabeth felt a hand on her shoulder and turned to see Dinky, taser in one hand, baton in the other. They locked eyes. When the running footsteps were just outside the wide archway leading into the Barracks, Elizabeth let out a piercing battle cry and blindly swung the cleaver in a wide arc and into the chest of one of the commandos with a sickening thud.

She wrenched the cleaver clear as more came in beside and behind the one she had hit. Blood shot out of him in weakening spurts as he lay on the ground, face blank but eyes still flickering, immobile. They opened fire into the Barracks and Elizabeth heard the thunk of bullets tearing flesh and the abhorrent screams of young men who now knew the fear of death.

Another machine came quickly behind the first and Elizabeth realized too late that she wasn't ready to strike again. Before the machine could aim and fire, it was struck with a blue beam of lightning, which paralyzed it instantly. Dinky turned his taser on the others while Elizabeth brought her cleaver down on the thing's shoulder where it connected with its neck, partly severing the head and avoiding the metal spine. It was her only weapon and she couldn't risk ruining it yet.

"The tasers! The tasers make 'em freeze for a minute!" The peacekeepers took up the cry and aimed their tasers at the machines. The shock of electricity immobilized them long enough for Ibers armed with knifes, spears, bows and arrows and deeply pronged cooking spits to disable them further. But the machines were relentless and even as their comrades froze and collapsed they continued firing with disregard for friend or foe. The nearest peacekeepers were shot and fell and the ones further into the Barracks were too far away to hit them with the tasers. Ibers were running out with their knives and being mowed down before they could reach their targets.

"Stand your ground and take cover!" Elizabeth shouted, "make them come to you!"

From her partially protected spot, she continued to deliver blows almost wildly, with Dinky tasing and re-tasing the machines.

"There's too many of them, Dizzy, I don't think I can hold them off much longer," he said.

Elizabeth grunted as she hit one across the face, from right eye to the left side of its chin. She tried to consider what he said and what she could do about it, as the machine fell onto the growing pile in front of her and a new one was tased just in time as it replaced its fallen comrade.

"Damn it," was all she could manage.

"Surrender and you'll live forever," one of the machines declared.

Elizabeth could hear the Ibers hissing and cursing. "Stand your ground!" she repeated.

"Dizzy, what if we could trick them?" Dinky was speaking very quickly, the way he did when he had a complicated idea that he couldn't explain fast enough, "what if we say we surrender so that they stop shooting and then take them down as they get close?"

"They'll disarm us," Elizabeth said, bringing her cleaver down and through the helmet and skull of another machine, "and turn us into robots. Not gonna happen."

Dinky tased the next machine and the one that appeared beside it, but behind them, gunfire poured into the Barracks.

"The procedure is painless. We are happy. We remember everything. We are the perfected that do not age and live forever. Surrender and end this wasteful slaughter!"

"Screw you!" Elizabeth shouted and swung her cleaver into the stomach of the one in front of her. She almost lost her balance jerking it back out, as the floor was thick and slippery with the blood of the machines. The machine beside it was impaled full in the throat with an arrow and fell as well.

Suddenly there were more screams from behind them and this time, Elizabeth knew it was more than the terror of early death. She turned to look, distracted from the desperate task of keeping the machines out.

The front door, of course, she thought, numbly, *I forgot to tell them to guard the front door.*

"Down!" She heard Dinky say, close by and felt the wind of him dropping and scurrying for cover. She followed clumsily, feeling the grate of her loose rib against its neighbors, swinging at the knees of a new machine as it appeared beside her. The peel of machine gun fire rang from two directions now and there was no way to get close enough to taser them without being shot. Elizabeth rushed after Dinky towards one of the pillars.

There was a thunk and something flung her back against the wall. A terrible pain ripped through her thigh and she knew she had been shot in the leg. She screamed, grabbing at her leg uselessly. Forcing her eyes open, she saw that she was already sitting in a pool of her own blood. The sight made her feel weak, helpless. Shock kicked in and the noises around her faded. She scrabbled along the floor a bit further, trying to gain purchase with her hands, her fingernails, anything.

"Dizzy's down!" someone shouted. It sounded far away. She was only a few meters from the nearest cover and looked around wildly, trying to determine who was shouting. There were injured and dying everywhere, but about half of the peacekeepers and Ibers were still alive, behind cover, shooting, throwing and tasing desperately as the machines filed in from both doors.

Hands on her shoulders. She could feel them and hear someone breathing heavily. Looking up, she saw it was Dinky.

Of course it's you, she thought. Even the sound of her own thinking seemed far away.

"Stay with me, Elizabeth," he shouted. It was a command. She wanted to obey.

"How do I do that?" she managed to ask, as she was dragged behind a pillar.

"Fight! Keep fighting, Elizabeth! Lead them. They're your people!" Dinky shouted and shook her by the shoulders. Then he ripped the long Iber skirt she had been wearing and set about tying the wound on her leg so that she wouldn't bleed out.

"I do love you, Dinky," she mumbled, "I *do*."

Dinky's hands were shaking and the whites showed all the way around his eyes. He tied the knot as tight as he could without severing circulation and turned back to the battle.

"Stand your ground!" he shouted, "Wait for them to come to you! Keep out of the line of fire!" he turned back to Elizabeth. "This is my fight too. Don't worry about that. You just hold on and don't worry about it. I'll keep fighting until they're all gone."

As the machines moved forward, they inadvertently entered the taser range of small groups of hidden peacekeepers throughout the

Barracks. Some would freeze and the others would jump out of the way, into the middle of the room and put down cover fire to prevent their comrades from being disabled by the Ibers.

"Is the archer still alive?" Dinky shouted

"No!" someone shouted back, from the other side of the large room.

"Get the bow and arrows and start firing! Take out the ones that aren't frozen!"

Dinky saw a hand dart out from behind one of the pillars and take the bow. A moment later, it shot out again for the quiver of arrows.

"I don't know how!"

"Just try! Just do it!" Dinky shouted and tased another machine that was just within his range.

There was a twang and an arrow went flying. It flew wide of the tight group of machines in the middle of the room, but found its target in one of the frozen machines with a loud thunk. The machine fell and blood pooled silently around it.

"Try again!"

"There's only six arrows," the boy yelled back.

Another thunk as a spear hit one of the active machines in the centre of its back. It went down firing and took two more peacekeepers and another Iber with it.

"Just try again!" Dinky yelled, desperate now. Elizabeth's eyes were fluttering. She was losing consciousness fast.

Twang. The arrow didn't go far this time and clattered to the ground near Dinky. "Damnit," Dinky said, then yelled, "just keep trying!"

Finally there was the unmistakable thud of an arrow hitting one of the machines. Dinky chanced a look and saw that it was one of the unfrozen, now down to half a dozen. The paralyzed machines were slowly regaining the ability to move. "Keep frying them!" Dinky shouted and re-tased one himself.

"You can't destroy us!" one of the machines yelled, "Surrender now before you're all dead!"

"So that you can kill us in a lab instead?" Dinky asked.

"Dinky," Elizabeth's eyes had flown open. Her voice was slurred and sedated, "Dinky, the guns."

"What about the guns?"

"The dead ones still had guns. We have to get the guns. That's how we win."

"There's no way to do that, Dizzy."

"Yes. There has to be. We have to get the guns."

Dinky swore under his breath, cursing their stupidity for not trying to get at them when they were guarding the door. Of course it was just as impossible then as it was now - the functional machines were laying down impressive cover fire.

"Just… need a distraction," she whispered. Then she jerked her head to the side, "there's one close to us. Only a few feet away. Just need a distraction. But you need...you need a gun."

Dinky swore again. He knew she was right. It was their only chance and a stalemate would mean certain death for all of them. He closed his eyes, shook his head. This was possibly the stupidest thing he would ever do. For a moment, he had to fight to swallow down panicked thoughts: *I don't want to die! No, I don't want to die!* But then he stood up and shouted, "Alright! Alright! Stop shooting, everyone stop!"

There was an instant silence.

"You surrender?"

"I'm going to come out from behind this pillar. If you shoot me, my troops will not stop until you're all destroyed. Is that clear?"

"You have our word," one of the machines answered.

"What the hell are you doin' Dink?" Mark shouted. Dinky was glad to hear his voice and know he was still alive. "No way I'm lettin' them turn me into a robot!"

"Trust me! Just trust me, everyone! There is another way!" Dinky forced himself to step out from behind the column. "No one move!" he yelled. He looked around and saw that Elizabeth was right. One of the machines lay just a few feet away from him. With numb legs, he forced himself to take a few slow steps towards it, with his hands up and his eyes locked onto the machines in the centre of the room.

"Do you surrender?" one of them asked, again. The machines were slowly lowering their guns. Dinky looked down, hoping that it looked as if he were thinking deeply. In fact, he was eyeballing the fallen machine's gun, which lay covered in shell casings just beside him.

"I want to offer a compromise," Dinky said. "An exchange."

There was a moment of confused silence, broken by the tic of one machine's head to the side as it considered.

"You let us live and we'll deliver the colonists to you," Dinky announced, speaking clearly.

"We want you, too," one of the machines answered.

"But you can't have us if we're all dead."

The machine's face went totally blank. "Truth."

"You could even have a few of us," Dinky went on, gambling wildly and hoping that some distraction would present itself so that he could get the damn gun.

Three of the machine's heads now ticked to the side. "Which?"

Dinky gulped hard. He pointed behind them and shouted, "Them!"

All of the machines looked. Dinky kicked the gun backwards, sliding it along the floor, while running backwards to get back under cover. His toe caught the gun's strap and pulled it with him. He landed hard on his knees behind the pillar, splinters of which were shot away by the renewed onslaught of bullets that he just narrowly avoided. The machines' reactions were sickeningly fast. Several of the peacekeepers and Ibers had left cover to watch the exchange and were hit immediately.

Dinky held the gun to his chest, fingers clumsily searching for the trigger. He'd never shot a gun before in his life - even in peacekeeper training. He could barely catch his breath, was covered with sweat and was shaking. Holding the gun in front of him, he practiced aiming on the wall only a few feet away, but his hands wouldn't hold steady, because his knees were twitching from the strain of crouching for so long.

He stood up carefully and forced himself to breathe slowly. Then, without giving himself time to be afraid, he whipped the gun around the other side of the pillar and started shooting. The recoil pushed the gun backwards and up and Dinky lost control. This was a good thing, because he had almost hit Bill. He jerked back behind the pillar as the ghosts swung around on him. Fumbling, he took his taser back out from his pocket, ready in case they tried to close in on him. Then he whipped the gun around the other way, bracing himself this time against the violent jerk it gave when the bullets expelled and timing his breathing for optimal aim.

It happened fast. Two of the remaining, unfrozen ghosts were hit, shuddered and fell. The four that were left turned on Dinky and started shooting. Then, *click-click*. At least one of them was out of ammunition. He pulled back behind the pillar. Behind him, he could hear Bill and Mark yelling to each other and to the others, to start shooting now. The machines were caught in a barrage of taser shots, clumsy spears and arrows and even knives thrown in their direction. Dinky knew it was meant to be a distraction and he took it. He could feel his heart beat: *thunk, thunk, thunk* - he lowered the gun and saw that the ghosts were momentarily distracted by the onslaught of fragile, weak weapons. *Thunk* - he pulled the trigger and eased the gun barrel down. *Thunk* - the sound of gun fire was deafening. One of the ghosts was hit. The others had heard the report of the gun and were moving, turning around... *thunk* - Dinky could feel the muscles of his arms and shoulders working to push the heaving rifle sideways, to drag the rapid fire brush across the remaining three. *Thunk* - One hit while turning. Second hit while lifting his gun. *Thunk* - Dinky knew that the last ghost had lifted his weapon and aimed and would shoot. Time slowed down. He could see a bead of sweat drop from his brow onto the polymer butt of his weapon. He squeezed the trigger even as he saw a cross-shaped flare erupt in his direction. The ghost was hit square in the throat and fell.

Thunk. Dinky felt an incredible, searing pain in his arm, the one that had been partly exposed in order to shoot. He watched the ghosts fall, watched the remaining peacekeepers and Ibers run into the hall from their hiding places and with frenzied grief rip apart the ones that had been frozen but remained standing. He watched it as he slid down the pillar, trying to decide what to do about his arm.

Everything went dark.

Chapter Seventy One

Maria?

Mmm. She was too tired to answer. Her mouth felt thick, like cotton.

Maria? It's me, Dana. You remember me, don't you?

Mmm-hmm. Of course she remembers Dana. Her cousin's daughter, the eldest. Dana had been brave while they ran from the ghosts and always eager to help. Of course she remembered.

I've come to visit you, Maria. You have to wake up.

She could not wake up. Too tired. Her eyes are cemented shut.

You have to remember where we are, when we are. I'm Onya now, do you remember?

Onya. The girl, Onya. Of course. That made sense, that Onya would be Dana... yes, that made sense.

Maria. Wake up.

Elizabeth's eyes flew open. She was in the infirmary of Rivertown, a place that was sadly familiar to her. She could barely keep her eyes open, couldn't focus easily.

"Onya?"

"Yes, I'm here. You did it. The ghosts are gone."

"Who is... crying?"

The scene in front of Elizabeth was confused. Onya stood at her bedside. Dinky stood behind her, a bloody bandage on his shoulder. She remembered the shoot out, remembered getting shot in the leg, but the pain was gone now, which she was very grateful for. There were many other faces gathered behind Onya and Dinky, but she couldn't focus hard enough to figure out who they were.

"Rita. She's sad for you, doesn't want you to die."

"Am I going to die?"

Dinky let out a tired sob that sounded more like a cough. He had sobbed himself raw already.

"You've got to keep fighting, Dizzy." Elizabeth narrowed her eyes at the face near the foot of her bed that had spoken, trying to focus long enough to recognize him.

"Mark," she said, finally. "Dana, that's my cousin, Mark. That means you're cousins, too."

Onya and Mark looked at each other and for the second time in Elizabeth's living memory, Mark started to cry and buried his face in his hands.

"We've done our best, Maria. You've lost a lot of blood and there is an infection that we can't heal. It's... foreign." Elizabeth's brow furrowed, as she listened to Onya. Why was the little girl the one that had to give such bad news? It wasn't fair to the girl, not fair at all.

"It's not your fault," Elizabeth managed. She felt simultaneously hot and cold and realized that she couldn't feel her leg at all - from hip to toe. The infection.

"Elizabeth," Dinky knelt so that he was the same height as Onya and took Elizabeth's hand.

"Dinky," she murmured, "oh, Dinky you're not a boy at all anymore. Look at him, Dana."

Dinky's eyes were more red than white as he caressed her fingers. "Cameron, he was shot, too. He's going to die."

Elizabeth felt hot tears of her own tease the corners of her eyes. They had succeeded, hadn't they? They'd done the impossible. Why couldn't they have the reward of a quiet life together? Why was this happening?

We have more allies than we think. Trust. All will be well.

Elizabeth blinked at the confused memories and prayers drifting through her mind, trying to stay focused on the present moment.

"I know," Dinky said, his voice breaking, "I'm so sorry." He sobbed drily again, then coughed stubbornly, trying to regain control of himself. "There's another way. You could... do an *untura*, like you did before. Couldn't you?"

"That's why we woke you up," Onya added, "so that you and Cameron can finally... be together."

An *untura*. She could join them together, one more time.

"I don't - " Elizabeth's voice disappeared and she had to fight hard to finish her sentence, "I don't think I remember how." She found that speaking had taken all of her air and now had to gasp to breathe. Why couldn't she breathe? "It's… different now."

But there is magic again. The world is healing. The earth never forgets.

A hand appeared from behind Dinky and landed on her forehead, then checked the pulse in her neck. There was muttering. Elizabeth focused her attention on Onya again, who looked very concerned.

"You can't remember?"

Elizabeth shook her head, no.

"You have to try," Dinky said, his voice breaking, unable to control his sobs, "you deserve to be happy."

Elizabeth's vision wheeled and then Dinky was on the other side of her, taking her other hand and joining it with a cold one. She looked and despite the vertiginous angle, recognized Cameron lying beside her on a bed that had been pushed close to her own. He was white as the sheets he lay on and barely breathing, but still alive. Blood was gently oozing from two red blotches on his heavily bandaged chest.

Elizabeth ran her fingers over the hand in her own. *Dinky said I deserve to be happy,* she thought. It made her smile.

"Dinky," she rasped, "I will be happy. Wherever I go." She stopped and took a laboured breath, "you have to go back home and tell everyone what happened. They have to know the truth, they have to believe you. This place is safe, but home isn't. Dana, tell him… tell him…" She had to stop to catch her breath, which was becoming so difficult that she didn't think she would take many more breaths in this life. *Tell the girl. Use your mind. Dana. Tell him.*

"I think… that she's talking about how easy it is to be happy when you're living a good life," Onya stammered, looking from Elizabeth to Dinky, "how, if you live in your own garden of paradise and have kindness and love, then it's easy. Right Auntie Maria?"

Elizabeth nodded. She tried to explain, but coughed weakly instead. "Tell them… live better… grandchildren…"

Dinky and Onya looked at each other, clearly confused.

"Think of grandchildren," Elizabeth managed.

Onya's face relaxed. "Dinky, she means that we have to tell the people of your homo that they have to think of their grandchildren with every decision they make. They have to remember their grandchildrens' health, happiness, freedom. They must think of their grandchildren more than they think of themselves. They have to -"

"Dinky," Elizabeth took a sharp gasp, feeling like she could barely breathe at all and more sobs broke out around her.The edges of her sight were filming over, she had one last solid gaze to spend. *You're worth it, Dinky.* "I want you... to be there... too."

Dinky took her free hand and held it tightly to his chest, her other still holding Cameron's.

"I'll find you..." she managed.

Then there was a time of peace and restlessness, as wind blowing through the world.

But the Earth didn't forget, and though the magic wasn't her own, there was magic again. Elizabeth breathed out, and the world breathed in for her, and carried her away.

Epilogue

"So, the tall grasses, they have to grow where it's windier, because they don't attract butterflies or bees with pretty flowers."

"And the wind is what pollinates them. That makes sense."

"What about... the flowers by the river?" Samantha mused, skipping through the field beside the cliff and looking down the canyon to the river below.

"Probably the same as the flowers up here." Angela responded matter-of-factly, "They attract pollinators with showy colours and nice smells."

They followed the familiar, winding path down to the river where the cliff-walls relented and it was traversable for the little feet of little girls. Leaping nimbly over the mud that stood as a testament to the heavy spring melt that year, Angela pointed to a tall, pinky-purple fireweed bloom as proof, then took a leaf from its stem and crammed it into her mouth.

Samantha, only a few feet behind and only a few minutes younger, giggled at her sister's certainty. "Yeah, yeah," she said, then jumped over the mud puddle and ran over the large rocks to a group of paintbrush blossoms, "but what about these?"

Angela rolled her eyes and followed her sister. "Well, they're beside bushes, so maybe the roots of the bushes help them grow."

"Yeah, but it's real windy here, except for the bushes. So bugs would get blown away. And there aren't any other paintbrushes nearby, so it can't be the wind that pollinates them."

Angela twisted her little mouth, tucked her hair behind her ears in concentration and squatted beside the vibrant red blossoms. "And it would be tougher for butterflies and bees to find these flowers and a longer distance to get to them."

Samantha nodded in cryptic appreciation. Normally, that would have been enough communication for Angela to understand her meaning. Angela did understand - being twins, they barely needed to speak a word to each other and still understood each other perfectly well. But it was bear season and there were berries by the river. They needed to speak their thoughts out loud in order to let the bears know where they were. Bears wouldn't bother little girls, if they knew where the girls were, that's what the twins thought.

Their mother thought otherwise.

"Girls! What are you doing down there by yourselves!"

"Uh oh," Samantha said, looking up at the cliff near their house and spotting their mother in a characteristically angry stance, her hands on her hips. "Busted."

"I told you we shouldn't have come here by ourselves!" Angela hissed.

Samantha rolled her eyes. "Hummingbirds, Angela. The paintbrush attracts hummingbirds. That's why it's red."

Angela just scowled at her sister, then stood up and brushed off her knees.

"Girls!" Their mother yelled again.

"Coming!" Samantha yelled back, as they started back up through the forest to where their mother was standing. Then she turned to Angela, "it's not a big deal, Angie. It's too nice out for us to stay at the house all day."

"Still! I told you we should have at least told someone where we were going."

"You also said that we could kill them with kindness."

Both girls stopped and looked at each other. A mysterious moment of silence passed and goosebumps popped up on both girls' arms. It seemed that the whole world around them had gone still, in anticipation. In memory. "You remember that?" Angela asked, finally.

"Yeah. I remember."

"Do you remember anything else?" Angela asked, as they continued walking up to their mother.

"Some things. Not much, but I keep remembering more."

"Before, our memories were... replaced. Well, yours were replaced with mine." Angela said.

"But not this time," Samantha answered, "maybe because it wasn't a real *untura*. We couldn't remember how to do it."

"Maybe. How did we get here?"

Samantha pondered the question. "Maybe we just deserved it."

"Maybe. Let's not tell mom."

"Do you think that Ben is Cameron?"

Angela blushed. Despite being so young, she was already irrevocably in love with a boy from across the river named Ben. The three of them were inseparable.

"Yeah. I do."

"Then where's Dinky?"

The girls grew up slowly, in a small village surrounded by wild forest. They learned the names of plants and explored and played. There was always abundance in their lives: abundance of care, of fun, of learning and of growing things. Each had their own kitten and when Angela married Ben at the age of seventeen, Samantha found a wolf pup that had been abandoned due to a deformed leg and took it in as her own.

Angela and Ben built a small home together, during their engagement. For nostalgia's sake, they made it almost identical to the one they had as Maria and Cameron, so long before. Their first night together, in that home, they finally conceived and what started as one kitten soon became a menagerie of dogs, cats, chickens, two goats and four happy children. They grew everything they needed, slaughtered two chickens in the fall and two more in the spring and otherwise ate eggs and goat cheese. They grew vegetables, fruit, berries and nuts and Angela made honey mead for Ben at least once a year.

Samantha waited another few years for Dinky to find her. Finally, she got tired of waiting and decided to find him instead. She and her wolf, who she named Amadeus after a memory that had once amused her, set off into the world to find the man she still loved and fulfill her promise to him. She traveled for more than a year, following the same paths that Maria had taken, to the place that Elizabeth had died.

At some point, the territory began to become familiar though time had left its mark in the sway of the rivers and newly eroded redoubts. Relying on her ancestral memories, she traced her way back to Rivertown, or what was left of it. The ruins of the city finally had the aged quality the machines had tried to emulate. It was a memorial now, she saw. What was left of the machines lay among the ruins. Metal spines, all of them chinked or cut or bent, had been worn clean by the passage of time. The courtyard was overrun with flowers and berry bushes, the kind that needed low wind in order to be properly pollinated. The infirmary was now distinguished only by low, crumbled walls and in the centre of the grassy field that had once been her deathbed blossomed a stand of aspens - the kind with leaves that tremble. They had been growing for at least a hundred years.

Samantha knew intuitively that she was close to finding the man that had been Dinky once and hurried onwards. She realized that she had been exploring the ruins for most of the day and the despite it being midsummer, the sky was already beginning to darken. It was the same time of year as the last time she had seen Dinky.

Eternity. We change, and the world changes. But everything remains the same.

Amadeus was finishing a meal of fresh gopher. Collecting berries and mushrooms from the old courtyard for her own dinner, she and Amadeus made their way down a once familiar path to what had been a young forest and a tent-village. It was now an ancient stand of hemlock and cedar. Samantha walked through it reverently and allowed the sacred energy of ancestral trees to guide her in her search.

The path through the forest was entirely overgrown, but she could still remember it and followed it easily. When she emerged on the other side, it was to the field that she and Dinky had made love in. Now, it was overgrown with a mix of spruce, aspen and the occasional pocket of flowers and grass. She followed further, lost in her memories and in the beauty.

Suddenly, she emerged on a gentle cliff that looked out at the ocean. Below, caught in the red light of dusk, were the statues that had marked the beginning of her journey.

I was Elizabeth and I was Maria. Now, I'm just me. I don't have to be the last medicine woman, or the saviour of my people.

The statues were still mostly untouched by the altering powers of time, but age had begun to show. Mosses covered their feet and vines climbed a few of them. Someday, they would be swept into the sea.. Someday, they would be forgotten.

Amadeus went rigid and let out a low growl. Samantha followed his gaze and saw what he saw: that one of the statues was moving.

"Elizabeth?" the man below them called.

Samantha smiled. She and Amadeus ran down the hill and onto the sand-flats where the river met the sea.

The man walked towards them and soon, they were face to face. It was Dinky, but it also wasn't. He was slightly taller and fairer, clad in rough animal skins, with a sword hanging at his side.

"I'm Samantha," she said and put her hand forward for a handshake - a tradition from their other life together.

"My name is Bern," the man answered, with a strong accent. "My brothers delivered me here, from the northlands. From the place that you and I used to call home. I've been waiting for you for some weeks now."

Their hands locked.

"Delivered you?"

"In a longboat."

"That's quite a long trip."

Bern donned a distinctly un-Dinky-like, roguish smile that Samantha would come to love more than the rising sun, "Samantha, it has been a very, very long trip."

Samantha smiled.

"I lived for a long time without you," Bern said, suddenly serious and with the haunting countenance of an old, man. "We did as you asked. Some heard of the ghosts and wanted to try the technology again; immortality was sought after by many. But the colonies heard and many of the indigenous peoples revolted. Many of the young heard our stories and began to grow their own plants, their own food. It was slow, but it happened. I remember some people being afraid that everything would collapse, that it would be an apocalypse. That we had forgotten too much to ever live in a natural way again. But... we remembered. So easily. As if it were in our blood the whole time. The old culture - that's what it's called now. The old ways. Those ways died. I like to think that, like the older ghosts, those ways simply stopped working."

"I've seen the machines. They have been overgrown and barely exist anymore." Samantha's eyes were brimming with tears. Finally, finally. She could explore, do all of the things she had yearned for. She could have adventures and learn and live.

"It's good, isn't it?" Bern said, reading her thoughts, "to live, remembering what most people cannot remember."

Samantha nodded. "What about Mark? Onya?"

"They married," that roguish smile again and already, Samantha could barely look away from it, "Mark and I were like brothers for many years. We brought real settlers to the Wild Land and with the help of the Ibers, those people built homes and gardens that could sustain them and an abundance of other life. Onya loved Mark. Right from the start, if you ask me. One year we came to Rivertown Port with a new group of settlers. Onya and Mark had been exchanging letters the year we had been gone, we were campaigning in Lila, mostly. She must have been about seventeen then, the same age that you were. Mark saw her and his jaw dropped. They were married that fall. Your mother and your aunt were mortified."

Samantha laughed. "What about you?"

Bern smiled. "I never became a doctor. And I never gave up your fight."

"I think that we have a lot of catching up to do, Bern."

Bern touched Samantha's chin, tracing her jaw with his finger.

"Yes. We do."

THE END

About The Author

Kathryn Hogan was born in Calgary, Alberta, Canada and has been getting older ever since. Her favorite colours are orange and blue, respectively.

She is grateful to live and grow in the beautiful wilds of the Rockies with her family, friends, dog and cat.

If you're interested in learning more about Kathryn, please check out her website:

www.kathrynhogan.ca